Something was bothering Tyler as he grabbed Dusty's leash.

The K-9 was up, alive with excitement. Tyler laughed at Dusty's exuberance, but still there was the nagging detail deep down in his gut that refused to surface.

What was it?

He hastened toward the conference room where Penny went. As they got closer, Dusty's nose quivered. Two more steps and she pulled on the leash, eager to get to the scent. An old one. One she'd remembered from before.

The scent left by Randall Gage and his black marker.

"Penny," Tyler shouted as he ran. "Don't open that box!"

Dana Mentink
and

New York Times Bestselling Author
Shirlee McCoy

Peril from the Past

Previously published as *Cold Case Pursuit*
and *Delayed Justice*

LOVE INSPIRED
INSPIRATIONAL ROMANCE

Special thanks and acknowledgment are given
to Dana Mentink and Shirlee McCoy for their contributions
to the True Blue K-9 Unit: Brooklyn miniseries.

LOVE INSPIRED®

INSPIRATIONAL ROMANCE

Recycling programs
for this product may
not exist in your area.

ISBN-13: 978-1-335-42462-4

Peril from the Past

Copyright © 2021 by Harlequin Books S.A.

Cold Case Pursuit
First published in 2020. This edition published in 2021.
Copyright © 2020 by Harlequin Books S.A.

Delayed Justice
First published in 2020. This edition published in 2021.
Copyright © 2020 by Harlequin Books S.A.

This edition published by arrangement with Harlequin Books S.A.

For questions and comments about the quality of this book, please contact us
at CustomerService@Harlequin.com.

Love Inspired
22 Adelaide St. West, 41st Floor
Toronto, Ontario M5H 4E3, Canada
www.LoveInspired.com

Printed in U.S.A.

CONTENTS

Dana Mentink is a nationally bestselling author. She has been honored to win two Carol Awards, a HOLT Medallion and an RT Reviewers' Choice Best Book Award. She's authored more than thirty novels to date for Love Inspired Suspense and Harlequin Heartwarming. Dana loves feedback from her readers. Contact her at danamentink.com.

Books by Dana Mentink

Love Inspired Suspense

Desert Justice

Framed in Death Valley

True Blue K-9 Unit: Brooklyn

Cold Case Pursuit

True Blue K-9 Unit

Shield of Protection
Act of Valor

Roughwater Ranch Cowboys

Danger on the Ranch
Deadly Christmas Pretense
Cold Case Connection
Secrets Resurfaced

Gold Country Cowboys

Cowboy Christmas Guardian
Treacherous Trails
Cowboy Bodyguard

Visit the Author Profile page
at LoveInspired.com for more titles.

COLD CASE PURSUIT

Dana Mentink

Brethren, I count not myself to have apprehended: but this one thing I do, forgetting those things which are behind, and reaching forth unto those things which are before, I press toward the mark for the prize of the high calling of God in Christ Jesus.
—*Philippians* 3:13–14

To my precious dog-loving reader friends...
thank you for your kindness and support!

ONE

Penelope McGregor shivered at the distant creak from the back of the house. Goose bumps erupted along her spine. Just the aged floorboards swelling from the falling October temperatures. It was as if the old Brooklyn home struggled under the weight of a new day. Penny knew the feeling.

She forced her attention back to her phone screen, scanning the party supplies. An image appeared and her lungs constricted, overcome by the crushing weight of terror. It was as if she'd fallen into a pit of ice that was freezing her breath away, one gasp at a time. The picture of the blue-haired clown mask leered at her, the mouth agape like a crimson wound.

It's just a picture. It's not real.

But it was as if she was four years old again, standing in the dingy kitchen, watching the blood pooling around the bodies of her parents while a man in a blue-haired clown mask stared down at her.

He'd leaned close, all those years ago, close enough for her to smell the tobacco on his breath. His voice was strange and muffled through the mask as he handed her a stuffed monkey. And in her childish confusion, she'd taken it, stunned at the sight of the blood and the terrible stillness of her mother and father. Too frightened to speak, too terrified to scream.

Annoyed with herself, she clicked the website closed. She'd been looking for inspiration for the October open house at the station. She wanted to make it a fun event for the police families at the Brooklyn K-9 Unit, the NYPD offshoot in Bay Ridge where she proudly served as the desk clerk and self-appointed morale officer. The muscles in her stomach remained tight, her ears still straining against the quiet of the Sheepshead Bay home she shared with her cop brother, Bradley, and his K-9 partner, King.

Lately she had been double-checking door locks, troubled by noises at night that kept her awake. She wanted to believe it was paranoia, but deep down she knew that the nightmare was coming to life again. She'd known it since she'd received the text from the man who'd slaughtered her parents. The text had been anonymous, sent from an untraceable number, but that hardly mattered. Even though the tech gurus at headquarters hadn't been able to pinpoint where the message had originated, she knew exactly who'd sent it last month, twenty years and six months after the murders.

Randall Gage, the killer clown.

She pictured him typing out the message, face hidden behind that horrible mask, except for his green eyes.

It was a mistake to let you live.

You first, then your brother, his text had promised.

Thanks to US Marshal Emmett Gage, Randall's cousin, there was finally DNA evidence proving Randall had killed Penny and Bradley's parents. The information had hit the news and caused a media sensation. Officers in the Brooklyn K-9 Unit, including Bradley, all reassured her that it was only a matter of time before Randall Gage was captured. He would never get close enough to hurt her family again, they said, and she tried hard to believe it. The text told her otherwise. For some reason she could not fathom, he was not going to give up until she was dead.

Peering out the window, she was relieved to see a police car driving slowly by for its hourly check. It had taken all her force of will to dissuade her brother from having a cop camped out in the house with her. For twenty years she'd struggled to prove to herself that she was not a helpless victim. She had to try to believe she was safe, in order to refuse Gage any more power over her.

But there was a second person's life hanging in the balance now, as well. Six months earlier, on the twentieth anniversary of the crime, another little girl was given a stuffed monkey by a man in a clown mask. She pictured Lucy Emery, the painfully shy child. How had she felt when she'd seen her own parents lying dead on the floor? Her heart constricted when she thought about Lucy. The two cases were eerily similar—the mask, and the fact that the girl had been neglected by her parents, just as Penny had.

Had Randall Gage made Lucy an orphan, too? Or was a copycat killer at work? As if one deranged clown wasn't enough. The thought of young Lucy just starting the terrible journey that Penny had been walking for the past two decades caused a churning in her stomach. At least Lucy been taken in by her aunt and K-9 cop

Nate Slater after the two had married. It was another strange parallel to her own life, since she and Bradley had been adopted by a retired NYPD detective and his darling wife.

Would Lucy get a chance to live free from the shadow of fear? Not until the case was solved and Randall Gage or the copycat killer was behind bars.

The creaking noise whispered from the back of the house, louder now. She willed herself to be still. Seconds ticked by. Nothing but the typical sounds of the two-story house they rented that was tucked between two other family homes. The aging fixtures and the charming wood were part of the reason she and Bradley had chosen the home. The small yard was perfect for King to stretch his legs, too.

Her cell phone rang. She jumped, then answered.

"Hello, Penny. I'm on my way to drive you to work." Detective Tyler Walker's tone was all business. She could picture the serious blond-haired, blue-eyed cop with his tracking dog, Dusty, by his side. A blush rose to her cheeks. The detective was seven years older than Penelope's twenty-four, but somehow she always felt like he saw her as not much more than a child. That man was six-feet-three inches of no-nonsense grit, emphasis on the *no-nonsense*. His smiles were rare, at least when she was around.

"No need for you to drive me. I can take the train," she said.

"It's no problem. Better for you to ride with me. Bradley is stuck on a case, and he doesn't want you traveling to work alone."

She knew it would do no good to argue. "All right. I'll be ready. I…" She stopped. Had she heard something inside the house? Or was it the wind in the trees outside? She'd already stewed in embarrassed silence when Tyler had scoured the house and yard the day before to find the source of a scratching she'd heard.

"It sounds like someone is trying to break in," she'd told him.

He'd insisted she wait in his squad car while he searched the house. Finally, he'd announced, *"You've got a squirrel on your roof, doing his best to store a pile of acorns in your gutter."*

She'd gone red-hot with mortification.

"Penelope?" Tyler's voice jerked her back to the present. "Everything okay?"

Should she tell him about the sound? But it was just the normal house noises, certainly. No way did she want to embarrass herself a second time in front of him. "Yes. Everything is fine. I'll be ready when you get here."

"All right. See you in fifteen minutes or so." He disconnected.

She'd be safe, with her babysitter Tyler en route. It was embarrassing, humiliating even, to be forced back into the helpless-child role. It was 180 degrees from the person she'd tried be.

Again, a sound in the rear of the old home made her tense. Bradley had told her the swiftly cooling October temperatures wreaked havoc on the ancient pipes. Tyler was on his way. She could call him back and ask him to come inside and check when he arrived, but the thought made her cringe.

Sticking her chin up and squaring her shoulders, she checked each room on the ground floor, Bradley's tiny study, his bedroom, the bathroom and even the hall closet. Her search ended in her bedroom—empty, as she'd known it would be. *You see, you worrywort? Perfectly secure.* Cool autumn air fluttered the blinds.

She stopped dead.

The window was open, the one she'd left closed tight and locked.

The shadow emerging from the closet was all too real.

A long-buried nightmare come back to life.

Randall Gage's expression was something between a smile and a frown. "It's been a long time, Penny."

Her blood turned to ice, the shock hitting her with the force of a physical blow.

She wanted to shout, to shriek at the murderer standing right before her eyes. Instead her voice came out hardly above a squeak. "Don't touch me."

Randall twirled a length of rope in his hands. His thick hair was disheveled, graying clumps standing up in spiky disarray. He was much thinner than she'd pictured, gaunt, and his cheekbones protruded from sallow skin. The green eyes burned as brightly as they had the day he'd shot her parents. Pure fright almost rendered her unable to move. Oddly, he smiled.

Her nerves shrilled an alarm. *Get out. However you can.*

She lunged for the bedroom door. Randall got there first, knocking her to the floor with a fist to her shoulder. He slammed the door and slid the bolt home—the bolt her brother had installed as an extra precaution.

On her back, she crab-walked away, scrambling upright, almost tumbling when her legs butted up against the bed. She should scream and try to alert a neighbor, but she could hardly force her lungs to breathe, let alone yell. Terror rippled through her in torrents that prickled her body in gooseflesh. She was too scared to think. Randall Gage could not be here, in her home, in her bedroom. It had to be another horrible dream.

Randall stared at her, head cocked slightly. "You turned into a pretty lady. You still have some freckles like you did when you were a kid. Same red hair. Looks nice with your brown eyes."

"What do you want? Why did you come here?"

He appeared not to hear the questions. "Penelope McGregor, desk-and-records clerk at the fancy new Brooklyn K-9 Unit." He shook his head. He was still smiling. "And you never even thanked me."

Her heart was thundering so loudly she wondered if she had heard him right. "What are you talking about?"

"I gave you a chance at a great life. You're a success now. Got yourself a respectable job…" He scanned the tidy bedroom. "And a nice place to live in a good neighborhood. I gave you all that." His reptilian gaze slid back to her. "You owe me, but lately I'm not sure about your loyalty."

She could only stare at him.

He frowned. "Your parents were terrible. They didn't care about you. Left you and your brother in dirty clothes, without regular meals, and they forgot about you at day care. Who forgets about their own *child*?" He shook his head. "I never would." He sighed. "They didn't love you, Penny."

They didn't love you. The very thought that was at the core of her deepest insecurity. *They didn't love you because you weren't lovable.* She clamped her jaw together as he continued.

"They were bad people. We were planning to rob the deli and they got cold feet. Did you know they intended to tip the police off and pin the blame on me? Scum, you see? No loyalty, no concern for others." He looked at her closer and his brow furrowed. "Or maybe you didn't know that. That's why you said what you did to the reporters. You didn't understand what I saved you and your brother from." He smiled, relaxing. "That's it. Don't know why I didn't think of it before."

What she'd said to the reporters? What was he talking about?

"My parents didn't deserve to be murdered," she blurted.

His jaw clenched. "Yes, they did. They were ruining your life and your brother's. They cost me everything, and they're gonna cost me my freedom, too."

She scooted a step back toward the window. If she could bang on it...

"Close it," he said.

"I..."

Now his voice was an angry bark. "I said close it. And lock it for good measure."

He came closer, so close she could smell cigarettes on his breath. She spiraled back to the bloody day when her world had spun out of control like a runaway carousel. Her parents lying murdered... Randall in his awful clown mask... The glittering green of his eyes staring at her.

"I won't."

"Cooperate and maybe I'll let you and your brother live."

He was lying, had to be, but all she could do was buy time. With shaking hands she slid the window closed and locked it.

"Even my own kin's against me now. My cousin,

the hotshot US Marshal, got my DNA." Randall started to pace. "He invited me to a diner, and I got wise and bolted, but I figure he got my prints or DNA from my water glass, so now they got me dead to rights for the murders. It's been on the news. I'm a wanted fugitive, and it's only a matter of time before they get me."

She couldn't tear her gaze from the rope as he twirled it around. "So what are you doing here then?" she whispered. "Why did you come back?"

His eyes narrowed to slits, and he thrust a crumpled newspaper forward so it was inches from her face. "Because you told them I was a monster."

Ah, now she knew what he'd been talking about. She remembered the reporter on the phone, pressing her, grilling her, demanding she provide her thoughts on Randall Gage in light of the probable copycat murder that was dominating the headlines. "He's a monster," she'd said, before slamming down the phone.

Randall was watching her closely. "I know it was a misquote. These reporters are always lying to juice up their headlines. Tell me you didn't say that, Penny."

She should lie, placate him, anything to buy time, but her self-control disintegrated against the onslaught of her fear and long pent-up rage.

"I did say it," she shouted. "I said it because it's true. You are a monster." Tears she hadn't felt coming rolled down her face. "You shot my parents in the back, and you took away my childhood and my brother's. You're not some sort of hero, you're a murderer and you belong in prison."

She heard his sharp intake of breath and she knew she'd made a grave mistake by telling the truth. His nostrils quivered. A vein in his temple jumped.

"So it's true then."

Her legs trembled. Was there something she could grab to fight him off? But her fastidiously uncluttered room offered nothing she could use to save herself. There was only a neat side table with her tattered Bible, next to a bed with a teddy-bear pillow given to her by her brother on her sixteenth birthday.

Randall stepped forward with the rope, mouth caught in a grimace. Moisture gleamed in his eyes. "After everything I did for you, you turn out to be a backstabbing double-crosser just like your parents. I'm going to kill you and your brother, like I should have done all those years ago."

"No," she said, forcing out the word. "You're going to prison. Like you said, it's just a matter of time. They know it was you, and they're closing in."

A slow, thin-lipped smile formed. There was no warmth in it, no humor—only the promise of death. "Then I'm going to make sure you both die before they put me away."

She screamed and lunged again for the door, but he loomed over her, holding the rope and reaching for her throat.

TWO

As he pulled up to the curb in front of Penny's Sheepshead Bay home, Detective Tyler Walker marveled at his partner's—Dusty's—unflagging energy. The golden retriever had been through a strenuous training session the day before to keep her tracking skills in good shape, and still she was looking at him in hopes that there would be a game of fetch in the offing. Humans should have such energy.

He could sure use a dose, more so now that his thirty-second birthday was looming ever closer. Why did ear infections suddenly strike his eighteen-month-old daughter, Rain, in the wee hours? The answer didn't matter. Four hours in a Brooklyn emergency room until the doc stuck an otoscope in her ear and prescribed a course of antibiotics. Feeling the usual stab of single-parent guilt, he'd kissed her sleeping cheek and tucked her into the cot in his mother's apartment, tiptoeing out to head to the station at 5:00 a.m.

Yawning, his mind returned to the question that had plagued him for six months. Was the killer clown who'd orphaned Penny and Bradley McGregor also responsible for the death of four-year-old Lucy Emery's parents?

Or was it a copycat killer using the clown-mask MO? The Emerys had been killed on the twentieth anniversary of the McGregor murders, which provided juicy fodder for the media. Randall Gage or a copycat? The copycat notion was favored by the cops.

Lucy was just too young to provide the police with much to go on. Tyler and Dusty had been beating the bushes trying to locate Lucy's "friend," some brown-haired guy named Andy, who might be a key witness. Recently, out of nowhere, the little girl had said she missed "Andy." But no one knew to whom she was referring. So far all Tyler had accomplished was to waste countless hours.

He got out and knocked on Penny's door, which was decorated with a wreath of fall leaves. Didn't surprise him. Penny was the one who made sure the fall decorations were up at the office and the "pumpkin spice" creamer was stocked in the fridge. The quiet redhead was relentlessly cheerful, and her optimism mystified him. She, above all people, had every reason to be hardened toward the world.

While he waited, he chucked a ball for Dusty. It rolled behind a garden pot bristling with rosemary. He knocked again and checked his watch. Five minutes past her typical time. Unusual for the rigidly prompt woman. He texted her and waited for a reply, but he got none.

A wisp of tension rolled through his stomach. He eyed the adjoined property. All quiet with the neighbors. He gently tried the handle. Securely locked, just as it should be. She might have taken a phone call. The cop on patrol had reported an all-clear from his earlier drive-by. Dusty had finally got the ball and pranced into her spot at his side as he headed down the alley between

Penny's place and the next building. Overhead, a leaf-filled gutter dripped. A drop of cold trickled down the side of his neck. He wiped it away.

Dusty brushed against his leg. *Work time?* she seemed to say.

"Just a routine check," he told her. He left the typical parade of cars and dog walkers behind as he plunged deeper into the alley. Side door secure. One frosted bathroom window, high up, small, was closed tight, as far as he could tell.

That left the rear corner.

Penny's bedroom window faced the alley. It wasn't a scenic view, but you took what you got in Brooklyn. He'd listened to Bradley tell his sister in no uncertain terms to keep her window closed and locked, and the curtains drawn. The autumn glow trickled between the buildings, dazzling his eyes as it reflected off the white paint. Shading his brow with one hand, he looked again. And then he heard it, the faintest muted scream. Alarm bells clanged in his mind, and he grabbed his gun and let himself into the gated backyard.

He tried the window and found it locked. He could not see anything through the drawn curtains. The screams continued, curdling his blood as he radioed. "Requesting backup at the McGregor house." He raced to the patio and grabbed a heavy metal chair.

"Stay," he told Dusty. The dog whined but obeyed, plopping down on the grass. Dusty was a tracking officer, not equipped to attack, and wasn't wearing body armor—he would not put his partner in harm's way.

He lifted the chair, adrenaline pumping. No time for stealth. With all his strength, he heaved the chair into the window, praying it would not hurt Penny in the process. Then he swung it in a wild spiral to break out the remaining glass. He gripped his gun and darted a quick look over the ruined windowsill. Randall stood facing the window, holding a rope around Penny's throat. Penelope's fingers clawed at Randall's as she struggled to breathe.

"Police. Let her go, Randall," Tyler shouted. He took aim, but he could not risk hitting Penny. Randall walked backward toward the bedroom door, dragging Penelope with him. When he reached the threshold, he threw her down and sprinted into the hallway. Penny fell to her knees, gasping. Tyler vaulted through the broken window.

He radioed an update and dropped to his knees next to Penny. He had one eye on the open door, his gun still in his hand. "It's okay, Penny. Try to breathe slow and easy." Settling her on the floor with her back against the bed, he raced to the front window in time to see Randall disappearing through the gate, headed for the alley. The rope he'd used to choke Penny was on the entry tile floor. Everything in him wanted to run after Randall and chase him down like the useless vermin he was. Right now, though, his task was to keep her safe until help arrived in case Randall tried to circle back to finish what he'd started. Gritting his teeth, he sent another radio update and a request for an ambulance. Then he turned back for Penny. She'd drawn up her knees, and was hugging them with her arms. Every part of her was trembling violently.

"An ambulance is coming." He eyed the red marks on her throat and rage prickled through his body. "Can you talk?"

She didn't answer.

He cupped her chin in his hand and gently tipped her face to his. "Are you hurt anywhere besides your throat?"

Finally she shook her head. "He was going to strangle me." She blinked, gulped. The whispered words held more terror than he'd thought possible. It infuriated him. No one should be able to terrorize anyone else, especially a decent person like Penny McGregor.

"We'll get him."

She didn't answer. Why should she believe him? Randall Gage had remained at large for twenty years. Even her adoptive father, Terry Brady, the lead detective on the case back then, hadn't been able to flush out the McGregor killer in spite of his dogged commitment. But now the cops knew exactly who the killer clown was, and the net was tightening. They would capture Randall Gage, no matter what it took. He squeezed her arm when a precinct cop arrived, hand on his gun.

Tyler filled him in. "I'll be back as soon as I can. Ambulance is rolling." As much as he wanted to stay with Penny, he couldn't take another moment to soothe her. Randall Gage might be slipping out of their grasp with each tick of the clock.

He hustled into the hall. Calling to Dusty, he let her sniff the rope before he jogged out the front door and charged into the alley. Dusty immediately put her nose to the ground and zoomed along, confirming for Tyler that Randall had indeed come this way. He might be able to fool his human pursuers, but he could not escape Dusty's relentless nose. No one could.

The alley was silent, a tidy corridor between the McGregor backyard and the set of nearby shared houses. It was empty save for a bike chained to a water pipe and three garbage cans hugging one wall. There was no other cover here. If Randall was hiding behind the cans, Tyler would just have to hope he wasn't armed.

He gripped the gun. This time, Randall wasn't going to get away. He was going to pay for what he'd done to Penny, Bradley and their family all those years ago. If he'd killed the Emerys, he'd pay for their murders, too.

Showtime.

Penny sat huddled on the small throw rug, shivering. *This is what shock must feel like.* The terror was so close to the surface it had sent her nerves into a kind of spastic pattern. A stupor took over her body, interrupted every few moments by a spasming of her muscles as her mind flashed through the details.

Randall Gage. His image was distorted and grotesque, like a fun-house mirror. She'd dreamed so often about his return and now that it had happened, she felt only gnawing disbelief. But this really was her home, and she truly was huddled into a ball on the little hook rug she'd made. Her neck ached where the rope had bitten into her skin.

It was a mistake to let you live.

You first, then your brother.

She tried to breathe slowly through her mouth to quell the rising panic. *I'm not a victim*, she repeated, but now the words rang false. Randall Gage was back, and he would have killed her if Tyler hadn't intervened. Maybe she really was a helpless child again, her life in the hands of the same horrible clown. Her throat throbbed and she fingered the abrasion as the fright bubbled anew.

"Penny," a voice thundered from the hallway.

"It's my brother," she told the cop.

Bradley pushed through, his Belgian Malinois, King, shoving in beside him, ears erect and nose quivering. He put the dog in a sit and crouched to hug her. His grip was so tight it almost hurt as he peered into her face.

"Are you injured?"

She shook her head. "Not badly."

He scanned the marks on her neck, his expression darkening to fury. "I heard the call and turned around. It was Randall? Positive?"

She nodded, gulping down a breath.

His grip on her forearms tightened. She saw her own tortured expression mirrored in his brown irises.

"He's angry that I called him a monster to the press. He—he believes we should be grateful to him for killing Mom and Dad."

Bradley jerked, his mouth flattening into a hard line. "This is going to end," he insisted and she could see the pulse throbbing in his throat. "He's not going to hurt you again."

His radio chattered. As much as she wanted to be consoled, to hug her brother tight, she knew the passing moments were crucial.

"Tyler went after him."

Bradley got up, squeezing Penny's hand one more time as another uniformed NYPD officer appeared in the doorway. She was followed a moment later by Sgt. Gavin Sutherland. He immediately took a knee next to Penelope, brow furrowed. "You okay, Penny?"

She forced her head to nod up and down at her boss, but she didn't think it was very convincing since her whole body still quivered with fear.

"You're safe now," he said. "Just try and keep breathing slowly, okay?"

She complied as best she could.

He maintained his reassuring touch. "The house is secure. Ambulance will be here in a minute."

She shook her head, mortified that the sergeant, a man she respected and admired, would see her in a puddle on the floor. "I don't need an ambulance."

"Her throat..." Bradley protested. "He tried to strangle her."

"It's okay," she said, barely managing to get out the words. "Tyler interrupted him before... I mean..."

"I'm going to back up Tyler," Bradley growled as he released King from the sit. The dog gave off as much energy as Bradley, pulling at the leash to speed their departure. King, like his master, lived to chase.

Gavin shot Bradley a look. "We have a team in place. Leave it to them."

Bradley's eyes blazed. "Is that an order? Are you commanding me to lay off pursuit of the man who killed my parents and almost murdered my sister?"

Gavin squeezed Penny's arm and rose to his feet. "No," he said calmly. "I won't make that order...at this time, but Tyler's the lead on this so you'll follow his direction." There was a touch of steel in his voice.

Bradley jerked his chin and blew out a breath. "Fair enough. Thanks, Sarge."

Penny could keep the panic inside no longer. "You should stay here. Randall said he's going to kill us both. Let the other cops track him." The words seemed to hang in the air. Bradley cast one glance at her. His expression was caught somewhere between ferocity and love.

"I'll stay with her," Gavin said quietly.

Bradley turned and ran out, King right behind him.

Penelope wanted to scream at him to come back. What if Randall killed him? Her only blood family, the person who had been her rock since she was old enough to remember?

Gavin spoke again to the other cops before he returned his attention to Penelope. "It's okay. We've got a dozen of New York's finest out there, including Tyler and your brother. They'll get him."

She could not answer through the crush of fear. All she could do was follow his advice and force her lungs to keep working.

"Front is secure, Sarge," said another officer from the doorway. "The house next door is unoccupied, family away on vacation. There's an elderly neighbor on the other side and we've got an officer with her. We've alerted Detective Walker. He radioed he's in pursuit via the alley."

Pursuit. She gulped. *Please, Lord, let them be safe.*

Sarge nodded. "Get the crime-scene team in here." He turned back to Penny. "Do you think you can stand?"

"Yes. I'm really not hurt," she said, trying to sound confident.

He grinned. "That's what your brother said after he got hit by a cab running down a purse snatcher. Must be a family trait. I'd like to have a medic check you out, anyway. You can wait in my vehicle."

Somehow she rose to her feet, leaning on Sarge's comforting arm. With every step her fear increased.

What if Randall Gage was lying in wait for Tyler and Bradley?

* * *

Tyler heard someone behind him. He jerked a look. At the mouth of the alley, Bradley and King were beginning their approach. He gestured for the pair to circle the block and cut off Randall's escape at the other end. They about-faced and disappeared. He followed up with a radio message. With dozens of cops, armed and amped to capture Randall Gage, communication was crucial.

Though he strained to listen, he caught nothing but the sound of the wind and the typical hum of Brooklyn traffic.

Tyler put Dusty in a stay and crept forward, weapon drawn. Inch by inch he got closer to the trash cans until he'd drawn alongside them. The metal sides were dappled with moisture and rust. He held his breath against the feral stink. An image of Rain flickered in his heart, tiny, so full of wonder at the world, so completely vulnerable and perplexing. She was his heartbeat, twined into the fabric of his soul, and he prayed God would give him another day to be her daddy. Right now, duty came before daddy—it was the most difficult part about wearing a badge.

One slow breath to clear his mind, and a count of three. He plunged around the cans, nerves firing on all cylinders, weapon cocked.

No one.

Breathing hard, he scanned past the garbage cans, spending only one more moment wondering before he called to Dusty.

The retriever leaped up, nose glued to the ground as she raced over.

"Track," he said, needlessly.

The vomeronasal organ in the roof of her mouth allowed her to "taste" certain smells. It took her less than fifteen seconds to solve the mystery. Pressed right up to a low basement window, she sat, bottom waggling. He surmised the window had been left unsecured by the vacationing family and Randall had used it to his advantage.

"Good girl, Dusty," he whispered. "We'll have playtime in a minute."

He radioed the update, and the first-in NYPD commander made a plan to seal off the perimeter. Tyler jogged with Dusty to take up a position at the rear of the house while a team alerted SWAT and prepared to make entry in the front. In spite of the cool temperatures, Tyler was sweating. Dusty barked as they approached the back corner of the house.

Tyler's mind raced. There was no way Randall could sneak through this police net. Not this time.

As he cleared the corner, some deep-down instinct screamed at him, but he did not have time to deflect the blow as Randall Gage swung a baseball bat at his head.

Penny didn't even remember the ride to the hospital. Her only thought had been that Tyler was hurt—to what degree she did not know. The waiting room was crowded with cops and dogs. Everyone was on pins and needles waiting for the doctor's prognosis.

Bradley leaned against the wall, King at his side. The anger blazed off him like a beacon, so different than his normal easygoing demeanor. He hadn't needed to tell her Randall had escaped the police net. That was clear from the barely contained rage emanating from him and all the officers gathered around waiting for word about Tyler. More trickled in with each passing moment. Raymond Morrow with his springer spaniel, Abby, and Noelle Orton whose accomplished yellow Lab, Liberty, was under threat from a drug smuggler who had a bounty on the dog's head. The team was a solid family, even though they were newly established. Her heart swelled at the thought.

Penny touched the abrasions on her throat, which had been pronounced minor. Bradley insisted on her being examined by a doctor, and she hadn't had the strength to argue. When Bradley's jaw was set, there was no use trying to change his mind.

Detective Nate Slater was engaged in an intense conversation with Sarge, who held Dusty's leash. The dog twitched forlorn eyebrows, watching every new arrival eagerly for signs that someone would take him to Tyler. Murphy, Nate's yellow Lab, was sprawled nearby in sharp contrast to Bradley's Malinois, King, who appeared as agitated as Bradley. Her brother bobbed his knee so violently that Penny wanted to shout at him to stop.

The digital clock read a few minutes after 10:00 a.m. No coffee, she thought with a start. She usually went into work early to be sure the coffee was properly prepared for the officers along with a plate of snacks on Wednesdays, if she'd had time to bake. It was her small way of helping them over the Wednesday hump. But she had not made it to the office, not today.

Don't be silly. The Brooklyn K-9 officers and staff were fully capable of providing for themselves, but it pained her that she'd not performed her self-appointed duty. The simple routine soothed her, reminded her that the world was still turning and she had a place in it.

"You had a good reason to miss work," she whispered to herself.

Fear pricked her skin again at the memory of Randall's green eyes, the clench of his calloused hands on the rope he'd looped around her neck. Any moment she felt she might wake up from a nightmare and find out none of it was real.

"He could be coming after Lucy again, too," Nate said.

Nate had even more motivation to see Randall caught than the other officers. He and his new wife, Willow, had adopted the orphaned Emery child.

Lucy, Penny thought with a shiver, the little chubby-cheeked innocent. If Randall really was the one who'd executed Penny's parents, not a copycat killer, would Lucy be in danger again, too? Then an image of another girl popped into her mind—petite, wild-haired Rain, Tyler's daughter.

That stopped Penny's thoughts cold. Penny was fine, Lucy was fine. Tyler was the one in the hospital bed, unable to go home to his toddler.

She knew all the cops in that waiting room were praying right along with her that Detective Tyler Walker would be okay. "Lord, please—" It was all she got out before the doctor shuffled in.

THREE

Everyone bolted to their feet, even the dogs, as the doctor approached.

"Detective Walker is going to be fine," she said, removing her green paper cap. The group all seemed to exhale at once.

Penny's knees almost buckled in relief.

The doctor continued. "The blow hit at an awkward angle instead of a direct impact to the temple, which would probably have killed him. He's escaped a serious concussion. We'll keep him for observation today and if his morning exam goes well tomorrow, we'll release him."

Gavin nodded. "Best news I've heard all day. Can I talk to him?"

She jotted something on a clipboard before nodding. "Yes, briefly. And he's asked to see Penelope and Dusty. I can show you to his room."

Gavin laughed as Dusty surged from the floor and yanked at the leash. "I think Dusty already knows where her partner is." He spoke to his officers, directing one to provide a ride to the hospital for Tyler's mother and Rain and dispersing the others back to their duties.

"I will let you know if I find out anything helpful." He turned to Bradley.

"You'll wait here for Penny, I assume?"

"You assumed right. We have to discuss safety measures we're going to put in place." He narrowed his eyes. "And this time she's not going to argue."

Meekly, Penny followed Sarge down the hall to Tyler's room.

Entering the tiny hospital room, her stomach jumped. It was so strange to see the strong and competent Tyler Walker prostrate and swaddled in a clean white sheet. His right temple was bruised, the eye blackened and puffy.

Dusty immediately got up on hind legs, front paws on the mattress, and began to lick whatever parts she could reach on her partner.

Tyler laughed and scratched his dog behind the ears. "I'm all right but couldn't you have warned me about the baseball bat?"

Gavin shrugged. "She probably tried to, but you were going pedal to the metal."

Tyler finally quieted the dog and glanced at Penny. "Are you okay?"

She blushed, hot to the roots of her hair. It was the curse of the ginger, the flush that stained her face at the slightest discomfort. "Yes. Perfectly fine. The doctor says you'll be okay, too," she said brightly.

"Yep," Gavin said, "and he'll have a restful couple of days while he's off duty recovering."

Tyler frowned. "No way."

Gavin straightened. "It's protocol. Don't fight me."

"Randall is close. You need every cop on this."

"We're covering all the major transportation systems

and bringing on extra cops for overtime. If he's out there, we'll get him." He raised a palm as Tyler struggled up higher on the bed. "Two days. You can spend your off time with your daughter."

His eyes blazed azure fire. "What about protection for Penny?"

"Bradley and I are working that out. I'll take Dusty with me. You're here until tomorrow and back on duty Friday, if the doctor approves. Copy that order, Detective?"

Tyler opened his mouth, then closed it. "Yes, sir." He heaved a sigh that seemed to come from his toes. "What am I supposed to do lying here in a hospital bed?"

Gavin offered a cheerful smile. "I'm sure there are some great cooking shows on TV you could watch. Your culinary skills are deplorable. We're all still recovering from the meal you provided at the last potluck. What was that called?"

"Spaghetti Surprise," Tyler said glumly.

"It was a surprise, all right."

Penny hid a smile as Tyler grimaced.

Gavin looked at his phone. "I'll check in with you soon. By the way, your mom and daughter should be here within the hour."

Tyler shot Gavin a dark look as he exited.

An awkward quiet unrolled between them. Penny pulled in a bolstering breath. "Umm, I am sorry. That you got hurt, I mean. I should have tried harder to get away." Her pulse went all skittery, the way it usually did when she tried to talk to Tyler.

"I was doing my job, that's all. Not your fault." He went silent.

She felt her flush deepen. Had she said something

wrong? Again? "Well, anyway, if there's anything I can do…"

"There is, as a matter of fact."

She brightened. A task was just what she needed. "What?"

"Can you please keep Rain from seeing me like this?" His blue eyes were pleading. "I know my mom is going to charge in with tears flowing, and I don't want my daughter to be part of that." He paused. "I was hurt once before, clipped by a car when Rain was an infant. My wife, she's my ex now, freaked out when she saw me in the hospital all banged up. She almost dropped the baby. Understandable, I guess. She was young, like you."

Penny felt the sting of that statement. She was young, but capable and mature. Wasn't she? It wasn't the time to try and change his perception. "I'd be happy to watch Rain while your mother visits," she said. "I'll just wait to intercept her in the hallway."

"Cops there? You shouldn't be alone."

"My brother is lurking with King."

"Don't go anywhere by yourself. It's too dangerous."

She tipped her head to one side and fixed him with a look. "You don't have to tell me that, Tyler," she said quietly. "I know better than anyone what Randall Gage is capable of."

Two spots of color rose on his face. "I apologize. I didn't mean to talk to you like—"

"Like I am a child?"

He sighed. "Yeah. Real sorry. Sometimes I lack tact, to put it mildly."

"It's okay. I'll go look out for your daughter."

"I appreciate it."

A moment or two of babysitting wasn't much to offer, considering the detective could have been killed trying to run down Randall. She let herself into the hallway. At least it was one small thing and perhaps Tyler might begin to see that she wasn't a helpless child herself if she could take care of his daughter.

Helpless child.

The flashback exploded in her skull—her parents lying on the floor, so terribly still. And she'd stood there completely vulnerable while Randall pressed a toy into her hand.

For twenty years she'd worked hard to convince herself she was not helpless, like she'd been at four years old, but now a deep well of uncertainty had opened up again inside, black and cold.

A warm palm stroked her forearm and she snapped out of her reverie.

"Lost in your thoughts?" Bradley said.

More like drowning in her nightmares. She didn't bother to force a smile like she would have with the rest of the world. Bradley would know. He always knew.

"I am telling myself that you all are going to catch Randall before he hurts anyone else."

"We are." Bradley's tone was clipped. "And while we're working on that, Eden Chang is hopefully going to extract the evidence to determine whether or not he's responsible for the Emery killings also. He'll go to prison for life."

Instead of comfort at his words, she felt the prickle of a panic attack starting up in her stomach. Randall was still at large. He'd promised to kill. Would they find him in time? Teeth set, she did a quick round of controlled breathing. *Lord, help me to be strong*, she silently prayed.

Because deep down she knew the nightmare was beginning all over again.

It took a good half hour for Tyler to calm his agitated mother. Francine Walker was a high-strung woman. It probably hadn't helped that her younger son had decided to enter into a dangerous profession after her older committed to a life in the military. She'd been a widow for two years, since Tyler's father died of a heart attack. She watched Rain for him faithfully and never wanted to take a day off from her babysitting duties, even when he practically strong armed her.

"Mom, I don't need anything, really."

She glanced around the hospital room and poured him water, anyway.

The concept of relaxation was completely lost on her, and unless she was performing some kind of service, she wasn't content. One time he'd paid for a weekend stay at a charming Brooklyn bed-and-breakfast for her birthday. She'd returned in a cab within three hours of her departure.

"I am sorry, Ty," she'd said. "I just can't lie there in a feather bed when I know you and Rain need help."

After straightening the tissue box and refilling his water pitcher, she shoved her silver chop of hair behind her ears and pushed her glasses up her nose. "Are you sure you don't want me to bring in Rain? She's just outside in the hall," she said, fretting. "It will help cheer you up to see her."

Nothing would help cheer him up except Randall behind bars. His head ached and his lower back twinged.

"No," he said firmly. "She shouldn't see her daddy with all these hospital trappings and his face all banged up. I don't want her scared. I'll be home tomorrow." He softened his tone. "Thanks for coming, Mom. I don't know what I'd do without you."

Tyler wasn't sure his father ever did love him or want him, but God had blessed him abundantly in the mother department.

She squeezed his fingers. "If only I'd been able to talk you into being an insurance agent or something."

He smiled. "I worked in an office for four interminable months before I went to the academy, you will remember. Believe me, everyone was happy I decided to pick another career. They told me I scared the clients."

"That's because you glower when you're irritated." Her tone was playful, but he could see the tightness around her mouth. He pressed a kiss to her fingers.

"I'm okay, Mom. Really."

"It's just that I know you're not going to stop." She shoved again at her hair. "You're going to keep after this killer, aren't you?"

"I have to. He gunned down Penny's parents and maybe another little girl's, too. I have to get this guy off the streets."

She sighed and moved away. "Since I would be wasting my time trying to cajole you into another career choice, I'm going to go talk to the doctor. Make sure he ran enough tests."

"The doctor is a woman, and she's done MRIs and X-rays of every square inch of my brain, what there is of it."

"Well, I'll just stop at the nurse's station and ask if we can have a nice chat, your doctor and me. She can tell me all about how to take care of you after you get sprung from here."

Before he could stop her, she'd scooted out of the room. As the door slowly closed, Tyler caught sight of Penny sitting with Rain in a chair. He heard a few bars of high-pitched singing.

Gingerly he got out of the bed and opened it a crack, comforted by the sight of Bradley and King standing close. Bradley was absorbed in a phone conversation, but his eyes didn't miss a thing. He winked at Tyler and continued talking.

Penny's long red hair was down, mingling with his daughter's fine blond curls that defied any type of containment. She had Rain facing away from her, guiding her chubby hands to clap the rhythm to some song about wheels and buses. Rain's grin was toothy and wide.

His heart lurched. An innocent passerby might have mistaken Penny for Rain's mother.

But Rain's real mother, Diane, had decided before her baby was even born that she didn't want to be a parent, not then, not to his child.

I made a mistake. I wasn't ready for marriage and I'm certainly not ready to have a baby.

They'd talked, fought, cried and talked some more, but Diane didn't love him or the baby growing inside her enough to stay. Diane was emotional, volatile, restless, a rolling stone—all the things Tyler wasn't. Those differences had been fascinating to them both at first. Gradually, he'd come to accept that he wasn't what she wanted, but he could never understand how Rain wasn't. His Rain, his beautiful daughter with the dazzling grin and the naughty disobedient streak that exasperated him, was worth dying for.

In the back of his mind, he'd been so sure Diane would have a change of heart when she held their baby for the first time. She hadn't, and he'd become mother and father to a squalling newborn who cried more than she was ever quiet.

Mostly he figured he was doing a pretty decent job of it, but often at 3:00 a.m. he would wake up worrying about all the mysterious things he didn't understand about women. Why did they cry when they were happy? How come they marched into the restroom in groups instead of alone? How could they be so incredibly strong and tender at the same time?

And most of all, how would he ever manage to teach Rain how to be a woman when he had no clue what made them tick? So absorbed was he in his thoughts, that it took him a moment to realize Penny had noticed him.

She smiled, blushing that cotton-candy hue.

He nodded, mouthed the words *thank you* and quickly closed the door again.

The sight of Penny cradling his daughter did not leave his mind as he climbed back into bed, pain throbbing through his skull. He felt more determined than ever to catch Randall before he could harm Penny, or Lucy, or any other person ever again.

God would give him what he needed to succeed. He was sure of it.

FOUR

Penny settled into her chair behind the front desk of the Brooklyn K-9 Unit on Friday morning. The beautiful three-story limestone building, with its neatly arranged work spaces, soothed her. Officers milled in and out on official tasks or guided their dogs to the training building next door, which also housed the kennel runs. The scent of her personally ground coffee mix perfumed the air.

She typed with machine-like precision, ruthlessly determined to keep her mind off what had happened two days ago. No, she would not be taking any more time off, she'd told her boss, Gavin "Sarge" Sutherland. Work was what she needed, what she craved. Trying for some sort of normalcy, she'd gotten up early, baked a pan of soft ginger cookies and ridden with Bradley into the office. It had been a long, quiet drive. Though she'd heard Tyler Walker was still off duty, she wondered what she would say to the serious cop when he returned. It had never seemed as though he had much interest in talking to her. What, after all, did they have in common? He was a cop, a single father, and she was a twenty-four-year-old desk clerk without even a niece or nephew to care for. What's more, he probably came from a normal, two-parent family, unlike her dysfunctional situation, scarred by violence. No wonder they had so little to talk about.

Gavin called to her from an open doorway. "Penny, would you come here a minute? There's someone I want you to meet."

To meet? Puzzled, she made her way to the conference room, where her boss stood, bending to scratch a fawn-colored dog with two enormous ears that flopped over at the tips. The dog immediately scuttled over and sat at her feet, tail thumping.

"Well, look at you," she said, kneeling to stroke his head. The dog whined, crowding closer, and she cupped his muzzle between her hands. His eyes were riveted on hers as though she was the only person on the planet.

"This is Scrappy," Gavin said. "He's some sort of German-shepherd mix, though we haven't done any DNA testing to see what the other part is. We found him scrounging for food, no collar, tags or microchip. You could practically see right through him he was so skinny."

An orphan, Penny thought, massaging the dog's ears until his eyes rolled in pleasure. A soft whine escaped him.

Sarge chuckled. "We thought he'd make a great K-9 cop, but he promptly flunked out of the Queens training program because he has a bit of a focusing issue." He sighed. "He just flunked out of a service-dog program, too, so it seems he's not cut out for public service. Since he gets along okay with King, I suggested to Bradley that maybe he'd be helpful to have around. Maybe, you know…a good companion."

Penny jerked a look at Sarge. "You brought him here for me?"

He nodded. "I will warn you he's prone to misbehaving. I had him in my office just long enough for him to devour the bologna sandwich I had on my desk. Incredible the way he opened the plastic bag and snatched the contents like a first-class thief. I also have yet to replace the pile of chewed-up pencils he left for me. Now that you've been told about his criminal tendencies, do you think you're up to the task?"

"I have no idea," she said. "I've never owned a dog before." She remembered as a child being completely infatuated with her daycare provider's terrier named Mr. Bigsley, who would be brought to the facility on special occasions. Mr. Bigsley had played with her sometimes, when she was the only one left waiting for pickup. He seemed to be watching over her. A shudder started up in her spine when she considered that Randall had been watching, too. And he'd almost killed Tyler Walker while trying to get to her.

Scrappy blew a breath through his nostrils and pressed his face into her stomach while she massaged his neck. Such trust, she thought. Incredible how dogs could decide in a blink to whom they would hand over their hearts.

"I'm just not sure I'd be very good at owning a dog."

Gavin considered for a moment. "He really needs someone to be his whole world, Penny."

His whole world? Tears pricked her eyelids. How could she be that when her own world had just fractured into millions of sharp-edged pieces? Randall was back, and her universe had been shaken so badly she could hardly string two words together, let alone take on a naughty dog.

But Scrappy wiggled his behind and kept his warm wedge of a head pressed close to her as if to say, *I am here to love you.*

To love you.

"I—I guess I could give it a try," she said.

Sarge smiled. "I was hoping you'd say that."

She closed her eyes to stave off the tears. On her knees, she circled her arms around Scrappy's sturdy neck and buried her nose in his fur. Too overwhelmed to speak, she hugged the dog and cried. Scrappy sat quietly and offered a gentle lick to her cheek. Instantly she knew she'd met the best friend she'd ever have.

With a soft click, Gavin gently closed the conference-room door and left her to share the moment with Scrappy. She suspected her boss felt sorry for her, and it made her cringe. She'd fought so long and hard to shed her "victim" identity. But in spite of the tidal wave of fear that threatened to overwhelm her, somehow she knew that this exuberant creature would remind her that she would never be alone as long as he was alive. Resolutely, she wiped her face and collected her wits. Scrappy wagged his tail in encouragement.

She got up and reached for the jar of dog treats in the cupboard, kept there in case a K-9 meeting went on a bit too long.

Scrappy watched her intently. "Okay, Scrappy. First lesson. Sit." She said it with conviction, like she'd heard the cops do.

Scrappy immediately rolled over onto his back, legs paddling in the air. She laughed. "That's not a sit."

Scrappy looked so cute, she gave him the treat, anyway. He hopped to his feet and gobbled the biscuit. "We'll work on that."

Scrappy's whole being broadcast such enthusiasm that she gave him another rubdown.

"Well, Scrappy, if we're going to be best buddies, this office is going to become your second home. Let's go get you settled in. I think I know where there's an extra cushion if you're not too picky." He scrambled alongside her, nose quivering.

She hoped the presence of her new dog wouldn't make her even more of a spectacle among her coworkers. Bad enough that there was now a brigade of officers constantly checking the house she shared with Bradley and plans afoot for an officer to bunk there whenever her brother was away. An alarm system was being installed that very afternoon under her brother's watchful eye. They arrived at the check-in area after she retrieved the spare dog bed.

"This is my desk, Scrappy. What do you think?" She placed the dog cushion in a quiet spot next to the water cooler.

Scrappy sniffed around for a moment. He trotted to his cushion and dragged it into the leg space below her desk, circled three times and apparently found the accommodations suitable.

She gaped. "Well, where are my feet supposed to go?"

He answered with a tail wag.

Laughing, she sat in her chair and tucked her toes under the edge of his cushion. Comforted by his solid furry weight draped across her feet, she breathed in the pleasure of her neatly ordered work space. Stapler, just so, neatly framed picture of her and Bradley at his

badge pinning and a lush indoor plant that Bradley had
dubbed "Frondy." Now that she had Scrappy for a desk
mate, everything felt perfect.

The second pot of coffee was perking in the kitchen.
The next shift of officers beelined straight for the coffee and creamers and helped themselves to her platter of cookies. She felt the knot of tension loosen ever
so slightly as her routine duties absorbed her mental
energy. Scrappy kept watch, ears swiveling, when he
wasn't snoring softly.

During her morning break, she even dove cautiously
again into plans for the October open house, mulling
over details as she let Scrappy have some exercise and
a few treats. She'd decided there would be a pumpkin-
decorating area as well as a craft table set up for the
children.

"We'll need the fat color crayons for the younger
ones," she murmured as she scribbled a note to herself
back at her desk. It was Rain she was thinking of. The
feel of her small hands in Penny's, her high-pitched
laughter, had awakened something unexpected. She'd
never allowed herself to think of having her own children. That was far too idyllic a picture for a woman
whose own parents had neglected and often forgotten
about their children. With her lifelong struggles against
insecurity and fear, she knew she was not proper mother
material, but for some reason it was extremely satisfy-
ing to tend to Rain.

FBI Agent Caleb Black startled her from her
thoughts. She jerked. A longtime member of the search
team hunting Randall, Caleb held up a napkin-wrapped
treat. "Sorry. I just wanted to thank you for the cookies. I came by to touch base with Gavin, and man was

I happy to see your home-baked goodies." He grinned. "Your treats are the best perk of having a temporary desk in this office."

"You're welcome. I…" Her voice trailed off as Tyler strolled through the door in jeans and a long-sleeved navy T-shirt. His temple sported a purplish bruise, but he looked much less haggard than before as he stood across the front counter from her.

Caleb quirked a grin. "What part of 'off duty' did you not grasp?"

"I'm not on duty. I was just in the neighborhood and I wanted to run something by you about Andy."

Penelope knew that Tyler and Bradley had been working overtime chasing down a lead provided by young Lucy Emery, who'd shared that she missed her friend Andy. The elusive Andy might just be the witness who could provide information about whether or not Randall Gage had killed the Emerys.

Caleb cut off her thoughts. "And I thought you just came in because Penny baked your favorite cookies."

Tyler inhaled deeply, eyes closed for a moment. For a quick moment, his face softened and he appeared younger. "Ah. That is the smell of those ginger cookies, isn't it? The ones with the sugar crystals on top?"

"Yes, those are the ones." Penny hadn't realized the cookies she'd chosen to bake were Tyler's favorites. Or had she remembered that, deep down? Was he lingering in her subconscious mind, too? She hadn't been able to stop thinking about him lying in that hospital bed. His battered face emerged in her mind. She fiddled with her stapler.

Tyler's gaze dropped. He let out a deep laugh, which further erased the weariness. "Easy, boy," he said to

Scrappy, who had come to stand on hind legs and peer at him over the edge of the counter, ears swiveling. "I'm a dog person, truly, but Dusty is out having her nails done so you might not recognize that." Tyler stood still as Scrappy gave him an exploratory sniff and he slurped a tongue over Tyler's offered hand.

"This is my new best friend, Scrappy," she said as the shepherd mix resumed his spot at her feet. She buzzed Tyler through.

He met her eyes as he moved to her desk. "I'm glad you have a buddy." His voice went soft. "How are you doing?"

"Fine, just fine." She straightened the stapler again, feeling the rise of heat in her cheeks at his intense gaze.

Caleb finished his cookie. "I've got a few minutes to chat, Ty, but if Gavin sees you here, I'm going to say you forced me to talk to you at gunpoint. I don't want any friction between the FBI and Brooklyn K-9 Unit."

Tyler smiled. "Fair."

She noted the tension in his wide shoulders. She realized he had not, in fact, let go of anything in spite of being ordered off duty.

Caleb headed off to the conference room but Tyler lingered. She could detect the fresh smell of shampoo from his hair.

"I just, er, I mean, wanted to thank you again for helping with Rain. She's been asking about you, in fact."

Penny looked away. "No problem. Is she doing okay?"

"Yes, except for her general misbehavior. The ear infection is better, and she felt well enough to flush a box of crayons down the toilet. That's her new hobby.

Flushing. The whole concept fascinates her. I think she's going to be a plumber."

Penny laughed. "I'll make a note of that when I babysit her again." She stopped abruptly. Had she said, "when" instead of "if"? Did he think she was insinuating she wanted him to ask her? As the heat threatened to paint her face in scarlet, Tyler spoke.

"Rain and I read about a million stories yesterday when I got sprung from the hospital, after I uncorked the crayon clog, but at bedtime she wanted to sing. My rendition of Johnny Cash's top ten hits did not do the trick. You'll have to teach me that bus song sometime, the one with the wheels and stuff."

"I'd be happy to."

"Okay. Uh, everything feel secure at your place?"

"Secure as Fort Knox."

"As is should be. Precious material inside."

Precious? Her? He seemed to be startled at what he'd said. "Well, anyway, gotta go get one of those cookies before Caleb fills his pockets."

"I can always make more."

"You'll never find anyone here to try and dissuade you."

He lingered.

She shuffled papers, still feeling his presence like the warmth from a lit torch, until her cell phone pinged. As she read the text message, she knocked over her tray, showering paper clips down upon Scrappy, who yelped.

She stared at the phone, unable to pull in a full breath. Terror pulsed through every muscle and nerve as she reread the text.

I almost got you. Next time, I'll finish it.

* * *

Tyler saw Penny bolt to her feet. The rolling office chair shot backward and slammed into the water cooler. Scrappy scrambled up, whining and circling her ankles, as Tyler surged forward and took her by the shoulders. "What is it? Tell me."

Her lips moved, but no words came out. Her face was bloodless. He walked her backward and settled her into the escaped chair. Scrappy pawed at her knees.

Tyler ignored the agitated animal. "Take a deep breath." A tremor rippled through her body as he held onto her forearms. She shuddered. Several other officers moved closer.

"Ambulance?" Officer Lani Jameson asked, worried.

"I'm not sure," Tyler said. "Give us a minute."

Scrappy could take it no more. He leaped into Penny's lap and shoved his nose to her neck. Her arms encircled him, and she tipped her cheek to graze along his ears. The dog seemed to poke through Penelope's fear, and Tyler silently thanked the funny creature.

She looked up and pressed her phone into Tyler's hand. He read the threatening text, and his gut hardened into iron.

Randall Gage.

Anger flashed hot through his bones as he thrust the phone at Lani.

Her voice was tight as she answered. "He never gives up, does he? I'll call Eden."

He brought Penny a glass of water and stayed close until the tech guru was summoned. Eden Chang chewed her lip as she examined the information on Penny's cell phone.

"It was probably sent from the dark web again, like

the first couple. I'll research it, but I doubt it's going to lead anywhere helpful. I'm sorry."

He'd learned that the "dark web" was a whole vast network of encrypted online content that wasn't indexed by search engines. Basically, it was a criminal's paradise for buying credit-card numbers, all manner of drugs, guns, counterfeit money, stolen subscription credentials and software that allowed them to break into other people's computers.

He put a hand on Penny's shoulder, earning an ear swivel from Scrappy. "Come sit in the break room until you feel better, okay?"

She shook her head, straightened in the chair and scooted Scrappy to the floor. "It's not time for my break yet." Her voice quivered.

"That doesn't matter. This is a unique circumstance."

Her lips pressed into a thin line. "It does matter. I'm going to stay at my desk until my break. I have a bunch of work to catch up on and the monthly reports."

"Don't be silly—" he began.

Her mahogany eyes sparkled. "I am not being silly. I am going to do my job." Each word was precise as cut glass.

That's when he realized her hands were balled into fists on her thighs and the sparkle in those luminous eyes was the precursor to tears. Why had he used the word *silly*, as if she was a child? Right now she was fighting to hold onto her independence, to preserve some shred of dignity in the face of a monster who was determined to kill her. Work was her life preserver and he'd just minimized that. *You're a real sensitive guy, Tyler.*

He stepped back a pace. "I'm sorry. I don't think

you're silly. I was concerned, but I should not have said that."

She nodded, body still stiff and taut as she stood, rolled her chair back into place and sat again. Scrappy trotted cheerfully to his self-appointed spot at her feet. He licked her ankle as he set up watch. "I'll need to work on my reports now." She gulped. "Please."

The tiny stroke of desperation in that last word lanced an arrow right to his heart. He forced a smile. "Sure thing."

She began to type on her computer, slim shoulders ramrod-straight. Anyone would think she was completely composed, save for the trembling of her fingers on the keys. Caleb walked over, clipping his phone to his belt. "I've got to take care of something on another case. We'll have to talk later, Tyler."

Noelle Orton joined them, her slight form made larger by the bulletproof vest. Her yellow Lab, Liberty, flapped her ears as she approached. The dog was a beautiful specimen with a distinctive black ear marking.

"I was talking to Eden when Lani called about the text." Noelle gestured to Penny, brow wrinkled. "She okay?"

"She's putting up a pretty good front."

Caleb shook his head. "Guy murders her parents and comes after her and her brother twenty years later? I'm impressed she can even leave her house. She's got amazing courage."

Amazing courage, his mind echoed. Far beyond her years.

Gavin arrived and spoke quietly to Penny. His eyes narrowed as he caught sight of Tyler.

"Walker…"

Tyler raised his palms. "Not on duty. I promise."

Gavin sighed. "Why am I not surprised? Meet me in my office and tell me what we have on this text."

Tyler filled in Gavin and met with Eden with no tangible result. An hour later he checked on Penny again and called Bradley to bring him up to speed. He could hear his friend's anger crackling in his tone.

"We gotta get him, Ty," Bradley almost shouted. "He's torturing my sister."

"I know. We will." Caleb approached as he ended the call.

"Bradley?"

Tyler nodded.

"How's he taking the text?"

"Let's just say his blood pressure is edging toward the roof."

"No doubt."

Caleb followed him down the hallway, and they ran into Noelle exiting her cubicle with Liberty at her side. Her expression was alive with excitement. "We got a tip on Holland."

Tyler froze. Ivan Holland was the Coney Island drug smuggler who had put a bounty on Liberty's head for messing with his operation. The dog had almost been run over in the latest attempt, along with Noelle, who had been walking her at the time. Everybody on the team was hankering to bust Holland for targeting a member of their police family.

"According to a tipster connected to Ivan's crew, they've turned on him after he killed that informant. They don't want to be a part of his police vendetta— it's drawing too much attention. He's got no one on his side now. Tipster tells me he's been hanging around Flatbush."

"When?"

"This morning."

Tyler's stomach rolled in anticipation. "Who's talking to the locals?"

"I will," Noelle said.

"I want to be in on it, too," Tyler said.

"Nope," Noelle said. "You're not even supposed to be here."

"I'll come in an unofficial capacity. Help you take notes." In fact, Tyler felt a burning desire to help Noelle bust Holland. It would be a big load off his plate and clear the way for him to devote most of his time to catching Randall.

Noelle arched an eyebrow.

Tyler pressed on. "I'll ride along as a civilian escort. Dusty needs an outing, especially after her grooming. She can't stand grooming days."

She was still frowning. "If Gavin finds out…"

"Tell him Tyler forced you to take him at gunpoint," Caleb said as he headed for the door. "We've already covered that."

Tyler held up his hands. "I promise. I'm riding along only. Purely a civilian thing."

Noelle laughed. "That's how you spend your day off?"

"If it gets Ivan Holland off the streets, I'll happily sacrifice. Can we stop at the training center and get Dusty?"

"No problem."

Tyler jerked a look at Penny. "I'll meet you outside in ten, Noelle. Got to check on something."

Noelle and Liberty walked outside. Noelle's brow was furrowed, and he understood her determination. Capturing Ivan Holland was personal.

Penny was still at her desk, staring at her screen.

She gave him that cheerful smile again, but he noticed the slight pinch of her lips.

"Doing all right?"

She nodded. "Bradley is going to have my cell-phone number changed. I'll be okay now. No more texts hopefully."

If only Randall's threats could be neutralized so easily.

"Is there anything I can do? Something you need?"

She fired a bright smile. "Not a thing. I'm surrounded by cops with a guard dog on my feet. Perfectly safe."

He wanted to press further, but she was already staring at her screen, typing with amazing dexterity.

"I'll be back in a couple of hours, well before you leave. At quitting time, I'll take you home, all right?"

Her fingers paused on her keyboard. "No need. My brother will escort me."

He wondered if she was still stinging from his "silly" comment. Or was she merely hanging onto the formalities of work because it kept her from thinking about other things?

It suddenly occurred to him that he himself had come into the office, to the comfort of work and routine, when he could just as easily have accomplished his discussion with Caleb over the phone. Then he'd inserted himself into a police assignment with Noelle. So who was clinging to the comfort of a work routine now?

He cleared his throat. "You have my cell-phone number, but if anything changes and your brother isn't available, call me, okay? Or, you know…if you want to talk or anything."

Pink suffused her cheeks. "Thank you. I will call you if I need to." He saw the muscles of her throat convulse as she swallowed. "That's very kind."

Still, he could not make himself walk away. "Promise me you won't leave without me or Bradley?"

"Yes, I promise."

"All right. I'll see you later." He'd cleared the counter, willing himself not to turn and look at her again, when she spoke.

"Tyler?"

He stopped. "Yes?"

"Randall has been at large for twenty years. What…?" He heard the hesitation in her voice. "What are the chances you are going to catch him this time?"

"This time?" He locked on her soft brown gaze. There was such vulnerability there, raw emotion shimmering in her irises. "One hundred percent."

Her whispered follow-up split his gut in two.

"Before or after he kills me?"

He walked back to her desk and kneeled there, earning a nose poke in his thigh from Scrappy. Pulling her hands away from the keys, he forced her attention to his.

"Penny, we are going to put Randall away before he hurts you or anyone else again. I know it's hard to believe, but now we know his identity and we will get him soon, very soon. You just have to hold on and trust."

The brown of her irises softened to a lighter café au lait. "Honestly, I don't know if that's possible. I've not really trusted anyone but Bradley since my adoptive parents passed." She paused, her mouth pulled into a thoughtful bow. "But I will try."

Without thinking, he pressed a kiss to her hand. "I won't let you down." And then he strode out, not wanting to detect any shock in her face from his gesture that had shocked him plenty.

Kissing her hand? Promising that he would keep Randall from ever hurting her again?

And strangest of all, feeling deep in his soul that he desperately meant to keep that promise, no matter what the cost.

FIVE

Penny walked Scrappy at lunchtime in the grassy area provided for the police K-9s. He pranced and sniffed, enjoying the cold autumn breeze. She was reassured by the constant parade of cops and dogs. They all checked on her solicitously.

She kept a smile fixed in place as she responded politely and later forced herself to eat her peanut butter sandwich in the break room. When she went to fill a glass with water, she returned to find the remainder of her sandwich gone. Scrappy swiped the crumbs from his lips with a satisfied slurp.

"You are a naughty dog, Scrappy," she scolded.

She grinned and caressed him. "How about tomorrow I bring you a chew bone so we can have a lunch break together, okay?"

She got a tail wag of agreement. Tummy full and energy depleted, he settled under her desk for a nap while she tackled the outstanding paperwork and ordered a box of supplies for the open house. By late afternoon, she'd almost forgotten the terrible text from Randall. A glance out the window told her that evening was coming. The growing darkness sent a chill cascading down her spine. She wasn't afraid of the dark, was she? No, not the dark, just the man hiding in it.

Bradley called a little after four.

"Sis, I'm stuck on a stakeout."

Her heart began to pound.

His voice cut through her fear. "Tyler's almost there. He's bringing your phone with the new number."

She swallowed and forced a calm tone. "But he's off duty."

"He grumbled so much that Sarge said he could take over your detail when I'm not around."

She remembered Tyler's kiss on her hand, a warm spot she imagined she could still feel. "But he's got Rain to take care of. I'm sure I could ask another officer…"

She looked up to find Tyler striding in with Dusty. He twirled a key ring around his finger. His eyes were shadowed with fatigue, she thought, or maybe frustration. The hunt for Ivan Holland had not yielded any results. Or perhaps he'd begun to regret his decision to be her babysitter.

She covered the phone. "Bradley told me you were coming, but really, it's fine. I can get…"

He shook his head, which seemed to make him wince. "No, I want you with me, but I have to pick up Rain from day care. Do you mind? I figured we can get some dinner at my apartment before your brother comes home."

He said it so matter-of-factly, but the very idea whipped up her nerves. Dinner? At his apartment? "Um, well, I've got Scrappy. Maybe I should…"

"My building has a dog run. We can stop with the dogs before it gets too dark."

Dark. Again, her stomach flipped. *Go home, lock the*

door and hide until morning, her mind yelled. But she would not live that way. She'd spent too long hiding in the shadows and fought too hard to make her way out of them. She forced back her shoulders.

"Okay." She ended the conversation with Bradley and disconnected. "I'll get my purse."

Her knees only shook a tiny bit as she left the secure station and stepped into the darkness with Tyler, Scrappy and Dusty. They walked quickly to his vehicle. Tyler's sharp gaze traveled along the street and between the vehicles.

Looking for Randall, she thought with a shiver. Gratefully, she slid into Tyler's civilian vehicle, an SUV.

She watched as Tyler settled into the driver's seat. The interior was meticulously clean except for a lone bag of fishy crackers lying on a car seat in the rear.

"Better grab that bag," she told Tyler, as Scrappy hopped in, nose quivering. "He's not very reliable around food. I found that out the hard way."

Tyler chuckled. "Neither is Dusty, but she does a great job tidying up anything Rain has dropped."

He turned on the engine and immediately a preschool counting song began to blast through the speakers. Tyler's face turned scarlet. "Oh, sorry. Uh, that's Rain's favorite at the moment. Something about turtles and goldfish."

Penny could not prevent her giggles from spilling out.

He quirked an eyebrow. "I don't think I've heard you laugh before. Not for a long time, anyway. It's nice."

Now it was her turn to blush. He paid attention to her laughter at work? He was always so focused, moving too quickly and purposefully to pay any mind to her, she'd thought.

They traveled the Belt Parkway at a snail's pace through the traffic until he pulled up to a four-story building with a yellow sign for Happy Tot Day Care stuck on one of the doors. Through the front window she could see small children climbing on a plastic play structure and playing with toy cars. High-pitched squealing floated through the air.

And in an instant, the long-ago sadness returned. A dull pain bloomed behind her ribs as her mind traveled back into the past. She recalled being the last child left at day care, her four-year-old nose pressed to the window in search of parents who had forgotten about her again. One by one the other children had been picked up until the facility went quiet. Penny had stayed among the abandoned toys, trying not to notice the lengthening shadows or the agitated pacing of the teachers. She recalled Miss Deborah's brightly painted fingernails clutched around the phone, a combination of annoyance and pity in her voice.

"How could they forget their own kid?" she'd whispered. "And they don't even wash her clothes or brush her hair. They probably don't feed her breakfast before they dump her off here, either."

It was the truth. Bradley, barely fourteen, was the one who toasted bread for her, cut it into triangles and added butter, if there was any in the fridge. He packed her after-school snack, too, a hastily assembled collection of whatever he could find instead of the neatly partitioned containers brought by the other children who shared her day care. She remembered the laughter of the other kids when she'd found half a baked potato in her bag for snack. She would have been perfectly content eating that potato, but she'd gone hungry rather than face the laughter of her peers.

Sometimes it was Bradley who'd come to retrieve her after he returned home from a full school day and a couple of hours at his part-time job to discover her missing. She remembered those long afternoons, looking into the eager faces of the parents as they'd hugged their children and hastened them to cars, admiring their crayoned pictures.

She'd tried taping her own painstakingly drawn pictures on the front of the dented refrigerator, hoping it would help her parents think about her, remember her… want her. If the pictures were good enough… If she just tried hard enough…

She heard Randall's words again. *Your parents didn't love you.* Tyler's touch on her shoulder made her jump.

"Sorry. You looked sad there, for a moment."

She blinked. "I…spent a lot of time in day care. Randall was a handyman and he did some work at the place. That's how he met my parents. They got into some bad things, together. Planned some thefts and scams and such."

Tyler listened intently, though he was no doubt privy to all the facts, anyway. For some reason, she felt the need to say it aloud. "Randall knew… I mean, he noticed my parents, uh, forgot about me sometimes. That's part of the way he justified killing them." She gulped. "He said they were bad parents and I suppose he was right. It took me a long time to understand that it wasn't my fault that they neglected me. I always thought if I was different, more appealing somehow, prettier, smarter…"

Tyler took her hand. His fingers were long and warm as he gently squeezed. "I'm sorry. None of that should have happened to you, or any child for that matter."

She shrugged, garnering strength from his big palm. "It's okay. I have a great brother, and my parents did what they could with what they had. Plus I had two amazing adoptive parents."

He still held her hand, warming it between his. "But you still have some past scars to work through, right?"

"I know my biological parents' behavior wasn't because of me, but sometimes the feelings creep up and I have to give myself a stern talking-to. I guess with Randall coming back it's natural I'd start to stew about things again." She flashed a smile at him, but his face remained grave. She gave his hand a jaunty wiggle before she let go. "Really, it's okay."

"I wouldn't have brought you here if I had known it would be so painful."

"It isn't. I'm all right."

His face still showed uncertainty.

"Well, Detective," she said, voice bright. "Since I know you aren't about to let me stay in the car, let's go get Rain. Scrappy and Dusty can hang out now that the fish crackers have been secured."

He paused, azure eyes troubled. "If it's too hard to go in there maybe I can have someone bring her out to me. I'll just make a phone call."

Warmth tickled her tummy at his thoughtfulness. "No. It's good for me to see all the kiddos at pickup time. It reminds me how families are supposed to be, how God made them to be."

He nodded, and she wished she had not shared something so deeply personal with him. He was, after all, only babysitting her.

Gulping in a deep breath, she walked with him into the day care.

Tyler carefully placed the still soggy finger paintings in the trunk area after strapping Rain into the car seat next to the two eager dogs. The artwork was a mishmash of yellow, all yellow. The teacher had said she could not be persuaded to try any of the other colors. Funny how that small girl knew exactly what she wanted. He wished he had such clarity.

Rain delighted in the new doggy, whom she called "Sappy." Since she insisted on her counting music, he turned up the sound and Rain and Penny sang together. He chimed in at the chorus for good measure, which earned him a brilliant smile from Penny.

That smile had to be a million watts and it left him speechless for a moment. What a splendid thing to possess so much joy when she'd endured a mountain of hardship. He resolved to try to coax a smile from her again soon.

On the drive back, he kept a wary eye out for Randall, but there was no one tracking them that he could detect. When they reached the brick apartment building, he parked and they let the dogs out for a rollick in the fenced dog run. Again, there was nobody around who shouldn't be.

He led the way to their third-floor apartment. "My mom lives downstairs," he explained in the elevator on the way up. "She joins us for dinner. Hope that's okay. I think the Friday-night dining tradition started as a way to ensure I was not poisoning her only grandchild with my cooking."

He was unlocking the door when his mother appeared in the hallway, a covered dish clutched between two pot holders. "Well, hello." Her eyes went wide as she took in Penny with the eager Scrappy at her shin. "I didn't know you had a dinner date, Ty."

Tyler grimaced as he let Rain inside. Scrappy and Dusty beelined in. "Not a date. Mom, you met Penelope McGregor at the hospital. She's Bradley's sister. You know, my buddy who manages to be over here every time you make fried chicken?"

"Of course. I always make a couple of extra pieces figuring Bradley will eat a few." He discerned a calculating look in his mother's eye that gave him pause. "So nice to see you again," she said as she walked after them and put her casserole dish on the counter. Pausing to clasp Penny's hand, she said, "You have the most lovely red hair, Penelope. Just the most attractive shade, like an autumn sunset."

Though he had a feeling his mom was about to meddle, he agreed. Her hair did remind him of a glorious sunset. He blinked.

"Thank you, and please call me Penny. But the red hair comes with a maddening amount of freckles, which got me teased plenty in school."

Rain brought Penny a stuffed rabbit. The toy's face was discolored by a set of ink eyebrows that she had drawn on after discovering a marker in Tyler's desk drawer. She bent and took it. "Who is this?"

"Babby," Rain said solemnly.

"Babby the rabbit. Shall I take care of him for a while?"

Rain nodded.

Penny cradled the bunny like a baby and Rain trotted off in search of another toy.

His mother beamed. "Rain must really like you, Penny. She doesn't hand Babby over to just anyone. Babby is her right-hand rabbit. Did you see that, Ty? Look how she's taken to Penny."

"Yes, Mom, I saw," he said. "Thanks for making the lasagna. It smells great."

"Tyler is the world's worst cook. If I left it up to him, Rain would starve or turn orange from an overdose of mac and cheese. I suppose that might be my fault since I was always the chief chef and bottle washer when my husband was alive. He always had to have things just so and I never wanted my boys to feel the pressure of trying to cater to his food whims." She paused for breath. "Do you like to cook, Penny?"

Tyler sensed again how the wind was blowing. His mother was shifting into full matchmaker mode. "Mom, would you mind setting the table while I fix a salad?"

"Oh, sorry, Ty. I can't. I have to run along."

He stared. "You're not staying for dinner?" He couldn't remember the last time they'd eaten Friday dinner without her.

"Nope. I'm so busy. I've got a zillion things to do."

Like what? he wanted to ask, but the door was already closing behind her.

Penny appeared to be trying to smother a giggle.

"My mom's not too subtle, huh?"

"I think she was hoping you had a date. I take it that's not a frequent occurrence."

He sighed and got out the salad bowl, fishing in the fridge for lettuce, tomatoes and carrots. "No. Dating is not on my agenda. I told her I have my hands full with Rain, but she won't accept that." He paused. "She feels bad. Her last matchmaking effort resulted in me marrying a woman who left two days after Rain was born, so our track record is terrible, anyway."

The giggle died away. "I'm sorry."

He shrugged. "It was a mess, of course, but I'm coming to realize that it was for the best. If Diane stuck around, she would have resented it and passed that feeling on to Rain. I wouldn't ever want Rain to feel like she was unwanted." He froze. "I… I'm sorry. I'm sure that's not how your mother felt." *Blockhead move, Ty.*

To his great relief, she smiled. "It's okay. I've had a lot of years to puzzle it out and I like to think my mom loved me the only way she could, even if it wasn't the way I wanted or needed."

He nodded. "I get it. My dad loved me, too, I suppose, but he was an unhappy guy, never satisfied with anything or anyone. Mom said she wouldn't ever hold it against him since he gave her two sons. Diane gave me Rain, so I'll always be grateful for that." A memory of Diane flicked across his senses, her blue-black hair fanning out across the hospital pillow.

Something in her expression when she'd been handed Rain after the delivery had finally hammered home the truth, even though he hadn't allowed himself to believe it then. He'd been so certain that she would react like he had. Tears had run down his face and his hands had shaken so badly he could almost not support the perfect life that had just emerged into the world. His daughter, a perfect baby, an undeniable delivery straight from God.

Diane had looked over her daughter. "She's beautiful, isn't she?" she'd asked.

He'd only been able to nod, the emotions stripping away his speech.

She's ours, he'd wanted to say until her expression stopped him.

She's yours, Diane said with her eyes.

And that's when the terrible realization began to sink in. Diane was not going to parent this baby. Further, she was not going to stay with him, either. Nothing had changed in that hospital delivery room, for her, anyway.

He found himself saying the words aloud. "I was sure Diane would fall in love with Rain once she held her, like I did. I think she was just too young to…" He trailed off.

"To be a good mother?" she finished softly.

Why was he always saying some dumb thing when he was around her? He heaved out a deep breath. "I guess that's what I told myself. The blaming hurt less than admitting she didn't love me or Rain enough to stick around. In retrospect, I wasn't the best husband. I didn't try to understand her very much and I worked around the clock."

He recalled one particularly nasty argument they'd had when she'd spent several nights in a row out with her friends. "I need a life, Tyler," she'd insisted. "My friends understand me better than you." But had he ever tried to get to know her friends? Join in their activities? He sighed.

"She said I didn't know how to have fun and maybe she was right. I know I could have tried harder."

Had he really admitted that? He'd never really formalized the thoughts until that moment, but it was true. It wasn't solely Diane's age that killed their relationship. He could have—should have—done better.

The divorce was wrapped around with feelings of intense shame. He didn't like to think of the conversations they'd had, the way he'd pretty much begged Diane to stay. The love had died on her end long before it ebbed away for him.

"Fun looks different for different people," Penny said.

He looked for judgment in her expression, but he didn't find it there. Penny was young, too, but he could already see she had plenty of maternal instinct. It shone in her smile and the soft brown of her eyes. His heart thunked against his ribs.

"Does Diane have much contact with Rain?"

"No. She sent a card on Rain's first birthday, but other than that, she hasn't checked in once. I haven't changed my cell phone or email addresses because Rain is going to want contact with her mother at some point. Frankly, I'm dreading the day I have to explain the situation to her. How am I going to tell her that her mother didn't want her?"

"You love her. You'll help her understand it wasn't about her. Some very kind people in my life helped me to see that."

Something about her sweet smile made him want to press a kiss to her lips. He was dumbfounded by his own thoughts. Penny was a colleague, Bradley's sister, and what's more he was supposed to be keeping her safe, not admiring her character or thinking about kisses. He stood there, addled, but she'd already begun to wash the lettuce for the salad.

Grabbing some paper napkins, he slapped them on the table. While the lasagna was cooling, the three of them gathered around the coffee table to build a block

Cold Case Pursuit

tower. It didn't get very high as Rain knocked it over once with her elbow and Scrappy did the same with his tail. They settled for making a block corral for Babby to sit in.

As Penny and Rain added the finishing touches, he stood to stretch the kinks out of his back. He went to the window and gazed down at the busy street below. It was almost fully dark outside. Somewhere out there, Randall was plotting to kill. He looked back at Penny and Rain bathed in the glow of lamplight. Their giggles filled the room with sweet music that had been missing for a long time. One false move, one careless moment, and Randall would snatch her life away. Though he knew there was really no chance anyone could see into his apartment, he pulled the curtain closed, anyway.

It gave him the sensation that the three of them were cocooned in the soft light. If he could only prolong the time, keep the thought of Randall far away from this happy moment. Penny had watched him close the curtains, then quickly refocused on the blocks. Randall would never be out of Penny's thoughts until Tyler put him away forever. After that, would she be ready for marriage? Would he ever be again?

Unsettled, he went about serving up the lasagna and pouring ice water into glasses and milk into a sippy cup for Rain. The dogs had been fed and lounged nearby. He guided Penny into a seat and slid Rain's chair, with the attached booster setup, close. Babby was given an honorary seat and even his own plate and spoon for his imaginary meal.

"What is Babby going to eat?" Penny asked.

"Candy," Rain said with a maternal nod.

"Nature's perfect food," Tyler said.

Penny grinned. "Babby gets to start with dessert and skip the vegetables. That's a pretty sweet deal."

As he began to say grace, the happiness of this family scene, so long missing from his life, clogged his throat. Embarrassed, he found he could not continue.

Penny smoothly finished the grace, and Rain added her own vigorous "Amen!"

He sent her a nonverbal thank-you and she acknowledged with a quiet smile.

He found himself staring at Penny as he ate his meal. Was there really a loving, sweet red-haired beauty sitting across from him, chatting with his daughter? She seemed so interested in what he had to say, in helping Rain to manage her dinner, almost like she belonged there. The cold note of reason intruded on his happiness. She wasn't here because of him…it was merely a safe place to land until her brother came and fetched her. She was here for protection, not because she was looking to get to know him and Rain any further. He swallowed wrong and coughed into his napkin.

Keep things cordial and professional. It was sage advice, but as the evening wore on, he found himself thoroughly enjoying her company. When the meal was over, he was sorry. He firmly declined her offer to help wash dishes.

"No thanks, I got this. I happen to be a master dishwasher even if I can't cook a lick. Rain looks like she's angling for a playmate. Feel free to defend yourself if she tries to drag you into the play area." He gestured to a corner partitioned off by a folding screen. "Don't feel obligated. I am making it my life's mission that my daughter will learn the meaning of the word *no.*"

Penny laughed. "I'm sure a bit of playtime with me won't upset your entire disciplinary agenda."

Penny and Rain trundled off to the play area with the two dogs. Soon he heard Rain snap on her kiddie music player and the clamor of cheerful music started up. While he washed and dried the dishes, his mind drifted back to Randall, who was even now making plans to murder the gentle woman who was playing dress-up with his daughter. He smacked a plate into the dishwasher harder than he'd meant.

Not gonna happen.

Bradley tapped on his door as he was drying off the counter. Tyler let him in.

Bradley inhaled with a look of rapture. "Man, it smells good in here."

Tyler laughed. "No thanks to me. It's my mom's lasagna."

"I figured you didn't make it if it smells this great."

"I will pretend I didn't hear that. Have some." He cut a square, plated it and handed it over along with a fork.

Bradley ate a massive bite and rolled his eyes. "Excellent. Where's Penny?"

He pointed to the corner. Another song about ducks and frogs began. "It doubles as the playroom."

Bradley nodded as he chewed, keeping his voice low. "Penny's a natural with children. I tell her that, but…" He stopped.

"But?"

"She's just not sure of herself. Thinks she wouldn't be a good mom because of our own parents. Scared it's in the DNA or something." He shrugged. "Never mind. I shouldn't be talking about her business. Thanks for pitching in while I was tied up."

"No problem. Happy to help." He would not tell Bradley exactly how happy he felt at having his sister around. "What did you find out today?"

He forked in another mouthful. "Nothing about Randall, but I talked to Lani on my way here. That guy Joel Carey says he's got a photo that will prove Brooke and her pups are his."

Ownership of the gorgeous stray German shepherd and her pups had been a source of controversy since they'd been rescued from an abandoned building site. The pups had become a favorite of everyone in the department. Brooke, the mama dog, and her clan had been getting meticulous care at the police veterinary center. The whole unit had fallen in love with the adorable, precocious puppies. Tyler had even taken Rain to see them.

Joel Carey insisted he was their rightful owner. He was mistrusted by all the cops, including Tyler. Carey's timing was suspicious since he came forward right after a heartwarming news piece aired featuring the dogs. The dog was named Rory, he claimed, and she'd run away when a fire broke out at his place. The fire had conveniently destroyed all of Carey's ownership records about the striking animal.

"I still don't buy it," Tyler said. "Carey's just looking to breed or sell them to make some money. We can't just hand them over."

"If Carey produces a photo of himself with Brooke, we're not gonna have much choice." Bradley wolfed down another bite of cheesy noodles. "Tell your mom I'm going to name my firstborn after her."

"That will be dicey if you have to call your son Francine."

"Good point. I'll hope for girls. What'd you and Noelle find on Ivan Holland?"

"Nothing concrete, but we're getting closer. He's in the area and he's getting desperate as his people turn on him. Matter of time." He waited until Bradley swallowed and addressed the elephant in the room. "Eden is working on the text he sent Penny, but…"

Bradley's eyes darkened. His tone hardened, like it had when Tyler had called to fill him in on the newest threatening text. "But she's going to get nothing, just like the last time."

"Randall might be playing with you and Penny. Maybe he's moved out of the area. It would be smart after what he pulled at your house. Could be he's just bluffing about trying again."

Bradley set down the plate a tad too hard. "You and I both know he's not going to stop. Getting her a new phone number is like putting a bandage on an arterial bleed. Have we got extra eyes on Lucy Emery, in case Randall is the one who took out her family, too?"

"Nate's arranged that with Sarge." He paused. "What does your gut say, Bradley? Do you think Randall also killed the Emerys?"

"I don't know, but that's secondary at the moment. We have to get our hands on him. Now."

Tyler nodded. "Copy that."

Bradley followed him to the play corner. Tyler's breath caught. Penny sat on the beanbag chair, Rain curled up in her lap. Penelope's arms were around Rain. Both were sound asleep. Dusty and Scrappy snored away, as well, sprawled on the throw rug. Scrappy's paws were thrust up in the air. He was dressed in a pink tutu. Dusty snored away, wearing a pair of Rain's dress-up butterfly wings.

Bradley chuckled. "You'd never catch King wearing dress-up clothes."

But Tyler had eyes only for Penny and Rain.

Emotion unfurled deep inside him, like a plant blooming after a long-awaited rain shower. His daughter and Penny were joined together, as if they were meant to be that way. But surely not. She was a deeply wounded woman, determined to hold together the unraveling strands of her life. And he was an older, world-weary single father, lacking the courage to risk his heart to make another family.

He took a picture with his phone of the two sleeping on the beanbag.

Bradley sighed. "All four of them sound asleep. Too bad I have to take Penny home."

Too bad, he agreed.

SIX

Penny slept fitfully, slogging through the Saturday morning chores at their Sheepshead Bay home. She missed seeing Tyler and Dusty in the backyard, but they were back at work. *It's Bradley's turn to babysit me*, she thought glumly. At least she required less supervision than Scrappy, who had already unspooled an entire roll of toilet paper all over the bathroom and down the hall. His irrepressible curiosity reminded her of Rain. A flush crept up her cheeks when she remembered how she'd fallen asleep in Tyler's apartment, right there on the beanbag with his daughter.

Way to show him you're a competent adult. She'd been awakened by her brother's gentle patting on her shoulder, and Tyler had then rolled Rain into his arms and carried his daughter to her bedroom. Why couldn't she have stayed awake a bit longer?

Still, the evening had been cozy and perfect, a shared meal and interesting conversation. Astonishing, how relaxed she'd felt. How long had it been since she'd enjoyed the company of a man to that degree? She did not date often, and when she did, she inevitably found a reason to break it off when the prickly panic began to creep in, the low whispers that told her she was not ready to let things progress any deeper. Marriage and family were not in her immediate future.

The squawk of a bird flying over the yard made her start. Did she even have a future anymore? With a killer waiting for his chance?

She slapped a slice of bread into the toaster to distract herself from the unsettling musings and poured a cup of kibble into Scrappy's bowl. "You are supposed to eat kibble, not peanut-butter sandwiches or toilet paper." He stared at her fixedly, but when nothing more enticing was added to the mix, he set about gobbling it up.

The house phone rang, a telemarketer she figured, but it kept right on ringing until she finally picked up the call.

"Penelope?" The quivering voice made her press the receiver closer.

"Mrs. Lawson? Is that you?"

"Yes, honey."

Penny lost the next few words until her neighbor got to "…flooding." The word was followed by sniffling. The elderly lady in the brownstone next door was a widow who rarely ventured out unless it was to deliver a loaf of her freshly baked cinnamon bread to Penny and Bradley. Widowed five years prior, she was a virtual hermit. Penny's heart sped up at the anxiety in Mrs. Lawson's voice. "You've got a flood, Mrs. Lawson?"

Bradley entered the kitchen, attention diverted from the coffee machine by her phone conversation. King regarded Scrappy with a watchful eye. He was tolerant of the mutt, but not completely accepting yet. Scrappy was smart enough not to challenge King in any way. She put the call on speaker so Bradley could hear.

"I was just drawing a bath in the tub to soak my feet in some Epsom salt, but the faucet handle snapped off and I can't shut off the water. I tried to pull out the plug, but I can't reach down that far without falling."

The sniffling grew more pronounced.

"On my way," Bradley said.

"I'm so sorry, Mrs. Lawson. My brother will come right over, okay? He's a whiz at fixing things. It will be all right, don't you worry."

Bradley fetched his toolbox, strode to the door and disabled the alarm.

"Stay here," he said to Penny. "Bolt the door behind me."

"I will." She dutifully turned the lock after he left.

Ten seconds later, the phone rang once more.

"I'm so sorry to call again," Mrs. Lawson said, her voice quavering. Penny had to press the phone closer to her ear as the woman continued. "But can you bring a tarp? I want to protect the legs of my oak dresser. The water is flooding the tub and soaking the carpet." Penny could hear Mrs. Lawson's quiet sobbing.

"Yes, of course. Be careful not to slip, okay?" She peered out their living-room window. "Bradley is on his way up the stairs right now, I can see him at your door. I'll get that tarp." She wasn't about to disobey Bradley's direct order, but she figured it wouldn't hurt to fetch the tarp from the cellar and text him. He could return and snag it after he'd turned off the water.

King would not follow her down into the basement. He was staring out the window, tracking his partner's every move. She knew Scrappy would be at her heels all the way down the steep, narrow stairs, so she let him out into the backyard. He shot outside, rump wiggling at the thought of a romp in the yard. She locked the sliding door before pulling her sweater more tightly around herself, then went to the cellar steps and flipped on the light. The cold interior smelled of mold and old cardboard. The darkness seemed to penetrate her body. Goose bumps rippled her arms as she peered down the staircase. For a moment she froze on the threshold, breathing hard.

Thoughts of Randall and his hideous clown mask stabbed at her. *Next time, I'll finish it.* Her feet froze.

There was nothing in that basement that could hurt her. At the bottom of the stairs, she strode purposefully to the neat shelves, where Bradley had a stack of tarps. She grabbed one and tucked it under her arm. The tension inside her turned to satisfaction. At least she could accomplish one small thing without turning into a quivering lump. She would put the tarp by the front door so Bradley could easily grab it.

She'd just reached out for the railing to start upstairs, when hands jerked her backward.

She wanted to claw the fingers away, but her arms were twisted behind her back and someone pushed her hard, her cheek hitting the clammy cement wall. She sucked in a breath to scream when her captor pressed a strip of duct tape across her mouth, sealing in her fear.

"Surprise," Randall said into her ear. "Did you think I forgot about you, Penny? Did all your cop friends convince you I couldn't get close again?"

His breath smelled of coffee and cigarettes. Disbelief filled her body even as she wriggled to get loose. How had Randall done it? Probably by intimidating Mrs. Lawson. Randall had obviously threatened her into making the initial call. Then he waited until Bradley was safely away from the house and forced her to phone again the second time, requesting the tarp.

As if Randall read her mind, he chuckled. "I saw your brother carrying the tarp through the cellar doors the last time I was watching your yard, checking things out until I was sure which window was yours. Neat trick, asking the neighbor call you to fetch it. The old lady was tougher than I thought. I had to hurt her a little bit to get her to cooperate."

Hurt her? The sweet and vulnerable widow? Terror and outrage sparked through her entire body. Her screams were caught inside her taped mouth.

"We'd better go before dear brother Bradley comes back." He leaned so close his lips brushed her ear. Disgust nearly gagged her. "I'm going to save him for a later date."

There was another rip of tape and her hands were fastened behind her back. Then she was being marched, stumbling, toward the doors that exited to the outside. Randall forced her through and outside. He didn't bother closing up. Instead he propelled her into the alley, where a small car was parked. As soon as she saw the car, her fear bucked even higher.

Her brother's words echoed in her mind. *Never let an abductor take you to a secondary location.* She knew with sick certainty that once Randall forced her into that car and sped away, she had no hope of saving herself. Pressing her heels into the asphalt, she resisted with all her might. Her shoes juddered over the rough surface. Randall stopped, but only long enough to change his grip. He turned her around, pressed his arm into her stomach and flipped her over his shoulder. Leverage gone, she thrashed wildly, trying to knock him over, or slow him down—anything to prevent her abduction. He merely grabbed her tighter and sped up his pace. Her silent screams abraded her throat.

Bradley must have surely known by now. He'd have found Mrs. Lawson and gotten the truth from her. He and King would come charging down the alley any moment. She just had to hold on for a few more seconds. With a sudden violent contortion, she tumbled free of Randall's grip.

Her knees struck the ground, causing a sharp jolt of pain. She ignored it, surging to her feet. All she had to do was get away for a split second. Legs churning, she could not maintain her balance with her hands trapped behind her back. A stumble slowed her. Randall dove at her, knocking her flat. The breath was pressed from her lungs as he pulled her to her feet and once again flopped her over his shoulder.

Her vision blurred as she was bounced against Randall. The black fabric of his windbreaker scraped against her cheek.

Stall! Fight as hard as you can for a few more seconds...

Blood pounded in her head and beat behind her temples. She kicked and bucked as if an electric current was passing through her body, but Randall was strong and determined, and this time he wasn't going to relax his hold.

Unable to scream, born along like a leaf in the current, she heard the pop of a latch.

No. This couldn't be happening. Bradley would see. Someone would come. Terror flooded her nervous system as she realized what was taking place. She was dropped into the gaping trunk of Randall's car right on top of a leering rubber clown mask.

The last thing she saw was Randall's crooked smile as he slammed the lid closed, leaving her in darkness.

Tyler smiled at Dusty in the back seat of his police car. She was curled up next to the soft pink sweater Penny had left at their apartment. Memories from their evening refused to leave his mind for very long. The dogs had seemed to enjoy their gathering as much as the humans. The two animals had tirelessly retrieved the toys Rain flung at them. He suspected both dogs had been tossed an ample supply of peas from Rain's plate when he'd taken his eyes off her. Penny might have noticed but she wouldn't rat out Rain to him.

He'd enjoyed the evening probably much more than he should have. It had been a very long time since he'd laughed so heartily and shared so much. For some reason, she hadn't seemed upset by his talk of his broken marriage. There was something about her that calmed him, soothed a part that had been broken when Diane left. With Penny, there was safety in letting down his guard, showing his silly side. And when he saw her with Rain asleep, as if they belonged together… He shifted on the seat. He had enough to think about right now trying to find the elusive Andy and tracking down Randall. Not to mention the case on Ivan Holland, which could break at any minute if the local beat cops spotted him.

There were way too many balls in the air to be preoccupied with thoughts of Penny. Still, he found himself guiding his vehicle along the road that would take him past the McGregor home. He'd just check in with

Bradley, make sure the protection schedule was complete, he told himself.

Dusty flapped her ears. "Yeah, I know we already worked out the schedule, but it couldn't hurt to double-check." Dusty blinked. Why did he feel like the dog could see right through him?

Why am I making excuses to see her outside of work hours?

He hadn't the faintest idea. Teeth gritted, he pulled to a stop a block before her home and let out a deep breath. Quickly he looked again at the picture on his phone of Penny and Rain sleeping soundly. Again, a sense of peace washed over him when he viewed the picture for the dozenth time.

He should turn around before he made an idiot of himself. He'd flipped on his turn signal when the call came in over the radio.

Abduction.

McGregor home.

A BOLO issued for a dark-colored sedan.

Penny.

Adrenaline swamped him as he turned on his lights and siren, then punched the accelerator. He screeched up to the curb. Bradley and King were sprinting from the alley, racing toward Bradley's car.

Tyler rolled down the window and shouted. Bradley froze, then turned and hurried to Tyler's car. His face was white and pinched. "Randall took her. I saw him getting into the driver's seat. Exited the alley westbound." Bradley swallowed. "I think he put her in the trunk."

Tyler fought to pull in a breath.

Lani braked to a stop behind them, red lights flashing. "I was a block away, taking a report. What happened?"

Bradley pointed to the neighboring house. "Elderly lady named Anita Lawson was threatened by Randall into setting us up. She's not hurt badly, but she needs care. And Scrappy's in the yard. I can hear him barking."

"On it," Lani said.

Bradley had already gotten King into the car when the second report came over the radio. A patrol officer from the 61st Precinct had possibly spotted the sedan speeding on the Belt Parkway.

Tyler listened, his heart slamming into his ribs. His spirit plummeted when the cop informed them he had lost his quarry in the long pocket of residential homes and shops sandwiched between the Belt and Emmons Avenue. Randall had headed into a sleepy Sheepshead Bay waterfront community close to the marina. With multiple units responding from different directions, they'd close in quickly and cut off his escape from Brooklyn. They'd locate the vehicle and make the bust. If he headed for the piers themselves between Ocean Avenue and East 26th Street, they could cut him off there, too.

His throat went dry as he finished the thought.

But would Randall kill Penny first?

SEVEN

In the cramped trunk, the darkness stabbed through her like an ice pick. Alone. She was completely alone, like she had been on the night she watched her parents die. Randall had left her then with a deep well of uncertainty that she should do something, anything. But four-year-old Penelope had not had the faintest clue what action she should take. The phone in their cramped unit had been disconnected for nonpayment, so she could not have called anyone even if she'd thought of it. So she'd huddled into a ball on the sofa, clutching the plastic-wrapped monkey, too afraid to look closer at what was lying on that worn kitchen linoleum. The fear had taken root deep in her soul. She'd been very hungry, she remembered. Stomach growling, shaking and alone, she'd waited for her brother.

Alone. Twenty-four-year-old Penelope fought hard against the buzz of panic that electrified her. Panic was not an option, and Randall hadn't won yet. She ordered herself to calm her breathing. It was a Herculean feat since her mouth was taped shut and her body was being jostled with the car's movement. The trunk interior smelled of gasoline and rust. The flabby rubber of the clown mask pressed into her back, where her shirt had ridden up. That horrible clown face, as if it had leaped from her nightmares into real life.

She would not cry. She was not a child and certainly not helpless.

Pressing her feet against the lid of the trunk, she kicked with as much violence as she could muster. Her heels thudded uselessly against the metal, sending pain through her bruised knees and shins. The trunk did not give, and the car did not slow. Where was he taking her? When would he stop?

She knew the answer to that question. *He'll stop when it's time to kill me*, she thought with a shudder.

She needed to attract attention.

Rolling onto her side, she desperately sought the soft glow where the taillights were positioned. She found one, wriggling as close as she could. If only her hands had been secured in front, she would be able to whack at the light until it popped free. Her only option was to try it with the heel of her boot.

Contorting her body drenched her in sweat. Inch by painful inch, she got her feet into position. Aiming her boot heel, she banged at the plastic. The crunch when it gave was sweeter than music. Another round of aerobics brought her face close to the empty hole. A puff of cool air bathed her. The sedan hit a bump and smashed her cheek into the frame. White-hot pain zapped at her. This time she braced her knee against the movement and peered out the hole.

Glimpses of paved road and the bumper of a car flashed by. A delicate whiff of the sea told her they must be near the marina. Faint hope stirred. The marina area was lined with piers housing recreational fishing fleets, dinner boats and, across the water, lovely houses she could never hope to afford. It was a vibrant place with seafood shacks, gift shops and bicycle rentals. Though it wasn't as bustling as it would be in the summer months, the October weather was still mild enough that there might be plenty of people still about. But at this hour? Another bumper appeared in her tiny view hole. After a moment, it vanished, turned into another lane perhaps.

What if no one notices the broken taillight? She had to try something else.

But what could she do with her hands taped behind her?

The rubber mask.

Groping and straining, she grabbed it, willing her fingers to grasp the symbol of her worst fear. She gritted her teeth. The thing that Randall used to terrify her was going to be her salvation. As she tried to turn herself into position, the car bumped and juddered, throwing her onto her belly. Was he stopping? Her time was ticking away.

Breathing hard, she jerked her body around and fed the clown mask through the hole. Maybe if she could hold it there, wave it like a signal flag, the movement might attract attention. A violent bump of the car caused her to lose her grip and the mask fell through the hole. She cried aloud.

She tried to peer out and see where it had landed, but she only succeeded in banging her face against the metal again. Gradually, an important detail eclipsed the feelings rampaging through her.

Every nerve telegraphed the dreadful message. The car was slowing. Randall was pulling over somewhere.

Her plan had failed and now he was coming to kill her, just like he'd promised. She heard the engine die.

Her brother would find her. Someone surely would come.

Footsteps crunched along the side of the car. She readied her feet to kick out, to knock him backward and earn herself a few precious seconds. The plan was unlikely to succeed, but it was all she had.

Help me, she silently prayed. *Don't let him kill me.*

A key scratched in the trunk lock.

She blinked back the tears. Whatever happened, she would not give him the satisfaction of seeing her cry.

Tyler braked to a stop at the entrance to the marina parking area and slammed a hand on the steering wheel. "Where is he?" Behind him, Dusty whined.

Bradley's increasing tension crackled over the radio. "I've checked the parking lots and we have units on both ends of the street. What's your location?"

"Parking lot by the piers. Nothing so far. I…" He stopped in midsentence. "Hold on a minute." He was out of his car and sprinting to the spot where a crumpled object was lying on the asphalt. A clown mask with blue hair and a slashed mouth. Had Randall stopped and opened the trunk? Continued on, or reversed and returned to the main road? There was only one way out of the parking lot. Either Randall had escaped the lot before Tyler had shown up, or he was somewhere nearby, perhaps behind the boathouses or the warehouse at the end of the long row of boat slips that lined the Sheepshead Bay waterfront.

He almost shouted in the radio pinned to his shoulder

as he broadcast the location. "I've got a clown mask. I'm going to have Dusty track."

"I'll be there in five," Bradley said. He didn't ask Tyler to wait. Tyler wouldn't have listened, anyway.

Unwilling to waste a moment lingering around for a reply, he released Dusty from his vehicle, clipped on her long lead and brought her to the mask.

"Track."

The command was unnecessary. Dusty was already nose-deep in the rubber recesses of the mask. Three long whiffs and she took off across the parking lot. He pulled his sidearm and followed.

Nose glued to the ground, she led him to the last row of cars. There at the very end was the black sedan. The rear taillight was missing. Pulse roaring, he put her in a stay and edged forward, weapon aimed at the driver's-side window. Another step closer and he darted a look into the front seat. Empty. Rear seat, also.

The trunk lid was slightly ajar. Weapon aimed, breath held, he jerked it open. Empty. A ragged breath escaped him. Tyler wasn't sure if he should be relieved or not. Penelope hadn't been left there for him to find. Did that mean Randall hadn't hurt her? Yet?

"All right, girl," he said, calling to Dusty. "Show off that champion nose, okay? Track."

She was already twitchy, nostrils vibrating as she followed the scent from the parking lot past the dock. A row of neatly painted warehouses with corrugated roofs lined the area next to the boat slips. There was no outward indication that Randall had passed this way, but Dusty had all the clues she needed. She led him right to the second warehouse, sitting obediently at the warped wooden door and beaming those soft eyes at him.

He gave Dusty a pat and whispered, "Stay. You'll get your treat soon—I promise."

As soon as he arrested Randall Gage and got Penny to safety.

Gripping his gun, he seized the door handle and counted to three.

Penny stumbled as Randall pushed her behind a stack of pallets in the old warehouse. The place smelled of oil and the far-off fragrance of the sea. She tried to stay upright but fell to her knees instead. Sharp pain cracked through her shins and she felt a trickle of warm blood ooze through her pant leg.

Her throat was dry and aching from her muted screams. She'd struggled, thrashed and gone limp, but to no avail. Not a single soul had witnessed Randall wrestle her from the trunk and march her into the empty warehouse. He'd covered her bound hands by keeping her to his side, as if they were a couple, strolling along the dock.

The skin around her mouth stung from where he'd ripped off the tape.

"It's too suspicious having you walk around with your mouth taped. If you make any noise, I will toss you in the water and hold you under until you drown." That thought made her weak. Drowning alone and helpless, sinking to the bottom of Sheepshead Bay to her silent death while Randall watched and gloated made her nauseous. Still, she would have risked shouting out, if she had seen a possible rescuer.

But there had only been a single dockworker, who'd been too far away to hear over the wind-tumbled waves. A couple had passed by on a boat, and her pulse quickened, but they'd merely waved a friendly hello. Randall had waved in return and the couple kept on going. Her last hope had seemed to fade away in the small vessel's wake.

She'd been praying with all her being that Bradley would catch Randall's trail. But he hadn't been able to rescue her, not this time. How would he feel knowing that he'd been tricked? It would eat away at him and the thought made her angry. Bradley should not have to shoulder any more grief. "You have no right to do this."

Randall jerked as if she'd surprised him. "I have every right. Your parents messed up my life. I saved you from them and you repaid me with betrayal, just like they did. You, your brother, your parents. The whole lot of you are a bunch of snakes who deserve to die."

She glared at him. "How exactly did we mess up your life? So my parents came to their senses and changed their mind about the robbery. You could have gone ahead without them."

His face went scarlet. "I did go ahead, and because your parents tipped off the cops anonymously, I almost got arrested. I had to lay low for two days and you know what happened in that time? Huh, Penny? Do you have the slightest clue what they cost me?"

She saw the rage simmering below the surface of his irises.

"My wife left me," he snapped. "One too many times I'd let her down. She warned me the next time I didn't come home, she'd hit the road." He shook his head. "I tried to phone, but she wouldn't take my call." His voice dropped. "On her way out of town she got in a wreck. Killed on impact." He took a knife from his pocket and pointed it at her. His fingers were gripping it so tightly, his knuckles went white. "That's on your parents. She's dead because of them."

Penny shook her head. "They didn't mean for that to happen."

"You were four years old. How could you possibly know what kind of people they were?" His eyes rounded. "I told you the truth, and you still defend them, like they were great people. It's unbelievable. They were dirty double-crossers who never cared for you. I saved you from that, and what did you do? You double-crossed me, too. Told the world I was a monster."

She pressed down the words bubbling up in her throat. Confrontation wasn't going to get her out of the situation. Instead she forced a conciliatory tone. "I'm sorry about your wife. That must have hurt you very much. I can understand why you feel angry."

"You understand?" For a moment, she thought she detected a softening in his face, but then he tipped his head back and laughed. "You looked just like your mother for a minute. She thought she could sweet-talk me, too." He bent close to her, the knife now inches from her cheek. "Know what that got her?"

Penny swallowed. She did know. It had earned her mother an execution. For the first time, Penny admired her parents for standing up to Randall the best way they could, for trying to make a better choice for themselves and maybe for her and Bradley. They'd failed as parents, but at the end it was possible they'd attempted to change. She longed to tell Bradley about her epiphany. Would she live long enough to share her thoughts? Her only option was to stall for as long as she possibly could.

"Why did you kill the Emerys? What did they do to you, Randall?"

He shook his head. "Not that again. Stop talking."

"Are you having trouble justifying why you orphaned Lucy Emery? Did you think you were saving her, too, by murdering her parents?"

He edged the knife closer. "I told you to stop talking. You're giving me a headache."

But talking was the only thing keeping her alive. "You don't have to kill me. I understand now why you're so angry. I didn't know about your wife, but now that you've explained it, I'll talk to the press and tell them your side of the story. They won't think you're a monster anymore after I tell them the truth."

Slowly, he shook his head, then grimaced. "It's too late. It's a matter of time before I'm sent to prison. You and your brother are the last two items on my to-do list. Or should I say, my to-die list?" He laughed again.

So much for the soft approach. Randall was obsessed with his mission. There was no point in pretending she understood his evil. She shrugged. "So you're just a coward, aren't you? It doesn't take a big man to shoot two unarmed people and kill a woman with her hands tied behind her back."

He glared at her. "Like you said, I'm not a man, I'm a monster."

She stumbled back several steps as he advanced.

He snapped his head to one side. "Did you hear something?"

She could only detect the harsh sound of her own breathing until somewhere in the back of the warehouse a door slammed open. Her pulse thundered.

"Police!" a familiar voice shouted. Randall swung around.

Penny didn't wait. She darted into the shadows of the

warehouse, almost falling over a low pile of rope. Catching herself in time, she raced down a row of shelves.

Randall was right behind her. "I'll kill you," he shouted. "It won't do you any good to run."

But she'd recognized the voice of the police officer who'd slammed through the door.

Tyler Walker was here, for her.

And she was going to do everything she could to keep herself alive long enough to make it to him.

EIGHT

Protocol dictated that Tyler should wait for backup, but that wasn't going to happen, not with Penny's life on the line. "Randall, it's all over," he hollered. A clatter from deeper in the warehouse indicated Randall, or perhaps Penny, was on the run.

He took cover behind three enormous fuel barrels and shouted again over his thundering adrenaline. "There's no way out of here. Give it up and let her go."

There was a crash from somewhere to his left. Tyler surged forward, sheltering himself next to an upside-down boat with a freshly painted bottom. He waited, straining to hear. The tiniest squeak—the sound of a rubber sole on the cement floor—alerted him. Randall must be at his three o'clock, moving quickly.

Tyler erupted from behind the boat. Past a pile of netting, he saw a flash of black. He pursued, skirting a rusted engine and a crate full of batteries. Motion ahead. Sprinting forward, he rounded a boat in the process of being refinished and stopped short.

Ten feet away he caught sight of Penny. She was half crouched, hemmed in a corner by piles of neatly stacked lumber. Her body was rigid with fear, and awkward posture indicated her hands were probably bound behind her. She snapped a look at Tyler.

He saw her mouth open as if she was about to shout to him, but a rustle from behind a pile of sailcloth snatched his attention. He aimed his weapon.

"Nowhere to go, Randall. Let me see your hands," he shouted.

Randall catapulted from behind the sailcloth. He sprinted toward Penny, his arm raised, gripping a knife.

"Stop," Tyler shouted as Randall charged. Penny screamed, twisting her body away. She created just enough of a gap between them. Tyler fired. Randall grunted, dropped the knife and clutched his side. A bloom of red appeared through the fabric of his shirt.

"Stay where you are," Tyler roared, but Randall ducked behind a row of shelving. Penny stood, eyes enormous with shock. Her gaze darted between Tyler and the spot where Randall had been a moment before.

He kept his voice quiet but commanding. "Penny, it's okay. Come toward me."

She walked as if she was on a pitching ship, each footfall a little unsteady. Everything in him wanted to crush her to his chest, but the situation was far from secure. He kept his weapon trained in case Randall appeared and tried to attack her again. When she got close enough, he took her wrist and guided her behind him toward the exit door, still searching for Randall. He felt her shudders go right through him. What could he say to comfort her? It was only by God's grace that he had gotten to her in time. But if he could take down Randall, right here, right now, it would finally be over. Freedom for Penny and Bradley.

Another cop was already through the door. Tyler handed Penny into his care. "Get her out of here."

The officer quickly escorted Penny away. Tyler could have called in Dusty to track, but as he edged around the shelves, he saw the trail of blood. As silently as he could, he whispered an update into his radio and crept forward. Following the droplets led him to a tiny office, the door ajar.

From far away outside, he heard the sound of barking, low and intense, but not Dusty… It was Bradley's dog, King. He eased open the door with his boot. A puff of sea breeze on his face sent his nerves skittering. He darted through the door. The office was small, a desk and a file cabinet jammed tight. Papers littered the floor. A small window above the desk had been slid open. A bloody handprint on the sill showed him Randall's escape route.

Smothering his frustration, he reversed course, radioing again as he went. He burst back outside, into a maelstrom of noise and activity. Penny was safe, he noted, sitting in the back of a squad car and guarded by two officers.

In the opposite direction, down by the water, Bradley was holding onto King as a cop tended to someone on the ground. *Yes, we got him*, Tyler silently crowed with satisfaction as Dusty joined him. They jogged to the dock. The closer they got, the more his instincts blared at him. Something wasn't right. His spirits sank as they neared. The prostrate figure wasn't Randall. It was a skinny young man, no more than a teen probably, dressed in jeans and a flannel shirt. An officer pressed a cloth to the man's bicep. Blood stained through the compress.

"The guy came out of nowhere and demanded my boat," the young man said, a look of outrage on his face. "I told him no way, and he cut me. Can you believe that?"

Boat? Tyler groaned as he saw the tiny motorboat growing smaller and smaller as it plowed through the choppy waves of the bay. He felt like shouting. This could not be happening. Randall could not be slipping out of their grasp again.

"Already called it in," Bradley grunted. Anger flamed in his eyes. "But he'll probably ditch the boat as soon as he can. Harbor Patrol is deploying and a chopper's en route."

Like Bradley had already noted, Randall would no doubt dump the boat within minutes to avoid being spotted from the air, so they were back to a ground pursuit. This time, they had an advantage, he thought grimly. "He's wounded. I shot him. There's a blood trail. I'll inform all the local clinics. He won't get far bleeding like that. He'll have to stop somewhere for medical attention."

Bradley's nod was curt as he locked gazes with Tyler. They both knew how close Randall had come to keeping his murderous promise to kill Penny. They made their way back to her. She bolted from the car when she saw Bradley and locked him in a tight hug. Then she wrapped Tyler in a similar embrace.

He clasped her tightly, feeling her tears on his neck, the wild beating of his heart, or was it hers? He could not tell. There were so many emotions tumbling through him he did not trust himself to speak.

"You're okay," she mumbled. "He didn't hurt either

of you." She sounded as if she was trying to reassure herself.

"We're fine." Tyler moved her back into the car and eased her onto the seat again. Her cheek was bruised, blood trickled from the corner of her brow. The knee of her pants was torn and bloody. "Tell me how you're doing."

She turned a stricken face to both of them. "I'm— I'm okay, I think. Is Mrs. Lawson all right? Randall said he hurt her."

Tyler nodded. "Lani said she's very upset, but fine otherwise."

Penny bit her lip and looked at her brother. "I'm sorry, Bradley," she said, tears caught on her lashes. "I thought it would be okay to get the tarp from the basement. I should have suspected..."

"None of this is your fault," Bradley said savagely. Tyler nodded in agreement.

"As a matter of fact, you showed some real smart thinking, kicking out the taillight and shoving the mask through." Tyler was going for encouragement, but his cheerful tone rang false even to his own ears. He was still reeling at what could have happened. Randall with the knife ready to plunge into her heart.

A look of utter defeat stole over her face. "I guess if I was real smart, I wouldn't have let him get to me in the first place." Her voice wobbled and she wrapped her arms around herself.

Bradley moved away to get King settled as another wave of cops arrived. Tyler knelt next to her.

"That's on us, Penny. We should have moved you to a safe house before this, insisted on it."

"But I don't want to..." She trailed off, defeat clouding her features. "You're right. It's the prudent thing to do." Her chocolate gaze met his. "But I can still work, right? My job…it's everything to me."

He heard in her question a mountain of desperation, the passionate need to hold the threads of her life together. Reaching out, he gently touched the soft skin of her forearm. If he'd been a moment later… Cold slithered along his spine. The best course of action was to settle her in a safe house, keep here there, and avoid the office since Randall knew all about her job. He looked up to find Gavin standing nearby. He must have heard Penny's question, because he gave Tyler a slight nod.

Tyler looked at Penny again, closely this time, past the fright. He realized at that moment that Penelope McGregor was, quite simply, beautiful. Not in the common way of television models and movie stars, but in the earnest curve of her mouth, the delicate sprinkle of freckles, the way her eyes shimmered with an intensity that made his breath hitch just a little. He swallowed the feelings and took her hand.

"If you want to work, we'll talk to Gavin and make that happen for you."

She sagged a bit, her fingers ice-cold in his. "Thank you."

He paused, weighing his words as he considered what she'd been through. Locked in a trunk, bound and helpless, almost murdered. *Lord, help me to be delicate here.* "There are people connected to the department, really good doctors I mean, who can help you…process what you've just experienced. They specialize in trauma."

"I know all about doctors who specialize in trauma, Tyler." She looked away from him for a long moment before she turned back. "They can't help me feel safe again. I will never feel safe again until Randall is caught."

He fought the growing desire to tear the city apart brick by brick until he got his hands on Randall. "You are a strong person, there's no question about it, but if you change your mind, all you have to do is say the word. I'll take you myself and—and I'll stay with you through it, if that would help. You wouldn't be alone unless you wanted to be."

For a moment, she was silent, clenching his fingers. She brought his hand to her face and rested her cheek against their twined fingers. He held his breath, hoping she would feel his determination, the tide of emotion that welled up inside, the ferocious need to protect, the fear at what might happen if he failed.

And there was something more. It was as if she touched some soft spot inside him, opened a vault down deep in a place he'd kept locked in shadow since Diane had left. He pressed his mouth to her knuckles and kissed her. "I am so sorry this happened."

After a final squeeze, he let go of her hand and stood, breaking the connection between them as a medic arrived.

It was a connection he could not afford.

Not now, not ever.

The safe house was not actually house, but a second-floor room in a boxy six-story redbrick hotel in Bay Ridge. Penny tried hard to banish the feelings of defeat as she surveyed her new residence. Bradley, of course, had wanted to stay here with her, but it would be foolhardy to place both targets in the same spot. To make matters worse, she was not convinced her stubborn brother was safe at their home, even with his devoted police dog, but there was no changing his mind about leaving. She wondered if he was secretly hoping Randall would show up again. The thought chilled her.

The hotel decor reflected a depressing beige color palette. One corner hosted a minifridge, a microwave and tiny coffeepot. The two double beds filled the rest of the space—one for Penny and the other for Brooklyn K-9 officer Vivienne Armstrong. Her border collie, Hank, slept on dog bed in the corner. Hank had better manners than Penny's exuberant companion. Scrappy wasted no time in jumping up on the bed as if testing the waters.

"Same rules here as home, Scrappy," she said, ordering him off the bed and onto a squishy dog cushion Tyler had brought from her house.

Vivienne looked around. "Not exactly the Ritz, but we'll make do, won't we?"

Penny gave her a bright smile. She knew Vivienne would probably rather be anywhere but a cramped hotel room, so Penny wanted to be as amiable a roommate as possible. "It will be just fine. I appreciate you staying with me."

Vivienne lifted a shoulder. "Happy to do it."

Penny endured a very long Sunday filled with cooking-channel shows, reading time and taking Scrappy and Hank out for supervised outdoor time. She sadly missed going to church, but she did some Bible reading on her own.

When things got particularly dull, she spent time peeking through a crack in the curtain at the crawling traffic below. Tyler called regularly to check in, but he did not ask to speak to her directly. The night passed in an agitated haze. Her sleep was peppered with snippets of terrifying memories. Once she awoke panting and crying, fearful that she'd been locked in Randall's trunk again. Scrappy dispensed with the rules and leaped onto the bed, trying his best to lick away her nightmare.

Vivienne comforted her and fixed them both a cup of midnight tea until Penny was able to try to sleep again. Resolved not to awaken Vivienne a second time, Penny focused on lying still, staring at the ceiling and trying desperately to keep her mind on open-house details. Her brain would not stay on track. It was only when her thoughts drifted to Tyler and Rain and their joyful dinner party that she finally relaxed into sleep.

On Monday morning, she made her bed, brushing off the dog hair that accumulated when Scrappy rushed to comfort her in the middle of the night. They had de-clined maid service, which was just fine with Penny since it gave her something to do. She was desperate to get to the office. She'd carefully pulled her hair into a loose ponytail and dotted a bit of makeup over the worst of her facial bruises, as well as a swish of light pink lipstick.

"At least it's convenient for us to get to work from here," she told Vivienne when she emerged.

Vivienne shoved her short black hair behind her ears. "Absolutely, and we have a great view of the street, easy to keep an eye on things."

Vivienne reached into a paper bag and pulled out a bagel. "Want one? Caleb got bagels. He delivered them while you were in the shower."

Caleb Black, Vivienne's fiancé, not Tyler. She felt a stab of disappointment.

She was about to say "no thank you," but instead she nodded. Food was fuel, she told herself, and she needed fuel to do her job. "Maybe just a half. Thank you."

She managed to eat half a bagel with some strawberry cream cheese by the time Vivienne had swallowed the last of hers.

"All right," Vivienne said, putting down her phone. "Got the all-clear. We're safe to take the back exit and head to the office."

Thrilled to the core, Penny clipped a leash on Scrappy and the two dogs followed them out of the hotel room. After a quick stop at the dog run, they arrived at the parking lot, where they found Tyler waiting.

Penny's pulse ticked up a notch, but at the same time the tension in her stomach dissipated a fraction. She recalled the warmth of his touch as she'd sat in the patrol car, wrists still smarting where Randall's duct tape had imprisoned her, the kiss on her knuckles… Tyler had been so kind, his blue eyes brimming with tenderness. Or perhaps it was just professional concern.

She offered a smile, but Tyler seemed nervous, detached. *I'm just a job*, she reminded herself, and Tyler was her brother's good friend, to boot. He was her cop babysitter, not anything more. The thought left a cold spot in the pit of her stomach. Their evening together with Rain had clearly not meant the same to him as it had to her. Vivienne drove her to the station with Tyler following in his vehicle.

When they arrived, she made a beeline for the kitchen, relived to find it empty as she set about making the coffee. Scrappy stayed close throughout the morning. Bradley and Tyler were on their phones, similar frowns etched on their faces. She knew they were chasing down leads at the local clinics and hospitals. The boat had been found within five minutes of her rescue. Randall had climbed into the back of a tarp-covered truck and escaped completely unnoticed, even by the driver, until he leaped out at an intersection and bolted.

She pictured Randall running at her with his knife raised over his head and her hands shook as she poured a glass of water in the kitchen. She was surprised to see Tyler's mother and Rain walk past toward the conference room. She put down her water and hurried to see them.

Francine beamed a smile. "Well, hello, Penny. Look, Rain. It's Miss Penny."

Rain waved a chubby hand. Penny sank to one knee and greeted her. "What are you two doing here?"

"Tyler said Dr. Gina was bringing Brooke and her puppies for a visit and who could resist a chance to see them?" Francine said.

Gina, the department veterinarian, had been taking care of Brooke and her puppies at the training center until the ownership issue was decided. Since the German-shepherd mother and pups had been found at the construction site, the whole unit had taken an interest in the canine family. Unfortunately, so had a man named Joel Carey, who insisted the dogs were his and intended to produce proof to that effect.

Penny had seen Joel at the station, loudly and brashly demanding his dogs be returned. She'd developed an instant dislike for the guy. Part of her hoped Joel wouldn't be able to prove the valuable dogs were his.

Penny made to follow Rain and Francine to the conference room, but Rain stopped her, arms raised, a bag of goldfish crackers in one hand.

Francine laughed. "I think she wants a lift. Better your back than mine."

Penny hoisted Rain, who immediately twined her fingers in Penny's hair. The heft of the child in her arms felt so sweet that Penny gave her a squeeze. Rain responded by resting her cheek against Penny's shoulder. It awakened in Penny a deep satisfaction, which startled her. She had never allowed herself to really contemplate mothering before. The subject of lasting relationships and children inevitably raised feelings of sadness, disappointment and neglect. Penny had decided early on that she would not risk imposing those feelings on a child. There might be something deep down in her DNA, a strand of genetic selfishness, that would reveal itself if Penny had children, as it had in her own mother.

Perhaps that was why she always broke things off before they could get serious. The thought was too exhausting to entertain at that moment. She snuggled Rain closer. It was okay to dote on the little girl because there was no developing relationship with her father. The notion gave her an odd prick of both regret and relief.

As they walked along, Scrappy fell in behind. A low chuckle made them all turn. Tyler was walking a few paces after them, sporting a wide grin. The smile lifted the corners of his vibrant blue eyes and her heart did an unexpected dance.

"Scrappy's catching those fishy crackers in midair," Tyler said. "Best game ever."

Penny realized that Rain had been sprinkling a trail of crackers behind them for Scrappy to snarf down. She and Francine laughed, too.

"No wonder Scrappy loves Rain so much," Francine said. "She's like a vending machine for canines.

I'm just going to pop into the ladies' room for a minute. I'll find you in a bit."

When she left, Tyler shot Penny an uncertain look. "Do you want me to take her? She can get heavy after a while."

"I'm happy to carry her." Penny blushed. Was he uncomfortable with her caring for Rain? Doubts assailed her. He knew how her mother had treated her. Maybe he thought she'd be like that with Rain. Maybe...

"Great," Tyler said, and his expression grew warm and relaxed.

She let loose a sigh. "I like hanging out with Rain. It takes my mind off things, and I think we're buddies now."

"Buddies for sure. I couldn't pick a better one for her." She searched his face for any clue that he was insincere, but she did not find any.

He moved nearer and pressed a kiss to Rain's head, which brought his mouth close to Penny's. She imagined for a moment that he lingered there, his lips so near hers.

Snap out of fantasyland. She soldiered on down the hallway, heart beating hard against her ribs.

They strolled into the conference room. Brooke and her puppies were enjoying pets and coos from the gathered officers. Scrappy sprinted to the nearest puppy, head down, bottom up, and began a playful tussle. Rain asked to be put down and was soon swarmed by two big-eared pups. Their button noses twitched in excitement and Rain's hearty giggle made Penny chuckle, too.

She and Tyler watched the canine chaos.

"I'm glad I got to see Rain today." Tyler sighed. "I'm away too much."

Penny had heard from Vivienne that Tyler had spent

almost all of Sunday, his day off, at the station trying to track Randall Gage.

"I'm… I mean, well, I was going to ask you if you'd made any progress, but I know you'd tell me if you could."

He grimaced. "Matter of time. Randall must have gotten help at a clinic somewhere. There was a fair amount of blood in the back of the truck he hitched a ride in. He was bleeding too heavily to patch himself up. I have a strong hunch, but the doctor I need to talk to had a family emergency. Waiting for a call back. I…"

He stopped at a wail from Rain. One of the puppies had gotten overenthusiastic and nipped her finger with needle-sharp teeth.

Penny immediately dropped to her knees. She took Rain's fingers in her palm and gently rubbed them. "There, see? I rubbed the ouchie away."

After a minute, Rain nodded and let Penny dab her tears with a tissue before she wriggled loose to resume her play with the puppies. Tyler extended a hand and helped up Penny. When she stepped on a dog toy and wobbled, he brought her steady against him with an arm around her waist.

"Where did you learn how to do that?" he said.

Her breath caught at the feel of his arm encircling her. "Do what?"

"That ouchie trick with Rain."

Penny stopped dead. Her heart squeezed as she struggled to reply. "My mother used to do that. I hadn't remembered until just this moment."

His face softened. "That's a nice memory."

"It is, isn't it?" The lump in her throat refused to budge. "I guess that means…"

"That she loved you."

Those three words hovered there.

She loved you.

And Randall's words chased behind them. *Your parents were terrible. They didn't care about you. Left you and your brother in dirty clothes, without regular meals, and they forgot about you at day care. Who forgets about their own child?*

She bit her lip and his hold fell away, except for his hand on her wrist. "Randall said they were bad parents, and he was right."

His tone was feather-soft when he spoke. "But they weren't bad parents because you were a bad child. I have thought about this topic a lot, you know, since Diane walked away from us. Someday Rain will come to me and ask why her mommy left. I will tell her that Diane didn't leave because there was something bad about Rain."

He caught her gaze, an earnestness on his face that made her reel.

Long-ago hurts flickered through her mind like an old-time slide show. Her parents had neglected her, forgotten her, left her craving love and acceptance, and she'd been worried that she was unlovable.

But here was this sweet and unexpected memory, her mother's tender touch, her desire to comfort. So what was the truth? The words echoed the question she'd asked God so many times.

Did they really love me?

She realized Tyler was watching her, one hand come to settle lightly on her shoulder. She blinked back into the present.

He leaned close, his mouth near her ear. "You are

lovable and loved because God says so. I tell Rain that every day and I think maybe you need to hear it, too." His fingers caressed her shoulder as his words warmed her heart.

How had he known that it was what she most deeply desired to hear? What she prayed about in the long nights when sleep would not come? The wonder of it traced a warm path through her veins. She blinked against sudden tears.

You are lovable and loved because God says so.

Bradley strode in, face steely, and Tyler pulled away. Bradley jerked his chin at Tyler and they moved to a corner, talking urgently.

Penny forced herself to keep her attention on Rain. Whatever they were discussing was only going to cause her more tension. She retrieved a rubber ball from the corner and rolled it back into the wriggling pile of doggies. In truth, she wanted nothing more than to think about what Tyler had said, to turn it over and over as if she was holding a translucent gem up to the sunlight and watch it tease apart the glorious rainbow of colors.

Tyler returned to her, jaw tight. "I've got to go. Can you make sure Rain gets back with my mom?"

"Of course." She clasped his arm as he turned to leave. "Is it about Randall?"

He covered her fingers with his just for a moment. "Yes, it's the lead I was waiting for. I'll keep you posted."

She didn't say all of the things that throbbed in her heart just then. *I'm afraid for you and my brother. Randall is a monster. Be safe.* Instead she nodded and moved closer to Rain. She couldn't do a thing to stop Randall herself, but she could take care of Tyler's little girl and say some silent prayers that this time, Randall would be stopped once and for all.

Tyler fought to keep his excitement in check as they hurried to their cars with the dogs.

"Doctor at a clinic right here in Bay Ridge finally got back to us," Bradley said. "She treated a guy matching Randall's description on Saturday night. Stitched up the wound on his side and provided antibiotics. He said his name was Aaron Fisher, but he was acting squirrelly so she covertly took a picture."

Bradley held up his phone so Tyler could see. The picture was blurry and dark, but it was clearly Randall Gage.

"Yes," Tyler said, adrenaline surging. "Finally."

Bradley continued. "He gave the doc an address in Bay Ridge that doesn't exist, but she remembered when she was locking up she heard him telling a taxi to take him to a location in Sunset Park."

It was the break they had been waiting for.

Tyler and Dusty followed Bradley's vehicle to a quiet street on the outskirts of the neighborhood. They stopped at the address the doctor had overheard, where a large four-story apartment building sat on the corner of an intersection. They found the building manager to be a young woman with a smile full of crooked teeth and a bright blue streak in her blond hair.

She considered their question. "Aaron Fisher? Yeah, he's lived here a while. I haven't seen him for a couple of days, but that's not unusual. He kept to himself. Not particularly outgoing."

"Do you have a phone number for him?"

She hesitated. "Is he in some kind of trouble?"

"Would you please call it, ma'am?" Tyler asked. "Right now."

A gleam of worry came into her eyes but she dutifully dialed the number. "No answer."

"Ma'am," Bradley said, "we are going to need you to open the door for us, if he doesn't answer our knock."

"I don't think I should do that. Privacy is—"

Bradley cut her off. "We have reason to believe he's murdered two people, maybe more. We can get a search warrant if we need to, but time is critical."

She blanched, swallowed and reached for a key. "I'll open it." They followed her to the last unit at the end of a dark hallway.

Tyler directed the woman to step few feet away from the door. He put Dusty into a sit next to her and pounded on the door. "Randall Gage? Police. Open up."

Silence.

He rapped harder.

"Open up right now or I'm sending the dog in," Bradley shouted.

Nothing.

He gestured for the women to unlock the door and then guided her out of the way. Bradley and Tyler drew their weapons. King was electric with excitement, quivering from ears to tail.

Tyler ticked off a count of three on his fingers and then shoved the door open with his boot. At Bradley's command, King barreled inside, tearing around the small studio apartment like a heat-seeking missile. Tyler and Bradley were right behind him. After a few moments, he sat dejectedly, tongue lolling. Tyler whistled to Dusty, who confirmed their suspicions that Randall was not there.

Nonetheless, Tyler and Bradley checked the small closet, the bathroom and under the bed until they were satisfied their quarry was not hiding.

"Clear," Tyler called to Bradley. Biting back his disappointment, he holstered his weapon and began to scan the littered kitchen counter. Boxes of empty takeout, soda cans and old newspapers covered the aged tile. An open pantry door displayed shelves empty except for a box of sugary cereal and some canned chicken soup. A kitchen drawer was partially open—there was a tattered folder with photos spilling out. Tyler pulled a pen from his pocket and eased open the drawer.

His insides jolted. Stomach knotted, he pulled on a rubber glove and laid the folder on the table, flipping it open. "Bradley, come look at this."

Bradley joined him in an instant. They stood there for a moment in silence, perusing the dozens of newspaper clippings, yellowed with age.

Killer Clown Slays Two
Killer Leaves Little Girl Alive at Murder Scene
Slaying Investigation Goes Cold

"He must have clipped every mention he could find. Sick." Bradley's fists clenched as he studied the photos. Tyler counted fifteen, all pictures of Penny. Some had been cut from newspapers. One had been printed from the internet, an image of her sitting in attendance amid dozens of cops at the opening of the K-9 command unit. She was smiling, clapping.

Bradley's face went scarlet. "He's been stalking her."

There were other photocopied photos from a few news articles—one had been written just after Lucy

Emery's parents had been killed, on the anniversary of the McGregor murders. The offset quote was Penny's.

Randall Gage is a monster and he needs to be behind bars.

One article had been stuck on the door with tacks. The paper was crisscrossed by angry black marks, slashes of permanent marker that had defaced Penny's image in the accompanying photo and left black streaks on the door, where his anger had overflowed. In the middle of it all, he'd plunged a knife so deep through her image that it was halfway into the wood.

Tyler felt as though his body was boiling from the inside out. Randall had taken so much from Penny and Bradley, but he would not be content with that. He wanted it all, down to her very last breath. The knife proclaimed that loud and strong.

"We'll get a team in here," Tyler said. "I'll take Dusty around the vicinity and see if she can get any traces."

But they both knew Randall had abandoned the apartment and would not be coming back. Since there was no sign of blood or bandages, he'd obviously come here, taken what he needed and cleared out after he'd gotten patched up at the doctor's office. His actions were getting bolder because he knew the cops were close and it was a matter of time before he was captured or killed.

Randall was getting more and more desperate to complete his mission.

And they had to stop him before he made Penny pay the ultimate price.

NINE

Penny finished her report that afternoon in spite of the anxiety crawling up her spine. Tyler stood a few feet behind her, arms folded, staring at a spot on the wall. It was all she could do not to plead with him to take a coffee break or go for a run. Anything to relieve his brooding silence. Tyler had curtly informed her that Randall had abandoned his apartment, but her instincts told her he'd left something behind, something that was too terrible for them to reveal. Whatever he and Bradley had found, neither of them intended to share it with her. What could have been so awful? Goose bumps marched up her arms.

Don't let your mind go there.

She would have preferred to stay later than four o'clock to finish a few lingering tasks and shave a couple of hours off her mind-numbing hotel time, but Tyler was clearly itching to take her home. Perhaps he was looking forward to having his babysitting duties over for the day so he could return to his investigation work. She sighed, considering the long evening ahead with Vivienne. It was probably hard for Vivienne, too, since she no doubt would rather be spending time with Caleb, discussing wedding details.

As she gathered her purse and a box of materials she wanted to organize for the open house, the office phone rang. It was not in her nature to allow a call to go to voice mail when it would likely only take a few seconds to answer and forward to the correct party. Penny picked up the receiver. "Brooklyn K-9 Unit. How can I help you?"

"I know where you can find Ivan Holland."

She jerked. Ivan Holland? The gunrunner who had tried repeatedly to kill Officer Noelle Orton and her K-9 partner, Liberty? Holland had put a bounty on Liberty's head after they'd foiled two smuggling operations at Atlantic Terminal and he'd made good on his threats to enact revenge. Holland was an ax hanging over Noelle and Liberty's head.

Stomach tight, she gestured to Tyler, who was at her side in three strides. "Who is this, please?" she said. She was afraid putting him on speakerphone might cause him to hang up, so instead she held the receiver between them so Tyler could hear.

"Never mind who I am. Ivan Holland is the guy who tried to kill your police dog. He put a ten-thousand-dollar bounty on that mutt's head, right? You want him or not?"

She tried to ignore the feeling of Tyler's muscled shoulder against her arm as he craned to see the number and wrote it on a notepad. He signaled for her to keep the conversation going.

"So you have information about Ivan Holland's whereabouts?" A rumbling screech sounded in the background. "It would help if you would give your name, sir. Then I can route you to the appropriate person to handle your information."

"You don't need to know my name. Ivan's time is over. We're not working for him anymore."

"Sir, if you'd just—" Penny began.

"I'm tellin' you where you can find Ivan right now. He's—" The caller stopped talking abruptly.

Penny gripped the phone. "Are you there, sir?"

"I have to go."

The phone went dead.

Tyler was already dialing the number he'd written down. Penny could hear the phone ringing endlessly, but it did not go to voice mail. He disconnected, then made a second call.

"Noelle? Tipster just called in about Ivan Holland's location. Wouldn't give his name and the call was cut off." He huffed out a frustrated breath. "No, I don't know where he was calling from. The number is a cell phone."

Penny bolted to her feet. "I know where he called from."

Tyler stared. "What? How could you know that?"

She grinned. "That noise in the background. Did you hear it? It's the Cyclone roller coaster at Coney Island."

He quirked up an eyebrow. "Are you sure?"

"Completely. I used to beg Bradley to take me. Once we rode it three times in a row until I got sick to my stomach. That sound is unmistakable. That's where the tipster is right now." If the caller was telling the truth, it was also very likely where Tyler would find the fugitive the unit had been seeking for more than six months.

"Noelle, meet me at Coney Island. I need you to make the positive ID and keep your distance. I'll handle the bust with backup. We won't risk him going after you or Liberty one more time," Tyler added to Noelle before he disconnected.

Penny and Tyler ran with both dogs in tow to Tyler's car. "I'll drop you at the safe house on my way," he said after she climbed in.

She shook her head. "That will take too much time. You have to go now or Holland might get away. I don't want to stay here by myself since most everybody is busy elsewhere at the moment, so I'll go with you."

He gunned the engine. "I'm not taking chances with your safety. I'll stay here with you until…"

"Call Vivienne. Tell her to meet us at Coney Island. I'll stay in the car until she gets there or until you're done."

"No way, I can't—"

"Yes, you can," she snapped. He jerked a look at her, eyes wide, but she plunged on. "This department has more to do than searching for Randall and babysitting me. Holland is a menace." In fact, he had murdered an informant, targeted Noelle and would have succeeded in killing Liberty if the dog had not been so well trained. She tipped up her chin and looked Tyler full in the face. "I'm not letting you risk a chance to catch this thug for my sake. We have to go right now."

His eyes were pained. "I can't…"

She squared off with him. "If I'm not safe in a locked police car in the middle of Coney Island with a seventy-pound dog on my lap, then I'm not safe anywhere. Drive, Detective," she insisted.

It seemed as if her command had left him stunned. After a long moment of hesitation, he flipped on the lights and siren. "Buckle up."

She already had. Surprised at her own forcefulness, she sat back in the seat and watched the road fly by. Tyler didn't look at her and she wondered if she'd offended him.

But she was right. There were more people that needed protection, besides her. If Ivan Holland got away because of her, she would not be able to stomach that. Clutching the door handle, she steadied herself as Tyler wove in and out of traffic on their way to Coney Island, squawking his siren to punch his vehicle through.

They pulled up to the boardwalk that divided the broad stretch of beach from the amusement rides and vendors. The place brought back memories for Penny, and she smiled in spite of the circumstances. Summertime and stolen days with her brother were some of her sweetest childhood recollections. Bradley had saved up his money and treated her when he could. They'd ridden every ride they could afford and stuffed themselves with Nathan's Famous hot dogs—hers smothered in mustard and the works for him. She'd never tasted anything as delicious as those greasy treats.

"Best thing ever?" Bradley had said, his own fingers sticky with condiments.

She'd nodded. "Best thing ever, best brother ever."

When Bradley's money ran out, they would walk on the shore, searching for shells cast up on the sand. He always constructed elaborate sand villages that she decorated with bits of driftwood and broken shells. Their sprawling structures inevitably garnered attention from the other beachgoers. Penny loved the beach just as much as the rides. There on the sand, no one cared if a person's clothes were too small or a kid's bangs were crooked after her teen brother had done his best to trim them. Moments at the beach were glorious and golden.

The beach and boardwalk were always magnets for families walking hand in hand or playing near the surf—mothers, fathers and their children. Funny how that had never bothered her on those long-ago days. She'd had Bradley and he was enough. He was the biggest blessing in her life. Randall's threat echoed ominously in her mind.

First you, then your brother.

Stroking Scrappy's thick fur for comfort, she resolved to do whatever Bradley or Tyler asked of her, anything that would help capture Randall and make sure Bradley would have a future.

The massive wooden Cyclone stood proudly at the corner of Surf Avenue and West 10th Street, as it had since it opened in 1927. Its arching ramps and twists were darkly silhouetted against the sky. How she'd squealed in delight over each heart-stopping drop. Noelle and Liberty had already arrived, and had parked on the street that was tucked between the monstrous coaster in front and Luna Park behind. Only two months before both areas would have been jammed with summer vacationers, enjoying the scorching temperatures, but now the area had far fewer visitors.

Before he got out, Tyler turned to her.

"I know, I know," she said before he could speak. "Stay in the car. Do not open the door under pain of death. Text you at the first whiff of trouble."

He paused and, after a moment, grinned. "Okay, yeah, that's what I was going to say and one more thing."

"What did I forget?"

"Nothing." Quickly he leaned over and pressed a kiss to her cheek.

She started, nerves tumbling. "What is that for?"

"I've been meaning to thank you for making Rain's ouchie all better." He fingered a lock of her hair that was draped over one shoulder. "Thank you. You are a very special woman."

Before she could say a word in response, he got out of the car. In a fog, she watched as Noelle handed him a plastic bag, which he opened to give Dusty a sniff. She knew it was an item from the warehouse where Ivan Holland had murdered someone who had informed on him. Dusty grew excited, tail lashing, and led Tyler in the direction of the boardwalk. Noelle and Liberty followed, Liberty's tail arcing through the air in unison with Dusty's.

Tyler's kiss still felt warm on her cheek. She put her hand there to convince herself she hadn't imagined it. He'd really kissed her? After she'd bossed him so terribly? When he'd thought of her as a child not too long before?

You are lovable and loved because God said so.

She realized that in the course of a few days she had glimpsed a whole new side of Tyler than she'd ever seen before. He was a gentle man, a father with a deep wound who was still able to comfort and minister to others. He was faithful. He was loving.

Loving? To her? He had probably meant nothing by the kiss—it was just an automatic gesture, some sort of token of friendship. But her stomach somersaulted, anyway, as if she was taking a ride on the mighty Cyclone again.

Unhappy with his confinement, Scrappy whined and

crawled into her lap, peering out the window to see where Tyler and Dusty had gone. Penelope clasped her arms around his stout neck and strained to do the same. Was Ivan Holland out there somewhere, lying in wait for Tyler and Noelle? Or perhaps the tip had been some sort of planned ambush by Holland's enemies.

Breathing gone shallow, all she could do was watch and wait.

Tyler did not allow himself to think about anything but Dusty as she scurried from spot to spot on the wide, slatted boardwalk. If he had, he would have tried to puzzle out just what in the world he'd been thinking kissing Penny.

To his left, past the boardwalk railings, was a wide expanse of golden sand with only two hardy individuals building castles in the autumn temperatures. It reminded him that Rain's upcoming birthday plan was to go to the beach in spite of the season. To his right was a line of ride entrances intermingled with pizza and hotdog establishments, gelato stands and souvenir vendors. The smell of popcorn filled the air.

He trailed Dusty, confident that nothing would derail her from her quarry. He'd called for backup on the way. Noelle was scanning the crowd. Since Tyler had never actually seen Holland face-to-face, he was counting on her to make the identification more quickly that he could from the photos he'd been shown. With her eyes and Dusty's tracking, they would get him if the tipster's information had been correct. The golden retriever's nose was working overtime trying to sort out Holland's scent from the millions of visitor trails crisscrossing the boardwalk. So intent was he on his dog that he almost didn't notice the towheaded boy who raced over to pet Liberty, oblivious to the Police Dog, Do Not Pet sign emblazoned on her harness. As Noelle tried to get between the boy and Liberty, Tyler looked for the mother. He suspected it was the woman so distracted paying for two hot dogs she hadn't realized her son had wandered off.

At that precise moment, Dusty whined and sat near a man with sunglasses perched on a metal bench. The man tried to look nonchalant, but Tyler saw his posture stiffen as he took in the police dog. Noelle's eyes widened as she signaled Tyler. No mistake. Holland's panicked look flicked from Dusty to Tyler and he shoved a hand in his coat pocket.

"Stop right there—police," Tyler called, drawing his weapon.

Holland leaped to his feet and darted behind an older woman, who looked up in surprise. At the sight of Tyler's weapon, she froze and let out a small scream.

The scream caused panic to ripple through the handful of visitors, who began to run in all directions. "Get down," Tyler shouted, but he lost sight of Holland behind the scurrying bystanders.

"Tyler." Noelle's voice was tight with tension. He spun to find Ivan Holland with his hand gripping the neck of the boy who had been on his way to pet Liberty. Holland had a gun pressed to the boy's head. Noelle restrained a barking Liberty with one hand and gripped her revolver in the other.

The mom turned toward the commotion, dropped the hot dogs and shrieked. "Stay there," Tyler shouted at her. "Holland, let the kid go," he commanded.

Holland's eyes thinned to slits. "No way. One of my people tipped you off, huh? Traitor."

Tyler took a step forward. The mother was sobbing now.

"Please, let him go," she wailed. "Don't hurt my son."

Out of the corner of his eye, Tyler saw two cops making their way along using the row of trash cans as cover. A couple steps closer and Holland would be surrounded, but the area was a target-rich environment with plenty of potential for injuries or worse.

"I'll kill this boy if you try to stop me from leaving," Holland yelled.

"You don't want to do that," Tyler said. "Let him go and we'll talk it over."

"Nothing to talk about. I walk or the kid dies." Holland gave the boy a shake. Tears coursed down the youngster's face.

"Stop," his mother sobbed. "You're hurting him."

One of the newly arriving cops reached an arm out to keep her from coming any closer, but she lurched around him and rushed at Holland. Holland instinctively stepped back, stumbling as he did so. Tyler sprang at Holland and knocked him over backward, away from the child. The gun tumbled loose from his grip. Noelle was there in a flash, kicking the weapon away and training her own weapon on the gunrunner.

The mother scrambled to her son, clutching him, tears streaming down her face.

Holland struggled, but Tyler overwhelmed him easily, rolling him onto his stomach. Dusty and Liberty were both barking up a storm. The man grunted and thrashed.

"Shoulda killed that dog," Holland spat, his cheek pressed to the dirty boardwalk.

"Now you'll never get the chance." As Tyler cuffed and Mirandized him, he felt a surge of intense satisfaction. Finally they had one fugitive in custody. Next on the agenda was putting the killer clown away for life.

Cops closed in from behind, keeping the crowd back and securing the loose weapon.

Breathing hard, Tyler looked up at Noelle with a grin. "About time, huh?"

She grinned back at him and lowered her weapon. "My thoughts exactly." She rubbed Liberty's ears. "Looks like the target is off our backs, sweetie." Liberty celebrated with a long lick to her partner's face.

Tyler and Noelle both took a moment to get their breathing under control and wipe the sweat from their brows. Adrenaline still swamped his senses, but he calmed as he rewarded Dusty with her favorite rope-pull toy and they enjoyed a quick game of tug. He tossed it for her, and she happily chased it down. Another job well done, another bad guy going to prison, where he belonged.

Tyler and Noelle waited until Holland was safely loaded into the back of a police car, and made sure the boy was not injured. To be on the safe side, they'd called in a medic to check over both the boy and the mother. Noelle arranged a ride for them back to the station to give their statements.

"That was scary, and I didn't even get to go on any rides," the boy said, face crumpling.

The dad in him pitied the disappointed child. "Well, how about if I ask the officer to show you the red lights and sirens on his car? How about that?" Tyler suggested. "He might even let you turn them on yourself."

The child's eyes lit up. Tyler escorted them to the waiting police car and asked the officer to take special care of his juvenile transport. Tyler heard the boy's enthusiastic chatter as the cop bent to talk to him.

Overhead the squeals of delight carried from the Cyclone, as passengers plunged down a turn at sixty miles per hour. The thought occurred to him that it had been far too long since he'd ridden the big wooden attraction. The last time was when he and Diane were dating. At the top of that roller coaster, he'd looked out over the ocean and thought his future was right on track with the woman he loved. Then there had been the gut-twisting plunge. He'd not been back to Coney Island since that day, and he'd thought he would never return. All of a sudden he found he was looking forward to giving it another try. Rain would love the colors and excitement, and someday she'd be big enough that he could take her on the Cyclone, too.

An unexpected thought intruded. What would it be like if Penny was with them, her red hair streaming out behind her against the blue sky? They'd share some cotton candy as pink as her cheeks and listen to Rain's squeals together, like a couple in love, a family. What? The daydream burst as quickly as it had formed, leaving him reeling.

His mind was giving out on him. First he'd kissed Penny. Now he was imagining family trips and thinking about love? What was the matter with him? Marriage was not some fairy tale and he was nowhere near wanting to enter into that tumultuous adventure anytime soon. Rain was more than enough of a challenge.

He shook his head and took a moment to gather himself.

"You okay?" Noelle asked.

"Perfect, just decompressing."

She nodded and headed for her vehicle.

In a few more moments, he made his way to his car with Dusty. As he drew closer, he considered Penny's command that he drive immediately to Coney Island. She had not sounded anything like an uncertain young girl. That was Penny McGregor at her strongest.

And at her most attractive. She was looking at him now through the car window, eyes wide. He recalled the feel of her satin cheek against his lips. The massive post-adrenaline reaction was getting to him, had to be. He did his best to push the thoughts away as he strode closer to his vehicle and opened the back door.

"Did you get him?" she asked.

"We sure did."

Penny's squeal of delight lit up his senses. That feeling came over him as he let Dusty climb in, the stomach-clenching sensation of being at the precipice of the roller coaster, ready for the drop. Teeth gritted, he willed away the feeling.

Been there, done that. Not doing it again.

He got inside and closed the door, firmly sealing out the noise of the giant roller coaster.

TEN

Penny was elated as they drove back to the safe house. Tyler's report about Holland's capture was no doubt missing many details, but she was thrilled that the gunrunner was in custody and there had been no injuries. Noelle and Liberty deserved some peace of mind. She wondered why Tyler did not look as happy as she felt. After a few quiet minutes rolled by, she asked, "Is something wrong?"

He shrugged. "Not really. I was just thinking about that boy. An act of violence like that can really mess up a child." He froze, jerking a glance at her. "Uh, I wasn't talking about you, Penny."

Her face burned. Is that what he saw? A grown-up version of a messed-up kid? It was exactly the opposite of what she'd worked her whole life to prove to herself, that she was not defined by what had happened to her at the age of four. "It's okay. You're right. Violence does damage children—adults, too. I'll pray for him." She fastened her gaze out the window.

"I don't think of you that way, damaged by what happened to you." His voice was soft and it drew her back to him, but the hurt remained.

"You probably don't think of me at all." Why had those words come out of her mouth? Like she was some self-pitying teen? Aghast, she knotted her fingers together and stared at her lap.

He sighed, low and quiet. "Oh, but I do. Lately I can't stop thinking about you."

Thinking about her? Did he mean the case? Randall's threats? But the gentle blue of his eyes made her feel that he was not referring to police work. "I guess the Randall case is on everyone's mind," she finally said.

"It's not the case, Penny." He cleared his throat. "You aren't who I thought you were."

"How so?"

He rubbed a hand over tired eyes. As his body relaxed from the tense situation with Holland, his defenses seemed to ease, as well, and his words came tumbling out. "I don't know, exactly. I've learned lately that I have a bad habit of putting people into boxes rather than finding out who they really are. I've been guilty of it since my marriage ended. Maybe it's a form of self-protection or a cop trait. I mentally boxed you up in the too-young category."

"Too young for what?"

He looked out the window, at his steering wheel, fiddled with the radio. "Ah, um, friendship, you know, or…things."

"Things?" It was not her imagination. He was flushed an embarrassed red.

Suddenly he looked as awkward as a teenager who'd tripped over his own feet. "Not that I'm in the market for…things, right now. I mean, Rain and I are doing great. I've got her and my job, so that's really all I can handle. But if I was, you know, well, I mean if the situation was different, you are the type of woman I would, uh…" He thunked his head against the headrest. "Can you please talk for a while so I can stop embarrassing myself?"

She laughed. "Sure thing. What should I talk about?"

"Anything, everything. Whatever you want so I can use my ears instead of my mouth."

"Okay," she said over her thudding pulse. "How about I tell you all my glorious plans for the office open house this weekend? That should be suitably boring." *And safe.*

"Excellent," he said, visibly relaxing. "I'm all ears."

Penny rattled on about the details, everything from the frosted fall leaf cookies to the coloring and dress-up activities for the kids. The conversation lasted all the way to the hotel safe house, where Vivienne was waiting just inside the rear entrance to ensure the hallway was clear.

"Thank you," Penny said automatically as she got out of the car.

"I should be thanking you." Tyler's smile was rueful as he walked her in. "You allowed us to bag Holland, and you kept me entertained the whole way home."

She shrugged. "Happy to do my part."

"Sorry for running off at the mouth." Tyler bid her a formal good-night. He seemed uncomfortable, unhappy, perhaps, that he'd shared his thoughts with her. "You're a one in a million and I really admire you. That's what I was trying to say."

She blushed.

And then he bent to hug her and wrapped his arms around her waist, her cheek pressed close to his. "You just don't know how special you are, do you?"

Her breath caught as her face tipped up to his. He was angling his head to kiss her when Vivienne opened the door for her and Scrappy. Tyler instantly stepped away, looking at his boots. "Okay. Well, I'll see you tomorrow."

"Okey doke." When Penny turned to look over her shoulder, Tyler was already striding away.

You just don't know how special you are...

She realized she felt exactly the same way about him. Thoughts of Tyler would simply not leave her head. But were they talking about different things? He'd considered her too young, ruled her out as a friend. Or was he talking about something deeper?

How did he really feel?

And how did she?

Back in the hotel room, Vivienne locked up and Penny poured a bowl of kibble for Scrappy.

Vivienne laid some paper plates on the table and unbagged some deli sandwiches. "Sorry, it's deli again. I wish I knew how to cook. Caleb will tell you he'll be wearing the apron in our kitchen after we're married."

Penny laughed and took a bite of her turkey sandwich. "You already have those roles all worked out?"

Vivienne's eyes lit up. "We talk all the time. He's the most amazing man I've ever met, my best friend in the whole world. We have chemistry." She sipped some grape soda and eyed Penny over the top of the can. "You know, it seems to me that you and Tyler have some chemistry also."

Penny coughed and quickly gulped some soda. "Us? No, we're just..."

"Friends?"

"I'm not sure of that, even, let alone anything else."

Vivienne's eyes took on a mysterious glint. "Oh, I'm a pretty keen observer of human nature and believe me, Tyler finds you fascinating. I see the way he was looking at you at the puppy play date. He gets this dopey faraway expression when he's watching you. And what I interrupted there when I opened the door…" She grinned.

Penny's face went hot. "Oh, well, I believe he thinks I'm too young for him."

She waved a hand. "His brain might think so, but his heart is listening to an entirely different story. Trust me. I'm a whiz about these things."

Penny managed to get the conversation switched to easier subjects, but that night, curled up with Scrappy, she allowed herself one moment to imagine that Vivienne's scenario was real.

She and Tyler together, a family with Rain.

She'd never allowed herself to conceive of a future with anyone.

Was it time to let herself believe it?

Or was she setting herself up for the biggest heartbreak of her life?

With Randall ready to kill her at any moment, it was sheer foolishness to be contemplating relationships with Tyler or anyone else for that matter.

Tyler finds you pretty fascinating…

Smiling, she closed her eyes and let herself relax into sleep.

Tyler woke up Tuesday morning determined to keep his mouth in check. He couldn't imagine why being around Penny made him go soft in the head to the point that he began to babble. At the usual time, there was a soft knock and he opened the door for his mom.

"Good morning, Mom. Rain is ostensibly tidying her room, which means it will probably be a bigger mess than it was before."

"We'll sort it all out. Are you going to see Penny today?" she said. "Can you invite her over for dinner maybe?"

He sighed. Might as well take the bull by the horns. "Mom, I know you've got your hopes up, but Penny and I are not in a relationship."

She hung her coat on the back of the chair. "You could be, if you wanted to."

"There are way too many obstacles between us."

"Mostly just one big obstacle, Ty, namely you."

"It's a bad idea."

She fixed him with an intense look. "Things didn't work out with Diane. That hurt you deeply, but you are meant to keep running the race, honey. God doesn't want you to seal yourself off from the love He puts into your life."

He felt his cheeks go hot. "I'm not sure God has put Penny in my path as a love interest, Mom."

"All due respect, Ty, but you are not always a fount of wisdom."

He jerked. "What?"

"Well, remember the time you let Rain take a brush to bed and it wound up so tangled in her hair we had to cut it out?"

"Yes, but…"

"And the enchiladas you forgot about in the back of your SUV for three days?"

He sighed. "Uh-huh."

"And the day you thought it would be a great idea to replace the—"

"All right." He held up his palms. "I get your point, but right now I have to hit the road. Vivienne had to go out on an assignment with Hank so I'm Penny's transport." He swiftly kissed her on the cheek. "Talk to you later. Let's go, Dusty."

"But Ty…"

He rushed out the door before she had a chance to formulate her follow-up questions.

His mother was well-meaning, but she didn't understand. It was his responsibility to protect Penny, not love her. Or was his mom correct and he was merely trying to protect himself from risking his heart again?

He picked up Penny up at the hotel and drove them to the K-9 Unit firmly committed to keeping things professional. Shoving aside his mother's words, he felt like his head was screwed on straight until the moment he ushered Penny and the two dogs into the police-department lobby. Penny stepped behind him and took something from his back pocket.

He looked in horror at a pair of fuzzy pink bunny ears, then snatched them up.

"You…" Penny started giggling. "This was in your pocket." She'd hardly managed to get the words out in between bouts of laughter that transformed her into the most breathtaking creature he'd ever seen.

Embarrassment warred with delight. Her laughter was exquisite, like water bubbling over river rocks. "Uh, Rain insisted we play dress-up this morning. I had to be the bunny." He groaned. "I can't believe I forgot to take it out of my pocket." She was still overwhelmed by giggles, and he found himself laughing along with her.

"I get it," she said. "Anything for Rain."

He chuckled some more. "Nothing is more humbling to the male ego than raising a daughter."

"You're a good dad. Real men aren't afraid to wear pink bunny ears," she said when her own giggles subsided.

Caleb strolled in checking a text on his phone. He did a double take at the bunny ears in Tyler's hand. He arched an eyebrow. "Are you working on a new look, Walker?"

Penny quickly took the ears and put them on her own head. "Just trying out something for the dress-up box for the kiddie corner at the open house. How do I look?"

"Fantastic," he said. "Those ears are perfect on you. Talk to you two later."

Tyler let out a breath as Caleb left. "Thanks for the save. He would never let me live it down if he knew I was carrying around pink ears in my back pocket and dressing up like a rabbit in my off hours."

"I guess you owe me one, Detective."

He reached over and tweaked the costume ears. "I guess I do." He willed the thought into words. "I, uh, I was wondering if maybe, you know, after we capture Randall, if you would like to go on an adventure with me and Rain. A museum trip, or maybe a kiddie movie or something like that." There. He'd asked her out on a date, sort of.

She gave him that incandescent smile. "I think that would be great."

"Great." He felt the silly grin spread across his face, but he could not wipe it away.

Penny took off the ears and headed for the coffee room. Tyler followed, feeling as if he was floating. She soon had the place smelling of fresh-brewed coffee and three cops were in line at the machine.

"We're here for your special pumpkin-spice blend, Penny," Lani said. "The weekend cops complain that they have to make do with plain old java on your days off."

"I'll have to try a weekend shift someday." Lani's eyes widened as Penny pulled a plastic container from her bag and transferred some goodies to a plate. "I had a batch of blondies in the freezer at home. Vivienne drove over and retrieved them for me."

Tyler noted in awe that the cops closed in for the sweets like moths to a porch light.

"Thanks, Penny," Raymond Morrow said. "I'm taking one for now and one for later."

"Aww, man. Love me some blondies," Henry Roarke added.

"Blondies?" Jackson Davison said, sticking his head in. "I'm just in time."

By the time Tyler finished pouring his coffee, every last treat was gone. "You guys are vultures," he called in mock outrage. "I didn't even get one measly treat."

"Snooze, you lose," Henry said, retreating to his desk.

Tyler's stomach grumbled, reminding him he'd skipped breakfast to get in that game of dress-up with Rain. He sat glumly at the table until Penny slid a napkin in front of him with a fat blondie in the center.

He blinked at the treat. "You saved me one?"

She nodded. "You need your strength for the next round of dress-up."

He laughed and took a big bite of the blondie, then rolled his eyes at the chewy pleasure. "And to think I might have missed out on this if you hadn't had my back."

Penny shrugged. "I don't like anyone to be left out."

Yet he hadn't seen her set aside treats for any other cop. She was giving him special consideration. *Gratitude for shuttling her around, probably, you dope.* But she'd said yes to a future date with him. Or maybe she'd only agreed because she liked his daughter? He sat staring at the blondie.

Darcy Fields entered and inhaled. "The smell of coffee is the only thing that got me out of an endless meeting. If the lab had coffee like this, I would probably never leave for any reason." She helped herself to a cup and sat at the table. "I'm so close to a breakthrough I can taste it."

Tyler straightened. He knew exactly what she was referring to. The forensic scientist had been tirelessly working to capture some DNA left at the Emery crime scene. Darcy would provide the definitive answer to the question they'd all been wondering.

Had Randall Gage killed the Emerys, too? Or did they have another killer at large?

He motioned for Penny to join them. "We're really counting on you, Darcy. I've gotten nowhere with Lucy's clue about the elusive friend named Andy, and Randall so far has not given us anything conclusive related to the second killings. It's looking like you're our only hope until he's in custody and confesses the way he did to Penny about her parents' murders. If he even is the Emerys' killer."

Darcy grimaced. "I'm working as fast as I can, but science is slow."

Penny patted her hand. "My brother always says you have to go slow to go fast."

"My slow pace is not going to be good enough if he gets close to you again. I heard what happened at the docks. Are you okay?"

Penny's smile was bright but forced. "Just a little banged up, is all. Tyler got there just in time." He saw the brave front she presented to Darcy, but the clenching of her hands gave her away. That cheerful demeanor did not completely hide the fear written underneath, not from him, anyway. It made him burn with urgency to neutralize Randall before he could inflict any more agony on the McGregors.

Nate Slater poked his head in the break room. "Some boxes delivered for you, Penny. They're stacked in the front office."

"On my way. Must be the tablecloths I ordered for the open house."

Tyler finished his coffee and put the mug in the dishwasher. "I'll help you move them."

She didn't decline his assistance and he was oddly pleased. He hefted the larger of the two cartons and she scooped up the smaller one with her name scrawled in black on top. "We'll just put them in the conference room until I get them sorted out."

They delivered the boxes. As much as he enjoyed staying with Penny, it was time to start another round of phone calls to follow every last clue he could that would lead him to Randall's whereabouts. "See you later."

"For sure." She waved the bunny ears at him. "What should I do with these?"

"Bring them over next time you come to play." He was out of the room before he wondered what she thought of his casual invitation. Would she think he was using her as a source of free babysitting for Rain? Flirting?

Was he flirting? He wasn't sure he even knew how.

He was a complete mess, he thought as he rubbed a hand over his forehead. Dusty greeted him with a tail wag from her cushion near his desk, but she didn't get up. "Maybe you and I need some exercise time to clear our brains, huh?"

Something niggled at his gut as he grabbed her leash. Dusty was up, alive with excitement. He laughed at her exuberance, but there was still a nagging detail deep down in his gut that refused to surface.

What was it?

He paused in the doorway, sifting through the details of the morning.

Bunny ears.

Packages.

Black marker.

His nerves fired. Black marker. It was probably nothing. *Check it out, anyway.* "Come on, girl," he said to Dusty.

He headed toward the conference room and as they got closer, Dusty's nose quivered. Two more steps and she pulled on the leash, eager to get to the scent—an old scent she'd remembered from before.

The scent left by Randall Gage and his black marker.

"Penny," Tyler shouted as he ran. "Don't open that box!"

ELEVEN

Penny tore open the cardboard flap at the same moment she heard Tyler's shouted warning. She screamed as a puppet exploded from the box. The crude felt figure reached the end of its spring and recoiled. Torn paper shreds flew out and fluttered to the carpet. Reeling, she fell onto the floor.

Scrappy shoved his concerned nose in her face. She clung to him, trying to understand what had just happened. Dusty raced in and sat, posture stiff to show she'd found a target. Tyler was next, blue eyes absorbing the scene before he sank to a knee at her side. Taking her elbow, he scooted her away from the settling debris until she was sitting with her back against the wall. The solid surface behind her kept her grounded.

Tyler looked over his shoulder and moved slightly, blocking her view of what had sprung from the box.

She gulped in a breath. "I want to see it," she said, craning her neck.

"I don't think…"

She gritted her teeth, the fear whipping her pulse into a frenzy. "Tyler, don't try and protect me from the truth. This is my place of work, it's my life, and I want to see what he's done." Her forceful tone sounded as if it was coming from someone else's mouth.

He studied her for a minute and then nodded. "All right." As he moved aside, she could properly make out the hideous contents of the package. Her senses reeled as she took it in. The puppet was still waving slightly from side to side on the spring. Where the facial features should have been was a cut-out photocopied picture of Penny's face. It must have been taken at a happy time in her life, she thought. She was smiling, the collar of her desk clerk uniform shirt showing. Perhaps she'd just gotten her job with the police department. Her eyes roamed the grotesque toy's body, which was covered with splotches of brilliant red paint. It took her a moment to realize the symbolism. The red was meant to resemble blood...her blood.

Randall's promise made visual.

In case she didn't get that message clearly, he'd made one more addition. She swallowed as she examined the rope noose strung around the puppet's neck. Scrappy poked at her leg with his wet nose, whining softly. She absently caressed his ears and held him close to keep him away from the macabre delivery.

Gavin arrived at a run, eyes wide, and from somewhere far away she heard Tyler explaining what had happened.

"I should have noticed earlier," Tyler said. "The black marker was similar to what we found in Randall's apartment. Dusty picked up his scent on the package as we got closer to the conference room."

Their words faded away as she looked down at the torn papers on the floor. What she'd mistaken for newspaper scraps were actually photocopied pictures of her, but the eyes were poked out and the papers were torn into pieces.

It should have been fear, she felt then, but instead it was a fountain of anger that bordered on rage, unlike anything she'd felt before. Randall's evil had invaded her place of work, her lone sanctuary, the hub of her cop family. She turned on Tyler. "What did you find at his apartment?"

He looked as though he was about to try to put her off the topic. Then he reconsidered. "Pictures of you, defaced, like this. Newspaper clippings of your parents' murders." He paused. "A photocopy of the interview when you called him a monster."

She got to her feet with a hand from Tyler. "He's been planning his revenge carefully, hasn't he? He's invaded every area of my life, even here."

Gavin cleared his throat. "Penny, I am going to ask something of you now that you're not going to like."

She braced herself. "You're sending me home, aren't you?"

He held up a placating hand. "Just for today, until we run down how this package was delivered here and set some things in place."

Her rage flared, high and bright. "So now he gets to take my job from me, too? He's stripped me of my home, my security and now this?"

"It's the safest choice," Tyler said.

Gavin patted her arm. "Just for today, okay? Let us do our jobs here and make sure our security is shored up so we can keep you and everybody here safe. Do you understand?"

And everybody here. It occurred to her just then that if Randall had sent a bomb or a chemical poison, everyone in the building might have been affected. It wasn't just about her anymore. She swallowed and willed herself to speak.

"Yes, sir," she said, hardly able to say the words. "I understand."

"All right. Tyler, take her back to the secure room at the hotel, and I'll alert Vivienne to meet you there. Staff meeting in one hour. I'll get people in here to photograph this mess before we clean it up." He looked at Penny again. "I promise. I'll have you back at work before you know it."

Penny didn't reply. She could not be certain the anger wouldn't burst from her just as the puppet had exploded from the box. Silently, she followed Tyler and Dusty to the squad car. Scrappy seemed to pick up on her emotional morass. His ears were down as he climbed into the vehicle. She felt Tyler sneaking glances at her, but he did not try to make small talk as they made their way back to the safe house.

"Vivienne will be here in twenty. I'll take you up and stay until she arrives, okay?"

Penny managed a nod. Back in her dreary hotel room, she could not force herself to sit. Instead she paced laps around the dingy carpet while Scrappy whined from his lookout post on the couch.

Tyler rubbed his palms on his pants. "Can I, uh, make you some tea or coffee or something? I know how to prepare beverages, at least."

She didn't even have the energy to force a smile. "No thank you."

"Penny…"

"This isn't fair." The words catapulted from her mouth. He jerked, startled.

His reply was gentle. "That's true. Not one single thing about this is fair."

"Why does Randall have the right to take so much from me?" Her voice was loud, echoing in the bare room. "My parents, my home, my job. What makes him so special that he can turn me into a victim for my entire life? How does he have that right?" She was almost shouting now, her fingernails biting into the palms of her clenched fists.

"He doesn't."

"But he's doing it, Tyler." Her eyes filled. "One day at a time, he's stripping it all away and he's going to keep going until I've lost everything." She gulped. "He's going to kill me and then he's going to kill my brother." Her voice broke on the last word.

"No, he's not."

"How can you say that? He's still running around loose." Tears splashed hot down her cheeks. "And I'm the one locked up in a hotel room. It's not fair." Now the sobs came out of her along with the tears that she no longer attempted to staunch. "Is God punishing me?" The horrible question rose again from the darkest place in her soul. *Am I unlovable? Do I deserve this?*

He took hold of her shoulders and drew her to him. Her sobs shook her, but his arms were steady, stroking her back, pressing his cheek to the top of her head, repeating over and over.

"This is going to end."

How? When? The questions remained locked inside and all she could do was cry.

He held her until her sobs died away and she was left sniffling. "I shouldn't be yelling at you," she whispered, taking the tissues he handed her.

"Yell all you want. I'm glad you can share your feelings with me." His embrace was tender and strong, comforting and encouraging. She breathed in the scent of his aftershave, felt the strong beat of his heart next to her cheek. She had the oddest sense that she belonged there, pressed close to him, allowing herself to let go of a burden that had been building since she was a little girl.

When the storm of emotion eased, she was left with both a reservoir of fear and an odd feeling of comfort. How was it possible to have both? She wasn't sure, but she knew that Tyler's arms around her had brought her closer to hope, and farther away from despair.

"I'm sorry," she said.

He tipped up her chin to meet his eyes. "You don't have to be sorry. You can rage and cry and vent all you need to with me."

"You don't want to hear all that."

His finger caressed her chin. "I am privileged to hear all that."

Tiny flickers of light danced through her bloodstream at his touch. "I… Thank you." She felt her face flush. "You don't have to…"

And then he was pressing a kiss on her lips and everything flew away in the tender rush of comfort. She felt his hand skim the back of her hair as he let the kiss linger for a moment before he pulled away.

"You just remember what I told you, Penny. You are lovable because God made you that way. You just hang onto that and we'll do the rest. Randall will not rob you of the things you love. I won't allow it."

Oh, how she desperately wanted to believe it, to believe him. His kiss had been so precious, just like his words.

Vivienne's knock on the door made her jump. Tyler cleared his throat, and let her in. After a brief conversation, he called for his dog, and then he was gone, leaving her to wonder at what had just passed between them.

Tyler grabbed a cup of coffee before heading to the meeting, hoping the strong brew would clear the buzzing from his senses. Every nerve in his body was at full alert. What had he done, kissing her like that?

You were comforting her, that's all.

But he knew it was a lie. Yes, he could not bear to see her distressed, but he'd also found himself comforted by that kiss. The oddest feeling percolated through him— the radical thought that Penny McGregor was meant to be his. The feeling was deeper and more profound than he'd ever experienced before, even with Diane.

Use your head, he warned himself. He began ticking off the reasons that anything more than a friendly relationship was a very bad idea indeed.

First of all, it was his job to protect her. He was a cop, and she was his duty. Period. Emotional attachments would only impede that. That was exactly why interoffice romances were discouraged.

Second, he was seven years older than Penny and the weary father of a child who'd already lost one mother. Dive deeply into another relationship now that Rain was old enough to form strong attachments? The thought of inviting a woman into their lives and then having her walk away was too much to consider. It would shatter his heart, but what would it do to a toddler to have a second mommy desert her?

Third...

Bradley's poke on his arm brought him from his reverie. "I just talked to Penny. She said you calmed her down. Thanks, man."

Tyler smiled weakly. Reason number three screamed across his brain: Penny was his buddy Bradley's sister. Bradley was fiercely protective, as he should be. Cops should not date other cop's baby sisters.

Bradley frowned. "What's going on? You're off in space somewhere."

"Sorry." He gulped some coffee, which burned his tongue.

Gavin stood at the whiteboard as the officers took their seats. "All right. We know Randall mailed the package using a fictitious return address. I've gone over procedure with the mail room and all packages will be screened there before they're delivered to the office."

Henry gestured to his beagle. "They'll call me if any odd packages arrive and Cody will do an explosives check."

Explosives. Would that be Randall's next attempt? Tyler noticed Bradley's jaw was tight.

"What leads to we have?" Gavin asked.

Caleb spoke up. "Got a possible tip putting Randall at a homeless shelter in Dyker Heights, but it looks like he cleared out, if that was him."

"Nothing further from the Emery crime scene?" Sarge asked.

Caleb shook his head. "Nothing conclusive until we get Darcy's DNA results."

"Nothing substantial on the Andy clue," Tyler said. "I'm half convinced Lucy's friend might be an imaginary one."

"So we still don't know if we're looking at one killer or two." The room went quiet at Gavin's words.

Tyler drummed his fingers on the table. "If Randall killed the Emerys also, why didn't we find many newspaper clippings about it at his apartment? There was only one. He'd practically built a shrine about the McGregor murders, particularly about Penny."

Bradley glowered. "He's obsessed with her."

"Or he hasn't had time to collect much on the Emery killings," Caleb added.

"In any case, time's ticking away. We need to bust Randall Gage before he makes good on his threats." Gavin looked at Bradley. "Probably wouldn't be a bad idea for you to go to a safe house also. This isn't just about your sister."

A vein in Bradley's jaw jumped. "No."

Tyler tried a cajoling tone. "Hey, man. Couple of days off with pizza and football to watch. Doesn't sound bad to me."

"I said no." Bradley's tone was clipped and hard. "I hope Randall comes after me. Better me than Penny because King and I are ready. He won't get a second chance."

Tyler wasn't surprised at Bradley's reaction. He'd have said something similar if it was his sibling on the line.

"Right, well the other item on the table is the fall open house on Saturday." Gavin leaned against the podium. "Makes most sense to cancel."

Cancel. That would be the final broken straw in Penny's life.

Gavin continued. "But that may not be necessary if we move all activities inside. We're getting some pressure from higher up to go forward with it so there will be photos and video clips to put on the web of our new command unit." He paused and cleared his throat. "They made the suggestion that we could go forward with the event while Penny is secured at the safe house."

There was an angry buzz around the table, but Tyler's voice rose the loudest.

"No way. Penny put her heart and soul into that open house. It's her event. If she isn't allowed to be here, we should cancel."

There were murmurs of agreement.

Gavin nodded. "That was my thought, as well. We can postpone the public-access segment for later in the year and continue on with the part which was intended for cops and cop families only. We'll know everyone on the guest list. No one gets past the front desk unless they're buzzed in. We can pull in some personnel on overtime and button this place down tight. Any objections?"

Tyler wanted to speak, but he knew it had to be a unanimous decision.

"Penny's worked so hard on it. I say we go forward," Henry said.

Gavin scanned the reactions from his officers. "All right. Let's vote on it. All in favor?"

Every person in the room raised their hands.

Tyler felt a swell of pride. All the cops in the unit respected Penny and wanted the best for her. She was one of their own. Her cop family would not allow Randall to strip this important day from her.

It was one small victory, but to her, it would be enormous.

He felt again the softness of her lips on his, the strange buzz of bliss at being close to her.

Straightening in his chair, he reminded himself of his excellent reasons for avoiding a relationship with Penny.

Falling in love with her was out of the question right now.

If only his heart would fall into line.

TWELVE

Penny was nearly beside herself with excitement when Saturday morning finally rolled around. The days of her pseudo incarceration had crawled by in painful slow motion. She'd been awake for several hours already by the time Tyler arrived. Her hair was neatly secured in a twist and she wore her fall-hued sweater. Vivienne told her the burnt orange and golds complemented her coloring. She thought about that remark while she added a bit of pink to her lips and the tiny glass acorn earrings her adoptive mother had given her years before.

Tyler's weary eyebrows lifted in appreciation when he saw her. "You look great," he said.

"Oh, thank you," she said. He rubbed his eyes and she felt a small pang of guilt that she'd required such an early pickup when he'd been keeping long hours working on the hunt for Randall. "Still waking up?"

He waved a hand. "Naw, I'm fine." He smoothed a hand over his jaw. "But is it really necessary that we get to the office at six thirty when the party doesn't start until noon?"

"Sorry, but yes. I have a million things to do. Can I make it up to you with a good cup of coffee when we get there? I've got my own special blend ready to perk up a pot."

He smiled. "A good cup of coffee will get you plenty of forgiveness from this cop. Throw in a muffin and I'm your devoted servant for life."

"You need to get yourself one of these brownies," Vivienne said as she entered, holding up a napkin containing a half-eaten, gooey treat. "Wait until you taste these caramel thingies. Francine was a rock star to help out."

He gaped. "My mom baked these?"

Vivienne grinned. "Yes and no. I got Penny the ingredients for her famous chocolate-caramel whopper bars and she mixed up two batches. Your mom baked them at her place since there's no oven here. Didn't you know?"

He shrugged. "I've been trying to follow up on some leads in the evenings when Rain is sleeping, so I'm kind of out of touch." He raised an eyebrow at Vivienne. "Brownies for breakfast, Officer?"

Vivienne sniffed. "Life is short, Tyler. One must not turn down the blessed gift of a homemade dessert no matter when it's provided."

Penny laughed. "You are easily pleased, friend."

"Never underestimate the power contained in a sweet treat made with love. I'll get my pack. Be right back." She popped the rest of the brownie into her mouth and disappeared into the bathroom.

"Vivienne is a good roommate," Penny said fondly.

Tyler smiled at her. "It's nice to see you looking so happy."

She shrugged. "I love party planning. It's going to

be so much fun to see everyone having a good time to-gether. Your mom and Rain are coming, right?"

"Mom will bring Rain over and drop her off with us on her way to get a tooth fixed and come back after to join us. They'll be there at noon when it starts." He yawned again. "I should just about be awake by then."

"A shot of coffee and a couple of these brownies and you'll be doing wind sprints," Vivienne said, return-ing. She picked up a bag filled with party supplies and Penny and Tyler each carried a box. They paraded down to the back parking lot with the three dogs in tow. Tyler made them wait in the building while he checked the lot before he signaled to them to come out. Dusty and Scrappy sprawled contentedly in the back of Tyler's car and Penny took a spot in the passenger seat.

Vivienne slammed the trunk closed and loaded Hank into her own vehicle. After a thumbs-up, she drove out of the parking lot first. Tyler waited a few moments for her all-clear report before he followed.

"My mom must really like you if she's baking up your brownies."

"I think she would do that for anyone."

"She's not much of a baker. There was one cake epi-sode I recall from my childhood that wound up with a fire-department response. I'm sure she was extra dili-gent with your treats. Somehow I think she'd do any-thing for you." He sighed.

"Because she's trying to set you up with a girl-friend?"

Now it was his turn to look chagrined. "It's her life mission to see me settled down. I told you before she feels responsible for how things ended with Diane. She got some worrying signals while we were dating, but she never spoke up because I was head over heels for Diane and I probably wouldn't have listened, anyway. My dad was a powerful personality, and I think she learned how to keep her opinions to herself. We all did."

She cocked her head in his direction. "That must have been difficult."

He shrugged. "Dad was never comfortable showing emotions, except for disapproval. Mom was the nurturer and she was more patient than you can imagine with two boys. Since my brother is in the service, she's focused all her energies on me and Rain. I'm grateful for that. I don't know how I would manage the single-dad thing without her. Anyway, she's determined to right the sinking Walker ship for Rain's sake. I'm sorry if it's made you feel awkward."

"I think it's had that effect more on you than me."

"Maybe so. I've been gun-shy of relationships, so I have my radar up all the time." He frowned. "Except when I'm with you." His tone was puzzled.

"Should I be flattered or disappointed?"

He flicked a quick glance at her before his gaze returned to the road. "I'm not sure I'm much of a prize."

"Why would you say that?"

"Cop hours, single dad…" He hesitated. "Jaded older guy. Not the most attractive package."

"You love your daughter. There's nothing more attractive than that."

He shot her a sidelong glance. "Do you really think so?"

She felt suddenly uneasy, and laced her fingers in her lap. She'd just told the man he was attractive. Her nerves fluttered. "I wouldn't have said it if I hadn't meant it."

"I…" His eyes fixed on something in the rearview mirror, narrowing for a moment.

She could detect nothing but the normal New York traffic as they drove along, but his hands tightened on the wheel.

Her stomach knotted in an instant. "What?"

"Probably nothing. There's a vehicle two car lengths back, a grey truck. Can't see the driver. Could be purely innocent, but it's been behind us for a bit now."

Randall? Could he have gotten hold of another vehicle? Of course he could—he was capable of anything. She forced her fingers to loosen their death grip. In the side mirror she could barely see the truck. The memory surfaced of being locked in Randall's trunk, hands bound and mouth taped, utterly helpless.

Not helpless, she told herself sharply. *You kicked out the taillight and helped Tyler find you.*

But if he hadn't…

If he'd been a moment later…

She remembered the glint of the knife as Randall ran toward her. His green eyes had told her with absolute certainty that he intended to kill her.

She tried to push down the rising wave of panic. Cold sweat prickled her neck.

Tyler pulled down a side street. Her pulse hammered as she watched out the side mirror. The seconds ticked by, and the grey truck did not follow.

Tyler turned left and left again, circling back as traffic allowed. There was still no sign of the truck.

"Looks like we're clear." Tyler offered a reassuring smile. "I didn't mean to scare you."

The profound relief dizzied her. "Better safe than sorry."

"Right."

But she noticed that Tyler still did not appear quite as relaxed as he had before. Guilt rose alongside the relief. He was on edge and it was because she'd insisted on having the open house. She kept telling herself it was for the officers and their families, how disappointed they would be if the event was canceled. The reality was that Penny would be the most devastated of them all.

"Tyler, am I being selfish?" she blurted out.

He blinked at her. "About what?"

"Insisting on staying at work? Going forward with this party?" She looked out the window rather than at him. She could not bear to see condemnation. "The open house could have been postponed, or..." She swallowed. "It could have happened without me."

"No," he said, taking her hand. His hands were strong and warm. "It couldn't. No cop in the unit would consider canceling. It's important to you and you're important to all of us. You've helped make us a family, Penny."

She blushed. "You'd be a family without me."

"No. A family needs a rallying point, someone to remind them that relationships are the most important thing. You do that for us." He paused and his voice pitched lower. "You do that for me."

She knew her face was pink with pleasure. Was that what he really thought? Could she actually be the person he saw? A woman who helped glue their police family together? She went warm all over at his last words.

You do that for me.

But confusion seeped in through the pleasure. Did he mean friendship? Or did his heart beat with something much deeper, as she felt hers doing? She had no idea what to say.

"I know this is a bad time in your life, but after it's over, you'll be free to go after your goals. What do you want, Penny?"

"A family," she said instantly. "That's what I've always wanted."

His hand squeezed hers and he started to reply when his radio crackled and he released her.

Could she possibly be a part of Tyler's family one day? It made her breath catch to think of it. She wanted to mull over his words and hold them up to the autumn sunlight, examine them like the spectacularly colored fall leaves, but they'd pulled into a spot in front of headquarters and her musings would have to wait.

Hurrying inside, she plunged immediately into preparing the coffee and putting out the brownies. The treat quickly drew the early shift personnel, who seemed to share Vivienne's idea that brownies were a perfectly acceptable breakfast food. Everyone volunteered to help with the setup and she put them to work.

Her next job was decorating the conference room, and she firmly put out of her mind the horrible puppet box delivered to the police station. Nothing like that would happen again. Randall was not welcome in her thoughts. Today would be a celebration, a time to enjoy her police family. Tyler's earlier words came back to her.

A family needs a rallying point, someone to remind them that relationships are the most important thing... You do that for me.

A little wisp of pleasure circled inside her as she covered the tables with festive fall cloths and added the tiny hay bales and smiling scarecrows. Jackson and Vivienne started prepping a lavish luncheon buffet in the kitchen so families would have plenty of choices. There would be everything from vegetarian lasagna to crispy fried lumpia. The dessert table was already crowded with pies and homemade fudge. Gavin's wife, Brianne, had brought two dozen of her famous caramel apples, spangled with sprinkles and chocolate chips. The pot of apple cider she'd set simmering on the stove would be the crowning autumn touch.

Another room was set up with activities for the kids. The pumpkin-cookie decorating station and dress-up clothes promised to be a hit with all the youngsters, especially Rain, she thought. And if all else failed, there was her surefire party pleaser—puppies.

Dr. Gina had already gated off a corner for a puppy play area and Brooke and her fuzzy babies were snoozing in an untidy pile of fat tummies and curvy tails. Gina had tied fall handkerchiefs around each animal's neck. Purely adorable, Penny thought. If that didn't make everyone stop and enjoy the party, nothing would.

Penny noted Gina gazing at the happy canines, a little crease between her eyebrows. She was probably wondering if Joel Carey would show up with proof that he owned the dog family, like he'd promised. Best not to dwell on that possibility at the moment.

The phone at her desk rang and she scurried to answer it. Technically, the office was not open for business matters on Saturday, but she was expecting a call from the local homeless shelter confirming that they would pick up all the leftover pumpkins to distribute to the children staying there.

"Brooklyn K-9 Unit," she said.

Silence.

"Hello? Is there anyone there?"

The connection ended. Her phone flashed the number from where the call had come. Local area code. Should she be worried? She no longer had the ability to distinguish worry from paranoia.

Henry called to her from the doorway. "Penny, where do you want this hay bale?"

"It's for the photo corner. I'll show you." After quickly texting Tyler about the hang-up call, she scurried back to the party plans.

"My guys are trying to get a location on that call," Caleb said. "Just in case it was Randall." Tyler found it disconcerting to talk to the FBI agent while he was dressed in overalls and a straw hat. Penny and Vivienne had talked him into being Farmer Black in the small pumpkin-patch area where the kids would be able to choose a pumpkin. "Beat cops are checking the area. No sign of Randall Gage."

"Could be unrelated," Tyler mused.

"Could be."

Lani appeared at his elbow. "Gavin pulled an extra unit to patrol the block until the party is over as a precaution."

Tyler relaxed a fraction. The building was secure. Even if it was Randall calling, he was not going to get anywhere near Penny, Bradley or anyone else. Still, he would keep his antenna on alert for the first sign of danger.

The office was buzzing with activity. A feeling of longing poked at him as he watched families arriving, moms and dads leading their excited children by the hand. Willow and Nate led Lucy in.

Tyler bent down to greet her. "Hello, Lucy. I'm so glad to see you. Rain will be here soon, and she'd love to play with you."

The child pressed her cheek into Willow's thigh.

"She's a little shy," Willow said.

"Totally fine." The girl had a right to be withdrawn. He saw in her what Penny might have been like as a child. Already the victim of neglect and then to become an orphan after witnessing her parents' execution? At least Lucy had an amazing couple to adopt her, as Penny had. He watched the threesome walk by. Nate hoisted Lucy up on his shoulders. Her squeak of laughter penetrated the party noise. A perfect family, he thought.

Why did he keep picturing himself and Penny squiring Rain around the festivities? Since Diane had left, he'd written his single-dad identity in stone, but something was chipping away at that stone at an ever increasing rate. A certain red-haired, freckle-faced, tenderhearted woman. She wanted an intact family, and so did he. She loved Rain, like he did.

But the rules...the solid reasons he'd pondered why dating Penny was a bad idea.

He blinked. "I need coffee," he said aloud. He'd turned in that direction as his mother arrived with Rain in tow. Thanks to Grandma, Rain's yellow pants and sweater actually matched and her hair was neatly contained in two curly pigtails. He was getting to be pretty masterful at wrestling her curly mop under the control of a half-dozen barrettes, but he was a long way from conquering pigtails. Babby was clutched under Rain's arm. She immediately reached for him. "Daddy."

Francine handed her over. "Be good, baby. See you soon."

Daddy. How he relished hearing that word. Someday she would look around and wonder why she didn't have a mommy like the other kids. That thought struck him hard until he reminded himself that for the moment Rain wanted him, adored him, favored him out of all other people in the world. That made his heart swell, until Penny walked in and Rain immediately stuck out her arms in her direction.

"Enny," she said.

Penny laughed and Tyler handed over his daughter, mildly offended and thrilled at the same time. It was clear that Rain adored Penny. That thought made his nerves tumble. His daughter was not afraid to open her heart fully to this woman. Should he follow suit? Embrace the images his imagination supplied of the three of them together, enjoying life? But what about his list of excellent reasons to shy away? And what if down the road Penny decided she did not love him enough to stay, just as Diane had concluded? His skin went cold.

"Earth to Tyler."

He jerked from his thoughts as Caleb shoved a large cardboard carton at him. "Congratulations, Detective, you've been nominated to go lug the other box of pumpkins from the storage room and bring them here."

Tyler chuckled. "I have? Why don't you do it? You're the big burly farmer."

"I know, and my muscles are way bigger than yours, but I'm busy pulling weeds and keeping the crows out of my pumpkin patch and that's a full-time job. Hop to it, Walker. The kids are waiting."

Tyler saluted. "Yes, sir, Farmer Black." He turned to Penny. "Is it okay if Rain stays with you for a while?"

"Of course. I'll help her decorate a cookie." She

snuggled Rain close, and Tyler noted how his daughter relaxed in her embrace, cheek pressed close to Penny's. Two peas in a pod, his mother would say.

Best not to think about that. In the storage room, he located the box of pumpkins and hauled it where he'd been directed. He, Caleb and Vivienne laid them out in the pretend pumpkin patch to the delight of the waiting children. Caleb, grinning from ear to ear, took his spot next to a bale of hay.

"All right, children," he announced in a booming voice. "Who would like to pick out one of my prize-winning pumpkins to take home? You won't find a finer set of pumpkins anywhere, I guarantee. Best pumpkins in the whole state of New York, maybe even the world." There was a chorus of excited voices and several children trotted happily into the patch.

Vivienne eyed her husband adoringly. "He's really getting into the role, isn't he? I even saw him looking at tractors online."

"Watch out or you'll be trading in your badge for a pitchfork," Tyler warned.

She laughed. "If that's where life takes us, I'm in. Police work or pumpkins. As long as we're together, we can do anything."

He felt the swell of longing again as he watched Vivienne join Caleb and press a kiss to his cheek. Tyler searched for Penny and Rain.

He spotted Penny at the decorating table, helping Rain select a sugar cookie from the pile. Of course, his daughter had picked the one on the bottom, so Penny was delicately rearranging the tower of treats to accommodate.

His cell phone buzzed with a text from Bradley. Call

me. His heart ticked up a notch. He caught Penny's eye, gesturing with his cell phone that he needed to make a call. When she nodded, he stepped out and went to his cubicle. Dusty followed along.

"Need some quiet time, girl?"

Dusty crawled into her crate near his desk and flopped down for a snooze while he dialed Bradley's number.

"You're missing a good party," Tyler said.

"I know. I'm on my way. Figured I'd call from the car but you didn't pick up."

"Sorry, I was hauling pumpkins. What did you get?"

"Remember the lead on someone named Andy, who was house-sitting for someone on the Emerys' street around the time of the murders? I finally tracked that Andy down."

Tyler's stomach tightened. Young Lucy Emery had told them her favorite person besides her Aunt Willow and Uncle Nate was someone named Andy, someone with brown hair. It was their only slim lead on a possible witness to who had killed the Emerys. Perhaps the "Andy" clue referred to the killer himself, someone bent on delivering Lucy from the care of her neglectful parents. Maybe Randall, maybe not. He held the phone tight. "Did you find him?"

"Yes and no."

He groaned. "You're killing me. Spit it out, Bradley."

"Yes, I found one Andy Spinoza, who was house-sitting six doors down at the time of the murder." He paused. "Andy is short for Andrea."

He blinked. "A woman?"

"Yep."

Lucy had been adamant that Andy was a male, but

she might have been mistaken. Tyler sat forward. "Does she have brown hair at least?"

"Nope. She's seventy-two and her hair is white as the driven snow. What's more, she claimed she'd never met Lucy Emery or her parents."

"Is she telling the truth?"

"Yeah. Her details check out."

Tyler had to restrain himself from not thunking his head on the desktop. "Another dead end."

"That's an affirmative. I'll be back at the office in ten."

"Copy that."

He pushed back his chair, slapping his thighs in frustration. He was becoming more and more convinced that the whole Andy thing was simple confusion or imagination from the mind of a traumatized child. At the moment, it was a lead that went nowhere in answering the question that burned in all their minds.

Was Randall Gage the Emerys' killer, too?

That's the number-two priority, he reminded himself.

His first mission was to capture Randall and lock him in a cell.

Permanently.

The murmur of party noise drifted down the halls, but suddenly he did not feel in a festive mood. The open house was a momentary distraction, but the danger remained undiminished. As soon as the party ended, he would redouble his efforts and beat the bushes for any meager clue that might lead him to his quarry.

With so many cops looking for him, Randall was living on borrowed time.

And that meant Penny was, too.

THIRTEEN

Penny helped Rain spread orange frosting on her pumpkin cookie. She held up the tray of decorations. "What do you want to put on your pretty pumpkin?" Rain scooped up a collection of goodies with her plastic spoon and festooned her treat entirely with orange candies and sprinkles. She refused any other colored item.

"Well, that's orange all right," Penny said with a smile. "Your daddy will like it." She glanced around but Tyler had not returned. She wondered if the call had anything to do with Bradley's absence. Her nerves tightened. She wished her brother would arrive soon. The longer he was away, the more her worry mounted. What if Randall changed his mind and decided to harm Bradley first? Her throat went dry.

"See?"

Penny refocused on Rain, who was holding up her cookie for Penny to admire. "What a great job you did."

"Daddy?" Rain said.

"He'll be back in minute. Are you going to share your cookie with him?"

Rain immediately shoved in a big bite that puffed out her cheeks.

Penny giggled. "Every good chef has to taste-test first, I guess."

Rain put down the cookie and climbed off the chair in search of the puppies. "Hold on there, sticky girl," Penny said, snagging Rain's gummy hand. "We have to wash first. Then you can see the puppies."

Rain complained. "Doggies."

"Frosting is bad for doggies," Penny insisted. "And besides we have some fun foamy soap in the ladies' room."

Relenting, Rain clutched Babby under her armpit and followed Penny into the ladies' room. Penny turned on the water and got the temperature adjusted correctly, but Rain was too short to reach. There was a stool in the tiny corner cabinet, where the other desk clerk stored extra sets of clothes for her one-year-old twin girls. "Hold your hands up for a second, Rain, while I get the stool. Like this." Penny demonstrated.

The little girl thrust her own sticky hands up high.

"Stay right there for just one minute."

Penny went to the corner and opened the cabinet door. She had to get on her knees to reach the stool. "Okay. Got it. Step up on…" Her heart jolted as she turned around. Rain was not there.

Immediately, Penny pushed open the two stall doors. "Rain?"

There was no sign of her. Whirling, she ran to the door. When she saw a sticky orange handprint indicating the child had exited, she went cold all over. Stomach clenched, Penny ran out into the hallway. Babby was lying on the floor and she snatched it up. "Rain?" she called. Scrappy must have heard her from where he was playing in the puppy area. He came bounding up quickly and skidded to a stop.

Vivienne appeared, carrying a roll of paper towels.

"What's up, Penny?"

"Rain's wandered off."

Vivienne frowned. "She couldn't have gone far. I'll check the kitchen."

"I'll go to the kid area." Penny sprinted down the hall. Surely that must be what had happened. Rain couldn't wait to have her hands washed. She'd gone on her own to find the puppies. Bursting into the room, she scanned the crowd. There were kids picking up pumpkins and others trying on tutus and cowboy boots. Three were busily absorbed in creating cookie masterpieces. None of them was Rain. The knot in her stomach tightened.

She whirled and ran out, plowing into Tyler in the doorway.

"What's wrong?"

"Rain."

His blue eyes darkened to steel. He clenched her forearm. "What happened?"

"I was washing her hands in the bathroom. I turned to get the stool and she disappeared."

His tone went flat and hard. "Where have you looked?"

"The hallway and here. I just…"

Vivienne poked her head in. "Rain's not in the kitchen. Jackson said she wasn't in the stairwell, either."

Tyler and Penny both sprinted to the larger conference room. Families were chatting away and eating platefuls of food. Gavin looked up from his bite of pasta, his eyes narrowing.

"Walker?"

"Rain's missing."

He immediately put down his fork and pushed back from the table.

Bradley was just sitting down with a plate of sliced brisket and potato salad in the spot next to Gavin. He bolted from his chair with King. "We'll search the parking lot, just in case she got outside the building. Seal it off. I'll check with the patrol cop."

"What should I do?" Penny almost sobbed.

"Nothing," Tyler snapped.

It was hard to breathe. "I could check outside, make sure—"

"No. I'll handle this." His expression turned to granite as he took Rain's bunny from her clutched fingers. "Stay here. I'm going to get Dusty." He ran toward his cubicle, returning in a moment with Dusty. Penny could only look on with her heart in her throat as the recrimination pounded her.

She had lost Tyler's daughter.

She looked up to find Willow touching her arm. "It's okay. They'll find her." Lucy was tucked in her other arm. So small, so dependent on her adopted mother. Rain had trusted Penny to care for her.

And Tyler had trusted Penny, too.

She choked back a sob as all around her cops began to search every square inch of the building. Tyler thrust Rain's bunny at Dusty. "Track, girl."

Dusty trotted down the hallway, nose glued to the floor. Penny followed Tyler on shaky legs. His back was rigid with tension. A million thoughts ran through Penny's brain. If Rain had gotten out somehow, wandered into the street... If Randall was watching the building... had lured her away.

She remembered what Randall had said about her parents. They were neglectful, bad parents. Was she bad, too?

Was that what she was destined to be? A bad mother? She slowed to dash the tears from her eyes. Vivienne raced down the stairwell. "She's not upstairs."

Visions swirled through Penny's head, each more far-fetched and terrible than the last. Rain hit by a car. Tumbling out an open window. Vanished, never to be recovered again.

The panic made her feel light-headed.

Vivienne reached out a hand. "Maybe you should sit down here for a minute."

She leaned against the wall to steady herself and prayed with all her might that Rain would be found. From the direction of the front office, she heard a shout.

"She's in here. I found her," Tyler yelled.

Found her. Hurt? Or worse?

Penny's knees went weak, but she forced herself to continue into the reception area. She peered at the cops gathered around, then edged past them with nerves quaking. Rain was there, curled up underneath Penny's desk on Scrappy's cushion. Tyler tossed a rope toy to reward Dusty, then sank to his knees next to his daughter.

Penny leaned on the door for support, her vision blurred with unshed tears. *Thank You, God.* Her heart quivered with gratitude and pain. Tyler had trusted her with his most precious possession and she'd let him down, let Rain down.

"That was very naughty," Tyler said to Rain. "You

should have stayed where Miss Penny told you and not left the bathroom."

Rain pulled a frown and stuck her sticky thumb into her mouth. She would not look her father in the eye.

"Daddy and Miss Penny were worried about you," he continued. "All the officers were looking everywhere. They were all feeling scared and sad because you were gone. I felt scared, too." Rain started to whimper, and Tyler pulled her into his arms, sticky hands and all. He stood with the child clinging to him. He leaned his face against her pigtails and Penny read in the lines of his posture the utter relief as the terror ebbed away. In a moment, he would turn around to face her.

She did not want to see the look in his eyes, the expression that revealed his disappointment in her, the woman who'd lost his daughter.

She'd neglected Rain, lost her, put her at risk.

Before he could say a word, she hurried out of the room.

Tyler kept his expression stern as he cleaned Rain's palms with a wet wipe. His pulse was still elevated, and the harsh tone he'd used when he'd barked orders at Penny rang in his mind. He hadn't faulted her for letting Rain slip away, not really. It had happened to him, too, and the sheer panic that erupted when it had happened pushed him into cop mode both times. Now he looked around for Penny as the partygoers relaxed back into the festivities. The expression on her face when she'd told him Rain was missing had been nothing short of unadulterated terror. He had to find her, had to apologize.

Tyler toted Rain and her bunny, determined not to take his eyes off his precocious daughter as he searched.

Ten minutes later, his mom arrived, and he'd still not found Penny.

"What's wrong?" she said. "You're worried about something, I can tell. What happened?"

"Nothing. Just a small glitch. Penny was watching Rain and she wandered off. That's all."

Francine frowned. "You didn't yell at Penny, did you?"

"No." He paused, grimacing. "Not exactly yelled."

She skewered him with a look. "As in 'not exactly but I used that horrible I'm-in-charge tone' that crops up whenever you feel like things are out of control?"

He huffed out a breath. "Probably."

"Probably?"

"Okay, I did use that tone, but I'm going to apologize as soon as I can. I've been looking all over for her."

Francine took Rain. "An excellent idea. Go find her right away and tell her your behavior was inexcusable and you're very, very sorry. It wouldn't hurt to order her some flowers later, too. Roses would be nice. I'm taking this kiddo straight to the bathroom for a good hand-washing. Get busy, Ty."

"Yes, ma'am," he said meekly. Bradley. He would know where his sister was. But Bradley was absent from the dining table.

"He went to the break room, I think," Vivienne told him.

Bradley was indeed in the break room, staring into a cup of coffee, his plate of uneaten food nearby. Penelope was not with him.

"Where's Penny?"

Bradley studied him coldly. "She needs some time alone," he said.

"No, that's not what she needs. She needs an apology from this blockhead for snapping at her."

Bradley didn't smile but his expression relaxed slightly. "If you were any other guy, I'd be reaming you out for hurting her feelings, but I know this is more about her than you."

He sank down in a chair across from Bradley. "How so?"

"Her deepest fear is that she is going to be like our mom and dad and she'll let her own kids down. That's why she breaks off relationships, I think. She's afraid to find out she's cut from the same cloth they were."

"That's nonsense. She's the most loving person I know."

"Yeah," he said with a thoughtful look at Tyler. "And she cares a lot about you and Rain. She's allowed herself to get close to you both, I've noticed. It required a lot of courage on her part." There was an accusation in his tone.

Tyler rolled his shoulders, suddenly weary. "And I shook her confidence, didn't I?"

"Probably, but I'm sure you can apologize sufficiently and she'll understand." He paused. "What I'm more concerned about is what happens from here."

"What do you mean?"

"If history is any indication, my guess is she's going to distance herself from you both."

A sharp pain cut at him.

"Is that what you want?" Bradley asked.

"Me?" Was that what he wanted? A simple way out of his emotional dilemma? It would be so much easier than having to deal with his untidy heap of emotions. "No," he said after a minute. "I care about your sister."

Bradley folded his arms. "That's what I thought. And she cares about you, too, so if you want her in your life, let me give you a word of advice. Don't let her walk away because she won't come back. If you do convince her to stay, you'd better mean it for the long term." Bradley stood. "That's all I've got to say. I'm going to go finish my lunch."

"Where is she, Bradley? I have to talk to her."

"She doesn't want me to tell you, but you know my sister." He offered an innocent shrug. "She's a hard worker. Any excuse to tidy up the files..." He let the words drift away.

Files. Tyler made a beeline for the small file room close to the front office.

Penny was there leaning against a cabinet, arms hugging herself. Scrappy hovered nearby. Her face was blotched from crying. When she saw him, she gulped and straightened. "I was just... I mean... I had a file to return so I figured..."

He stepped close. "Penny, listen to me. I am so sorry. My tone with you was unnecessary. I absolutely don't blame you for losing track of Rain. She's a crafty one, for sure." He tried a smile, which she did not return.

"Perfectly okay," she said brightly. "I never should have turned my back on her. I probably shouldn't have thought I could take care of her in the first place."

"No, really, Penny. I get it. It's happened to me. It wasn't your fault and you didn't do anything wrong or neglectful."

The word seemed to slap at her. She jerked back as if to keep the maximum distance between them. "That's nice of you to say. Thank you. I need to get back to the party."

He reached out a hand. "No, please, Penny. Listen to me. I…"

The phone rang in the outer office. "I'd better get that. Waiting on a call from the homeless shelter."

"Penny…"

But she'd skirted around him and darted into the outer office. He followed.

Whatever damage he'd caused, he had to show her that the fault had been his and his entirely.

If he didn't succeed, he had a feeling she would drift right out of his life for good.

FOURTEEN

The phone at her desk rang a third time before she got there. She wanted to grab her purse and head right out the door, but she could not leave the open house, not until everything was cleaned up and the last guest had left. At least if she could tackle the phone call, maybe Tyler would leave and she could regain her composure.

She sucked in a breath and steadied herself as the phone rang again. Work would restore her purpose. Work would salve the raw place in her soul, the place that said, "You'd be a bad mom, just like your own mother was."

She grabbed the phone. "Brooklyn K-9 Unit, how may I help you?"

"Hello, Penny," Randall said. "Why didn't I get an invitation to the party?"

Ice flashed across her nerves, freezing her an inch at a time. Tyler must have read the shock in her posture. He ran to her side and hit the speakerphone button.

"Who is this?" he demanded.

"Hello, Detective Walker. I'd recognize your voice anywhere. This is the guy you shot at the docks. My side's still killing me, by the way."

Penny realized she was still holding the receiver and she set it softly down on the cradle, fingers shaking. "What do you want?"

"Lots of things, but I'm not going to get any of them. The cops have done an excellent job sealing off the area. There's nowhere for me to go, not even to my apartment. So what's left for me? You know the answer to that, Penny. Only one thing, or two, to be specific."

Tyler leaned close to the phone. "You're not going to get it," he growled. "Give yourself up. You'll get a fair trial at least."

"Not likely, when you are all busily trying to frame me for the Emery murders, too."

"Same clown mask, same MO. Give us something to prove it wasn't you."

There was a pause. "What do I get in exchange for doing your work for you?"

"What do you want?" Tyler asked.

"A get-out-of-jail-free pass."

Tyler grimaced. "Not possible, but going to jail for one set of murders is preferable to two sets, isn't it?"

"Okay, how about I tell you I wasn't even in the area when those two got offed?"

"Got an alibi to that effect?"

Bradley and King hurried in. Penny put a finger to her lips.

"I was visiting a lady friend in the Catskills the night the Emerys were killed. I was there a few days. You know I go up there sometimes—it's where I conked your fancy-pants FBI agent on the head and knocked him out back in July, remember?"

"It's all about timing," Tyler said. "You could have killed the Emerys before you fled there in April."

"My bus ticket proves I wasn't anywhere near the Emery home when they were shot."

"Anyone can buy a bus ticket."

"Don't treat me like an idiot. Bus stations got video. Do your job and find yourself another killer. It's enough for me to get rid of the McGregor family. The parents deserved to die. How many times did I see the kids wandering the streets while their worthless parents were out getting drunk? Whoever killed the Emerys might have noticed that kid being ignored, too. Maybe you should be thanking that copycat killer for getting rid of a couple of losers who didn't deserve a kid, anyway."

Penny swallowed convulsively. She thought of her parents, the woman who kissed her ouchies and the father who would play his harmonica from time to time. They didn't deserve to be murdered.

"That wasn't your decision to make," Tyler said.

Randall snorted. "Well, I made it, anyway, didn't I? So what do I get for all that information?"

"You get nothing except a trip to jail," Bradley snarled.

Randall laughed. "Is that you, Bradley? Sorry, kid. You have to wait your turn until I take care of your sister."

Bradley looked as though he was going to snatch the phone up and break it in half.

"Did you like the puppet, Penny? I made it just for you. Figure I'm going to be seeing you real soon."

Tyler's chin jutted out. "Why don't you meet me face-to-face? You got a problem with the McGregors? Tell me all about it in person."

"I am not interested in you, Detective. I made a

promise and Penny knows that I keep my promises, don't you?"

She swallowed. Her voice came out in a whisper. "You're never going to stop, are you?"

"Not until you and your brother are dead. I'll have that to keep me warm at night when they put me away." He laughed again. "You know what they say. In for a Penny, in for a pound. See you soon."

The connection ended.

There was a sound of breaking glass from outside. Tyler pulled Penny down below the counter. "Stay low."

He ran out the front door, Bradley right behind him with King.

Her body went numb with fear. Randall was out there, watching. She'd been a fool to think all the protection they'd put in place would dissuade him. All of her family, her police family, including Rain and the children, had been put at risk because of her. She had been selfish, she realized, and there was only one course of action to take.

But first, she pressed her hands together and prayed for the safety of Tyler and her brother. Minutes ticked by and there was a buzz of movement, radios and cell phones going off as word spread through the open house.

Tyler and Bradley returned. Bradley was carrying King. Penny's heart dropped.

"Get me some paper towels," Bradley called, holding King's paw. Horrified, she saw red dripping onto the entry tile. Vivienne rushed over with a roll of towels. "I'll get Dr. Gina."

"He doesn't need a vet, it's paint. Randall threw a glass jar full of it at Tyler's vehicle. That was followed by a rock with a bus-ticket stub attached. King stepped in the paint splatter before I could stop him but I managed to keep him away from the glass shards."

Tyler grunted. "Cop out front said Randall was in a grey truck. He took off. They're trying to track him." He held King's leash while Bradley wiped off the paint.

"You're okay, boy," Bradley said to King. "He needs a bath before he starts licking his paws. Let me hose him off and I'll get Caleb. We'll help with the search."

"I'll go now, too." Tyler looked at Caleb. "Call me when the scene's processed and I'll start chasing down that bus-ticket information."

Before he headed for the door, Tyler's eyes found hers. Randall was close, and he'd singled out Tyler's car. The target had widened from Penny and Bradley to Tyler, too.

There was only one decision left for her to make.

It wasn't until hours later that she went in search of Gavin, pain impossibly heavy in her heart.

She found him behind his desk, peering at his computer screen. His phone rang and he gestured her into a seat as he picked it up.

"No, the police department has no statement at this time other than what you got from our public information officer." He hung up the phone. It rang again and he let it go to voice mail.

"Sorry. It's been ringing pretty steadily. I don't know how the media gets hold of details almost as soon as they happen. They are all circling like sharks, hoping to dig up some headlines." He folded his hands. "How are you doing? It's been an eventful day."

She nodded, her throat closing up.

"The party was a success," he said gently. "In spite of…everything."

She sucked in a steadying breath. "That's why I'm here. I wanted to have this party so badly, I didn't consider that I would be putting people at risk."

"Randall didn't hurt anyone."

"But he could have. He got close enough to throw paint. He might have been shooting instead."

Gavin listened intently. "Penny, we are going to get Randall Gage. It's a matter of time, but if you need some days off to ease your mind then—"

"I'm going to resign."

He raised both eyebrows. "That's not necessary."

"Yes, it is." She explained the details of her plan.

"Take a leave of absence instead. Let things settle."

"And you'll keep me in a secure room at the hotel until they do? For weeks? Months? Randall's been at large for more than two decades already. My brother and Tyler can't get anything done while they are watching me around the clock."

"Penny…"

She got up. "I don't want to leave, Sarge. This is my home. I…" She swallowed hard. "It's what I need to do."

She did not wait for his reply as she scurried out the door.

On Monday morning, the cops were all laser-focused on Tyler as he readied his report. He felt conflicted about what he had to tell them.

"Randall's alibis for the Emery murders check out. The bus driver remembers him and there's video footage of him getting on the bus the day before. He was on his way to a friend's place who let him stay. Convenience-store clerk in Monticello also has footage of Randall buying cigarettes the evening of the murder."

Gavin exhaled. "So it's certain then. We've got ourselves a copycat murderer."

Nate Slater had gone pale. "Lucy could still be a target."

"We'll get them," Gavin said. "Similar motives perhaps. We're looking for someone who knew firsthand how Lucy was being neglected by her parents, so it was someone with easy access to the situation."

Tyler winced, thinking about Penny. He'd tried to see her on Sunday, but Vivienne said she was in bed with a headache. His calls had gone unreturned, along with his texts.

Jackson drummed his fingers on the table. "We've discussed that neglect motive. We'll move forward with that line of thinking now that we've ruled Randall out."

An office clerk popped her head in. "Bradley, reporter on the phone for you, looking for an interview. Her name's Sasha Eastman."

Bradley grimaced. "Tell her thanks, but no thanks."

The clerk nodded and left.

Gavin stood. "There's another announcement."

Tyler noticed that Bradley's gaze was cemented to the tabletop. Whatever it was, he already knew about it. An alarm bell began to jingle way down in Tyler's gut.

Gavin blew out a breath. "Penny has given her notice."

"What?" Tyler said. He almost leaped to his feet.

"I told her she can use her vacation days for her two weeks as long as she comes in for a little gathering so we can say goodbye properly. She feels that she is drawing unwanted attention from the public, which is distracting from our work and possibly jeopardizing our safety here at the station, and that of her brother, by continuing to work here."

"That's not—"

Gavin stopped Tyler with a look. "I don't want her to go any more than you do, but the fact is, Randall's gotten close, too close, too many times."

"For how long? Until Randall's caught?"

Gavin's mouth twitched. "She's seeking a position with a K-9 unit in the Bronx, pending our capture of Randall. She's asked me for a recommendation, and I've provided her with one. If she is hired, I would imagine she will not be returning to her employment here."

Tyler sat back in his chair. Disbelief circled inside him, along with sorrow and anger. So she was leaving him, too, just like Diane, without a backward glance for him or Rain. Abruptly he got up and left the conference room, stalking toward his cubicle.

Bradley caught up with him. "If it means anything, she doesn't want to leave."

"Then she shouldn't," he snapped. "Or at the very least she could have talked about it with me."

His eyes narrowed. "Maybe she thought you'd get angry just like you are now."

"Don't I have a right to be?"

"I don't know," Bradley said. "Do you?"

"What are you saying?"

Bradley folded his arms across his chest. "What does she mean to you?"

Tyler stopped, mouth open. *Everything.* For some reason the thought stripped him of the power of speech. He stood there, gaping and mute.

"You said you wanted her around and I told you she

would bolt if you didn't give her reason not to. What re-assurances have you given her, Tyler?" Bradley let the silence go on for a moment. "Penny is more sensitive than most women and there are plenty of legit circumstances that made her that way. If you haven't given her any clear indication of how you feel about her, then like I said, she's got no reason to stay."

"I tried… I mean…" What had he given her? The vague sentiments about wanting to date her, spend time with her after Randall's capture? Nothing concrete—he hadn't had the spine. His mouth snapped shut.

Bradley's lips thinned into a tight line. "She's giving up everything she loves because it's best for everyone else. Don't make it harder on her, Tyler. If you're not willing to risk a relationship, then back off. She doesn't deserve any more pain."

Tyler watched Bradley go. What was happening? Why was his world turning upside down again? Why did he feel as though his heart was being yanked from his body in one quivering chunk?

He knew two things. First, he had to talk to Penny. But more than that, he needed to figure out the answer to Bradley's question.

What does Penny mean to you?

FIFTEEN

Palms sweating, he knocked on the door of the hotel safe room. Vivienne answered. "Glad you're here. I need to go take Hank out for some exercise. He's climbing the walls."

Though he wanted to tell her she didn't need to leave, he was secretly relieved she was stepping out. He had no idea how the conversation with Penny would go, but it would be harder with a third party in the room. She hastily departed. After a fortifying breath, he stepped inside.

Penny was folding clothes and stowing them in a pile resting next to her on the sofa. Her hair was caught in a soft ponytail. "Hello, Tyler." She did not look at him after her polite greeting.

"Hi. I heard from Gavin that you were quitting."

She seemed to curl in a bit on herself. "Yes."

"And looking for another position?" He hadn't meant for it to be such an abrupt statement, but it came out that way nonetheless.

"As soon as Randall is caught," she said. "It's for the best."

"Why? If he's caught, you'll be safe. No more threats to you or Bradley."

She sighed. "I need a fresh start, Tyler."

"Why didn't you talk to me about it?"

She stopped and shot him a quick glance. "I needed to think with my head, not with my heart."

He blinked. "But we can still see each other, even if you don't work in Brooklyn, right?"

Her long pause told him everything. She wasn't just leaving her job, she was walking away from him. He heaved out the breath he hadn't realized he was holding. "I see."

"I don't want to go, but I have to. I—I will be sad to leave you and Rain. I care about you both."

"And we care about you, too. I'm sorry if I was too scared to lay it out clearly, but—"

"I can't," she said, tears glistening. "I can't stay and risk hurting you or Rain."

"You won't."

"I have a murderer tracking me who will never give up. And even if I didn't…"

"What? What is it? Say it." He felt a growing desperation.

"I'm not sure I will ever be confident enough to be a fixture in Rain's life and I would never be able to stand it if I let her down."

"Penny…" He tried to grab her hand, but she pulled away. "You wouldn't do that."

"You can't know that. I'm doing what's best."

"So you're going to leave us." He fisted his hands on his hips. "Without a word."

"I didn't want to make matters worse."

"And you were afraid I'd try and talk you out of it."

He shook his head. "You should have talked to me. You're leaving just like…" He broke off, his insides burning as if he'd swallowed poison.

Now she turned her chocolate gaze on him. "I think you mean 'just like Diane did.'"

He sucked in a breath. "This has nothing to do with my ex-wife."

"You're right. It doesn't. And this isn't about you or Rain or how I feel about you both."

He could not contain the bitter laugh. "Believe it or not, that's exactly what Diane said before she dumped us like last week's trash."

Penny winced. "I'm very sorry."

"She was sorry, too, but not sorry enough to stay."

Her eyes flashed with emotion. "Don't lump me with your ex-wife. I am not Diane."

Hurt, betrayal and, most of all, a terrible sense of failure enveloped him. "You might as well be."

She flushed red. "That is totally unfair."

"I'm a single father and I shouldn't have let you become a part of our lives. I should have known you were going to leave us." His voice almost broke on the last word.

"Tyler…" Her shock hung in the air. "I didn't…"

His hurt came from a deep-down place because he now knew the answer to Bradley's question. What did she mean to him? She meant everything and now she was leaving him, leaving them. The pain tore at him until he could almost not get a breath. It was his own fault. He hadn't done enough for her to want to stay.

"Please…" she said, but he turned to go.

I want you to stay. I want to love you, and make a life with you and Rain. He wanted so many things, but now he knew their ending would be just like it had been with Diane.

"I hope you'll be happy in the Bronx, Penny." Then he escaped, practically running from the room as fast as he could go.

In his car, he rested his head on the steering wheel. What had he just done? How in the space of a few minutes had it all fallen apart? He wanted to get in his car and drive away somewhere quiet, where he could think, but his mom was waiting for him to pick up Rain. *You're a father. That's what's left for you, Tyler, nothing more.* Heart heavy as a stone, he returned home.

His mother looked up from her crocheting when he entered the apartment. "What's wrong?"

He sank on the sofa with a groan. "Where's Rain?"

"Napping. Tell me what happened."

He didn't bother wondering how she knew. "Penny's quitting."

Her fingers stilled on the crochet hooks. "For good?"

"Seems that way. And she's going to get another job, move on to another life." He closed his eyes. "I can't believe this is happening again. I cared about her, I really did."

"Do."

He opened his eyes. "It's over, Mom. You can't make someone stay. I learned that the hard way."

"Did you ask her to stay?"

He felt a rise of irritation. "I'm not going to beg, Mom. It was enough to do that with Diane."

She stabbed the hooks into her ball of yarn. "Tyler William Walker, you listen to me and you listen well."

He sat up straighter.

"Penny is not Diane. What's more, you are not the same man you were two years ago."

"I know that."

"Do you?" Her eyes blazed at him. "Because from where I'm sitting, you are so busy looking back that you're losing a treasure right in front of you."

"You're beginning to sound like Bradley."

"I always knew that young man was smart." She picked up her yarn ball and purse. "You know what? I didn't speak up to your father as much as I should have because I didn't want to make waves. And I didn't express my misgivings about Diane for the same reason. Well, I'm speaking up now, Ty. Stop looking behind you. God gave you two eyes in the front of your head, not the back, for a reason." And with that, she walked to the apartment door and slammed it behind her, leaving him gaping.

What was he supposed to do next? The apartment settled into quiet. He lied down on the couch, his mind alive with snippets of conversation.

What does she mean to you?

Stop looking behind you.

I care for you both.

He closed his eyes and folded his hands. The most important conversation he needed to have at this moment was between him and the Lord.

Penny fought against tears as she carefully loaded the personal effects from her desk into a cardboard box the next morning. The photo of her adoptive parents and her brother on the day he'd earned his badge made her pause. She'd nearly burst with pride at that moment. The second photo was one of her standing next to him in her uniform shirt. It had seemed on that day that maybe she had finally restarted her life on a path that would lead her into the future, away from the sadness and tragedy that had defined her past.

That had all come to a violent end when Randall had shown up. Everything was crumbling around her. The biggest blow was having to leave her police family.

And Tyler…

His image came uninvited into her thoughts. She'd been trying valiantly to forget his harsh condemnation.

I should have known you were going to leave us. It was all so shocking. She hadn't known there was an *us* except in her imagination. Worse than the words, worse than any of it, had been the catch in his voice when he'd said it.

He'd painted her with the same brush as Diane… as an immature woman who'd walked out on him and Rain. She didn't know what to do, how to fix it, except to leave the whole situation behind. Was she being cowardly or kind? She had no idea.

She was jotting down notes to discuss with the person who would be taking over her job, when Joel Carey, the man who insisted Brooke and her pups belonged to him, came through the door. Since her replacement was grabbing a cup of coffee, she plastered on a polite smile.

"How can I help you, sir?"

He waved a photo triumphantly and slapped it on the counter. "I'm here to claim my dogs. Take a look."

She peered at the grainy photo of Carey standing next to a German shepherd. He was not smiling in the picture. The dog was a beautiful specimen, as far as she could tell.

"See? The dog's mine and so are her puppies. I want them now."

"One moment, please." With a sinking stomach, Penny quickly summoned Gavin and Dr. Gina, who were settling some paperwork in the back room. They both arrived on the double.

Carey waved the photo around and Gavin and Gina examined it.

"It's a little blurry," Gina said. "That could be any dog. It doesn't have to be Brooke."

Carey's eyes narrowed. "Rory is her name and it's not just the photo. That homeless guy told you he remembered me calling to her, trying to get her back, but the traffic was too bad. And you promised that if I brought proof, the dogs would be turned over. Here's the proof. Are you reneging on your word?"

Gavin blew out a breath, his eyebrows knitted together. "No, you've produced the photo and we will release the dogs to you."

Gina went stiff and Penny could see the anguish in her face, but she did not contradict Sarge.

Carey gave a satisfied nod. "Let me have 'em."

"Not right now," Gavin said. "I'm sure Dr. Gina needs to wrap up a few things before she releases them."

Carey fisted his hands on his hips and glowered.

Gina nodded. "I'll need to keep them for a few days. They need their next round of shots."

"No way…" Carey began.

Sarge stared him down. "You want what's best for these pups, don't you, Mr. Carey? You wouldn't want to compromise their care in any way, after you've worked so hard to get them back."

Carey squirmed. "All right. I'll be here next week on

Monday morning to pick them up." He smiled. "Take good care of my dogs," he called before he left.

Gina sagged as the door closed. "He's just going to sell them. I can feel it. He doesn't love these dogs. That photo might be another dog entirely."

"I'm sorry, Gina, truly I am," Sarge said, "but we have no grounds to keep them from him any longer."

He touched Gina's shoulder and walked back to his office.

Penny went to Gina and hugged her. Gina sniffled against the tears. "I guess I knew it would come to this, but I hate the thought of turning them over to a guy like that. I was hoping he'd give up and leave them with us."

"You've taken such wonderful care of Brooke and her babies." Penny squeezed her and let her go to hand her a tissue. "Everybody will be crushed around here," she said. *Especially a little curly-haired tyke named Rain.*

She remembered Rain's squeals of delight as she tumbled and played with the pups, and the tender moment when she'd been able to soothe the child's hurt fingers.

How would Tyler explain that the puppies were being given away? She swallowed. What would he tell her about why Penny wasn't around any longer? A lump formed in her throat. Tyler was a good father and even though thinking of him unleashed a ferocious pang of pain inside her, she hoped he and Rain would find their own happiness.

She whispered a prayer that Tyler's heart would heal, even as her own felt like it was falling into pieces.

On Penny's last official Friday, the officers ordered a massive goodbye cake and presented her with a bouquet of pink roses. Tyler wasn't sure he should attend the party after what he'd said to Penny, but he made up his mind to go, anyway. He would do his best not to make her feel any more uncomfortable than he already had.

Penny was dressed in civilian clothes—a soft pink sweater and slim brown pants—and her hair was tied in her favored loose ponytail. Two high spots of color stood out on her pale cheeks. For one moment, her gaze locked with his, but she quickly looked away. He took a seat at the far end of the conference room and tried to wear a pleasant expression.

She picked at her cake and offered rounds of smiles and hugs, but Tyler saw her blink back tears. He was ashamed of himself for adding to her pain, for his childish need to hurt her to vent his own wild sadness. After his outburst at the hotel, he'd spent time with Rain and in prayer. Nothing soothed the lancing anguish in his own heart. Hour upon hour, he'd paced the nights away, until exhaustion drove him to sleep. But something had clicked in those endless minutes—a tiny flame had ignited that showed him the truth.

Somewhere in those turbulent hours, he'd come to understand without any doubt that he'd let the scars of the past tether him. A failed marriage and Diane's abandonment hung around his heart like twin anchors, weighing down his soul in a way God had not intended. It shamed him to think of it, to consider how he'd unburdened that heaviness on a beautiful person like Penny.

Why hadn't he been stronger, like her? She'd soldiered on bravely in spite of what Randall had done to her and her family. She dared to see herself as a light in the world instead of a victim. Part of him knew deep down that she'd even perhaps considered stepping further away from that past and embracing something new when she'd reached out to him and Rain. Could there be any clearer example of courage than that? And his own fear had kept him from reaching back.

Breathing shallow, he thought about his plan. He did not know if he could undo the damage he'd caused with Penny. It was a good possibility that she would head to a new job and a new life no matter how eloquent his words, and he would never see her again. All he knew was he'd prayed fervently that morning for God to help him make things right between them. He needed time alone with her, but that proved to be a problem with a roomful of cops gathered around.

He'd offered to drive her back to the safe house, still her home for the uncertain future, and she'd declined, of course. Bradley had already volunteered for the job. Unbeknownst to her, he'd taken over the task from Bradley, anyway. He humbled himself and explained to Bradley what he was going to attempt.

"You sure you know what you're doing, Walker?" Bradley had said.

"No, but I'm going to give it my best shot to make up for how I've hurt her."

"All right," Bradley said with a wink.

Tyler felt suddenly nervous. "Got any advice?"

"Don't say anything stupid." He whacked Tyler on the shoulder and walked away smiling.

Tyler swallowed against the tightness in his throat. The ride would be his last chance to undo some of the damage he'd done to himself and to her. He prayed God would help him find the right words.

After the office goodbyes were done, Gavin was

the last one to hug Penny. "You know that if you ever change your mind, you have a job here waiting."

Penny kissed his cheek. "I appreciate that so much, Sarge."

He touched her shoulder. "We'll get Randall soon. Don't send out that resume yet, okay? I'm still hoping we can change your mind."

"I know you'll catch Randall, but I think it's time for me to start over somewhere new, without so many memories. It's better this way."

Tyler's heart cracked open a little wider.

Penny shouldered her tote bag and took Scrappy's leash. Bradley followed behind with King after they got the all-clear from the patrol officer outside.

Her eyes rounded. "I thought Bradley was taking me."

"I took over the assignment."

He could tell she wanted to ask why, but he wasn't prepared to tell her, not with Bradley right behind them.

"Move it, Walker. Quit slacking," Bradley said.

In spite of Bradley's forced cheer, Tyler saw Penny's pain mirrored in her brother's face. *And you probably were the final push in getting her to quit*, he thought miserably.

"Okay." Bradley held King's leash. "Meet you at the safe house. We can discuss your plan to go stay with your friend in Florida."

Tyler cleared his throat and opened the passenger-side door for Penny.

She kissed her brother on the cheek. "It's okay if you have work to do. We don't need to talk about it now." She opened the rear door to let Scrappy and Dusty into Tyler's back seat.

Bradley waved her off. "Nah. I've got a hankering for chow mein. I figured we could do takeout. That's…"

Tyler heard the screech of tires. In a blur of motion, a grey truck roared up the street. A squad car followed the speeding car—code three. The noise from the chase bounced off the walls of the police station and echoed along the narrow street.

He knew it was Randall behind the wheel, even before the truck jumped the curb and careened onto the sidewalk.

Penny screamed.

Bradley reached for his weapon, but he had no time to react. The truck's front bumper struck him with a sickening thud that sent him sailing backward onto the pavement. He landed in a limp heap. King avoided the collision, barking at a fever pitch. The truck slammed to a halt when it plowed into the back of Tyler's vehicle. Dusty and Scrappy launched themselves out of the car through the open door.

Penny's mouth was open in shock, her eyes riveted on her fallen brother. He was lying completely still, one arm flung above his head.

"Bradley," she shrieked, her voice almost unrecognizable. Tyler tried to pull her behind him as he reached for his revolver. She wrenched herself from Tyler's grasp and ran toward her brother. King was loose, barking and jumping in a frenzy. Frantically, he snatched at King's leash, hauling him back, while trying futilely to aim his revolver at the crumpled truck.

Just as he was ready to squeeze off a shot at the opening truck door, Penny crossed into the line of fire. He eased up and Randall seized the moment to dive from the truck. A gun flashed in his hand as he headed toward Penny and grabbed her by the wrist.

"Drop the weapon, Randall," Tyler hollered.

Tyler still could not risk taking a shot since Penny was between him and Randall. She was pulling and flailing at her captor.

King's barking reached ferocious levels as he lunged and jerked at the leash. He had a target now. Randall Gage, the man who had taken down his partner. If Tyler released King, would Randall shoot? A bullet at this range might kill Penny, Bradley or King.

Scrappy circled Penny, teeth snapping, as Randall wrapped his arm around her neck, gun pressed to her temple. Dusty barked at full volume, too, adding to the melee.

"Call off those dogs or I'm going to shoot her right here," Randall screamed.

Scrappy continued to yelp and bark. Randall shot wildly, the bullet plowing into Tyler's rear tire.

"Stay," Tyler thundered at the dogs. The command had no effect on King, but Dusty sat and, mercifully, Scrappy froze. He did not sit, but he stood in place, whining, the scruff on his neck raised like King's, every nerve in his body taut.

Randall jutted his chin at King. "Him, too. Call off the big one." Randall's green eyes were wide with fear and rage as he shouted over King's ferocious barking. Tyler felt as though King's yanking was about to dislocate his shoulder. Penny clutched at Randall's arm.

"He won't back down," Tyler yelled. "I'm not his handler."

"You get that dog away from me or she's dead." Randall dug the gun in hard, causing Penny to cry out.

"Okay," Tyler said. "Give me a minute. I'll secure him in the car."

Backing slowly, he dragged the frantic King back toward his vehicle. The dog fought him at every step. "See? We're doing what you want, Randall," Tyler called over his shoulder. "There's no reason to shoot again."

It took all his strength to march the dog back where he could clip his leash to a hook in the car. King thrashed and barked so loudly Tyler's eardrums vibrated. At least Dusty and Scrappy stayed put for the moment.

Sweat beaded on Tyler's forehead. Cops were streaming from the office now, moving as close as they could to provide support. Randall would soon be surrounded, his capture inevitable. Tyler knew he had only seconds before Randall would kill Penny as his final act of vengeance.

Back toward Randall, he noticed a piece of broken asphalt on the ground near his open car door. An idea sizzled through his brain. What he was going to do might instigate a bloodbath. Randall might be arrested, but he could take many lives before that happened, including Penny's. There was no more time to think it through.

Now or never, Walker.

In one fluid motion, he grabbed the chunk, turned and fired the rock as close to Randall's head as he could manage without hitting Penny. It caused Randall to flinch. At the same time, Scrappy launched himself at Randall, who staggered backward, the gun sailing from his hand. Quickly Tyler released King, who flew like a missile toward his partner's attacker and clamped onto his leg.

Randall screamed and batted at King and Scrappy.

"Stop resisting," Tyler shouted to Randall, but he continued to thrash and swear.

Penny fell and immediately scrambled up again. Sobbing, she staggered toward her brother. Scrappy turned and raced to her. She was yelling Bradley's name, lurching the last few feet to reach her brother. Bradley was still lying on his side, blood pooling around his head.

It took all of Tyler's will and repeated orders from Jackson to get King to release. Finally, the dog did so and Jackson took charge of him. King whined pitifully, trying to get to his fallen partner.

Henry secured the weapon and cuffed Randall.

"I should have killed Penny twenty years ago and then come back for her brother," Randall screamed.

Bathed in sweat, Tyler waved in the ambulance. A medic raced over and began work on Bradley as another saw to Randall's wounds. A ring of officers watched, horror on their faces, as Penny clutched her brother's hand, sobbing silently until Tyler gently pulled her away.

"I want to stay with him. Please…" she cried.

"We have to let the medics take care of him now," Tyler said, holding her tightly so she could not run to her brother.

Bradley was loaded onto a stretcher and whisked into an ambulance. Tyler watched over Penny's shoulder. Bradley had still not moved at all, his face a stark white except where it was smeared with blood.

When the ambulance had departed, Tyler released Penny, but kept his arm around her. She remained on the sidewalk, gripping Tyler's arm, her body quaking with emotion. When Scrappy licked her face and she collapsed to her knees, Tyler kneeled next to her.

Her breath came in shuddery gasps. "My brother," she moaned over and over again. Tears poured down her pale face and her eyes were mirrors of grief and shock.

"Listen to me."

She trembled and would not look at him.

Tyler cupped her cheeks and gently tipped her face to his. "Penny, Bradley is alive. He's breathing on his own. Those are two good signs. The hospital will give him the best care, I promise."

She clasped his forearms and that shimmering caramel gaze met his for the first time in days. Tears clung to her long eyelashes like diamond chips. "Tyler, I'm scared. I'm so scared."

"I know. Me, too." And then he folded her in his arms and prayed soft and low, oblivious to the cops gathered all around, the red lights strobing, the whine of the dogs. He prayed with everything in him that Penny would not lose her brother. She nestled against him, shivering, crying, listening.

He had the dim sense that crowds were gathering, thrill seekers and passersby that stopped to discern what had just taken place. Looking up, he discovered that the Brooklyn K-9 officers had formed a tight circle around them, cops and their dogs, shielding Tyler and Penny from the curious glances. They stood shoulder-to-shoulder, protecting their own. His heart swelled.

Closing his eyes, he pressed Penny closer, hoping she could feel her police family gathered around her, praying that Randall Gage had not accomplished his deadly mission.

SIXTEEN

Penny and Scrappy walked the hospital hallways as the hours ticked by in agonizing slow motion. They were never alone. When she felt like talking, Tyler or Vivienne was there. When she simply wanted to cry, Gavin strolled along with her, handing over tissues and a bottle of water, or cups of weak hospital coffee. Jackson brought King, after he was checked out by the vet. The dog whined forlornly.

It was all terribly familiar. When Tyler had been brought here, she'd known him only slightly, a no-nonsense cop who thought her little more than a child. Now he stood next to her, tenderly anticipating her every need, his presence more comforting than she could have ever imagined. In the rare moments he'd left her side, she'd heard him quietly singing a song to Rain over the phone. It was an off-key version of the bus song she'd taught Rain. He didn't get very many of the words right, but the rhythm was perfect.

His words circled through the numbness in her mind.

I'm a single father and I shouldn't have let you become a part of our lives. I should have known you were going to leave us.

Yet he was caring for her now, but not the way she'd yearned for. It wasn't love, it was duty to Bradley, respect and care for a colleague's kin.

Not love.

It would not be that.

When they got the word that Bradley would be okay after he recovered from a concussion and two broken ribs, her knees buckled. All she could do was hold onto Scrappy's collar while he licked the tears that dripped from her chin and the officers crowded around her.

Randall Gage had not taken her brother away.

She thanked the Lord from the bottom of her heart, from the depths of her soul. Tyler stroked a hand across her back and pressed tissues in her palm. She saw that there were tears in the brilliant blue of his eyes, too.

"Randall is behind bars?" She said it to Tyler more to make it real in her mind than anything else.

"Yes, ma'am. And he's going to stay there forever. He'll never hurt you or Bradley or anyone else again."

"I can't even make myself believe it."

Gavin smiled. "You've had twenty years to worry. It may take some time for the truth to sink in."

She went silent. Tyler's fingers pressed comforting circles on her back as her hand stroked Scrappy's soft fur before he helped her to her feet and into a chair. She managed a watery smile. "Scrappy turned out to be a pretty big help, didn't he? Not bad for a police school dropout"

Tyler smiled, but it faded quickly. His hands fell to his lap. "Penny, I know this isn't the time, but…"

The door opened and the nurse appeared. "You can go in…" She hadn't finished her sentence when King surged forward, yanking the leash out of Jackson's hands, hurtling away to find Bradley.

Gavin went after him, apologizing to the startled nurse, and the cops laughed and broke into clusters for private conversations.

Penny followed Gavin, turning to look at Tyler. "What did you want to tell me?"

"It can wait," he said. "Go on. Your brother needs you."

She had to stop herself from running to Bradley's room.

Her brother was going to be okay. Gavin was doing his best to hold back King, who was straining to leap onto the bed with Bradley. Sarge finally succeeded in getting all four of King's paws back on the ground.

When she got a good look at Bradley, she nearly collapsed again. Gripping his bed rail, she pored over the face of her handsome brother. His head was muffled in bandages and his right eye was swollen shut. Tubes and monitors connected him to a variety of beeping machines.

"I'm going to take this big galoot out of here and let you two have a minute alone," Gavin said.

Penny nodded gratefully. She bent close to Bradley and gently touched his undamaged cheek. He smiled wanly and then grimaced.

"Hurts to smile."

"I'm sorry. I'm so sorry."

He raised the hand that was free of the IV. She clasped it, tears flowing freely. "Sarge told me they made the arrest. It's finally over, sis."

She had to bend to hear him. Over. Could it possibly be true? "I can't wrap my mind around it. All I care about is that you're going to be okay."

"I am…and so are you. We can start over now. Randall is out of our lives."

She swallowed hard, trying to make it real.

"So you don't have to quit," he croaked.

She didn't have to because of Randall, but there was still the mess in her heart left over from what had happened with Tyler. It was not going to be possible to see him every day at work, watch his little daughter grow right before her eyes, witness daily what she could not be a part of.

She reached over and kissed her brother gently as his eyes started to close.

"Rest now. We can talk about this later."

When his breathing relaxed into a regular rhythm, she said a prayer of profound gratitude that the Lord had spared her brother.

On Bradley's third day in the hospital, Tyler went to see him, smuggling in a plate of his mother's lasagna.

"Oh, man," Bradley said, sitting up, "am I ready for real food."

"That's a good sign." It was also a good sign that his bruises were starting to fade slightly. The cuts on his arm were scabbing over, as well.

"How's King doing with Jackson?"

"Jackson's been taking him to the office with him and every morning he runs to your cubicle expecting to find you there. Jackson says he's cranky, pure and simple."

"Aww. He's the best partner."

"Next best thing to a golden retriever."

"In your dreams." He peeled back a corner of the foil-covered plate and inhaled. "Your mom is a culinary genius."

"I'll tell her you said that." They made small talk until Tyler shifted and cleared his throat. "I've been thinking."

Bradley looked up from his perusal of the lasagna. "Yeah? About what?"

"About the question you asked me before." Tyler swallowed. "About what Penny means to me."

Bradley set aside the plate and folded his hands across the blanket. "And what is your answer to that question?"

He took a deep breath and let it out slowly. Time to make it all real. "She means everything to me, and I want her to be in my life forever." Breath held, he waited to see how Bradley would react.

For a moment, Bradley's face seemed to be made of stone. Slowly a smile replaced the scowl. "Well, it's about time, Tyler the Timid. The guy who gets Penny is going to be the most fortunate man in the universe and you almost let her get away, you big dope." He rolled his eyes. "I thought I was going to have to knock some sense into you."

Tyler felt his whole body relax. "So you think I'm worthy of her?"

"Not by a long shot, but you can spend the rest of your life trying to be worthy of her." He grinned. "And that means taking care of her brother, too. You know, bending to my every whim, bringing me fresh-squeezed orange juice and giving me your parking place."

Tyler let him go on awhile. "But what if I can't change her mind?"

Bradley rolled his eyes. "Then I guess you aren't trying hard enough. What are you doing wasting time here? Get on it, Detective. She's planning on sticking around until I'm on my feet again, but after that, she'll split unless you change her mind."

There was a knock on the door and a slim blonde lady popped her head in. "May I come in?"

Tyler raised an eyebrow as Bradley straightened and sat up higher on the bed.

"I don't know if Officer McGregor is up for visitors," Tyler said.

"I'm Sasha Eastman. I work for a local news station and I want to do an interview with Bradley and Penny McGregor."

Tyler thought Bradley looked a bit crestfallen that the beautiful lady had an agenda. "A reporter?" he said. "No thanks. You called the office already and we declined."

She smiled. "And you avoided my call, too. I never even got to speak to you."

Bradley's cheeks flushed. "I'm not interested in providing an interview."

"You haven't heard the whole idea. I want to do a show about your parents' murders."

"No thanks. My sister and I learned a long time ago that we don't talk to reporters."

"I'm not your run-of-the-mill reporter, Mr. McGregor." Her smile was warm and gentle. "I believe by telling your story we can draw out information about the copycat killer. Maybe even help you make an arrest."

Bradley frowned. "Like I said, Penny and I don't talk to reporters. Sorry."

Tyler took that as his cue. "I'll walk you to the elevator, Ms. Eastman. Thanks for stopping by."

"All right." She laid a business card on Bradley's table. "But I'm a pretty determined lady. I think we'll be seeing each other again."

Bradley didn't answer as Tyler led Sasha out of the room. Before the door closed, he turned back to Bradley.

"Do you want me to ask her to bring your fresh-squeezed orange juice? She's way better looking than I am."

A balled-up paper napkin hit the door as it closed on Tyler's chuckling.

Penny breathed in the pure joy of being back in their Sheepshead Bay home. She steeped herself in the pleasure of tending to her struggling plants and cleaning out the fridge before she restocked it with Bradley's favorites. She'd tackled the cooking by storm, first baking Bradley's favorite blueberry muffins, then working her way on to a pot of beef stew and even firing up the bread machine with a loaf of herbed Italian bread. Bradley's appetite had not yet fully returned, but she was determined to change that. Each day she produced a new batch of his favorites, surreptitiously sliding a portion into the freezer for him to eat later.

Then she set about refreshing the old house with vases full of fall mums, a fat scented candle for the tiny kitchen table and a fall-patterned kerchief for Scrappy. Each and every detail brought her both pain and pleasure, when she considered her future.

Penny figured on delaying her start with the new K-9 unit another month while Bradley settled into his three weeks of recuperation leave. They had graciously agreed to give her all the time she needed to tend to him. She was Bradley's self-appointed chef and errand runner, but when Bradley returned to full strength, she intended to make some changes. He was not adjusting well to lying around. King, on the other hand, seemed perfectly content to sprawl on the floor at Bradley's feet, snoring or watching basketball on the big-screen TV. Scrappy occupied a spot on the other side of the room, enjoying a beam of fall sunshine.

"You don't have to quit," Bradley had said again just that morning.

"I feel like it's the right thing to do." He'd pressed her for a reason, but she'd changed the subject. It was too difficult to explain to her brother all that was going on inside her heart and mind.

Though she was devastated at leaving her Brooklyn K-9 Unit family, she knew it was time to start a new chapter on her own. Randall had finally been excised from their lives. She'd survived his horrors and come out stronger. It would be good for Bradley, too, to restart his life without his sister always hovering nearby.

A fresh start…a new life. Why did her stomach squeeze when she considered it?

Because she had been afraid for so long that she didn't know what to do now that she wasn't.

Or was it the real reason, which she would not admit even to her brother…? Tyler. He'd made it clear that he regretted the feelings he had for her and that left a hurt that would not dissipate. How could she work at the same office with him? See him and Rain on a regular basis and not mourn the love she had for them?

Love—it was the correct word. It floored her to think it, but she had fallen in love with a man who didn't want her. When tears pricked her eyes, she straightened her shoulders. Soon it would be all over and the memories would recede into the past, where they would not hurt so much.

"There's nothing on TV," Bradley said now. "Why can't I take King for a walk?"

"Because the doctor said you're supposed to lie down and rest."

He rolled his eyes. "How does he know what's good for me?"

"Because he has a degree in medicine. You, on the other hand, believe that an ACE bandage can fix everything from a broken arm to sudden organ failure."

"ACE bandages are very versatile," he grumbled, watching her walk toward the hall closet. "Where are you going?"

She shouldered her bag. "To Coney Island. Rain is having a birthday party and she invited me to come. Just a casual thing." She was still feeling all kinds of awkward around Tyler, but she figured a birthday party would hold enough distraction to keep her from having to make conversation with him. She tucked the neatly wrapped present into her bag.

"A birthday party? I wanna go." He made a move to sit up. "I'll just sit quietly with King and…"

She pointed a finger at him until he sank down again. "You'll do no such thing. I will be back in a couple of hours and if there is cake, I will bring you a piece if you're very well behaved."

He groaned, and she walked back and kissed him on the forehead. "You're a real drill sergeant."

"A drill sergeant who loves her brother." She stroked his hair. Tears welled in her eyes when she recalled him sprawled on the sidewalk, plowed down by Randall's car.

He caught her hand. "I love you, too, sis. Have a good time."

She rubbed Scrappy's ears and clipped on his leash. When she reached for the window to peek out through the curtains, she caught herself. Randall was in jail and that's where he would stay. She had her life back.

Bradley was looking at her. "Go on," he said softly, as if he understood exactly.

She blew him a kiss.

Though her insides were jittery at the prospect of seeing Tyler again, she was still wrapped in gratitude that her brother was safe and sound. Straightening her shoulders, she headed for the door.

SEVENTEEN

Scrappy watched avidly out the window as they drove to Coney Island. It didn't matter if they were going to the beach or the Laundromat. Scrappy was her ever-eager assistant. "You're always ready to go anywhere with me, aren't you?" Her gratitude toward Gavin for allowing her to formally adopt Scrappy was boundless. The dog was her devoted companion and no matter where life took her, he would always be right by her side, a treasured part of her family. Along the way, she caught herself glancing in the rearview mirror every so often.

Randall's gone, she repeated to herself. She wondered how long it would take her to fully believe it. Maybe the new job in Bronx would erase the lingering memories.

She parked and walked Scrappy along the boardwalk to Nathan's Famous hot dogs, where Tyler stood with one hand holding Dusty's leash and the other wrapped around Rain's little fingers. When Rain saw Penny, she broke away and ran to her. Penny scooped her up.

"Happy birthday, big girl."

Rain carefully held up each of her pointer fingers.

"Two years old? Wow." Penny kissed her on the

cheek and eyed Tyler uneasily. "Where are the guests? Am I early?"

"You are the only guest she wanted to invite."

Her cheeks flooded with heat. "Oh. Well, you didn't have to do that. I could have dropped a present by your house. No need to—"

"I wanted to see you, too."

He had? Why? she wanted to ask, but he continued.

"I'll just get us some hot dogs. Do you two want to find a bench to sit on?"

Penny hesitated. The last time she'd been in charge of Rain, the child had disappeared. Cold rippled through her along with the October breeze. "I…"

He nodded firmly. "We can sit and eat our hot dogs and watch the surf." He held up a plastic bucket and shovel. "I promised her we would make a sand castle."

She swallowed and took Rain's hand and the plastic bucket. "All right." She and Rain settled on a metal bench, where they could look out on the wide stretch of sandy beach.

"Castle?" Rain said.

"Yes, Daddy says we are going to build a castle right after lunch."

Rain occupied herself watching the seagulls that swooped down toward the foamy waves. Scrappy tracked their progress, too, his whiskers twitching.

Tyler returned and put Dusty into a sit. He handed Penny a hot dog with mustard only. "Bradley said you're a purist, a mustard-only kind of gal."

She wondered why Tyler and her brother had been discussing her condiment choices.

His hot dog was loaded with every condiment that

would fit, and a third plate held a hot dog sliced into small pieces with a puddle of ketchup for dipping.

Rain happily began to eat her hot dog slices. Penny nibbled at her own lunch, wondering why Tyler had arranged for her to be a private guest at Rain's party. Surely Francine had wanted to come.

"I wanted to talk to you," Tyler said, after a bite of his messy hot dog. "But you've been hard to find lately."

"I've been on nursing duty."

"How's Bradley as a patient?"

"The worst. I've been tempted to handcuff him to get him to keep still."

Tyler laughed. "Not surprised. He wants to get back to work to track down the Emerys' killer now that Randall is headed to prison." He went quiet for a moment. "Penny, what I want to talk to you about is…"

At that moment, Rain suddenly pointed to a seagull flapping nearby. Her gesture collided with Tyler's hot dog and it splatted directly against his chest with a messy squelch.

He jumped up, dropping the hot dog and knocking over Rain's lunch. A seagull swooped in and snatched away Tyler's fallen food. Scrappy gulped up Rain's.

"Oh, Scrappy," Penny chided.

The dog didn't look the slightest bit guilty as he swiped a tongue across his fleshy lips.

Rain began to cry. Tyler dabbed at the colorful mess staining his long-sleeved navy shirt.

"I'll run and get more napkins." Penny jogged to grab a handful from the restaurant and, when she returned, Rain had already stopped crying, and was clutching her bucket.

"Castle," she insisted.

Tyler took the extra napkins and managed to wipe off most of the debris, but the mustard and relish had left a wide smear across his chest. He surveyed the damage. "That looked much better on my hot dog than on my shirt."

"Messy," Rain said.

Penny smothered a grin.

Tyler nodded ruefully. "Yep, that's messy all right. Well, I guess I'm done with my lunch."

"You can have mine," Penny said, handing over her hot dog. "I'm full, anyway, and it looks like Rain doesn't want anymore."

Tyler gratefully accepted and finished her hot dog in two bites before they walked down to the sand.

They watched the rolling waves for a few minutes, while Dusty and Scrappy sniffed the landscape. Rain started to fill her bucket with dry sand. When she dumped it out, she grew perplexed that the sand did not stick together.

"We need some wet stuff," said Tyler. "I'll get it." He took the little yellow bucket and moved toward the surf. A couple of shovel scoops and he had filled it. As he stood up with a grin on his face, Dusty barked at a nearby seagull. Both dogs raced after the bird, so close to Tyler that he stumbled back a pace, stepping into the hole he'd just made in the sand. He went down on his backside, just as a wave rolled in from the ocean. His shoulders contracted as a foamy crest of water doused him completely.

Penny clapped a hand to her mouth as he sprang up, soaking wet and blinking.

"Oo-o-o-hhh," Rain said. "Wet."

Tyler retrieved the bucket and shovel, then returned

to the dry sand. "Here you go," he said to Rain with a completely straight face, handing over the bucket. "I can guarantee this is the wet stuff."

Rain happily took the sand and dumped it out. Then she set to work refilling the bucket, completely absorbed in her task.

Tyler looked so comical standing there with his clothes soaked and the stain of condiments on his shirt that Penny started to giggle.

"I'm sorry," she said. "I shouldn't laugh, but…"

He chuckled. "That's okay. This hasn't exactly gone like I planned."

Both of them began to laugh outright until their merriment died away.

"Rain doesn't seem to mind the birthday mess," Penny said.

"Her birthday is actually Monday and she's bringing cupcakes to her tiny tot class. Today's celebration was just a reason to get you to come out with me."

She looked at him, puzzled. "Why did you want me to meet you?"

He drew close and held his hand out. "I'm waterlogged and messy, but I have something important to say and I'm going to say it, even though nothing has gone right today."

Heart beating fast at the intensity of his eyes, she took his hand. His fingers were cold and sandy. Automatically, she pressed them between hers and tried to rub some warmth back in them. He stared at their joined hands as if he saw something incredible there.

"This is why," he said.

"Why what?"

He raised her hand in his. "This right here. The way

you offer comfort to everyone, the way you nurture and love. It's in your DNA, it's who you are."

She stared. "I... I'm not sure."

"I'm sure. More sure than anything else I've ever known. Penny, you are a one in a million."

She blushed and tried to move her hands away, but he grabbed them.

"And I love you."

Her eyes went wide. "But..."

"I love you. I was afraid to say it because of my past failures. I mean, look..." He surveyed his shirt, gritty with mustard and sand. "I planned this perfect romantic situation so I could tell you that and this is how it turned out. But it's okay. If every plan I make in the future goes bust... I can live with that, as long as you're with me."

Shivers erupted up and down her spine. "The things you said..."

"Were untrue. I wanted to blame you for leaving me, but that wasn't your fault, it was mine. I've been dilly-dallying around, too scared to tell you how important you are to me. Tyler the Timid."

She raised an eyebrow. "Where'd you come up with that?"

"Your brother's nickname for me, but he's right." He pulled her closer. "I'm done being timid. I'm going to lay it all out there and tell you that I want you to stay at the office, in Brooklyn, with me. I want to marry you. I want us to be a family."

It was hard for her to believe it could be true. This man, the man who would not leave her thoughts, was offering her a life with him, the future that she'd always wanted. Her gaze traveled from his riveting blue eyes to Rain. "I'm not… I mean, I don't know how good a mother I would be to Rain."

"Look at me, Penny."

She dragged her eyes back to his face, lower lip between her teeth.

"Do you love me? Can you love me now that you know what a…" He looked at his shirt again. "What a mess I can be? After I hurt you and pushed you away? Do you love me?"

Tears blurred her vision. "Yes," she whispered. "I do, and I love Rain, too."

He gulped audibly. "Do you love us enough to step into this messy life with me and my daughter? I can't say it will be smooth sailing. As a matter of fact, I'm sure it won't. But I can promise you that I will love you every day of my life and I will try to be worthy of the amazing woman that you are."

She looked out at the waves, so much less vivid than his eyes. Rain dumped her bucket and started over. Penny took in the intensity of her knitted brow, so like her father's as, she began again on a new structure, better and stronger than the one she'd built before. When Penny looked at Tyler again, he was on one knee, holding a velvet box that held a slender gold band with a glittering, square-cut, pink diamond.

"Not a plain diamond, not for you. It's not good enough, I'm not good enough, but I'm asking you to accept it. Will you marry me?"

"Yes," she whispered as he slid the ring onto her finger. "I love you, Tyler."

"I love you, too, Penny."

Scrappy barked and he and Dusty raced again to the

edge of the surf. Rain upended the bucket and clapped as the lopsided sand castle stood strong.

Tyler grabbed Penny up in a hug, twirling her around, sand flying, his wet shirt dampening her jacket, the scent of mustard and relish clinging to him. As he kissed her, she knew her life would be here in Brooklyn with her police family, her brother and Scrappy, and Tyler and Rain, the family God had put in her path to teach her how to love like Him.

* * * * *

Aside from her faith and her family, there's not much **Shirlee McCoy** enjoys more than a good book! When she's not hanging out with the people she loves most, she can be found plotting her next Love Inspired Suspense story or trekking through the wilderness, training with a local search-and-rescue team. Shirlee loves to hear from readers. If you have time, drop her a line at shirleermccoy@hotmail.com.

Books by Shirlee McCoy

Love Inspired Suspense

Hidden Witness
Evidence of Innocence

FBI: Special Crimes Unit

Night Stalker
Gone
Dangerous Sanctuary
Lone Witness
Falsely Accused

Mission: Rescue

Protective Instincts
Her Christmas Guardian
Exit Strategy
Deadly Christmas Secrets
Mystery Child
The Christmas Target
Mistaken Identity
Christmas on the Run

Visit the Author Profile page
at LoveInspired.com for more titles.

DELAYED JUSTICE

Shirlee McCoy

It is joy to the just to do judgment:
but destruction shall be to the workers of iniquity.
—*Proverbs* 21:15

To the wonderful authors who wrote the books before this one. You are rock stars, and I love you all.

And to Melissa Senate, a woman I have never met, but who edited this manuscript and helped me add in all the details that tied it to every continuity book that came before it.
Melissa, from the bottom of my heart, thank you.

ONE

Sasha Eastman had never been afraid to stand on a crowded street corner in Sheepshead Bay, New York. She'd waited at crosswalks hundreds of times, standing amid throngs of people all staring at phones or streetlights and then flowing like lemmings across the roads. She knew the ebb of city life—the busy, noisy, thriving world of people and vehicles and emergency sirens. Since her father's death two years ago, she found the crowds comforting. Each morning she walked out of her quiet apartment and reminded herself that she wasn't alone, that there was a city filled with people surrounding her. She didn't need more than that. She didn't want more. She liked being free of the emotional entanglement relationships brought—the highs and lows, joys and heartbreaks. She'd lost her mother at fourteen years old, lost her ex-husband to another woman after three years of marriage. She'd lost her father to cancer, and she had no intention of losing anyone ever again. Being alone was fine. It was good. She was happy with her two-bedroom apartment and the silence she returned to after a long day of work. She had always felt safe and content in the life she had created.

And then *he'd* appeared.

First, just at the edge of her periphery—a quick glimpse that had made her blood run cold. The hooked nose, the hooded eyes, the stature that was just tall enough to make him stand out in a crowd. She'd told herself she was overtired, working too hard, thinking too much about the past. Martin Roker had died in a gun battle with the police eighteen years ago, shortly after he had murdered Sasha's mother. He was *not* wandering the streets of New York City. He wasn't stalking her. He wouldn't jump out of her closet in the dead of night.

And yet she hadn't been able to shake the anxiety that settled in the pit of her stomach.

She had seen him again a day later. Full-on face view of a man who should be dead. He'd been standing across the street from the small studio where she taped her show for the local-access cable station, WBKN. She'd walked outside at dusk, ready to return home after a few hours of working on her story. The one she was finally ready to tell: the tragedy of losing a family member to murder and the triumph that could come from it. Her mind had been in the past, her thoughts dwelling on those minutes and hours after she had learned of her mother's death. She'd been looking at her phone, wondering if she should visit the police precinct to ask for the case file on her mother's murder. When she looked up, he had been across the street.

And now…

Now she was afraid in a way she couldn't remember ever being before. Afraid that she would see him again; worried that delving into past heartaches had unhinged her mind and made her vulnerable to imagining things that couldn't possibly exist.

Like a dead man walking the streets.

She hitched her bag higher on her shoulder, determined to push the fear away. Martin Roker was dead. He had died eighteen years ago—a forty-year-old man who had forced the police to shoot him. He couldn't possibly be stalking her. Even if he had lived, even if he had decided to hunt her down for some twisted reason, he wouldn't still look like a forty-year-old man. He would have aged.

Her cell phone rang and she glanced down, dismissing the number as a solicitor's. When she looked up again, the light had changed and the crowd was moving. She stepped off the curb, scanning the area, her heart jumping as she met cold blue eyes.

He was there! Right in her path, looking into her eyes as if he were daring her to come closer. Hooked nose. Blondish hair. Taller by a couple of inches than the people around him.

She turned away, heart in her throat, pulse racing. She glanced back, sure that he would be gone. He was crossing the street with long, determined strides, his cold gaze focused on Sasha. Hands deep in the pockets of his coat, shoulders squared, he moved through the crowd without breaking eye contact. Terrified, she ran back the way she had come, dodging the throng of people returning home after work. The studio was three blocks away. She'd go there and call for a cab, because she couldn't call the police and say a dead man was stalking her.

Could she?

She glanced back again, hoping he had been a figment of her imagination and that maybe she was simply exhausted from too many nights thinking about the past and her mother's murder.

He was still there! Moving quickly and gaining on her.

This was real!

He was real!

She ducked into a corner bakery, smiling at the man behind the counter as she ran to the display case and pretended to look at the pastries.

"Can I help you?" he asked.

"Just looking," she murmured, her mouth dry with fear, the smile still pasted on her face. She knew how to fake happiness. She knew how to pretend everything was okay. She'd done it after her mother's murder because she hadn't wanted her father to worry. She'd done it after her ex-husband, Michael, had told her he was in love with another woman, packed his bags and walked out of their apartment. She'd put on her smiles and she had faked her happiness. She was ready to be more authentic. She wanted to be.

She wanted to tell her story and share her experiences. She wanted to hunt for the good in New York City's crowded streets and boroughs and give people something to smile about.

Had her determination to do that caused the past to be resurrected?

She could think of no other reason for a man who looked exactly like her mother's killer to be stalking her. The producer of the local cable news show she worked for had insisted she tell viewers about the two-day special report she was working on. The story of her mother's murder and the aftermath of it. After all these years, Sasha was eager to let the world know that her mother had been a wonderful woman who had made a terrible mistake. A mistake that had cost her life. Following that tragedy, Sasha had become determined to fulfill the dream she had spent so many hours talking to her mother about. Even at a young age, she had known she wanted to be a journalist. Telling her story was part of that.

But had it put her in the crosshairs of a madman?

She shuddered, still staring into the case and wishing she didn't have to walk outside alone.

The door opened behind her, the quiet whoosh making her skin crawl. She didn't dare turn around. She was too afraid of what she would see. Her shoulders tensed as someone walked across the tile floor.

"Hey, Bradley! You're in early tonight. You want the usual?" the man behind the counter called out cheerfully.

He obviously wasn't seeing a ghoulish monster.

Sasha moved to the side and let her gaze drift to the figure that was stepping up to the counter. Suit. Button-down shirt. Shiny leather shoes. A dog on a leash standing calmly beside him, its dark brown eyes focused on Sasha.

She nearly sagged with relief.

She knew the dog, and she knew the police officer. Detective Bradley McGregor's parents had been murdered in their home twenty years ago. Their four-year-old daughter, Penelope, had been left unhurt. Their fourteen-year-old son, Bradley, out on a sleepover at a friend's apartment, had been the prime suspect. The double homicide had been a hot topic on the local news channels back then. Recently, it had become one again. Earlier this year, a copycat killer had murdered a couple, leaving their young daughter as the only witness. The similarities between the cases had been obvious enough to make people talk.

Sasha had listened.

She'd been young at the time of the McGregor murders, and the details had been blurry. After doing some research and realizing that stories of Bradley's guilt had still circulated for decades after he had been taken off the suspect list, she had known she wanted to interview him for her show.

A local son raised by neglectful parents and suspected of their brutal murders becomes a well-respected K-9 police detective.

What wasn't feel-good about that?

Last week, she'd visited Detective McGregor at the precinct, hoping he'd agree to an interview. She'd tried to talk to his sister, Penny, but the young woman, who was the front desk clerk at the Brooklyn K-9 Unit, had said *No comment* at least five times.

Sasha hadn't given up.

She would return to the precinct and ask again, but now wasn't the right time to try to talk Bradley McGregor into an interview. Not when he was watching her tensely, obviously braced for an onslaught of questions and requests.

"Detective," she murmured, refusing to allow his lack of warmth to send her rushing from the bakery. Right now, this was her safe spot. She would hang around until McGregor left. Then she would walk outside with him.

"Ms. Eastman," he responded, his gaze shifting to the man behind the counter. "I'll take my usual, Jack. Throw in a couple of éclairs for my sister."

"Won't be long, she'll be moving out, hey?" the man said. "Heard she's getting married."

"You heard right."

"Can't believe the little kid you used to bring in for muffins and juice is old enough to fly the coop." He shook his head, his attention jumping to a point beyond Sasha.

He frowned.

"You got trouble, young lady?" he asked.

Startled, she turned and saw her worst nightmare staring in the storefront window. His cold eyes and dead expression were too familiar, his smile chilling as he pulled his hand from his pocket and pointed a gun in her direction.

She screamed, bumping Detective McGregor as she tried to duck away. The crack of gunfire echoed through the bakery, the window exploding into a million tiny fissures that crawled across the glass.

Detective McGregor shouted for her to get down, but she was already on the floor, scrambling for cover behind the counter. The door opened and closed, and she had no idea if McGregor had run outside or if Martin Roker had entered. She cowered behind the counter and waited as the sounds of sirens and people shouting drifted in from the street.

Detective Bradley McGregor raced down the crowded sidewalk, dodging pedestrians as he shouted for the gunman to stop. His Belgian Malinois partner, King, trained for protection but excellent at tracking and at suspect apprehension, loped beside him. Head up and ears pricked, King was waiting to be issued the command to attack. If the streets had been empty, if there weren't dozens of people around, Bradley would have already given it. The perp was a half block ahead, dark coat flapping like bat wings as he sprinted past stunned onlookers. He had tucked his gun away or tossed it. Both his hands were free. Bradley could see the paleness of his skin and the long, thin length of his legs. Dark slacks. Black coat. Short blond hair.

Armed.

Dangerous.

He called for backup, his radio buzzing with life as officers responded. He could count on his team to be there swiftly, but he wanted the perp off the streets now, before anyone was hurt.

"Police! Freeze!" he yelled as he dodged a woman with a baby in a carrier who was desperately looking for an escape route. People were panicking, short high-pitched screams and anxious shouts creating a cacophony of noise that rivaled the normal raucous sounds of rush hour in the city.

The perp veered to the right, sprinting into one of the narrow alleys that opened between buildings. This was where things got dicey. No visual of the perp. No way of knowing if he was running or preparing an ambush. They were near Ocean Avenue, the busy thoroughfare surrounded by newer multifamily dwellings. Closer to the bay, older homes dotted the quieter streets.

He slowed as he reached the alley, staying close to the brick facade of an apartment building as he called in his location. Whoever this guy was, whomever his target had been, he needed to be stopped.

"Police! Come out or I'm sending my dog in." He gave one last warning as he unhooked King's leash.

The Malinois was a mild-mannered, high-energy pet at home, but he became a fierce weapon out in the field.

King snarled, teeth bared, body tense. His scruff was up, his ears back. He was ready.

"Hold on, Officer. I'm coming!" a man yelled out from the alley.

"Slowly! Hands where I can see them!" Bradley responded, keeping hold of King's collar. The dog was scrabbling at the pavement, barking wildly. King loved anything to do with his job, but this part of the game? When he was let loose to do what he had been trained to do? It was his favorite.

"I'm coming, man! Hold the dog!" Someone shuffled into view. A man in his fifties or sixties. Scruffy gray beard and pallid skin. Dark blue sweatpants that hadn't been washed in a while. Oversize coat hanging from a too-thin frame. Not the perp. This guy had just been in the wrong place at the wrong time.

"Step to the side," Bradley commanded. "You see a guy run through that alley?"

"Tall dude? Blond hair? Yeah. He ran past me. I said hello, but he didn't give me the time of day otherwise," the man said, his focus on King, his dark blue eyes wide with fear. "You're not letting him go, are you?"

"No." Bradley's response was terse, his focus on the alley again. The perp was heading toward Sheepshead Bay and deeper into the quietest areas of the community. 1920s houses converted to apartments. Single-family homes on small lots that abutted one another. A nice residential community in Brooklyn, Sheepshead Bay wasn't known for its high crime rate. Once a fishing town, it offered a more suburban feel for city dwellers who wanted it.

It also offered plenty of escape routes.

He hooked King back to his leash and ran through the alley, bursting out onto the next street as the sun ducked behind rows of brick apartment buildings. There was a chill of winter in the air that blew in from the bay, hinting at the holiday season that would soon envelop the city. Bradley dreaded it the same way other people dreaded trips to the dentist.

Thanksgiving first. The holiday where families and friends gathered to give thanks for their blessings and for each other. Then Christmas, where the same thing played out. It wasn't that Bradley didn't enjoy gathering with people he cared about, but holidays were a reminder of what life could have and should have been. He and Penny growing up in a loving home with loving parents. No murder to taint their memories. No need for a loving adoptive family to take them in.

There had been blessings that had come out of the pain, but Bradley couldn't help wondering if there had been a purpose behind the struggles and trials. He had certainly learned a lot about life and about himself, but he had also had to work hard to overcome his rough beginning.

Aside from valuing what he had, loving deeply the people in his life, mostly he had learned to protect himself by building an impeccable reputation in the community.

Even that hadn't been enough.

He had heard the whispers after a copycat murder had rocked the community—a husband and wife killed, their three-year-old daughter the only witness. Even after all these years, after all he had accomplished in his work as a police officer, people had still wondered if he was responsible for his parents' murders.

Now that the perpetrator had been caught, there was no doubt of his innocence. The whispers had stopped, but the sting of them hadn't left him. He loved New York City. He loved Brooklyn and Sheepshead Bay. He had served the people of the city faithfully for more than a decade.

And still they had doubted him.

He frowned, scanning the street, and spotted the perp dashing across the pavement, his black coat flapping behind him. There were still too many people to safely release King. Protection-and-apprehension dogs were trained to take down the threat. They were not trained to differentiate the scent of the threat from the surrounding population. A straight and clear path between the dog and the suspect was necessary for safe deployment.

Right now, Bradley didn't have it.

He called in his location again as he sprinted across the street, dodging a bicyclist and several motorists who were surprised to see a police officer and dog darting through evening traffic.

Bradley knew the area well. The suspect ran through a packed parking lot, jumped a small retaining wall and kept going, ducking into a parking garage connected to one of the newer apartment complexes. He followed, moving more cautiously as he stepped into the dimly lit interior. There were too many turns and angles, too many cars, too many places where the gunman could be lying in wait. He kept a wall to his left shoulder and King to his right as he scanned the area. No sign of the gunman. No sounds of him fleeing. Bradley gave King the command to find and let the dog lead him through a maze of parked cars. There was a stairwell in the far wall, and King lunged into it, straining against the leash and barking wildly.

"Police! Come out with your hands where I can see them," Bradley commanded.

There was a flurry of movement on the landing above. A door opened and slammed closed, and King scrabbled at the cement steps.

"Let's go!" Bradley raced up the stairs, slamming his hand into the closed door and rushing out onto the third level of the parking garage. A car engine revved as he and King sprinted across the paved lot. King swung around, barking wildly as tires squealed and a small blue car sped around a corner and aimed straight for them.

Bradley shouted for the vehicle to halt, then pulled his service weapon, firing at the front tire of the vehicle as he dived for cover.

TWO

Martin Roker was alive.

He had been outside the bakery.

He had fired a shot through the window.

Sasha hadn't gone crazy.

She wasn't imagining things.

Her sleepless nights and long hours of work weren't making her hallucinate.

She frowned.

She had seen Martin three times in a week. Each time, she'd been convinced he was an unaged version of the man who had murdered her mother. Forty years old. Tall and angular. No wrinkles visible on his thin face.

"Impossible," she whispered as she watched several police officers collect evidence outside the bakery. When they'd arrived, she had been asked to have a seat and wait. Forty minutes later, and she was still waiting. The sky had turned navy with twilight, the city lights flickering on. Cars inched by the police barrier that had been erected at the curb, blue and white lights flashing on windows and pavement.

The man who had been stalking her had caused all this.

Martin Roker?

It couldn't be. Not an unaged, unchanged man in a world where everything aged and everything changed. Eighteen years was a long time. If Roker had lived, he would be close to sixty, with some gray hair and at least a few wrinkles. He'd have changed the way everyone did. Life left no one unscathed.

"He's dead," she muttered, reminding herself of the most important fact.

Martin Roker had been killed in a shoot-out with the police. Recently, she had looked through the files and the evidence that had been collected after her mother's murder. She had seen photos of Roker's body, lying where it had fallen, the area cordoned off by yellow police tape. She had felt for the wife and little girl he had left behind, and she had considered contacting them for her story.

She hadn't wanted to dredge up a past that she knew had been as painful for them as it had been for her. They were not responsible for Roker's actions, and their suffering in the aftermath only made his affair with Sasha's mother, the murder and his suicide-by-police all the more heartbreaking.

She had left them alone.

Despite her journalistic need for all the facts and all sides of the story, she had shut herself off from that part of the past.

But now she wondered if she had been wrong to do so.

Roker couldn't be stalking her through the streets of Sheepshead Bay. He couldn't have fired a gun at her.

But someone was. Someone had.

Who?

She needed to know. The only way she was going to find out was to dig into Roker's side of the story. Look into the life he had lived before he had murdered her mother.

Somewhere in the past was a clue about the present. She just had to find it.

"Are you okay?" the bakery attendant asked, plopping a bottle of water on the table in front of her before she could respond. "You look pale."

"It comes with the blond hair," she responded, offering a shaky smile.

"More likely comes from being shot at."

"That, too," she murmured, opening the bottle and taking a sip. Her hands were shaking and water sloshed onto her coat and the table.

"Who is he? An ex?"

"Ex?" She swiped at the drops of water, flicking them from the table before she dropped into a chair. She didn't consider herself to be easily scared, and she certainly wouldn't label herself as someone who got overly excited in chaotic situations. She tended to be the calm in the storm, the person people turned to when they needed a clear mind and a focused approach.

Right now, though, she was shaken.

Deeply.

"Ex," the man responded, pulling out a chair and sitting across from her. "Husband? Boyfriend?"

"Oh. No. It isn't anyone I know," she replied, glancing at the activity outside the window. What evidence were they collecting? What were they looking for? Shell casings? Bullets? Some clue that would give them a name and location for the perp? "Do you have security cameras outside?" she asked, falling back into old habits from her days as a newspaper reporter working the crime beat. That had been her first job. She'd learned a lot about law enforcement and the criminal justice system during those five years.

She'd also gotten burned out.

Too many hard-luck stories.

Too many atrocities committed against humans by humans.

She'd spent a lot of time praying back then, a lot of time writing in her journal, listing people who desperately needed answers or closure or healing. She had wanted to help all of them, and she had wanted to understand what caused a person to hurt someone else.

She hadn't been able to do either of those things.

In the end, she had walked away rather than become jaded and cynical. She hadn't wanted the job to change her.

"I'm afraid we don't. Place is too old-fashioned for that."

"Old-fashioned? It looks nicely updated," she responded absently, years of interviewing people making the conversation almost rote.

"Oh. It is. We keep up with the times, but I never felt the need for anything more than a lock on the front and back doors. People in the neighborhood know my shop, know me. Why would they want to do anything to hurt what my family built?"

"They wouldn't, and there are plenty of other businesses on the street. I'm sure some of them have security cameras." She took another sip of water. Her hand was steadier, but her heart was still beating rapidly, her pulse racing.

The man couldn't have been Martin Roker.

So, who was he?

Why had he been following her?

Why had he fired a shot at her?

"True, but I'll still be getting a security system and camera in the next few days. Not going to have riffraff causing problems around the bakery. We've worked too hard to keep this place going."

"I'm really sorry this happened."

"It's not your fault." He smiled jovially and stood. "I'm going to the kitchen. Probably won't be able to open tomorrow. Might as well clean up and get ready to end the day."

He walked into the back of the store.

She stayed where she was, facing the window and the lights, the dark evening sky and the familiar street. She had made Sheepshead Bay her home a decade ago, moving into an apartment that was within walking distance of the subway station. She'd just graduated from college, was newly married and searching for a job in journalism. Life had been exciting and filled with possibilities.

Ten years later, she had achieved some of her dreams. She had reached for others only to see them slip through her fingers. She had lost her father to cancer. She had lost her marriage to infidelity. She was still in the apartment and still working in journalism, but her focus had changed.

She didn't want to change the world so much as she wanted to cheer it. She couldn't take away pain or heartache, but she could put positive stories out into the world.

Or at least in the small area of the world her cable show reached.

She didn't reach for big dreams.

Not anymore.

She prayed for small successes. That God would use her to touch a heart, to ease a burden, to lift a spirt— those were the things she wanted. She had thought she was making progress toward that. Her life had fallen into a nice routine. Early-morning walk to work. A few hours of prep. Produce a live cable show that highlighted the good things that were happening in the community. A late lunch. A few more hours of work. An early-evening walk through Sheepshead Bay, enjoying the cacophony of city noise and the frenetic pace of life.

And then Martin Roker had appeared.

First outside her apartment at twilight, standing across the street as she walked home. The light had been dim. She had told herself she was mistaken, that it wasn't him, but her stomach had churned with anxiety.

She had dreamed about her mother that night, waking bathed in sweat with her heart tripping and jumping, terrified and not sure why.

She pushed away from the table, tired of her circling thoughts and her dead-end reasoning. She knew what she had seen. There was no doubt about it. What she needed to find out was who the Martin Roker look-alike was.

She stepped outside, smiling at a female police officer who was standing on the sidewalk a few feet away.

"I'm not trying to rush the process, but I was wondering how long I'm going to have to wait to be interviewed," she said.

"We're finishing up. If you'll go inside and wait a little longer, we should be with you shortly," the female officer said. She had green eyes and a kind smile. Sasha guessed her to be in her early twenties. Probably new to police work.

"Have you heard anything from Detective McGregor?" she asked, ignoring the subtle request to leave.

"I'm not that high up on the food chain," the officer responded.

"Is there someone here who is?"

"My sergeant. He's next to his cruiser." She pointed to the corner of the street and three uniformed officers who were standing at the curb.

"Thank you." Sasha skirted crime scene tape, her energy amping up, her nerves simmering down. Action was better than idleness. That had been her father's mantra after her mother died. Keep going. Keep moving forward. Keep the mind and the body occupied so the grief doesn't win.

"Ms. Eastman!" a man called.

She swung around and was surprised to see Detective McGregor striding toward her, his canine partner at his side. The dog seemed relaxed, tongue lolling out, bright eyes focused on Sasha.

McGregor, on the other hand, looked unhappy, his jaw tight, his expression grim.

"Were you leaving?" he asked.

"I was looking for you. Any success catching the gunman?" she asked, certain from the expression on his face he hadn't had any.

"How about we go inside to discuss it?"

"That's fine." She followed him into the bakery, staying a few feet away from his Malinois. Aside from what she had seen on television, she knew nothing about police dogs and how they worked.

"Don't worry," Detective McGregor said as he pulled

out a chair and motioned for her to sit. "King doesn't bite unless he's told to."

"I wasn't worried."

"No?" He took the seat across from her and stared into her eyes. She resisted the urge to look away. Face-to-face interviews were her thing. She knew how to meet eyes and make polite conversation, but she felt off-balance as she met McGregor's gaze. He was different from other police officers she'd interviewed.

Or maybe she just perceived him that way because she knew his background and because she understood how difficult it was to break away from the past. She admired him for his success. Professionally and personally. To have had such a rough beginning and to have created good things from that was something she was interested in exploring in her work.

"I don't know much about police dogs, but I'm not afraid of them. Much," she admitted, watching as King settled down beside Bradley.

Bradley laughed. "A little caution around a dog like King isn't a bad thing. He is trained in protection and apprehension. A powerful tool and a very good partner. Unfortunately, we couldn't catch the gunman. We tracked him to an apartment parking garage. He had a vehicle there, and he was able to escape." He didn't look away as he spoke. His eyes were the darkest brown she had ever seen, his hair a rich chestnut with hints of auburn. She hadn't noticed that when she'd gone to the precinct to ask for an interview, and she probably shouldn't be noticing now.

"Did you get a look at his vehicle?" she asked, following the same line of questioning she would have used if she had still been working the crime beat. She needed answers. Bradley might have them.

"Yes. We're also getting security footage from apartment management. It may take a little time, so I wanted to fill you in and let you know—we're working as fast and as diligently as we can."

"I appreciate that, Detective."

"I'm sure you'll also understand and appreciate the fact that I have some questions I'd like to ask. If you're up to it."

"I am." She pulled her coat a little tighter, cold with the thought that the man who looked like Martin Roker was still free. She had been hopeful he would be caught. That this would be over as quickly as it had begun. She had work to do, feel-good stories to tell.

And her own past to explore.

With Thanksgiving coming up, it had seemed as good a time as any to explore her heritage. Her grandparents had been gone for years. She had no aunts or uncles. No family members who might remember her parents as children. She had been contacting old friends of her parents, interviewing teachers who remembered them, trying to put together the beginning of the story that had become hers.

She didn't want to be here, the victim of a crime.

She wanted to be figuring out her past so that maybe she could begin planning a future that involved more than going to work in the morning and returning to her empty apartment each night.

"So, let's get started," he said, taking out a small notebook and a pen. "Did you get a good look at the perpetrator?"

"Yes."

"Good enough to pick him out of a lineup?" he asked, jotting her answers down.

"Absolutely."

"Did you recognize him?"

"Yes."

He stopped writing and met her eyes.

"Want to tell me who he is?"

"I can tell you who he looks like."

"Okay, how about you do that?" he said, a hint of impatience in his voice.

"He looks just like the man who murdered my mother."

He set the pen on the table, crossed his arms over his chest, his dark eyes spearing into hers. "Let's back up. Your mother was murdered?"

"Yes."

"Recently?"

"No," she said, offering a quick, emotionless account of what had happened.

When she finished, he nodded. "I think I remember hearing about the case. The murderer was killed by the police."

"That's right."

"And yet you think he was here tonight? Firing a gun?"

"I think someone who looks exactly like him was."

He frowned. "Why?"

"Why do I think that? Or why would the dead ringer for my mother's killer stalk me?"

"Stalk you?"

"I've seen him twice before today," she explained.

"What's the name of the man who killed your mother?" he asked. To his credit, he didn't voice doubts, didn't tell her she was imagining things or ask if she might be mistaken.

"Martin Roker."

He nodded. "All right. Wait here. I want to make a few calls, and then we'll talk more."

He told King to stay, walked outside and stood near the door, cell phone pressed to his ear, gaze still focused on Sasha. She knew he thought she was delusional. She would think the same if she'd heard the cockamamie story she had just told.

She stood, restless and uneasy.

King growled, the sound just enough of a warning to make her drop into the chair again. She wasn't afraid of the dog, but she wasn't willing to take chances around him, either. She would wait. Maybe McGregor would return with information that would make everything she had experienced make sense.

A dead man stalking and shooting at Sasha Eastman? It wasn't possible.

She seemed very aware of that fact. Yet she had still told him that the shooter was a dead ringer for her mother's murderer.

Bradley kept his attention focused on her as he called the precinct and asked for information on Martin Roker. It only took a few minutes for a clerk in the records office to confirm that Roker had murdered his ex-love, Natasha Eastman, and was killed in a shoot-out with the police.

The evening had taken a confusing turn, but there was one thing he was certain of—dead men did not fire guns.

On the other hand, Sasha didn't seem like the kind

of person who was given to imagining things. After she had visited him at the precinct, he had made it a point to watch her cable show. He'd been curious and then pleasantly surprised by the upbeat, hope-filled stories she presented to viewers. He would never have guessed that she had been through the tragedy of losing a parent to violence.

But then, most people wouldn't guess that about him. Not that anyone in Sheepshead Bay would need to guess. Anyone who had been in the community for any length of time knew the story of his parents' murders. A man, wearing a clown mask with blue hair, had broken into his parents' home. He'd shot Anna and Eddie McGregor but hadn't hurt their daughter, Penny. She had only been four at the time. Instead of harming her, the perpetrator had given her a stuffed monkey. Both unemployed at the time of the murders, Bradley's parents had been small-time criminals who liked to go out and party. They had been neglectful regarding the well-being of their kids. By the time of their murders, Bradley had been fourteen and well used to his parents' selfishness and indifference. He hadn't cared about it for himself, but he had been angry that Penny was often left alone with no food while he was at school. When his parents had the money to bring her to day care, they often forgot to pick her up at the end of the day.

Bradley had been determined to make certain Penny didn't suffer, he had been angry at his parents, he had wanted them to do better, but he had loved them. That he'd been considered a suspect in their murders, even briefly, had hurt. Worse, he'd been the prime suspect for just long enough to cement the community's distrust and suspicion of him, even twenty years later. The case had gone cold and would have been long forgotten if a copycat killer hadn't struck on the twentieth anniversary of the killings. Another couple, also neglectful of their young daughter, was murdered in their Brooklyn home. Little Lucy Emery had been left unhurt and given a stuffed monkey.

Same MO.

Different killer.

He knew that for a fact, because the perpetrator of the Emery murders was still on the loose.

His parents' murderer, finally identified through DNA, was now rotting in prison, awaiting trial.

Bradley was very much looking forward to seeing Randall Gage face justice. For his parents. For Penny.

For him.

Sometimes he still felt like that fourteen-year-old kid being interrogated and watched. It had hurt to have people he admired and trusted whisper when he walked by. It had been painful to realize that they could so easily begin to question his honesty and integrity. He'd spent the past twenty years proving who he was to the community. His parents may have been low-level criminals, but that didn't mean he had to follow in their footsteps. Thankfully for him and Penny, the detective on his parents' case and his wife had taken them in, giving them stability, room to grieve, to be confused. Bradley had taken the hard road—college, career, helping raise his younger sister. He had no regrets, but he had never forgotten the sting of being suspected of a heinous crime. He thought about it every time he worked a case. He never wanted to be responsible for tainting a person's reputation without cause, and he certainly wasn't going to treat Sasha like she had lost her mind because of her allegations.

The shooter had been very much alive. Bradley had gotten a good look at him. He planned to return to the precinct and search for photos of Martin Roker. It had been eighteen years since his death and since Sasha had seen him. It was possible the shooter looked similar enough to confuse her.

He walked back into the bakery and called King to heel.

"I verified Roker's death," he said as Sasha approached.

"I already knew he was dead. What I'd like to figure out is how a dead man could possibly be stalking me through the streets of Sheepshead Bay." She had a direct gaze and a straightforward approach to communication that he appreciated.

"You of course know that isn't possible."

"I do. I also know what I've seen. The man who is stalking me is Martin Roker's doppelgänger."

"I'll do everything I can to figure out who he is. Until I do, it's probably best if you stay close to home. Keep your doors locked. Don't go out alone."

"I have a job, Detective. I can't just blow it off."

"Your life is more important than your job, Ms. Eastman."

"I'll be careful, but I can't spend an indefinite amount of time locked in my apartment. Speaking of which—" she glanced at her watch and frowned "—do you think I'll be allowed to go home any time tonight?"

"I just need your contact information, and then you're free to go."

She rattled it off, then handed him a business card. "It's all here."

"Thanks. I'll keep you updated on our progress."

"I appreciate it, Detective." She walked to the door, her expression cool. Her hand shook as she tucked a stray strand of hair behind her ear. She wasn't nearly as unaffected as she pretended to be.

And he wasn't going to be able to let her walk away knowing that she was terrified.

"How about King and I escort you home?" he suggested, following her out into the cold November evening.

"I'd tell you that isn't necessary, but I'm a little shaken by what happened. I'd appreciate the escort," she responded.

"You said you've seen the gunman before?" he asked, moving so that he and King were positioned between Sasha and the street.

"I saw him as I was leaving work one day and then again when I was walking home a few days later."

"And you thought it was the man who murdered your mother?"

"I didn't think it was him. Not really. Roker would be close to sixty. The man I saw was more like forty. The same age Roker was when he murdered my mother." She shuddered.

"A family member maybe," he commented, wondering if Martin Roker had a twin who might have had a son.

"I suppose so."

"You don't sound convinced."

"The resemblance was uncanny, but..." She shrugged.

"But what?"

"I don't believe in ghosts, Detective. Obviously, if Martin Roker died, he couldn't be stalking me through the streets of New York City." They turned a corner onto a quiet residential street lined with stately brownstones that had once been summer homes for the wealthy. Now they were apartments rented by young professionals and growing families.

"It's possible he had a twin. Or a sibling."

"He was an only child. Raised by a single mother. If he had biological siblings, they'd have been on his father's side. Based on the research I've done, I doubt they would have known him well enough to want revenge for his death."

"Research?" he asked as she pulled keys from her bag and hurried up the cement stairs of one of the brownstones. The four-story house had once been a stately single-family dwelling. Now it was split into several apartment units.

"I'm telling my mother's story on the cable program I host. I was a teenager when she was killed, and a lot of the details are hazy. I guess I put them out of my head." She punched in the code and ushered him into a narrow stairway. "My unit is on the second floor. You don't have to accompany me. I'll be fine from here."

"I like to finish what I start," he responded, following her up a flight of stairs to the second-floor landing.

"Me, too." She unlocked the only door on the second level and stepped inside, hanging her bag from a hook near the door and slipping out of her coat.

"Would you like coffee? Soda? Water?" she asked, draping the coat across the back of a bright yellow chair.

"Water. If you don't mind," he responded. He wasn't

thirsty, but he did want to spend a few more minutes in the apartment. Get a better feel for its security strengths and weaknesses.

"For you and the dog?" she asked with a smile that softened her face and made her look a decade younger than he'd imagined her to be.

"King would probably appreciate that."

"King? I thought maybe his name was Cujo." She stepped into the galley-style kitchen. The living area and kitchen flowed together, all of it decorated in grays and yellows.

"I tried to name him that, but my supervisor refused to allow it," he said, crossing the room and looking out one of the large windows. Not much of a view, but a fire escape jutted out from the window.

"Did you really?" she asked, filling a plastic bowl with water and setting it on the floor.

"What do you think?" He checked the window lock. Sturdy but not unbreakable.

"You're much too serious to make a joke out of your partner's name."

Surprised, he turned to look at her. "Why do you say that?"

"Am I wrong?" She grabbed two bottles of water from the refrigerator and handed him one.

"Probably not."

"You don't know?"

"I suppose how serious I am depends on the situation." He dropped King's lead and watched as he trotted to the bowl and lapped up water like he hadn't had a drink in months. "I'm very serious about my job."

"I got that impression when I visited you at the precinct," she said, glancing out the window and frowning. "Are you looking for something?"

"Easy access points. Weak locks. Ways that someone might be able to get into the apartment."

"I keep the windows locked."

"How about in the bedrooms?"

She frowned. "To be honest, I've never thought about it. I'm two floors up. A person would need a ladder to get to the windows, and I can't imagine anyone being bold enough to put a ladder up and break in."

"Someone was bold enough to fire shots into a bakery where a police officer was standing," he pointed out.

"Point taken."

"So, how about we check those windows before I leave?" he suggested.

"Sure. Why not?" She led him into a short hallway. Two doors on one wall. One door on the other. She opened one, motioning him to follow.

The room was small. Maybe ten by ten. One window. A closet opened to reveal a file cabinet and shelves lined with boxes. A secretary desk stood against one wall, papers strewn across its surface, a stack of newspapers beside it. "Excuse the mess. I'm juggling a few different projects. Lots of research."

"For your cable show?"

"Yes."

She walked to the lone window, opened the shades and checked the lock. "This one is secure. There's a sliding glass door in my room. It opens to a balcony."

"Can I take a look?" he asked.

"I'm confident in my ability to know a locked door from an unlocked one, but if it'll make you feel better, you can." She sidled past him and hurried into the hall.

He was surprised by her rush to get rid of him. She wanted a story from him. *The* story from him. The one about his parents' murders, about the way it had felt to be a suspect in their deaths, about the years since then. The hard work he had put into building his reputation as a good police officer and a trustworthy person. He had no intention of sharing that with the world. He rarely shared it with friends. Even his sister, Penny, had no real idea of how much those few days of suspicion had cost, how difficult it had been for Bradley to face friends and family who had—even if only for a moment—wondered if he had killed his parents. He'd been cleared not long after the murders, but he'd had to wait twenty years for the killer to be identified and caught. Everyone was relieved that Randall Gage was in prison awaiting trial, but for Bradley, the echo of those long-ago accusations still rang loudly in his mind.

He followed Sasha into a room that was smaller than the office. A double bed took up most of the space. A narrow dresser stood between it and the wall. Six drawers. A lamp sitting on top, a framed photo beside it. He glanced at it as he walked by. An old church. Sasha in a wedding dress. An older man in a dark suit standing with his arm around her.

"Your wedding?" he asked, touching the white frame.

"What gave it away? The fancy hairdo? The church? The wedding dress?" She added the last with a quick smile.

"My keen powers of detection," he responded.

She laughed. "You do have a sense of humor!"

"You're surprised?"

"Maybe." She pulled back bright blue curtains and gestured to a sliding glass door. "It's locked."

"You might want more than a lock," he said, opening the door and stepping onto the balcony. King followed, nudged close to his leg, his rangy body relaxed. He didn't mind balconies, escalators, elevators. He'd been trained indoors and out, run through courses in a variety of situations designed to test his environmental tolerance and confidence. Like other K-9s, King had excelled during training and in his work.

The balcony was three feet wide and six feet long. A gate on one end opened to stairs that led to a small patch of grass at the side of the house. From where he stood, Bradley could see a corner of the street and a portion of the neighboring yard. "This would make an easy access point if someone wanted to gain entrance," he said, opening the gate and stepping onto the wrought steps. They clanged under his weight. "Have you considered a security system?"

"No, but it's probably a good idea," she responded, her gaze shifting from Bradley to the yard. "I don't spend much time on the balcony. Especially not lately."

"Too chilly?" he asked, probing the darkness just beyond the yard. Several trash cans sat near the neighbor's fence. Nothing alarming about that, but he was on edge and antsy.

"Too exposed," she replied.

"You've been nervous lately?" He grabbed her arm, tugging her back to the door.

"Wouldn't you be, if someone who looked like your mother's murderer was stalking you?"

"Yes," he conceded. He had spent two decades wondering if his parents' killer was somewhere close by.

That had made him pay attention to his surroundings and study the people around him. He wouldn't say he had been jumpy, but he had certainly been very aware of the possibility that danger could be close by.

King growled, his scruff suddenly up, his body stiff. Ears pressed close to his head, tail high and taut, amber eyes focused on the tiny sliver of street.

He sensed something.

Bradley gave Sasha a gentle shove into the house. "Close the door. Lock it. Stay away from the windows."

"What's going on?"

"Close the door and lock it," he repeated.

She frowned but did as he asked, sliding the door closed, snapping the lock down. He waited until she had moved away from the glass. When she was gone, he grabbed King's leash and headed down the balcony stairs. The night was quiet, the muted sounds of traffic and city life drifting on the brisk fall breeze.

King's ears perked, his scruff still raised as he sniffed the air. He growled, his attention focused on the house across the street, its yard dotted with large bushes and tall trees.

Someone was there.

King was issuing a warning, and Bradley would be a fool not to heed it.

"Police," he called. "Come on out of there."

No response. Not even a rustle of leaves or whisper of fabric.

"I said, come out!" he called again. "If you refuse, I'll send my dog in." It was a warning he was required to issue. Most criminals responded by surrendering or running. Dogs like King were known to be well trained and vicious when they attacked. There would be no hesitation and no backing down. If King was sent to apprehend a suspect, he got the job done.

Still no response.

Bradley unhooked King's lead, checking the surroundings to be certain no pedestrians were around.

The street was empty, the night settled heavy and dark on the surrounding houses. Long shadows undulated as trees swayed in the November breeze. A few houses still had jack-o'-lanterns and potted chrysanthemums sitting on their stoops. A few cutout cartoon turkeys graced the windows of several homes. The vibe was peaceful, people tucked safely inside, planning the coming month, looking forward to Thanksgiving meals and holiday prep. They had no idea that danger was lurking outside their doors.

"Last chance!" Bradley called. "Come out!"

Nothing.

He released his hold.

King bounded forward, snarling viciously as he sprinted across the street.

THREE

Sasha stood at the sliding glass door, nose nearly touching the glass. The road was visible from her apartment, the well-lit pavement a slash of slate against cement curbs. She'd watched as Detective McGregor and King had raced across the street and out of sight. Had they found her stalker?

Whoever it was hadn't made a secret of the fact that he was hunting Sasha. He had allowed himself to be seen three times. Then he had fired shots into a bakery, not caring that there had been witnesses inside.

"Who would do something like that?" she muttered, walking to the file cabinet that sat beside the antique desk she had inherited from her father. It had been her mother's. Natasha had loved old things. Books. Furniture. Clothes. She'd had a vintage style that had made her the cool mom in Sasha's group of friends.

The cool mom who had cheated on her husband.

Who had nearly wrecked their family.

Who had paid with her life.

Sasha had spent too many years dwelling on what might have been *if only*. Since her father's death, she had done her best to focus on what was and to live with the same grace and forgiveness for her mother that he had always demonstrated. Anders and Natasha had been Russian immigrants. They had arrived in the United States as college students, had met, fallen in love and married. Sasha could still remember the early years of her life, when her parents had seemed so happy and so perfectly suited for one another.

"No one is perfectly suited for anyone," she reminded herself as she opened the top drawer of the file cabinet and pulled a folder out. Filled with information about her mother's murder case, it also contained photos of both her parents when they were kids. She had compiled everything she could, hoping to use it on her show.

Her show?

The cable station's show.

It might be a small-budget program, but she was passionate about her vision for it, her goal. Her boss hadn't been as keen, but Prudence Landry was nothing if not open-minded. She had given Sasha a year to prove that the people of Brooklyn really were desperate for good news. Of course they were. When the Emerys, a young married couple, were murdered in their Brooklyn home months ago, their little girl left an orphan, residents of the borough had been shaken enough. Then to learn it was a copycat killing on the twentieth anniversary of the original double homicide—the murders of the McGregors, Bradley's parents. With that old case solved, the McGregors' killer in prison, Brooklynites could breathe a collective sigh of relief. But the Emerys' killer was still out there.

Sasha's show felt essential to her.

So far, the ratings were good. People around Brooklyn approached her at the store and on the street to offer feel-good stories about local people doing kind and generous things.

That was what the world needed.

Not the negative, sad and depressing news that network stations often featured. She dropped the folder onto the desk and thumbed through its contents, scanning news articles for information about Roker. Not that she needed a reminder of what the folder contained. She had spent hours poring over it. She knew Roker had been married but separated at the time of the murder. She knew he had left his wife and young daughter in the hopes that he could win Natasha back. When that hadn't worked, he had begun stalking her, showing up at her place of employment, standing in the street light outside their house at night. He had sent cards and letters for months, the tone of them becoming darker and more threatening. Natasha hadn't shown the letters to anyone. They had been found in her dresser after her death.

Sasha had memorized the cold facts of the case.

She hadn't had to try to understand the impact on the victim's family. She had lived it. Telling her story was supposed to be about letting go of the darkest chapter of her life.

She had really thought she could do that.

Instead, the past refused to die.

She thumbed through photocopied news articles, found the one with a photo of Martin Roker and shuddered. That was him. The man she had seen on the street.

She pulled it from the pile. Roker and the man who had been stalking her had the same nose. The same light-colored hair. The same cold blue eyes. Was there a difference in the chin? In the tilt of the head?

She studied the photo, her heart thumping painfully. She didn't want to think about Detective McGregor and King chasing an armed man. She wanted to focus on Roker's face and try to prove to herself that he and her stalker were not the same man.

"Of course they aren't. Martin Roker is dead," she muttered, carrying the photo to the balcony. It had been published by a tabloid, his face taking up most of the front page. The article was a long one. More a sensationalized account than a factual one. A Russian immigrant. An affair. A scorned lover. It was all perfect fodder for tabloid news.

"There has to be more personal information about him." She scanned the article, hoping to find a gem of information hidden amid the gossip. Nothing. An estranged wife. One daughter.

At least, Sasha thought she would have.

She jotted a reminder on the pad she kept beside her computer, pulled the sticky note off and stuck it to the mirror above her dresser. There were several other notes there. Her to-do list seemed to get longer every day. Her done list was nonexistent. The last week had been filled with anxiety and constant questions to herself about whether she was losing her mind.

Dead men did not walk the streets.

And yet she had been certain she had been seeing a dead man.

His son.

A brother's son.

None of which he had, according to records. Martin

had been an only child, so no identical twin. He also had only one child, a daughter, with his estranged wife. So no look-alike son.

Regardless, she couldn't understand why anyone related to Roker would come after her. She'd been fourteen when her mother died. She hadn't ever met Martin Roker. She hadn't even known about his existence until after the shooting. She had done nothing to call attention to herself or her past.

Yet.

Could someone have found out that she planned to tell the story on her show? Could that person be trying to stop her?

She jotted another note. A reminder to speak to the detective who had been in charge of the case. He might know if there was anyone who would be impacted if she dredged up the past.

Someone knocked on the door, the sound breaking the silence and sending her pulse racing again.

She hurried to the peephole and looked out into the hall, nearly sagging with relief when she saw Detective McGregor.

She yanked the door open, stepping back so he could enter the apartment. "What happened?" she asked breathlessly.

"He had a car parked at the end of the street," Detective McGregor said, crowding close as King trotted past and settled near the sofa. The dog was panting, his tongue lolling out to the side, his bright brown eyes focused on his partner.

"You saw it?"

"Yes. We almost had him," he growled, his frustration obvious.

"He had a good head start. You can't be too hard on yourself for not catching him."

"Sure I can," he responded, offering a quick smile that took some of the gruffness out of the response. "I radioed in a description of the vehicle. Unfortunately, there was no license plate."

"A stolen vehicle?" she asked.

"Probably. We've issued a BOLO. I don't think it will be long to track it down. I doubt he'll be with it."

"Did you see him?"

"He was tall and thin. Just like the guy who fired the shot into the bakery. I didn't see his face, but if I were into guessing things, I'd guess it was him."

"It's a reasonable guess."

"Maybe. But I like facts. Not speculation."

"After what you went through as a teen, that's not surprising," she said, regretting it immediately. She had done her research. She knew that he had been a suspect in his parents' murders. He had been cleared quickly, but the stain of it, the whispers that had followed him for years, had given him an excuse to be bitter and angry. Instead, he had worked hard. He had devoted himself to law enforcement. He had made a name for himself with the NYPD. She wanted to tell the story. One of overcoming and thriving.

But when she had visited the precinct to ask him for an interview, he'd given her a flat no and walked away.

"I'd rather not discuss my past, Ms. Eastman."

"Sasha," she said. "Everyone calls me that."

He nodded. "You don't have a security system here, and I don't feel comfortable leaving you alone tonight.

It would be too easy for someone to break through the sliding glass door."

She wanted to believe no one would be that bold, but after what had happened at the bakery, she couldn't.

"Do you have family you could stay with? A friend? Maybe somewhere outside of Brooklyn? Outside of the city would be even better."

She had plenty of acquaintances, but she had spent the years after her divorce caring for her sick father. What friends she'd had left after the divorce had drifted away as she spent all her free time driving her father to chemo and doctor appointments. She did have a few college friends who would be willing to let her stay, but they lived in other states.

"No family, and I wouldn't want to put my friends in danger." That was true, but it would have been nice to have someone she could turn to. If not for a place to stay, then at least for emotional support.

"It'll have to be a hotel, then. If you want to pack a few things, I can give you a ride to one."

"I can take a taxi," she responded, walking to the spare room and pulling a duffel from the closet. A few of her father's things were still there. The old satchel he'd carried to work for decades. His favorite tie. A couple of shirts with quirky graphics that he'd loved to wear.

"Do you have a roommate?" Detective McGregor asked, his gaze on the tie that hung from a hook.

"My father lived here for a while."

"I thought you had no family?"

"He passed away. Cancer."

"I'm sorry," he said, his dark eyes warm and understanding.

She looked away, focusing on getting the duffel, because she wasn't used to sympathy. Until recently, she hadn't told many people about her mother. She had wanted it to fade like a bad dream. Coworkers knew about her father, but they had tiptoed around the cancer diagnosis and treatment like it was a taboo subject. "Thank you. It was hard to lose him, but I was glad I got a chance to say goodbye," she said as she carried the bag to her room.

"That's the hardest part about losing someone to violence. You don't have a chance to say goodbye or to offer another *I love you*."

Surprised that he would be so open about something so personal, she met his eyes. "That was one of the most difficult things about losing my mother. It felt unfinished. As if the timer had been stopped before the end of the game."

"That's a good way to put it." He smiled, crossing the room and closing the curtains. "King and I will be out in the living room when you're ready to leave."

He walked into the hall, King padding along beside him.

Instead of opening her closet or dresser and grabbing the things she needed, she watched him leave. She had wanted to interview him for her show. Now she just wanted to talk to him. To find out more about how he had grown from his tragedy into a successful, compassionate person.

"Don't even think about it, Sasha," she muttered, tossing a few things into the duffel and telling herself she wasn't at all interested in getting to know Bradley McGregor on a personal level.

* * *

Sasha knew how to get ready quickly. She had a duffel packed and was out of the bedroom in just under fifteen minutes.

"I'm ready," she said as she walked toward him, gripping her bag in her left hand. No ring on her finger. He noticed. Not because he was interested in dating, but because noticing details was what he did. Partially because he was trained to do so. Partially because he had learned how important details were the year his parents were murdered. He had been the primary and only suspect for just long enough to make him paranoid about keeping track of his whereabouts, noting the people who were around him, what they were wearing, doing, how they were acting. What was said by whom at what time. His mind was constantly humming, cataloging details of everyday life, keeping lists. Just in case he ever found himself on the wrong side of the interview table again.

It was a great tool in the work he did as a detective for the NYPD, but it didn't always serve him well in his daily life. He'd had more than one person tell him he was too serious, that he didn't know how to have fun, that he was too devoted to his job, too focused on making sure the justice system worked the way it was intended to. He got the bad guys off the street. The court system made sure to keep them there.

In a perfect world, that would work perfectly.

But it wasn't a perfect world.

Sometimes, the bad guys slipped through the cracks and did more damage, caused more hurt. Sometimes, innocent people were tried and found guilty. The day he'd joined the police force, he'd promised himself that he would do everything he could to prevent either of those things from happening.

Yes. He took his job seriously, but that was because he understood just how damaging false accusations and arrests could be.

"Are we waiting for something?" Sasha prodded, her smile a little too bright.

She was nervous, her foot tapping impatiently on the floor, her knuckles white from her too-tight grip on the bag.

"That's not much," he said, gesturing to the duffel. "Are you sure you don't want to pack a suitcase?"

"I can come back, if I need to be away for more than a couple days." She strode to the door and held it open. "I'm not trying to rush you, Detective, but I start my day early."

"Your cable show airs in the morning?" he asked.

He knew it did.

He'd watched it a few times since she had visited the precinct and tried to get him to agree to an interview.

"Yes. I usually leave my house by five." She hiked the bag onto her shoulder, her bright-colored coat riding up her slim hip.

"That will work out well."

"In what way?"

"Tomorrow is my day off. I can pick you up at the hotel." He stepped into the hall, allowing King to move ahead of him, and watched as the Malinois sniffed the air.

"There's no need for you to go to the trouble, Detective."

"You can call me Bradley. That's what my friends call me."

"I appreciate your help tonight, but I can't expect you to keep escorting me from one location to another."

"Do you have a better plan for staying safe?" he asked. King seemed relaxed, his scruff flat, his tail wagging, but he was watching Bradley intently.

"Not now, but I'll think of something before tomorrow morning."

"And if you don't?"

"I'll figure something out. I'm resourceful." She smiled, walking downstairs and to the front door.

"How about this? If you come up with a better plan, call me. If you don't, I'll pick you up at 4:30." He took out a business card. It was time for their evening run, an activity that they both needed after a long day of work. Once he got Sasha safely to a hotel, he'd go home, change and run down to the bay front. At night, this time of year, it was chilly and damp near the water. Not weather most people enjoyed being out in, but Bradley enjoyed the relative quiet of early autumn evenings. Compared to long summer days when warm weather drove Sheepshead Bay residents to the shore, fall was a deterrent that allowed him to have the solitude he sometimes craved.

She nodded, not agreeing to the plan, but taking the card and shoving it in her coat pocket. He thought she was going to open the door and step outside, but she hesitated with her hand on the knob.

"I hope he's not out there," she murmured, pressing her eye to a peephole in the door.

"If he is, I doubt he'll try anything with King and I so close."

"He did when we were at the bakery," she pointed out.

"We were in a building. He was outside. The windows and walls between us gave him a false sense of bravado."

"Or he is crazy enough not to care about being caught."

"He cares. If he didn't, he wouldn't have run when King and I went after him. Ready to go?"

"Sure. Why not?"

Bradley was relieved. He understood her desire to stay in her apartment. As she'd pointed out, she had a life to live. A job, friends, people who depended on her. Continuing with her routine and going about her daily activities probably felt like the right thing to do, but it would be dangerous to live life as if a stalker wasn't after her. The fact that she was willing to go to a hotel was a step in the right direction, as far as protecting her went.

But she would also be alone.

No friends or family who could offer her a safe place to stay until her stalker was caught.

That had surprised him.

She seemed upbeat, peppy and warmhearted. The kind of person who probably attracted a lot of attention everywhere she went. Not because of her looks—though she was beautiful—but because of her bright eyes and wide smile. She exuded kindness the way others exuded hate and animosity. He'd worked in law enforcement for so many years, he sometimes forgot people like Sasha existed. Then he would meet someone like her and be reminded that not everyone had an angle or an agenda. Some people were just good-hearted.

Unless she did have an angle.

She had wanted his story.

She had asked for an interview.

It was possible she was still after those things.

The cynic in him was all too aware of that fact.

He reached past her and opened the door, motioning for her to stay where she was as he and King stepped outside. The evening was quiet aside from the soft hum of distant traffic and muted honk of horns. New York City never slept, but neighborhoods like this one did.

He watched King, noting the Malinois's relaxed body and perked ears. King gave no indication of danger as they made their way to the cruiser. An intelligent and protective dog, he had been trained to do what he was bred for: protect and apprehend. If there was danger, he always let Bradley know. As far as partners went, he was as good as any human partner Bradley had ever had.

He opened the back hatch of the cruiser. King jumped into his crate and settled down for the ride.

"He knows the routine," Sasha commented as Bradley opened the passenger door and waited for her to climb in.

"We've been working together for a couple years. He loves his job, but he also loves the end of the day when he knows we're heading home for our run." He took the duffel from her hands and set it in the back seat.

"He runs after a full day of work?"

"He has to. Otherwise, he'd be getting me to play ball all night." He smiled and closed the door.

The night was still quiet, the soft chirp of crickets mixing with the muted sound of traffic. To Bradley, it was the music of autumn, the brisk air and crunch of dry grass under his feet reminding him of his childhood. He had grown up in the city, and he loved it. The first fourteen years had been rocky. His parents had been drug addicts who cared more about their next fix than they did about their kids. He had been constantly hungry and constantly trying to find ways to keep his sister fed and healthy. Ten years younger than him, Penelope had been four when their parents were murdered. She had been the sole survivor of the crime. He had been the first suspect.

He tried not to let those early years of neglect and hunger and want affect him. He tried not to dwell on the fact that he had been suspected in his parents' murders before he was even old enough to drive. He didn't want that to change his attitude about people. He didn't harbor bitterness or hate. His parents—the ones who had raised him and his sister after the murders—had taught him grace, forgiveness and love. But there was no way to un-live those first few days after his parents died. There was no way he could ever forget the way the people in his community had looked at him—with suspicion and unease. For years after he was cleared of the crime, there had been rumors about him. Those rumors had ramped up again after the copycat murder several months ago. That case had led to the arrest of his parents' killer. Randall Gage was now behind bars. Where he belonged. However, the copycat murderer—someone who had killed a married couple and left their three-year-old daughter as the sole witness—was still at large.

Right now, finding the killer was Bradley's focus and mission. The little girl, Lucy Emery, had been able to give a vague description of the killer—just as his own sister had twenty years earlier: a man wearing a clown mask with blue hair. But a couple of months ago, Lucy had started saying she "missed Andy." Her aunt Willow and her husband, Detective Nate Slater, Bradley's colleague at the Brooklyn K-9 Unit, who'd taken Lucy in, had said there was no one named Andy in Lucy's life. Maybe Andy was someone from the neighborhood who knew Lucy. Maybe he'd seen how neglectful her parents had been. Maybe Andy was the masked killer.

For months, the team had been questioning people in the Emerys' neighborhood, trying to find someone who was familiar with Andy. Bay Ridge was tight-knit and often close-lipped, but the people there wanted the killer caught. Most had been forthright about what they had seen and heard the night of the murder. Thus far, not one person knew of an Andy who had hung around the Emery house or who might have known Lucy and her parents.

Chasing one dead-end lead after another was frustrating, but Bradley wasn't willing to give up. Someone knew something. That was the way it always was with crime. Sooner or later, he would get the answers he was looking for.

He was hoping for sooner.

He didn't want Lucy to grow up in the shadow of the unknown as he and Penny had. He wanted to give her and her aunt the answers they deserved.

With Sasha safe in the passenger seat, he stayed outside the vehicle to make a quick call to his sister, Penny, just to check in. Something he did every day when he hadn't seen her much that day and always would. Even though his kid sister was a grown woman and engaged now to a great guy and someone Bradley trusted with her life, Detective Tyler Walker, he still liked to touch base and make certain she was doing okay.

Growing up in a neglectful and unloving home had

made him conscious of the importance of expressing and showing love to the people he cared about. He hadn't wanted Penny to ever feel like he had—that she was an afterthought and expendable.

Tyler had been instrumental in getting their parents' murderer thrown into jail, and Bradley was confident he would spend the rest of his life making certain Penny never felt alone or unloved.

But he still made his phone call.

She didn't answer, and he left a brief message. He slid into the driver's seat, scanning the cars parked along the street as he pulled away from Sasha's apartment. No headlights went on. No car pulled out behind him. The man who had been outside Sasha's house had disappeared into the night, but Bradley knew he would be back. Stalkers didn't give up hunting their prey.

"I appreciate you doing this, Detective Bradley," Sasha said, breaking the silence.

"It's no problem," he responded. "Any thought as to what hotel you want to stay at?"

"I probably should have one, but I've been preoccupied. I guess whichever one is closest."

"How about one that's close to the K-9 unit?" he suggested. "We may need further information from you. That will make it easy to pick you up and escort you to the offices."

"That's fine."

"Great," he said, turning in that direction.

Traffic was heavy, rush hour well underway.

It would have taken less time to walk the few miles to the hotel he had in mind, but he didn't want to risk it. He had no idea where Sasha's stalker lived or how far he had gone when he'd run from King.

Better to be safe now than to be sorry later.

He'd drive her to the hotel and escort her inside.

Then he would go home and try to put the day's events out of his head. Just for a little while. Clear his head as he pushed his body to run, because he didn't want to be consumed by his job the way his parents had been consumed by their addictions. He wanted to live a life dedicated to more than that. His sister would be getting married soon. She'd be moving out of the house they had shared for years, and he would be living alone for the first time in his life.

He hadn't decided how he felt about that.

He only knew that changes were coming. For better or worse, life would be different. He wanted to embrace it, enjoy it and appreciate it for what it was.

But he also wanted to pursue justice.

He wanted to make certain the community he loved was safe.

That meant putting murderers like Randall Gage in jail—which he'd done last month with the help of the Brooklyn K-9 Unit and unexpected sources, like Randall's cousin Emmett Gage, a US marshal now engaged to his coworker Belle Montera, a K-9 officer. A DNA match on a genealogy site had led the K-9 unit to Emmett, knowing he was a relative of the killer. And hard as it had been for Emmett to accept that someone in his family was a murderer, he'd gotten Randall Gage's DNA so that it could be matched against a sample taken from evidence left at the crime scene. Finally, after twenty years, a very cold case had been solved.

Keeping Brooklyn safe also meant finding out who Andy was.

And protecting innocent people from danger.

Tomorrow was his day off. He planned to spend part of it questioning the Emerys' neighbors again. The rest of it he'd spend making sure Sasha's stalker didn't have another chance to take a shot at her.

FOUR

Sasha's alarm went off at 3:30 a.m.

She was already awake. She had been for hours.

The hotel room was quiet and clean, the bed comfortable, but every time she had shut her eyes, she had seen Martin Roker's face. The hooked nose and light blue eyes, slumped shoulders and rangy body.

She shuddered as she ran a brush through freshly washed and dried hair and pulled it back into a high, tight ponytail. The woman in the mirror was pale, her eyes deeply shadowed. Fine lines fanned out from her eyes, and what looked like a frown line marred the skin between her brows.

She rubbed at the spot, grimacing a little at the visage in the mirror. She was just a few years younger than her mother had been when she had died. She couldn't remember her having wrinkles and lines. She remembered her smile, her laugh. Sometimes, she remembered her voice.

But wrinkles?

No. Her mother hadn't had those.

"But you sure do," she muttered.

A little mascara and some lip gloss, and she was as ready as she was going to be for work.

She brushed her hand down her cotton blouse. Royal blue with long sleeves. No pattern. She'd donned a black pencil skirt that hugged her curves without drawing attention to them. She wasn't on cable television to bring attention to herself. She wanted to draw the public's attention to the good things that were happening in the community. To bring a little brightness into what could sometimes be a dark and frightening world. The show was low-budget. She didn't get paid much for her work, but Sasha didn't care. For the first time in years, she felt like what she was doing mattered.

She glanced at her watch. Ten of four.

She'd have the hotel concierge call her a taxi. That would save Bradley a trip to the hotel. She wasn't sure if he lived in Sheepshead Bay. It didn't really matter. He'd said this was his day off, and she didn't want him to get up early to escort her to work.

A taxi there. A quick run into the building.

She would be fine.

And she would be avoiding spending more time with a man who had taken up too much of her thoughts during the long sleepless night. Bradley McGregor was not what she had expected. The brief meeting they'd had at the K-9 headquarters a couple of weeks ago had given her the impression that he was gruff, hard-edged and serious.

She still thought he was those things, but she had seen compassion in his eyes. She had heard warmth in his voice. He wasn't as hard as he might want people to think, and that had made her more curious than she should probably be.

She wasn't in the market for a relationship.

She certainly wasn't going to get involved with someone when her life seemed to be spinning out of control.

That being the case, staying away from a guy like Bradley seemed prudent.

She fished in her coat pocket, searching for and finding his business card. She hated to call so early, but she wanted to catch him before he left to pick her up. Before she could dial the number, someone knocked on the door.

She jumped, the card falling from her suddenly numb fingers.

"Who's there?" she called as she hurried to the door.

"Bradley McGregor."

She peered out the peephole.

He was standing a few feet away, hands in the pockets of a wool coat, King standing beside him.

She unlocked the door and opened it, stepping back to let them in. "I was just going to call you," she said, the words coming out too quickly.

She was nervous.

She didn't know why.

She talked to people all the time.

Interviewed men, women and children without giving a thought to the fact that they were strangers.

Right now, though, looking into Bradley's dark brown eyes, she felt tongue-tied and discomfited and gauche, all her well-rehearsed icebreakers gone.

"Were you?" he asked, giving King a command to lie down as he closed the door.

"I didn't want you to waste your time coming out to get me. You did say 4:30. I thought I'd catch you before you left."

"Do you have a ride?" he asked, his gaze dropping from her face to her pencil skirt and stocking-clad feet.

"I was going to call a taxi." She hurried to the duffel, pulled out her heels and slid into them, using that as an excuse to stop looking into his eyes.

"A taxi?"

"One of those vehicles you hire to take you places?" she quipped, turning to face him again.

He was in casual clothes. Faded jeans, a long-sleeved T-shirt, scuffed leather work boots and a wool coat that he'd left open. He looked relaxed, his hands tucked into the pockets of his coat, a smile tugging the corner of his lips. "Thanks for the lesson in city transportation," he said. "But I'm wondering why you were planning to call a taxi when you knew I was coming to pick you up."

"Like I said, I didn't want you to be bothered. Especially not on your day off."

"I don't mind being bothered," he responded. "And I'll feel better knowing that you had someone walk you through the hotel and outside."

"That's nice of you, but I'm used to doing things on my own. I've been living in the city for ten years. I've got things figured out."

"During how many of those years was a stalker after you?" he asked.

"That's been a recent thing."

"So, maybe having an armed escort should also become a recent thing," he replied. "Do you need more time to get ready? King and I can wait in the hall. I only knocked because I saw the light under the door."

"No. I'm good." There was no sense putting off the inevitable and no good reason to send him away. He was already awake. Already out of his house. She might as well accept that and move on. Stalker or not, she had a job to do.

"Anything happen last night?" he asked.

"No. It was quiet. To be honest, I felt safer here than I've felt at home the last few days."

"You've been worried about the Roker look-alike."

It wasn't a question, but she nodded. "How could I not be? He looks just like a dead man."

"A dead man who murdered your mother."

"Exactly. I have no idea what he wants with me, but I can't believe it's anything good."

"He proved that yesterday."

"Did your team find any useful evidence at the scene?" she asked as they stepped into the hall.

"Nothing that is going to help us identify him. No DNA evidence. No fingerprints." He frowned. "Once your workday is over, I'd like you to stop by the K-9 unit. We'll need your formal statement. I'd also like you to look at a lineup of suspects."

"I thought you said your team wasn't able to get evidence that would lead to identifying the man?"

"They weren't, but we may have some ideas."

"I can stop by after work. That's not a problem," she said. King was a few feet ahead, his tan fur soft-looking, his tail high. He loped rather than walked, his lithe body seeming to hum with pent-up energy. If he noticed anything unusual, he didn't indicate it. That should have made her feel better, but she was still anxious as Bradley pushed the elevator button and she waited for the doors to open.

She wasn't sure what she expected to see.

Maybe Martin Roker standing in the elevator, a gun in hand.

But when the doors slid open, the elevator was empty.

She stepped in, edging back as King and Bradley followed.

"You're still nervous around King," Bradley commented.

"Why would you say that?"

"Because you're staring at him as if you expect him to jump up and take a chunk out of you."

"I don't. It's just..."

"What?" He pushed the lobby button, and the doors slid closed.

"I haven't spent much time around dogs. We didn't have one when I was a kid, and I haven't had time for one as an adult."

"You work a lot of hours?"

"I do five live programs and tape two shows for the weekend. That takes time. Plus, research and prep work. I do a lot of that at home, but it still takes a lot of my time and attention."

"Your boss won't let you bring a dog to work?" he asked.

"I never asked. She probably wouldn't mind. Prudence is happy as long as my ratings stay up, and I'm getting my job done. I'm just not sure it would be fair to have a puppy in an apartment."

"You mean like most dog owners in New York City?" he asked with a smile that took any condemnation from his words.

He had a nice smile. One that made laugh lines appear at the corners of his eyes and softened the hard edges and sharp angles of his face.

"Yes. I suppose I do," she responded, laughing a little. "I've always wanted a dog. I just don't know much about them, and I have no idea what would be a good fit for my lifestyle."

"Most dogs are very happy to fit into whatever lifestyle they're offered. Take King, for example," he said.

The Malinois turned his eyes, his mouth opening in what looked like a doggy smile.

"He loves to work. He loves to play. He loves anything that requires him to be on the go. He's a perfect working dog, but he also is a great companion at home. Once he wears off some of his energy. I take him for runs to make certain that happens. On our days off, we go to parks and hike. I let him jump in ponds and act like the goofball he is. He thanks me by not tearing apart my furniture and walls."

She laughed again, trying to picture the serious dog acting like a puppy. She wanted to ask how long the two had been working together, how old King was and how Bradley had gotten involved in K-9 work, but the elevator doors opened, and all his warmth and good humor seemed to slip away.

Even in casual clothes instead of a suit, he suddenly looked like a detective, his focus sharp and intent, his gaze scanning the lobby as they walked through it.

She hadn't thought she needed or wanted him there.

She had been convinced that she could make her way to work on her own with only a small twinge of fear and anxiety, but her heart was slamming against her ribs as he led her into the hotel parking garage, her mouth dry with fear.

"I'm glad you came," she said, the words slipping out unintentionally. She was glad, but she didn't want to sound needy. She certainly didn't want him to think that she expected him to play bodyguard to her.

"Scared?" he asked.

"I'd be lying if I said I wasn't."

"Caution isn't a bad thing, Sasha. I don't think the man who has been stalking you knows you're here, but that doesn't mean we shouldn't act as if he does."

"I don't want to live in fear. I did that for a while after my mother died. I was almost too afraid to function. Knowing that she was alive one minute and gone the next changed my sense of safety and security and my view of the world." She shrugged, not wanting to say more. She had never told anyone about the dark months after her mother died. About the way she had jumped at shadows, woken from nightmares and expected the boogeyman to jump out of every closet. Even her father hadn't known. He had expected her to soldier on. Just like he had. "I didn't want you to be bothered on your day off."

"I understand that. I had similar feelings after my parents' murders." He frowned. "That's off the record."

"Bradley, I would never use anything you told me on my show. You've already made it clear you don't want to be interviewed, and I respect that."

"Sorry. I'm a little jaded about the press."

"You weren't treated fairly after your parents were murdered, so I understand."

"How do you know? You were what? Five?"

"Twelve, but I don't remember the news story. I did research before I visited you and your sister at the K-9 unit. I'd heard a lot of murmuring from people who thought the Emery murder case was related to your parents. Twenty years after the fact. A preschooler the only witness. The clown mask, the stuffed monkey. You've got to admit, it was eerily similar."

"Trust me, our team spent a lot of time discussing the similarities."

"Then you'll understand the community's fascination and interest. I wasn't planning to contact you or Penelope, but your name kept popping up, and I got curious."

"You know what they say about curiosity, right?" he asked as he led her to a white Jeep and unlocked the door.

"It killed the cat, but you know what they say about cats, right?"

"They have nine lives." He opened the passenger door, gesturing for her to climb in. As soon as she did, he leaned in so they were face-to-face, eye to eye. She could see threads of deep red in his auburn hair and tiny lines fanning out from his eyes. "Just remember, Sasha. You're not a cat."

He backed away and closed the door.

She waited while he loaded King into a crate in the back, closed the hatch and did a circuit of the vehicle, leaning down a few times to look underneath.

Sasha was antsy, her fingers tapping her thigh, her body humming with the need to move. She was used to going top speed all day, five days a week. Even her Saturdays were busy. Cleaning, errands, research.

Sundays, she tried to rest, but there were always things to be done before and after church. Coffee with the Bible study group. Doughnuts for the worship team. She often stopped by the hospital where her dad had spent so much time during his last year, bringing treats to the nursing staff.

That didn't leave much time for introspection.

That was how she had always liked it.

Lately, though, as she researched her mother's murder case and readied herself to tell the story most people had never heard, she had wondered if she were still running from fear and sadness. Every time she tried to record her story, she found reasons to not do it. She had told her producer she would air it as a two-part show on a weekend. Prudence had suggested it be presented on the anniversary of her mother's death, and Sasha had foolishly agreed.

That date was looming large.

Just two weekends away, and she had nothing recorded.

So, put it on your calendar, and get it done, she told herself, pulling out her phone and making a note as Bradley climbed into the driver's seat. "Everything okay?" she asked absently, not really expecting an answer.

"Just checking for a bomb," he replied.

Dead serious.

Not a hint of humor in his voice.

She met his eyes. "You're kidding."

"I don't kid about things like that." He started the engine and backed out of the space without further comment.

She was left to her own thoughts.

None of them pleasant.

She had spent days and nights convincing herself she was wrong about being stalked. She could no longer pretend that was true. She could no longer hide her head under the blanket of her busy schedule and hope that the monsters would go away.

She needed to face this head-on, figure out who was after her and why. Only then could she get back to the life she had spent so much time and energy building for herself.

A life she was no longer certain she wanted.

She loved her job. She liked the people she worked with. She enjoyed her neighborhood and city life, but there was a part of her that longed for the family she no longer had and a piece of her heart she wasn't sure could be mended. She wanted to go back to the suburban community she had grown up in and the tiny church where her parents and their parents were buried. Not to stay, but for a visit. She wanted to see it all through the eyes of a mature adult, and she wanted to remember the good times rather than focusing on the dark ones.

Somehow, more than anything, she wanted closure.

The end of the old life that was tied to heartache and tragedy. The beginning of a new one.

She wasn't sure how she would accomplish that, but she thought the very first step was finding out who was stalking her and stopping him.

At this time of the morning, the streets were clear, traffic sparse. A few pedestrians made their way along the sidewalks, staying close to the buildings as they navigated the still-dark world.

Bradley kept his eyes peeled as he pulled up in front of the building that housed Sasha's cable program. Unremarkable but for a small sign near the door, it was in a row of brownstones that had been refurbished and turned into office buildings. Decades ago, the properties on this street had been neglected, windows broken or boarded up, doors listing open from broken jambs. Now it was an upscale area with an eclectic group of shops and a few private residences.

"No need to park or walk me in," Sasha said just as he pulled into a metered space. "The cable programming runs all night. I won't be alone in there."

She seemed to think he planned to drop her off and drive away.

He would have told her that wasn't going to happen, if she'd asked.

"I'll walk you in," he said, getting out of the vehicle and feeding the meter before he opened the hatch and let King out of his crate.

"It's really not necessary, but if you feel the need, that's fine." Sasha hurried past, jogging up cement steps that led to the door.

She used a key to open the door, not that the locked entry made Bradley feel better. Stalkers always found a way.

Even if he didn't know about her stalker, he'd have worried about her coming in before dawn when the area was so desolate—no one around to help her should someone be lurking. "You do this every day?" he asked as he stepped into the building behind her.

"Monday through Friday. Saturday and Sunday are taped during the week. The producer runs them. I usually come in Saturday to prep for the week."

"But it's not required?"

"No. Honestly, my producer would probably be fine if I spent less time here during the week. As long as I'm ready for every broadcast, she's only a stickler for the Monday afternoon meeting."

She strode down the hall, her heels clicking on the tile floor. She'd dressed in a slim-fitting skirt and blouse, her hair pulled back in a ponytail that hung to the middle of her back. Even in heels, she moved quickly.

He walked a few steps to her left, King on the lead beside him. The building seemed empty, the hallway dimly lit, brighter lights flickering on as they moved through. The developer who had refurbished and remodeled the building had done an excellent job, leaving dark wood trim and the ornate 1890 details. The bottom floor had been converted to upscale offices, signs hanging from the closed doors announcing the businesses in stylized letters.

"Nice building," he commented as they jogged up a staircase to the second story. The design here was the same: ornate woodwork and closed doors. On this floor, there were windows that looked into the offices. The lights were off in all but the one near the end of the hall.

"It really is. I'd love to take credit for choosing it for the cable show, but it had nothing to do with me."

"How long have you been working here?"

"A few years. I took the job after I stopped covering the crime beat for a newspaper."

"You worked the crime beat?"

"You sound surprised."

"Just surprised I didn't meet you during that time."

"I was covering Manhattan, so I'm not surprised we didn't run into each other," she responded as they reached the door at the end of the hall. A fire exit was beside it, a poster plastered across it warning that it was alarmed.

"What made you switch jobs?" he asked.

"My father."

"He thought it was too dangerous?"

She gave a quiet laugh and shook her head. "Hardly.

My father loved what I was doing. It had been a secret dream of his to be an investigative reporter. He had high hopes that I would one day fulfill that dream for him."

"But?"

"He got sick. Pancreatic cancer. We were on borrowed time, and I didn't want to spend what we had working all hours of the day and night. I quit the job and took a job here. At the time I was just assisting the producer. Normal nine-to-five hours. Not a whole lot of take-home work. She understood my situation, and she gave me ample leave. It worked out well."

"I'm sorry that you lost him to cancer."

"Me, too, but at the end, he was ready to go. Anxious even. He would talk about Mom all the time, about how he was going to see her again soon." She blinked, and he was certain he saw tears in her eyes.

"It still hurts."

"Not as much as it used to, but yes. I'm sure you understand."

"I wasn't close to my folks, but my adoptive parents were wonderful people. I miss them every day."

"I hadn't realized you were adopted."

"Yes, by the lead investigator on my parents' case. He and his wife took my sister and me in. They were the only people willing to take a chance on a fourteen-year-old boy with a chip on his shoulder. Everyone else who showed interest was willing to take my sister, but not me." He still remembered how it had felt to move in with them, the distrust he had had, the way he had tested their love and their boundaries.

"That's a wonderful story."

"And a true one, but it's—"

"Off the record," she cut in, her hand on the doorknob, her back to him. She was lean and muscular, her body more angular than curved. The kind of woman who would be in a fashion magazine or on a runway rather than a local cable news program.

"I was going to say it's the truncated version. There were a lot of tough times before there were good ones. I gave everyone who met me a run for their money. But you're right. It's all off the record."

"Like I said, I heard you loud and clear when you said you didn't want to do an interview or tell your story. I respect that. We'll have to be quiet when we go in. They're shooting a program, and it's not a large space. Sound carries, if we're not careful." She stepped into the office, holding the door so he and King could follow.

It was as bare-bones as he'd seen in any building. A love seat under the window that looked into the corridor, a chair sitting against one wall. An old wooden coffee table sat in the center of the ten-by-twelve reception area, a few thumbed-through magazines cluttering its surface.

A reception desk blocked access to several file cabinets and a door that led into a hallway. No receptionist. Just a phone sitting dejectedly near a powered-down computer.

"The receptionist doesn't arrive until nine," Sasha said quietly as she shrugged out of her coat and hung it from a hook on the wall beside the desk.

"What are her duties?" he asked, wondering if they actually received calls at a cable show of this size.

"She's basically the producer's assistant. She does whatever is required. Answers phones. Makes appointments. Corresponds with viewers. It's harder than you'd think."

"I didn't think it was easy." He'd be bored out of his mind with a job like that. Not because it was easy, but because he'd be stuck in a tiny office all day long with nothing to look at but the walls and the outdated artwork.

"Just a side note, Detective," she said.

"I thought we'd gotten past the formal titles?"

"*Detective* suits you," she replied with a smile. "We'll go to my office. It's really just a glorified closet, but I'm glad to have it. No talking in the hallway when that red light is on." She pointed to a light above the door that glowed bright red.

"Got it."

"I'm more worried about King."

At the mention of his name, King's ears perked up, and he grinned.

"Don't be. He only barks when there is something to bark about."

She nodded, but didn't seem convinced, her dark eyes focused on King, her lips pursed. "Behave, King," she said.

King's smile widened, his tongue lolling out.

Sasha laughed quietly and opened the door, stepping into the hallway and moving silently across the carpeted floor. She rounded a corner and opened a door, gesturing for Bradley and King to walk in ahead of her.

She shut the door and sighed. "There. Now we don't have to worry as much. You can have a seat, if you'd like. I'll make a pot of coffee."

She flicked on a coffee maker that sat on a corner of her desk.

If it could be called a desk.

It looked like one of the fold-up tables they used at

church when there was a potluck. White top. Metal legs. A laptop computer closed on top of it. A stack of papers to the left of the computer. A coffee cup to the right. There were three file cabinets pushed up against the wall, a small package sitting on one of them. Two chairs were pushed under his side of the table. He pulled one out and sat in it, wincing as he pushed back and hit the wall.

"I told you, it's a glorified closet," she said with a grin.

"At least you have a window," he responded, pointing to a window that seemed centered on a wall.

"Half of one," she pointed out, still grinning. "That's a faux wall the producer got permission to put up. She thinks privacy is good for the creative mind."

"What do you think?"

"I do prefer working alone, so this job has been a great fit."

"What about the production crew? They don't get in the way of your creativity?" he asked, giving King the down-stay command.

"Production crew? You're looking at it. My show is basically live feed. We have a studio and a camera. I set everything up. We have one cameraman who sets up the camera and presses Record. Then he walks out and monitors via a television screen in another room."

"I didn't realize that. I watched the show a couple times, and I was convinced you had an entire team producing it."

"That's nice to know. I always wonder if the people who watch can tell I'm the only one doing everything." She picked up the package. "Wonder what this is."

"Did you order something?"

"Not anything that would be delivered to my office." She set it on the desk and sat, opening the laptop and booting it up before lifting the package again.

"A fan, maybe?"

"They send letters. Not packages."

"Maybe it's an early Christmas gift?"

"It's the beginning of November." She pulled tape from the top of the package. "No return address. I won't be able to thank them."

Something about that made him lean forward.

Most people included return addresses.

People who didn't preferred to remain anonymous for any number of reasons.

The reasons he was currently thinking about weren't ones that made him comfortable.

"Wait—" he said, but she'd already pulled brown paper away from a white cardboard box. If it had been a bomb, it would have exploded from that alone, so at least he could relax on that end.

"Why?" she asked, using scissors to cut through tape that held the box closed.

"With a stalker, you need to have all packages checked out first. Just in case."

"In case…?" She lifted the lid, her eyes widening, her face draining of color.

"What is it?" He stood, the abrupt movement alarming King. The dog growled, his scruff up, his eyes focused on the door.

Sasha pushed the box in his direction, then stood and walked to the window, staring out into the darkness.

He expected to see something horrible. A dead mouse. A snake. A threatening note. Instead, there was a flame-colored rose. Orange with burnished red edges to the petals. A little wilted. Otherwise, there was nothing startling about it.

"A rose?" he asked, resisting the urge to lift it from the box.

"My mother's favorite. My father used to give her a dozen just like it for every anniversary and birthday."

"Aside from you," he asked, keeping his tone even and his voice calm, "who else knows that?"

"Now? No one."

"You've never told anyone?"

"Who would I tell?" She turned, her eyes swimming with tears she didn't let fall.

"A boyfriend? Husband? Friend? Coworker?"

"I don't currently have a boyfriend. I've been divorced for years. And, honestly, I feel pretty confident when I say you're not someone who likes to talk about the details of your parents' murders. You did, after all, tell me that several times."

"I don't. Not unless I have to."

"It's been the same with me. I've made it a habit to not talk about my mother's murder unless I have to. I'll be telling the story on my cable show, but my focus is going to be on the good that came out of the heartbreak. Certainly not on the details of the loss. There's no way I'd bring those things up while out with friends."

"Murder is definitely not a good dinner conversation."

"Not just murder. Losing anyone you love and talking about it makes people uncomfortable."

She was right.

He could count on one hand the number of people who hadn't shifted uncomfortably when he had mentioned that his parents were murdered. Not that he did often. It wasn't a subject he enjoyed going into, and most people wanted to ask questions he had no intention of answering.

Until recently, he couldn't answer.

Who did it?

Why?

Those questions had haunted him for two decades. Now that their murderer had been apprehended, he wanted to feel closer to some sort of resolution. All he felt was empty. Knowing who had killed his parents didn't change the fact that they were dead. It certainly didn't change him back to the young kid he had been before he had been suspected of their murders. He had hoped to feel closure, and he supposed he did, but he also felt as if the justice he had chased after for so long did nothing to fill the empty parts of his life. The parts that had once been filled with his need for answers, for justice. Maybe even for revenge.

"You think someone who knows about your mother sent this rose?" he asked.

"I have no idea, but it's…odd. Don't you think?"

"Looks like there's a note under the rose. Do you have sterile gloves?" he asked, wishing he'd driven his cruiser. He wanted to read the note, but he didn't want to contaminate evidence.

"In the office first-aid kit. Give me a minute. I'll be right back with them."

She stepped out of the room and ran down the hall.

He followed.

No way was he going to let her wander around an unsecured business on her own. The front door was locked, but there was no doorman as there was in many office buildings. They stepped into the reception area, and she rifled through a desk drawer, pulling out a pack of disposable gloves. "Will these work?"

He nodded and they headed back to her office.

King was still on the floor, head on his paws, eyes fixed on the doorway. He didn't look happy to have been left behind. "Sorry about that, pal," Bradley said, offering him a dog treat he pulled from a bag he carried in his pocket.

"I can't believe he didn't follow us," Sasha said as she pulled gloves from the pack and put them on.

"How about you let me handle that?" he said. "If there's a note that needs to be reported to the police, the packaging, box and everything in it are going to be evidence. We want to do everything we can to preserve them."

"All right." She stepped aside, watching as he put on gloves and carefully lifted out the rose.

Beneath it, a white envelope had been taped to the bottom of the box. He opened it, easing out a sheet of lined paper that had been folded several times. His stomach lurched when he realized what he was looking at.

Letters written in dried blood, scrawled across the surface in thick, jagged strokes.

You're next.

FIVE

If Sasha still had a job by the end of the day, she would be surprised. Fifteen minutes after Bradley read the note, the office building was teeming with K-9 police officers and their K-9 partners. Her producer, Prudence Landry, had watched things unfold with a laser-like focus.

Either she wasn't a dog person, or she wasn't a police person, or she simply didn't want to have the morning programming interrupted by a police investigation.

Now she was pacing the hallway, her gaze darting to the recording studio and the green light glowing above its door.

"I hate to try and rush the process, but we have twenty minutes before the next live programming is scheduled to begin," she yelled above the quiet hum of voices that had filled the normally quiet office.

Her husky voice seemed to bounce off the walls, but it had little impact on the officers who were dusting Sasha's office for fingerprints.

"Officers!" Prudence tried again. "Is there a timeline for when you'll be finished here?"

"Sorry about this, Ms....?" a dark-haired cop said

as he moved through the hall, a chocolate Labrador retriever at his side.

"Landry. But you can call me Prudence. We're casual around here. Although, not usually casual enough to allow this many dogs at one time." She smiled, but her movements were stiff as she extended a hand.

"They're very well trained," he responded with a charming smile. "I'm Officer Jackson Davison. Emergency services. This is my partner, Smokey."

"It's good to meet you both, but, as I'm sure you'll understand, we have a tight production schedule, and—"

"No worries, ma'am," a female officer said as she packed a few items in a small bag. "We're finished here."

"You are?"

"Aside from the work Smokey and I have to do," Officer Davison said, his gaze skirting past Prudence and landing on Sasha. "You're Sasha?" he asked.

"That's right."

"Mind if Smokey and I take a look at the gift you received?"

"I wouldn't exactly call it a gift," she muttered.

"It's in here," Bradley said, his hand settling on her shoulder, his fingers warm through the soft cotton material.

Her cheeks heated, her stomach doing a crazy little flip.

She wasn't happy with either response, and she stepped away, making room for Smokey and Officer Davison to walk into her office.

The hum of people had faded, officers and their K-9s leaving as quickly as they had come. She assumed they were outside, discussing what they had found. Or maybe they would go back to the K-9 unit first.

"We may as well see what they're doing," Prudence said, hooking an arm through hers and dragging her into the tiny room.

She didn't seem angry.

If anything, she seemed excited and pleased.

"If you don't mind staying there," Officer Davison said without looking their way. Smokey was still on the leash, but was sniffing the floorboards near the desk, working his way to the chair and up the leg of it.

Sasha had no idea what he was sniffing for.

She wanted to ask Bradley, but he was near the desk, his gaze focused on Smokey, King lying at his feet.

Smokey's tail wagged twice. Then his head popped up, his nose moving closer to the edge of the desk. He put his front paws on the chair, extending his head over the desk, before he retreated, trotted around the desk and repeated the process.

Once.

Again.

Around the desk. Up. Sniff. Drop down.

Finally, he seemed to home in on the box that had been placed smack-dab in the middle of the desk. He clawed at the table, trying to get closer.

"Work it out," Officer Davison said.

Smokey hopped onto the chair, front paws on the table, nose centimeters from the box. He sniffed, his tail wagging furiously, then dropped to the ground, lying on the floor and staring at Davison.

"Good boy!" Officer Davison said, pulling a ball from his pocket and leading the dog from the room.

"Good dog, for what?" Prudence asked, her gaze on the box.

"Smokey is a cadaver dog," Bradley explained.

"I hope you're not going to tell me he smells a body in that box," Sasha said, her voice shaking at the thought.

"No, but he just indicated on the box. That means there is more than an excellent chance human blood was used to write the note."

"Human blood?!" Prudence's husky voice was high with surprise.

"That doesn't mean someone died. It just means a small amount of blood was used. The great news is, we can run a DNA test, see if we have a match in the system."

"And if you don't?" Sasha asked, stomach heaving as she watched Bradley place the box in a plastic evidence bag.

"Then we'll find him another way."

"How?" she asked, arms across her chest.

He stared at her.

She stared at the evidence bag.

She'd never been squeamish about blood, but she felt a little sick and very scared.

She had seen the note.

She knew what it said.

You're next.

And she knew who it was from.

Martin Roker's look-alike.

"I need to figure out who he is," she muttered, stepping to the side as Bradley walked into the hall.

He turned quickly, the evidence bag in hand. "You need to do your job, and you need to let me and my team do ours."

"What's that supposed to mean?"

"You're an intelligent woman, Sasha. I'm sure I don't have to explain it to you."

"I'm an intelligent woman who is perfectly capable of making up her own mind about what she should be doing."

"I hate to break in on this little love quarrel," Prudence said wryly, "but your boyfriend is correct. You have a job to do here. Your show airs in two hours, and I haven't seen the script for it."

"First, he's not my boyfriend. Second, my story is prepped and ready. Just like always."

"I'll be back in a few hours, Sasha," Bradley said, ignoring her boss. "If you need anything, though, anything at all, you call me or text me. Okay?"

She could still feel the tension between them, but at least he still had her safety front and center. "I will. Thank you."

She watched him walk away, then turned her attention back to Prudence, her boss's patience clearly low.

"And the story about your mother?" Prudence asked. "I have that scheduled for next Saturday and Sunday. I haven't seen the rough-cut video yet."

"I'm working on it." She was. She just hadn't made much progress.

"Can you have it to me by the end of today?" Prudence asked. "Tomorrow at the very latest."

"Tomorrow is Saturday," Sasha reminded her.

"Yes. Which leaves less than a week for any changes and edits you and I might want. Not to mention that the story of your mother's murder is a hot topic in the news right now."

"It is?" Sasha had avoided watching the news last night and this morning for good reason.

"It started airing on local late-night networks, and it's still running hot this morning. Apparently there was a shooting in Sheepshead Bay last night, and you were involved in it."

"I'm afraid so."

"Don't be. It's great publicity. I have a feeling the ratings for your show are going to skyrocket. Make sure you mention that you'll be telling your story on our cable station next weekend when you broadcast today. I'll leave you to get ready. And I'll make sure the recording studio is empty this afternoon. That way you'll have plenty of time to finish the project." She turned on her heels and marched from the room, obviously more pleased with the chaos in the studio than Sasha would have imagined.

She shook her head, watching as Prudence rounded a corner and disappeared from view.

The office building fell back into its normal quiet. Nothing but the soft hum of the heater to break the silence. She knew she wasn't alone. Prudence was in her office. Darius Warren was in his, putting together notes for his programming the following week. A professor of economics, he broadcast an early-morning State of the Dollar address, highlighting economic trends and giving advice on long-term savings and retirement. After his program, the station ran two hours of paid commercial programming. Mostly advertisements for miracle vitamins or exercise equipment designed for an older crowd. Sasha's program followed that. She usually spent the two hours prior reading over her notes and making sure video clips were ready for her segment. Today's story was on a local teenager who worked odd jobs to earn money to donate to the local animal shelter. Feel-good story about a hardworking teen and cute animals. It should make her audience happy.

She sat at her desk, pulling out her file folder and thumbing through the notes. She needed to focus, but she kept jumping at every sound, her gaze darting to the door, her breath held as she waited for a monster to open it.

"He's not going to enter the building while the police are congregated outside," she reminded herself as she reread a sentence for the tenth time.

Unless he was in the building before you arrived, her brain whispered. Maybe he'd found a way to break in. Or had gotten ahold of a key somehow. Anything was possible.

Her mother had been in a school parking lot when she had been shot. Three of her colleagues had witnessed the murder. Roker hadn't cared. He had been on a mission, and he would have died to achieve it.

He *had* died.

Was Sasha's stalker as driven?

She didn't dare dwell on that. She didn't want an answer to the question. She had a job to do, an audience that was waiting for the next good-news story from New York City. She might not feel cheerful, but no one had to know that. She might be scared out of her mind, but she wasn't going to let that stop her from doing what she had set out to do when she had pitched this idea to Prudence.

"Do your job, Sasha," she muttered. "Then you can worry about everything else."

She pushed every thought from her head that didn't

have to do with cute dogs and sweet kittens and guinea pigs squealing in their homes, focusing her energy on something she could control rather than all the things she could not.

Two hours later, she was ready, sitting on the only prop she used—a comfortable velvet-covered armchair that had once belonged to her father. He had never had a chance to see her program, but he would have approved. Each time she sat in the chair, she was reminded of his kindness, his faith, his strength in the face of all that life had brought.

He had never remarried. As far as she knew, he had never even dated after her mother's death. He had poured himself into making certain Sasha felt loved, valued and secure. If she could spread a little of his kindness and optimism, it was the best way to preserve his legacy.

"Ten seconds," the cameraman said, his gruff voice cutting into her thoughts.

She nodded, sliding the folder of notes off-screen, straightening her skirt and blouse, and smiling straight at the camera.

The cameraman held up three fingers. Two. One.

The program began, and she lost herself in the story and her telling of it.

By the time the K-9 team cleared out of the cable news office, King was impatient, whining softly as he sat on the sidewalk beside Bradley. This was their day off. They usually spent it hiking trails at local parks or exploring waterfront areas. King needed the time to run off his energy with a long game of Frisbee or a few laps around a dog park.

"Sorry, boy. I know this isn't what we typically do when we're not on duty, but today is a different kind of day. We have another kind of job." For the past few hours, he'd walked around the building with King, gone around the block in every direction a couple of times, gone into the coffee shops and corner markets that opened up early. No sign of the stalker.

Now he gave King the command to heel and walked up the steps of the brownstone that housed Sasha's office. The sun was rising, the sky tinted gold as the new day stretched across it. Cars whizzed past. Horns honked. Sheepshead Bay was waking, the residents heading to work or returning home after night shifts.

Until yesterday, Bradley had planned to sleep an extra hour, do some laundry and then take King to the dog park. He'd figured they could spend an hour there and then walk to the beach to watch the gulls swoop across the brackish water. That was one of King's favorite pastimes, and Bradley enjoyed watching the Malinois bound across the sand. After that, he had thought he'd wander around the Emerys' neighborhood, listening to gossip and hoping for a lead, particularly on the "Andy" that little Lucy Emery had mentioned, that would bring the K-9 team a step closer to finding the person who had murdered the couple.

Now his focus was on getting Sasha through her workday and back to the hotel without her stalker following them.

He glanced over his shoulder as he rang the buzzer on the intercom panel for the cable channel. His white Jeep was where he'd parked it. Once he made sure Sasha was safely tucked away in the hotel, he planned to go to the K-9 unit to review video footage from several security cameras near the bakery. Yesterday's shooting had been caught on tape. He was certain of that. What he was hoping was that there was a clear view of the perp's face.

The street behind him was filled with commuter vehicles and taxis, all vying for a position in the burgeoning rush-hour traffic. Dim morning light filtered through a thin cloud cover. It would be a rainy, windy day in the city.

If only bad weather kept criminals at home.

"WBKN," a woman's voice said through the intercom. "May I help you?"

He identified himself and was buzzed in, not liking that anyone could get inside by saying he was a cop. Inside, Bradley jogged up to the second floor. Sasha wasn't in her office. She broadcast live at eight every morning. He glanced at his watch, then walked the hall until he located the broadcasting studio. A large window opened into a spare room. White walls and a backdrop that hung from the ceiling near the far wall. No exterior windows. A camera set on a tripod pointed at a lone chair, a man behind it hunched over and focused in Sasha's direction. She sat in the chair, leaning forward and staring into the camera's lens as if she were looking into the eyes of her best friend.

Bradley couldn't hear what she was saying, but he watched her hands move as she smiled into the camera. She was animated and filled with enthusiasm for her subject. The kind of television personality people would feel connected with and want to continue watching.

Had her show put her in the crosshairs of a madman?

She was being stalked and taunted by someone.

Bradley had consulted with the team. None of them

believed the gunman had been trying to kill her. She had been close enough for a clean shot. Even through the storefront window. So, what had been the point? To terrify her? To bring the stalker to the forefront of her mind?

Obsession was the hallmark of a stalker's personality, and the person who had sent the rose was obsessed enough to have found out information that Sasha was certain only she knew.

Obviously, she was wrong.

Someone knew about her mother's love of that color rose. The package was proof positive. The note had been sent to the forensic lab and would be swabbed for DNA. Maybe that would bring them some answers. In the meantime, Bradley would question Sasha again. Maybe she would remember something important. A person she had spoken to. A place where her mother had been mentioned. Perhaps she'd talked about it during one of her broadcasts without realizing it.

He frowned.

He could believe a lot of things, but not that. When he spoke of his parents' murders or even just his parents, he remembered. It was something he didn't do often enough for it to become commonplace. It certainly wasn't something he would do without giving it serious thought.

He had a feeling Sasha was the same. She had said very little about her mother's murder, providing just enough information to explain who she thought she had seen.

Martin Roker.

A dead man.

Impossible, and yet she had been lucid in her description of the man who she had said looked exactly like her mother's killer.

Unaged.

Unchanged.

Well, if the blood on the note did link to DNA, they'd soon know if Roker had an identical twin no one had known about. Or maybe a similar-looking son. There wasn't much information on the guy other than him having an estranged wife and daughter.

She finished speaking and settled back in the chair, her ponytail hanging over her left shoulder, her hands idle in her lap. Her smile slipped away as a monitor high on the wall to her left flickered to life, showing a quick glimpse of Sasha before switching over to a news clip featuring a local humane society and a teenage boy who was wheeling a wagon filled with bags of dog and cat food through the door.

Sasha's focus was on the screen, her body tense as she watched the clip. As it ended, she brushed her ponytail back off her shoulder, focused on the camera and smiled.

The cameraman lifted his arm, showing three fingers.

Two.

One.

Sasha began speaking again, her smile bright and animated. She looked nothing like the tense woman who had watched the video clip. Whatever she was feeling, whatever she'd been thinking, was well hidden behind her peppiness.

He watched until the end, waiting as she settled back into the chair, her eyes on the flickering monitor on the wall. A few credits appeared, there and gone so quickly he wasn't sure anyone would have time to read them.

After a moment, the screen went black and she stood, stretching a kink out of her neck, her body lithe and slender, her hair sliding along her shoulders. She rubbed her neck and stifled a yawn, lifting a folder from the floor to her left and saying something to the cameraman. Bradley thought he heard a deep chuckle and a higher, more feminine one.

As if she sensed his focus, Sasha's attention shifted to the window, her eyes widening.

She waved and smiled.

The cameraman turned toward the window, then stalked to the door and opened it.

"Who are you?" he demanded as Sasha edged out behind him.

"He's…a friend of mine."

The cameraman scowled, his ruddy face nearly covered by a full mustache and beard. "I don't like strangers wandering the halls. Even if they are strangers other people know. After that shooting last night, everyone in Sheepshead Bay is on edge. Including me."

"You heard about that?" Sasha asked.

"Who hasn't? I'd have mentioned it sooner, but I figured if you wanted to talk about it, you'd say something."

"I appreciate you giving me time and space to process things," Sasha said, not giving any further details or answering the questions Bradley sensed the cameraman wanted to ask.

People were curious by nature.

When bad things happened, they wanted the details.

Not just so they could ogle and gossip, but because they wanted to understand the causes and avoid them.

Sometimes, though, horrible things couldn't be avoided.

Even the best-lived life was sometimes filled with heartache.

Bradley had seen it time and time again. He'd spent one too many late nights or early mornings listening to the heartbreaking sobs of a mother who had lost a child, a father whose daughter wouldn't be coming home, a husband whose life partner would never again kiss him good morning. So many innocent victims of horrible crimes. There were nights when he couldn't sleep, thinking about the heartbreak and sorrow. Only knowing that he could offer help and closure to victims kept him going. The knowledge that there was something better beyond this life was comforting when he stood with grieving loved ones and watched their children, spouses, sisters, brothers or parents being buried.

It was also the impetus that kept him going when he was in the middle of the toughest cases.

Like the murders of the Emerys.

The couple had been killed in front of their three-year-old daughter seven months ago. The sole witness to the crime, Lucy Emery hadn't been old enough to give the kind of details needed for identification or apprehension of the killer beyond the clown mask. The K-9 unit had spent months pursuing one dead-end lead after another.

At first, the residents of Sheepshead Bay had been so busy whispering that the McGregors' killer was back at it, murdering couples with young children and hoping to get away with it like he had for twenty years, that they hadn't been focused on anything else. Such as the fact that there was a copycat killer at work. But there was such little evidence and nothing to go on. The K-9 unit had been relying on the community to provide insight and information about the Emerys. Whom they associated with, what they did and how they lived their lives were all important factors when it came to tracking down their killer.

Right now, a man named Andy, someone who Lucy had said she missed, was the prime suspect. Clearly, the man had been kind to her in some capacity. But after investigating all possibilities for a couple of months now, the K-9 unit still had no idea who this Andy was or his connection to Lucy or the Emerys. At three, Lucy was just too young to further explain, and talking about him seemed to upset her into silence.

Lucy had been through enough. That was why Bradley had been hoping the people of Lucy's old neighborhood would come through.

Unfortunately, the community hadn't been up-front with information. Every week, Bradley visited the neighborhood and spoke to the people he saw there. Every week, he prayed that there would be a new piece of the puzzle revealed and that, eventually, he'd have the full picture of what had happened the night the Emerys were killed.

So far, it hadn't happened.

Bradley wasn't giving up hope.

After twenty years, his parents' murders had been solved. If that could happen, anything could.

"Right," the cameraman finally said, his bright blue eyes focused on Sasha. "Do you need me to stick around and give you a lift home? After what happened last night, I figure you might not want to walk."

"I appreciate the offer, but I'll be fine," she responded kindly, smiling to take any sting out of the rebuttal.

"You weren't fine yesterday," the cameraman pointed out.

"Yesterday, she didn't have a police officer escorting her," Bradley cut in.

The cameraman shifted his gaze, his expression unreadable as he met Bradley's eyes. "You're with the police?"

"Detective Bradley McGregor. Brooklyn K-9 Unit."

"Good to meet you, Detective. Glad you're going to escort Sasha home. I'm always telling her the streets of Sheepshead Bay aren't as safe as they once were. A beautiful woman like her can't be too careful. Don't you agree?"

"Sure," Bradley responded.

Sasha's cheeks were pink with embarrassment, her fingers curled so tightly around the folder, it was wrinkling beneath her grip.

"Good. Good. Glad we agree. I've got to get ready for the next broadcast. See you tomorrow, Sasha." He threw the last sentence over his shoulder as he walked away.

Sasha didn't respond.

She was already walking back to her office, feet padding lightly on the carpeted floor, skin a shade too pale, shoulders tense.

"Are you okay?" he asked as they stepped into her office.

"Just a little tired. I didn't sleep well last night."

"Ready to head back to the hotel? Maybe you can get some rest?"

"I thought I had to stop at headquarters to give my statement?"

"If you're tired, it can wait."

"Not that tired. More worried than anything. Seeing that rose shook me."

"I'm sure that was what it was intended to do."

"Why?" she asked, dropping into her chair and setting the folder on the table beside her computer.

"Why am I sure?"

"Why would someone want to shake me up?"

"To get your attention. To make sure you know he's there."

"Trust me, I know," she said wryly, her hand shaking as she poured coffee into a white mug near the carafe. "Would you like a cup? I meant to offer it earlier, but things happened."

"I'm good," he responded, watching as she emptied three creamers into the mug, poured several packets of sugar in and stirred it listlessly.

She did look tired, the circles under her eyes dark against her pale skin.

"I don't understand any of this," she said, taking a quick sip of coffee and setting the mug down on the table. "It's been nearly nineteen years since my mother's murder. By this time, I'd think I would be the only person who remembered it."

"It made the headlines when it happened," he reminded her.

"Yes. The scandal made it big news. A woman killed by her ex-love." She shook her head. "My mother made some mistakes. She may have made a lot of them, but she was a good mother, and she did love my father."

"You don't have to explain your family dynamics,

Sasha," he said, hating to see the sadness in her eyes. He understood it all too well. He knew the hollowness of loss, the empty place where parents should be but weren't. He'd been fortunate to have adoptive parents who filled that spot better than his biological parents ever had, but just listening to Sasha talk about her mother helped him understand the relationship they'd had. Unlike his parents, Sasha's had loved and cared for her. The affair that had led to murder didn't change that.

"I know. I just think about it sometimes. Especially now that I'm trying to tell my story. I want people to know there is hope after heartache, but the truth is, I'm still broken from the loss of my mother. Death is hard enough, but murder under circumstances like my mother's makes it difficult to mourn properly."

"I understand that."

"Do you?" She sighed, sliding the folder into one of the file cabinets and pulling out another thicker one. "Here is all the information I've collected about my mother's case."

"That's a thick folder."

"The police investigated thoroughly, and they were happy to give me copies of what they had."

She pulled out a crime scene photo, wincing a little as she handed it to him. The second photo she held out was one of a beautiful blonde woman holding a little girl. Both of them were smiling into the camera, their dark eyes dancing with humor. "That's me and Mom. I was five. She was twenty-nine. She was only thirty-eight when she died."

She pulled out a third photo and crowed triumphantly. "Here it is! The picture of Martin Roker."

She slid it across the table, tapping her finger on the

face of a gaunt man who was smiling half-heartedly, his attention focused somewhere to the right of the photographer. Blond hair. Hooked nose. Stooped shoulders.

"The man who's been stalking me, who shot at me, looks exactly like him."

"We know he didn't have an identical twin or any siblings. Maybe he has a look-alike son."

She frowned. "He only has a daughter."

"I'll have our tech guru do some digging into Roker's past. Something's not adding up here."

She nodded. "I wish I knew what he wants with me."

Bradley thought the note had made it clear.

Sasha was next on the kill list of a madman.

He didn't say that. Just pulled out his phone and took a picture of the photo of Roker. "I'm going to send this to both Eden Chang, the tech guru, and my sister, Penny. She's the front desk clerk, but she helps out in record keeping, too, and will get this in your file."

"I spoke with her last week," Sasha said, reminding him of her unscheduled visit and the attempt she had made to get him to agree to an interview.

He hadn't thought much of her then.

As a matter of fact, he had been more angry than he'd let on. His parents had been gone for twenty years, the killer finally caught, but their murders still seemed to cast dark shadows across his life. No matter how hard he tried, he couldn't seem to get out from under them. "Right. Eden can run this through some face recognition software. Maybe we'll get a match for a current criminal in our data banks."

"That would be strange, don't you think?" She stood, tucking the folder under her arm as she grabbed her coffee.

"What?"

"Roker having a doppelgänger that is a criminal just like him."

"Strange, but not an impossibility. Do you want to go to headquarters now?"

"I hate to keep you here longer, but Prudence is going to have my head on a platter if I don't give her a rough copy of next weekend's story."

"You're going back to the studio?"

"Not the live studio. We have a recording studio. I'll work there. Once I'm finished, I'll set it aside. Tomorrow, I'll cut and edit. If you'd like to wait here, that's fine."

He had the impression that was exactly what she'd like him to do. He might have considered it, but the building was large, the hiding places limitless. There were doors everywhere. Bathrooms on each level. Probably other cubbyholes he hadn't seen.

He had a feeling Sasha's stalker was familiar with the space, that he had been there before, moving down the halls as if he belonged, testing doors, searching for the perfect spot to hide and to spy. Which meant he'd definitely found an easy way in: he had a key.

If he was there now, hiding behind one of the closed doors, King didn't sense it. He walked beside Bradley, his body relaxed, his tail wagging slowly. No stress. No hint that there was anything amiss. Bradley trusted his partner's senses more than he trusted his own, but that didn't mean he was going to let his guard down. Sasha had every right to feel safe. She had every right to move through her life without threat of harm.

For as long as Bradley could remember, he had rooted for the underdog and fought for the rights of those who couldn't fight for themselves. He thought it came from his early years, when his little sister was a baby, and he was ten, listening to her cry from hunger in the middle of the night while his parents were out partying. He had learned to make bottles. He'd learned how to change diapers. He had learned, by trial and error, to do all the things a good parent should.

He had learned to care for a helpless infant, and from that, he had learned everything else. Compassion. Empathy. Love.

He had built on them during his years with Joe and Allison Brady. Strong Christians who had lived their faith, his adoptive parents had taught him invaluable lessons about forgiveness and loyalty. He carried those things with him every day, using them to be the best law enforcement officer he could be.

Sasha stepped into a room, flicking on a light to reveal stark white walls and the same backdrop he'd seen in the live studio. A camera stood on a tripod against a wall, and she moved it toward the center of the room, focusing it on a comfortable-looking easy chair that sat in the middle of a blue-and-white area rug.

"You can sit in one of those chairs," she said, pointing to two folding chairs that leaned against the wall. He grabbed one and opened it, sitting on the metal seat and giving King the down-stay command.

The Malinois did so reluctantly, offering a quick yawn and soft whine in protest. He wanted to be out chasing gulls. They'd do it eventually. For now, Bradley's focus would stay where it should be: on keeping Sasha safe.

SIX

She spent an hour taping her story, the words pouring out in a rush she hadn't expected and didn't want. So much for the modulated, cheerful voice she had cultivated. Her voice cracked as she explained the way her mother's murder had ripped away her sense of security and destroyed her faith in human nature. It had taken years to overcome that.

And then it had been destroyed again by her ex-husband's infidelity.

She didn't mention that.

It wasn't part of her mother's story. It certainly wasn't something she wanted the world to know.

She didn't want Bradley to know it, either.

He was sitting in a chair, his legs stretched out and crossed at the ankle, his arms crossed over his stomach. His gaze hadn't wavered since she'd begun speaking, and she found herself, more than once, talking to him instead of the camera.

That wouldn't make for good programming.

Like her modulated voice, she had worked hard at making just the right amount of eye contact with the camera. Not too long or too short. Relaxed mouth and jaw. Easy smile. All the things that made a person seem approachable.

That had been what she had wanted—for people to feel welcomed by the show, drawn into it. She had wanted them to feel encouraged and motivated. She had her show be a call to action and a forum from which people could gain ideas about how they could make a difference in their community.

Prudence often said she had been successful in meeting her goals.

As a matter of fact, there'd been talk of another slot during the day. Prudence had been toying with the idea of giving Sasha a chance to explore local happenings and do feature stories on book festivals, grand openings, school theater productions.

Sasha had liked the idea, but she hadn't been as excited by the potential opportunity as she had thought she should be.

That was what she'd wanted, right? To build a career in the news industry, working as a journalist who saw the world through a different lens and reported on it?

She had thought so.

Until she had begun digging into her own story.

The more she had uncovered about her mother's murder, the more she had learned about her past, the less certain Sasha had been about her future. Looking through her mother's things, reading through old journal entries, seeing the soft looping handwriting and the flowery phrases, had reminded her of the things she'd once jotted in her own journal, the dreams she had once had.

She had wanted to be a photojournalist, traveling the world to take pictures of exotic locations and animals and people. She had wanted to use a camera to capture the world and give it as a gift to other people.

Instead, she sat in a small room, making a video recording of her mother's story.

Her father's.

Hers.

They were interconnected, held together by their family relationship and by tragedy.

She was the last person alive who had seen her parents during their happy years. After the affair, before the murder, they'd been working hard to rebuild their marriage.

Sasha had been old enough to notice the way they had looked into each other's eyes, the secret that passed silently between them. The smiles. The passionate kisses they hadn't realized she'd seen. Their love for each other had made her feel secure and safe. The ending to the story was a tragic one, but there had been a lot of beauty in the middle of that.

She planned to convey that in the recording, but her voice wobbled as she attempted to describe the love between her parents, her eyes burning with tears.

She wasn't a pretty crier.

She was the kind with the red nose and the blotchy skin.

Definitely not something the world needed to see, but she couldn't seem to pull it together. The more she tried not to cry, the more she wanted to do it. She could almost picture her mother as she'd been the last day. They'd both been heading out the door. Sasha had been in her sophomore year of high school. Her mother had been a creative writing teacher at the local middle school. They'd said goodbye as they'd walked out the door. Exchanged hugs and "I love you"s like they did every day.

Everything had been normal and good.

And then it hadn't been.

She cleared her throat, forcing herself to keep talking, spewing out the script she had written and memorized. She felt like she was choking on the words, her throat clogged with the disappointment and grief she hadn't allowed herself to feel in years.

She stood up, blindly walking to the camera and turning it off. She'd had enough for today. Maybe for every day.

"You okay?" Bradley asked quietly. He had moved from the chair to her side and was studying her face as if there were secrets he could read there.

"I'm fine. Just tired." Her voice was still husky, the words sandpaper-rough.

"Do you always cry when you're tired?" he asked, brushing a tear from her cheek.

"Only when I'm talking about my mother." She swiped tears from her face, impatient with her weakness and embarrassed that Bradley had seen it.

"You're braver than I am," he commented, cupping her shoulder and urging her into the hall.

"How so?"

"You asked if I'd do an interview for your show. I refused."

"Because you're a private person who doesn't enjoy his past being dragged into the present," she said.

"That's only part of the reason."

"What's the other part?"

"Talking about it is too painful. Not just because my parents were murdered, but because their deaths barely left a hole in my life. The truth is, there were days after they died when I was thankful they were gone, because I was certain my sister would have a better life with just about anyone else than she'd had with them."

"What about you?" she asked.

"Me?"

"Did you think you'd have a better life?"

He studied her solemnly, his dark eyes shadowed with memories of the past. "At the time, Penny was my sole focus. I'd been taking care of her the best way I could from the time she was an infant, but I was smart enough to know it wasn't enough. She didn't just need a big brother who made sure she ate and bathed and had clean clothes to wear. She needed a stable environment, a home where there weren't empty beer cans lying on the floor and used needles in the bathroom trash can."

"I'm sorry, Bradley. That's no way for a child to grow up."

"No, it isn't. I wanted better for her, but I had no idea how to provide it."

"I wasn't talking about your sister. I was talking about you," she corrected.

His jaw tightened, his lips pressing together.

She thought he was going to speak. Instead, he opened the door and urged her into the hall. "Do you need to go back to your office?" he asked.

"No. I've got everything I need to work on here." She held up the folder. "And I packed my home laptop. I can work from the hotel room."

"Do you need anything at your house?"

She could think of several things she would have liked to get. A couple of books. Her e-reader. The photo of her parents that she kept on her bedside table.

"No," she said, deciding against mentioning any of those things. Bradley had spent his entire morning babysitting her. They still had to stop at the K-9 unit before he dropped her at the hotel. The last thing she wanted to do was give him more to do on his day off.

"You're sure? I don't mind stopping there."

"I'm sure."

"If you change your mind, let me know. It shouldn't take long to take your statement. Then I'll drop you off at the hotel."

"I appreciate all you're doing for me. If I can ever repay you—"

"You can," he cut in, his voice a little sharper than it had been.

"Okay. Name it."

"Everything I said to you back there? It stays off the record. Don't use it for any human-interest story or feel-good pieces, okay?"

The fact that he had to say that to her, that he felt the need to remind her of something he had already said twice, told Sasha everything she needed to know about his opinion of her.

She stopped as they reached the exit, looking straight into his eyes as she spoke. "Just so we're clear, Detective, I didn't hire a man to stalk me, shoot at me and leave notes written in blood on my desk so that I could draw you into my web and trap you there."

His eyes narrowed, the muscle in his jaw twitching. "What's that supposed to mean?"

"Exactly what it sounded like. This isn't some elaborate ruse to get close to you so that I can do a story about the family's tragedy and you and your sister's triumph over it."

"I don't recall saying that it was."

"The fact that you have reminded me three times that our conversations are not on the record said it for you." She pushed open the door and stepped outside, blinking as watery sunlight filled her eyes.

She had forgotten that the sun was up, the street bustling with activity. That time had moved forward while she broadcast her story and recorded a session for next weekend's show.

She strode forward, dodging several pedestrians, and hurried to the Jeep. She wasn't thinking about Roker's double, gunfire or roses the color of fire. She was thinking about getting to the police station, giving her statement and getting away from Bradley as quickly as possible.

She heard the familiar beep as the doors were remotely unlocked. She would have yanked the door open, but a warm, furry body was suddenly pressing against her legs, nudging her away from the door.

"King?" she said, looking down at the tan dog. He was staring into her eyes and growling low in his throat.

She stepped back, tripping on the curb and falling into Bradley's firm chest.

His arm wrapped around her waist, holding her steady as she caught her balance.

"Sorry," she murmured, reaching for the door again.

King butted against her legs, growling and then barking, the ferocious sound scaring her into retreat.

She stepped away from the Jeep. "I don't think he wants me to ride with you," she said, not meeting Bradley's eyes.

She was embarrassed by her outburst and by the

anger she'd felt when she had realized how little he thought of her.

She had no reason to feel that way.

They barely knew each other.

She certainly didn't expect him to understand the ethics and morals she lived by, and she knew there were plenty of journalists who would do whatever it took to get a story that would sell.

"I don't think that's the problem," he responded. "What's wrong, King?" he asked.

King barked again, his scruff raised, his tail rigid.

She had seen the dog relaxed and happy.

She had seen him ready to work.

She wasn't sure what she was seeing now. She only knew King wasn't happy.

She stepped onto the sidewalk, watching warily as the dog paced back and forth in front of the Jeep. His nose was to the ground. He'd stopped growling and barking and seemed focused, his head down, his ears back.

"What's he doing?" she whispered, as if talking too loudly might interrupt the dog's concentration.

"I'm not sure," he replied. He was watching King, tracking the dog's movements as he rounded the car and returned. "Something is bothering him. That's all I know."

"Is he sick?"

"No. He's concerned."

"How can you tell?" she asked, her embarrassment fading as he watched the dog work his way from one end of the Jeep to the next. Up onto the sidewalk. A few steps toward the building. Back again.

"The way he is pacing and sniffing. He's trying to

work out a problem, but he's not sure what." He dropped to his knees and studied the chassis. "I think I see something."

"What?"

"I'm not sure, and I'm not going to reach in to figure it out. I'm going to call in my sergeant and ask him to come out with one of the detectives who also has bomb detection K-9."

"Bomb detection?" she repeated, because the words didn't make any sense.

There was no way there was a bomb underneath the Jeep.

Was there?

She backed away a few more steps, nearly bumping into a pedestrian.

"Careful," Bradley warned, taking her arm and tugging her back to his side as he pulled out his cell phone.

She tried to hear what he was saying, but traffic was heavy, engines roaring, horns honking, someone yelling. She couldn't hear above the sounds of city life and her own galloping heartbeat.

Bradley escorted Sasha back inside before the bomb squad arrived. He didn't want her standing out on the sidewalk. If she did, she might as well have a neon sign plastered to her back that read Sitting Duck. A gunman with good aim and the right weapon could take someone out from hundreds of meters away. Sasha could be standing in the middle of a battalion of police officers and still be murdered.

Just the thought made his blood run cold.

"What's going on?" she asked as he led the way to her office.

"I'm not sure."

"You must have some idea, or you wouldn't have called for the bomb detectors."

"I saw something attached to the Jeep's chassis. Looked like explosives, but I couldn't get a good enough view to be certain." He had gotten a clear enough glimpse to be worried, but he hadn't dared slide underneath to investigate further. There were too many people on the street. Cars. Bicycles. Pedestrians on the sidewalk. If the Jeep exploded, it wasn't just the vehicle that would be taken out.

"Explosives? As in, a bomb?"

"I'm going to let the experts decide," he responded. King walked beside him, his scruff still up, his ears back. He may not have seen what was attached to the bottom of the Jeep, but he had smelled it.

And he hadn't liked it.

That was enough to concern Bradley.

His boss, Sergeant Gavin Sutherland, had agreed to bring his bomb-detecting dog, Tommy. He'd also said he would bring Detective Henry Roarke and his K-9 partner, Cody. Roarke was a former military explosives expert. Cody was a high-energy beagle with a nose for detecting bombs. If there was something there, Tommy and Cody would know it.

"Experts?" Sasha asked as they reached her office.

"Two of our bomb-detecting dogs are the best in the business. If there are explosives around, they'll know it."

"And if there are?"

"We'll shut down the street and call in the bomb squad. The dogs and handlers should be here soon. I need you to wait in your office until I return for you."

"Which will be when?"

"Hopefully not long."

"That's vague."

"I wish I could offer a firmer timeline, but I can't. Sometimes the dogs locate a source quickly. Sometimes they take their time."

"If you'd like, I can call a cab and go to the hotel."

"Do you really think that's a safe idea? After everything that's happened already today?"

He thought she might be offended by the question, but she sighed. "You have a point. I'll wait in my office."

"No wandering the building? No heading out the back door to run errands?"

"Nope. I'll be sitting at my desk working on next weekend's show."

"You're sure?" he prodded, suddenly worried about leaving her.

"I'm sure."

"There's a lock on the door," he pointed out as he walked back into the hall. "Use it, okay?"

"Okay," she agreed, offering a quick smile.

She closed the door, and he waited until he heard the lock turn, then hurried outside. Gavin was already there, his vehicle parked in a no-parking zone a few feet away and angled purposely so that traffic had to take a wide path around. His boss stepped out of the vehicle when he saw Bradley.

Bradley liked and admired Gavin Sutherland. The dedicated cop had previously worked at the NYC K-9 Command Unit in Queens and had been promoted to sergeant of the Brooklyn K-9 Unit when the new team was formed back in the spring. If there was a bomb around, the Sarge and Detective Henry Roarke were two hardworking cops you wanted working on the case.

"We're working to block traffic on both ends of the block," Gavin said. "Once we get a clearer picture of what's going on, we can make decisions about evacuating businesses."

"I'm not even sure it's a bomb, Sarge," Bradley said, giving King the down command as Gavin got Tommy out. The springer spaniel jumped down excitedly, prancing on his leash impatiently. Like all the dogs on the team, he loved his work and looked forward to doing the job he had been trained for.

"I'll walk him around your Jeep. See if he indicates. Looks like Henry is pulling up. Why don't you fill him in? Once I finish, he can bring Cody over."

Bradley nodded, leaving King where he was as he strode toward the marked K-9 vehicle pulling into a no-parking zone a few yards away. He waited as Henry exited the vehicle, watching as he opened the back hatch and allowed Cody to jump out. The beagle shook with excitement, his happy baying sounding over the roar of traffic.

He was ready to work and anxious to do it, but he'd have to wait his turn.

"How's it going?" Henry asked, his focus on the Jeep and Tommy.

"It'd be better if I hadn't had to call you and the sergeant out here."

"You really think someone planted a bomb under the Jeep?"

"I don't know, but I'm worried enough to call in the experts."

"Not experts. Just trained," Henry corrected with a

clap on Bradley's back, following Sutherland and Tom-my's progress around the Jeep.

Bradley would trust Henry Roarke with his life. A colleague and a friend, the former soldier knew exactly what it was like to be accused of a crime he hadn't committed. Earlier in the year, Henry had been investigated by Internal Affairs for "unlawful use of force" against an unarmed suspect. He'd been on desk duty for months, but the good news was that not only had he been fully vindicated, but he'd found love with the investigator on his case.

He and Henry walked around the front of the vehicle, Tommy dropping his head to sniff the bumper, the tires, behind the license plate. His tail was raised and his paws scrabbled at the pavement as he went to the driver's side of the vehicle.

"He's on to something," Henry said. "It's good you called us. You have an enemy gunning for you?"

"Just every criminal I ever locked up, but I think this has more to do with the shooting yesterday."

"And the note this morning? I was on a case this morning, but I heard about it."

Bradley nodded. "The victim's mother was murdered eighteen years ago and the shooter is a dead ringer for the killer."

"Relative?" he asked just as Tommy let out three quick barks. "He's found it. Guess it's Cody's turn."

He led Cody to the Jeep, gave him the command to find and followed along, leash in hand, as the beagle sniffed the underside of the Jeep, ran to the driver's side. Sniffed again. Howled.

"Same place," Gavin commented. "I'm going to block off the road and call in the bomb squad. In the meantime, let's start clearing the sidewalk. I know that you're off duty, but can you run caution tape to block the area? Backup will be here soon."

"No problem." He called for King to heel, then grabbed the caution tape from the sergeant's vehicle and used it to cordon off the sidewalk three hundred yards in every direction.

Sirens blared, police cruisers making their way to the scene. At the end of the block, the bomb squad van was trying to find a path through bumper-to-bumper traffic. The road was a mass of honking horns and curious onlookers. People darting across the road in front of vehicles that were attempting to get out the way of emergency vehicles.

It was a bad situation. One the perp might use to his advantage. Often criminals returned to the scene of the crime. It was possible Sasha's stalker was hiding in the crowd, watching the drama unfold.

Bradley glanced at the building where Sasha worked.

A few people stood in the doorway, watching as chaos erupted. Sasha wasn't there. She had said she'd be working behind the locked office door. He and King would do a quick circuit of the area, searching for a Martin Roker clone.

Not a twin. They knew Roker had no siblings. Hopefully the unit's excellent tech guru would get back to him soon with the information she'd dug up. If there was any.

Maybe someone who just happened to look similar to Martin Roker had become fixated on the case?

DNA from the note might lead to answers, but the lab was notoriously slow. Fortunately, Bradley had connections. Men and women at the lab who had known his adoptive parents, who knew his story and who were always eager to help when they could.

He pulled out his cell phone as he and King walked toward the crowd of bystanders, dialing the number for the lab as he scanned the faces. It didn't take him long to convince his adoptive father's old buddy to expedite the testing on the note.

Bradley needed to find the person who was stalking Sasha and get him off the street. Sasha had every right to live her life without fear. She should be free to walk to work and home, to take public transportation, shop, move through her life without fear that she might be attacked.

Bradley would make certain she was.

He was as dedicated to that as he was to every case he worked, but he had to admit, there was something about Sasha that made him want to get more deeply involved. Her strength and courage, her determination to make a good life out of the tragedy of her past, were things he admired. He had lived through his own tragedy. He knew how hard it was to overcome trauma, to work through grief and to move on. Though he'd been long cleared as a suspect in his parents' murders, a part of him never forgot what it had felt like to be accused, whispered about. To be thought capable of something so heinous. When the copycat murders occurred, rumors had run rampant, and he'd felt that old shame and powerlessness that he had felt when he was considered a suspect in his parents' murders. Irrational as that was. Bradley had worked hard to make a name for himself in law enforcement. He had established himself as someone with integrity and honor.

But all the old pain and anger had risen up in him at the double murder so eerily similar to his parents'.

He'd been reminded of being the scared, orphaned fourteen-year-old—and how people couldn't be trusted, that no matter what he did, how much he had accomplished, he would always feel like the teenager who was suspected in his parents' murders.

And his need to prove himself? It had never diminished. He wondered if that was what Sasha was trying to do with her feel-good stories and her cheerful on-air persona. Maybe she wanted to stop being the teenager who had lost her mother in a scandalous tragedy and prove herself as someone who found the good and right and wholesome in the world.

Whatever her motivation, the job had put her in the spotlight, and that might be the reason she had become the target of a lunatic.

Bradley scowled, making another circuit of the area as the bomb squad van finally arrived. The perp might be hiding in plain sight.

If he was, Bradley and King would find him.

SEVEN

Sasha wasn't sure how long she'd been working, but her neck hurt, her eyes burned and her stomach was growling.

She stood and stretched, glancing at the clock on the wall and frowning. It was after noon, the light filtering in through the window casting long shadows across the floor. She had silenced her phone, and she checked it, wondering if Bradley had left a message explaining why he hadn't returned.

No voice mail.

No message.

Nothing but glowing numbers announcing the time and reminding her that she hadn't eaten breakfast that morning. She had barely slept the night before. She was hungry. She was tired. She was finished with most of the prep work for next week's story.

Any other day, she would have turned off her computer, grabbed her coat and headed home. This wasn't any other day. Bradley was worried someone had planted a bomb under his Jeep, and she was waiting to be told it was safe to leave the building.

She did a quick scan of local news and found a blurb

about the bomb squad being on scene near Ocean Avenue. There was a picture of her building and the black bomb squad van. No information about what had been found.

If anything had.

She rubbed the back of her neck and opened the file cabinet closest to the window. Her emergency supply of chocolate and energy bars was depleted. There was a chocolate protein shake. She shook it half-heartedly as she paced to the door.

The building seemed unnaturally quiet. No voices. No footsteps. No buzz of activity as the evening broadcasting crew arrived to begin prepping.

Had the police shut down the building?

She tried calling Prudence, but it went straight to voice mail. Bradley's phone did the same.

She unlocked the door, peering out into the hallway.

The studio light was green. Nothing was being broadcast.

From what she could see, the room was empty.

"Anyone around?" she called, leaning out of her office. She didn't want to take chances, but she didn't like the idea that she might be in the building alone, that the police might have evacuated the entire area, and she could be the only person left within blast distance of the bomb.

"Bradley would have called you," she reminded herself. "Even if he forgot, Prudence certainly wouldn't leave you behind if the place was evacuated."

Not if she knew Sasha was there.

Most days, Sasha left the door to her office open, the tiny space making her feel claustrophobic when it was closed. If Prudence had walked past on her way out of the building, she would have assumed Sasha had left for the day.

"You're being ridiculous," Sasha murmured, but she couldn't shake the feeling that she had been abandoned, and that the best thing she could do was leave as quickly as possible.

She closed the office door and moved down the hall, nearly running as she passed one closed door after another. As she'd suspected, the offices were empty, the normal daytime crew gone.

She grabbed her coat as she flew through the reception area, shrugging into it and stepping into the silent corridor. She hurried toward the stairs, certain she heard voices somewhere below. She relaxed a little, slowing her pace, telling herself there was nothing to be afraid of.

She passed a small alcove where two chairs and a table sat. A good place to eat lunch when it was too rainy to go outside, it wasn't usually empty at this time of day. Still, she was surprised to see a man, his back to her, standing in front of the window. Not something alarming or even worth noting.

Until he turned and moved toward her. Quickly. Decisively. Hand clamping over her mouth as he pulled her into his chest.

She saw his face.

Just briefly.

Just enough to know that her worst fears were coming true. Martin Roker. Whispering in her ear.

"I've been waiting for you, Sasha."

She tried to slam her head into his chin, but his grip on her tightened, the hand he'd slammed over her mouth pressing so hard that she bit the inside of her lip and tasted blood.

"None of that, okay?" His breath was a fetid mixture of alcohol and tobacco, his palm sweaty and cold. She gagged.

He shook her. Hard.

"You'd better get yourself together, or you won't live long enough to see tomorrow. Understood?"

She nodded.

"Good. Good. This wasn't what I planned, but we're going to make it work, right?"

She didn't respond as he pushed her back through the corridor, away from the stairs and the voices.

"Good thing I'm good at improvising. Those explosives were a stroke of genius. Perfect distraction for the cops, the dogs and everyone in this building. People are so predictable, gawking at the misfortunes of others while they whine about their own."

She wasn't sure if he was talking to himself or to her.

His grip shifted from her mouth to her throat, his hand pressing against her windpipe and jugular as he pushed her through the hallway, one hand wrapped around her torso, holding her arms down tight to her sides.

She couldn't breathe.

Could barely think.

She wanted to scream, but there wasn't enough air for that. Not enough energy in her body to fight. Her legs went weak, and she would have collapsed if he hadn't been holding her waist so tightly.

"Walk!" he growled.

"I can't breathe," she managed to choke out.

"As if I care," he responded, but he shifted his palm, his fingers sliding into her hair and fisting there.

She took a deep breath, ignoring the burning pain of her hair being pulled from her head. She didn't care if she went bald. As long as she could breathe.

They reached the end of the hall and turned left, moving into a narrow corridor that led to the building's only elevator. An emergency exit was there, too. Just a few short steps away.

If she could get there and push open the door, an alarm would sound. Help would come.

She hoped.

Please, God, she prayed silently. *Give me an opportunity to escape.*

She imagined her mother had done the same when she had seen Martin Roker pointing a gun at her across the parking lot. Sasha had tried, over the years, to block those thoughts from her head, to not think about the last moments of her mother's life, to not contemplate the terror she must have felt, the desperation to survive.

Now she couldn't stop thinking about it.

She couldn't stop wondering if her mother had turned and run or tried to reason with her killer. There had been witness statements given to the police, shocked coworkers who had given hints of what had happened.

Martin calling her mother's name.

Her mother turning.

A shot ringing out.

Sasha steeled herself as her attacker tried to press the elevator call button with his elbow.

He cursed under his breath and tried again without success.

"Push the button!" he demanded. "Now!"

She almost did, her arm twitching and then falling to her side.

"I can't," she lied. "You're holding my arms too tightly."

He cursed again, loosening the arm that held hers down. Not completely. But enough.

"Push it!" he nearly screamed.

She jabbed at the button, then shoved backward and slammed him into the wall. The thud seemed to shake the floor.

His arms fell away, and she ran to the exit, slamming her palm against the bar that opened the door, stumbling through as a siren shrieked and he snagged her coat.

She teetered on the metal landing of an exterior fire escape, her heels stuck through holes that allowed rain to drain through the floor.

She kicked out of them, throwing off her coat and whirling around, slamming both arms into Roker's chest. He stumbled back. She tried to run, but he snagged her ankle, pulling her leg out from under her. Her chin hit the metal railing, and she saw stars, tasted more blood.

She didn't have time to think about it.

Didn't have time for anything but action.

She kicked hard, slamming her foot into Roker's head and scrambling away, the siren still screaming. A dog barked. A man called out.

Roker was gone, metal clanging and shaking as he ran up the fire escape.

Bradley pulled his firearm as he and King ran up the fire escape. He didn't dare shoot. Not with Sasha between him and the perp. His heart raced as he watched a blond-haired thin man sprint up the fire escape, step onto the roof and disappear from view. He couldn't see a face or features, but the build, hair and height seemed to be the same as the guy who had fired into the diner.

The Martin Roker look-alike had been inside the building while they were out disarming the bomb he'd planted. The fact that Bradley had allowed himself to be distracted was infuriating. He knew what people were capable of. He understood how dangerous the world could be.

His mistake could have cost Sasha her life.

She lay still on the second-floor landing, her stockinged feet hanging over the edge of the first step.

Had she been injured?

Worse?

King reached her side and darted past, his desire to apprehend the suspect superseding everything else.

He bounded up to the next landing, heading toward the roof.

Bradley didn't dare let him go farther. Not with other officers and security personnel racing through the building and heading up to the roof. Anyone on the move would be King's target.

"Cease," he yelled as the Malinois jumped onto the roof.

No fear. No worry. No concern for the three-story drop.

As if a switch had been flicked off, King stopped.

"Come!"

King reluctantly returned to the fire escape and headed back down the stairs.

Bradley got to Sasha's side and reached for her neck,

his fingers brushing over warm flesh as he searched for her pulse.

"My heart is beating just fine," she muttered, flipping onto her back and looking into his eyes. There was blood dripping from a deep cut on her chin, but she looked more angry than hurt, her eyes flashing. She sat up.

"Not too fast," he said, putting a hand on her shoulder to make certain she didn't topple over.

"If I fall over and give myself another gash in the face, it will be my fault. I can't believe I did something so stupid." She grabbed her coat and pressed it against her chin. "I'm sorry about this, Bradley."

"Why should you apologize because a lunatic is hunting you?"

"Because if I'd stayed in my office like you'd asked me to, he wouldn't have had a chance to grab me," she responded, using his shoulder to push herself to her feet.

She seemed steady enough, her bloodied, bruised knees flashing through holes in her stockings.

"I should have called and let you know what was going on," he replied, impressed by her willingness to own her mistakes.

"You can fill me in after you get that guy," she replied, pointing to the roof. "He can't have gone far."

He didn't tell her that he could have gone any number of places—back inside the building, down another fire escape, onto another roof. The buildings in this neighborhood were close enough together that someone brave or foolish enough might make the leap.

"You guys okay up there?" Henry called, Cody baying excitedly as they both headed up the stairs.

"She needs an ambulance," Bradley replied.

"What she needs is for you to stop hovering over her and go chase the perp," Sasha corrected.

"I'm glad to see that the knock on your head didn't damage your ability to argue," he said, smiling as she scowled.

"I'm not arguing. I'm simply pointing out that, while you are standing here babysitting me, the guy who fired the shot into the diner and planted a bomb under your Jeep is escaping."

"We've got officers heading up to the roof, ma'am," Henry said as he reached the landing. "Once the alarm sounded, we figured the perp might be trying to make his way out of the building without being spotted."

"He's escaped before," Sasha pointed out, pulling the coat away and probing the still-bleeding wound. "Doesn't feel like it needs stitches. Maybe some superglue. I've got some at home."

"Superglue?" Bradley asked, leaning in for a closer look.

"Sure. That's what I did when I was a kid and my father was working. If I cut myself, I'd clean it out and glue the wound shut. Works like a charm."

Henry snorted. "I'm heading up to the roof. Don't forget, McGregor. You're off duty."

He didn't need the reminder.

He was very aware that he and King were sidelined. There were plenty of K-9 teams and police officers who could give chase, but he could admit he wanted in on it. He wanted to find the guy who had hurt Sasha, and he wanted to make him pay.

He frowned as he watched Henry and Cody race up the fire escape.

"You're upset," Sasha commented.

"Frustrated."

"Because?"

"King is one of the best apprehension dogs in the nation. It would be great if we could go after this guy."

"You really don't have to stay with me, Detective," she said, glancing down at the crowd of EMS personnel gathering in the alley below them. "There are plenty of people to keep an eye on me until you get back."

"That's not the way things work. I'm off duty. When I'm off duty, King and I don't get to chase bad guys."

"Then what do you get to do?"

"Chase seagulls, Frisbees and squirrels. Turn the local dog park into a dog wrestling ground. Laundry."

She laughed, wincing as she pressed the coat to her chin again. "Aside from the laundry, that sounds like a fun day."

"You think so?"

"Of course. Who doesn't love chasing seagulls, Frisbees and squirrels?" Her eyes were deep amber in the sunlight, her lashes thick and dark. She had a few freckles on her nose and cheeks that stood in stark contrast to her pale skin.

"Do you need to sit down?" he asked, alarmed by her pallor.

"No. I need to get myself cleaned up and get to police headquarters. I want to give my statement and look at the lineup."

"That can wait, Sasha."

"Until?" she asked, taking a step down and then another.

"You're feeling better."

"You know what will make me feel better, Detective? Figuring out what all this is about, knowing the guy who's been stalking me has been caught and is behind bars, moving on with my life." Her voice shook, and he touched her shoulder as he followed her down the stairs. Close enough to catch her if she fell. Far enough away that she might not realize he was hovering.

"It's going to be okay," he said.

"Of course it will be," she responded. "It's always okay eventually, but for right now, it isn't. For right now, I need answers."

"I understand."

"Do you?" she asked, as she reached the first-floor landing. Several EMTs were rolling a gurney through the alley, the wheels bouncing over holes in the asphalt.

"Yes. Are you familiar with the Emery murders?"

"Who in Sheepshead Bay isn't?"

"You probably also know there were a lot of similarities between that double homicide and my parents' murders. Until we figure out who killed the Emerys and why, I'm not going to be able to rest."

"Your K-9 unit caught your parents' murderer last month, didn't they? And everyone seems to think the Emerys' killer was a copycat."

He nodded. "I was cleared of being a suspect in my parents' murders a long time ago, Sasha. But the murders of the Emerys brought it all back for me for exactly that reason—a copycat. Sometimes, late at night, I wonder if people are thinking, 'Hey, maybe it was Bradley McGregor wearing that clown mask this time around, getting revenge on another neglectful set of parents, getting revenge for being considered a suspect when he wasn't the killer.'"

"Oh, no, Bradley. That's awful. No one thinks that."

He shrugged. "Probably not. But that's what goes

through my mind in the middle of the night when I can't sleep. I need to catch the Emerys' killer so that I can finally move on."

"I'm sorry you're going through this," she said, her eyes filled with sympathy that he hadn't expected.

He was used to people assuming that his childhood and his life had made him tough. He cultivated a gruff persona that convinced people he wasn't easily hurt, but that was because he had been hurt. It was because the wounds were still there, open and raw. Never healing because the gossip and whispers had never stopped in his own head. No matter how hard he had worked or how upright a life he lived, he couldn't stop thinking that some people were going to believe he was cut from the same cloth as his parents. He wished he could let it all go. Wished he could believe it when his colleagues told him how respected he was in the community, in the K-9 unit itself.

"I didn't tell you so you would be sorry," he said gruffly. "I told you because I want you to know that I understand how much of a hold the past has. I know what it's like to want answers. To *need* them."

She reached street level, stepped off the fire escape and turned to face him as EMTs swarmed around her. "I'll help you find what you're looking for," she said.

He had no idea what she meant and no chance to say that every officer on the K-9 unit had been helping him for seven months. The EMTs began looking at her cut, asking her questions, getting medical information that they were relaying to the hospital.

He wanted to stay behind and wait for news about the perp's apprehension.

Or his escape.

He also wanted to stick close to Sasha's side.

He liked her positive attitude, her determination, her drive. And he wanted to know more about her life, her job, her friends and hobbies. She interested him in a way few women had in the past decade. He'd spent years pursuing his career as he helped raise his sister. Their adoptive parents had been in their sixties when she graduated from high school. Joe and Allison Brady had given everything they had to make certain Bradley and Penny had the love and support they needed. They had died within weeks of each other—Allison from cancer, Joe from a heart attack. Losing them had left a gaping hole that Bradley had spent the past four years trying to fill. He had supported Penny as she finished her education, encouraged her as she pursued her career. He had given her a place to live rent free, and he had enjoyed her company, enjoyed knowing she was safe in bed at night.

He hadn't had time for more than that. Not with his hectic workload. But Penny would be getting married soon. She'd move out and create a whole new life for herself. It was what Bradley had been wanting, what he had been praying for—that she would have whatever life she wanted.

He was happy for her. Happy for himself, too. He had accomplished what he had promised he would when his parents had come home from the hospital with a tiny little girl wrapped in one of his old blankets. He had known then that he would have to protect her, care for her and give her what he knew their parents wouldn't. He had promised himself that he would make sure she grew up, got her education and had a better life than the one she had been born into.

Done, done and done.

Now he could focus on pursuing his dreams.

Whatever they might be.

Work, sure.

He'd known from the day he had been cleared of his parents' murders that he would go into law enforcement.

But there were other things he'd dreamed of while he was a young beat cop working his way up the ranks. Friendship. Love. Someone to go home to at night.

Maybe that was why he noticed how attractive and intelligent Sasha was. Maybe his subconscious mind was reminding him that he had a life to live, too. At thirty-four, it wasn't too late to achieve the life he had put on hold while his sister pursued her education and established herself as a vital part of the K-9 unit.

He followed the EMTs as they escorted Sasha to the ambulance.

He could hear her soft voice through the more strident tones of the men and women who were treating her.

"Seriously, just hand me some superglue and let me be on my way," she said.

He smiled as one of the EMTs explained that the cut was going to require more than a couple of dabs of glue.

"Then just bandage me up. I have places to be."

Bradley's grin widened as he jostled his way through what seemed like an army of medical professionals.

"Tell them, Detective," she said as she caught sight of him. He thought she might have smiled, but it was hard to see through the gauze bandage that was wrapped around the lower part of her face.

"If King can ride along, we'll escort you to the hospital and then to headquarters once you're stitched up," he replied.

"That wasn't what I was hoping you'd say," she muttered, but she seemed to give in to the inevitable, allowing herself to be helped onto the back of the ambulance.

He flashed his badge at one of the EMTs. "Mind if my partner and I ride along?"

"Not a problem, as long as he isn't planning on taking a chunk out of the crew."

"He's too well trained for that," he responded, jumping on board. King followed, sitting down beside him, his head on his paws, his expressive eyes conveying just how disgusted he was with the turn of events.

"Sorry, buddy," Bradley said. "I'll make this up to you tomorrow."

"With a trip to the beach to chase gulls?" Sasha asked, leaning her head back against the side of the ambulance and closing her eyes.

"That and a trip to the dog park," he responded. "If you're up to it, maybe you'd like to join us." The invitation slipped out, and her eyes flew open.

"So you can keep an eye on me?" she asked.

It would have been easy to agree, to let her think he wasn't thinking about other things—like getting to know her, spending time with her, enjoying a relaxing afternoon with someone who didn't seem to have any agenda except kindness.

"What would you say if I said there were other reasons?" he responded, because he believed in shooting straight and speaking plainly.

She eyed him for a moment, the white gauze making her expression difficult to read.

Finally, she nodded.

"You know what? I'd like that," she said, and he was surprised at just how happy that made him.

"Me, too," he said as the ambulance lurched forward and headed to the hospital.

EIGHT

The cut on her chin hadn't been nearly as bad as everyone had seemed to think it was. The doctor at the emergency room had cleaned it, glued it and pressed a gauze bandage over the area.

Nothing she couldn't have done herself.

She fingered the bandage as she paced her hotel room. Bradley had escorted her there after she had given her statement and chosen Martin Roker from a picture lineup—with the added explanation that the man stalking her had been a carbon copy, not Martin Roker himself, of course. Bradley had insisted on walking her to her room and checking every corner of it. Then he had stood on the threshold, his jaw dark with a five-o'clock shadow, his eyes red-rimmed with fatigue, and made her promise to stay locked inside until he returned the following afternoon.

For their...

Appointment?

Meeting?

Date?

She shied away from the last word, refusing to acknowledge it. She didn't date. Michael had cured her of the desire for male companionship.

At least, that was what she always told herself.

Her college sweetheart, Michael had been exactly the man she had thought she wanted in her life—charismatic and charming, caring and compassionate. His faith had seemed stronger than hers, his understanding of the Bible impressive. He had taught men's Bible studies at college and been a youth leader at his church.

She had fallen for him quickly when they'd met at church during her sophomore year. He'd been a law student, getting ready to take the bar. She'd been studying communications, hoping for a career in journalism. He had swept her off her feet with phone calls and flowers and little notes to tell her he was thinking about her.

It had felt like the real deal, the happily-ever-after.

They'd married two days after she'd graduated. He had passed the bar the following week. On paper, they worked. A power couple ready to make a difference in the world. She had adored him, and she had thought he'd felt the same about her.

She had been wrong.

He had cheated on her twice during their short marriage. She had forgiven him the first time. The second time, he had chosen to walk away. Five years of marriage, and he'd fallen in love with someone more exciting, more interesting, more passionate. At least, that was the way he'd described it. Sasha figured he had simply gotten bored with his straitlaced life. He had walked away from the Bible studies and joined a fitness club. He had traded Bible quotes in for inspirational speeches. He practiced law, but his real passion was encouraging people to live their best lives, and his best life had not included staying with someone who believed in traditional marriage and traditional values.

Boring.

Michael had used the word over and over again as he had explained why he was packing his bags and filing for divorce.

She had wanted to deny it, but there had been a small part of her that had thought he might be right. She had been in her twenties and working hard to balance being married with building her career.

Working long hours, returning home to spend frantic minutes tossing together a meal she and Michael could eat together. Wearing flannel pajamas to bed. Throwing her hair up into a ponytail every day. Her mother's murder had taught her that life could be unpredictable, and she had made it a habit to do everything she could to protect herself from the unexpected.

Maybe her marriage had died because of it.

Or maybe Michael was just a lying, cheating jerk.

She frowned, the skin on her chin pulling painfully. She walked to the mirror and pulled off the bandage.

The cut was on the underside of her chin, the skin around it bruised and swollen. She had nearly died a few hours ago. One misstep and she would have.

She touched a dark smudge on her cheek. A fingertip-sized mark that had probably been made when Roker dug his hand into her face to keep her from screaming.

There were several more on her neck.

She'd changed into pajamas after Bradley left, and her pale legs peeked out from beneath the hem of oversize sleep shorts. Her knees were raw and bruised, but she was here. She was breathing. She had more time to pursue the plans God had for her.

Whatever they might be.

She sighed, dropping into a chair and grabbing her laptop from the desk. She typed in her password, typed the name Emery into the search bar and watched as hundreds of articles popped up. Sheepshead Bay had been consumed by the story, caught up in the way history had repeated itself.

A copycat murder twenty years to the date the Mc-Gregors had been killed. A young survivor the sole witness. Not enough physical evidence to pin the crime on anyone. Like everyone else in the area, Sasha was familiar with the case. She knew the Brooklyn K-9 Unit had been working tirelessly to apprehend the person responsible.

Her job required her to search for good-news stories.

This certainly wasn't one. Lucy Emery had been neglected by her parents. There were a few articles about neighbors who'd seen the little girl playing alone in the front yard at just three years old. People coming and going from the two-family house. The litter that cluttered the yard. The broken toys she was often seen playing with.

Sasha could recall reading that Lucy's aunt Willow, her father's sister, had constantly tried to intervene and was constantly turned away by her brother and sister-in-law. In fact, the day of the murders, Willow had gone over to the home to give the Emerys an ultimatum about Lucy and the lack of care. She'd found her brother and sister-in-law dead. Her niece crying and alone. Now Willow and her husband, another detective on the K-9 team, were raising Lucy in a safe, loving home.

Sasha skimmed several articles, jotting notes and making a list of neighbors who had been willing to talk to the press. She knew the neighborhood. She'd covered several feel-good stories there, highlighting the good that came out of poverty and struggle. Maybe people would be willing to tell her things that they hadn't wanted to say to the police. She knew from news conferences that local authorities were searching for someone named Andy. Someone that Lucy Emery insisted was her friend, and who the police wanted to speak to regarding the Emery murders.

If Andy was a friend of Lucy's parents, perhaps he or she knew something that would lead investigators to the murderer. Sasha had no intention of sticking her nose in where it wasn't wanted, but she didn't see any reason to not visit the neighborhood, take a few pictures of the crime scene and see if any of the neighbors were willing to talk to her.

She could do a story on it. A switch from her normal, but still with a happy ending. A neglected child finding love and security after her parents' deaths.

It was a story that had played out before.

One she had been fascinated with since she had heard about the seeming connection between the Emery and McGregor murders. Bradley and Penelope McGregor could have chosen to go down the path their parents had taken. Both had been neglected. Bradley had been his sister's primary caregiver during the years their parents were alive. When they died, he had been accused of the murders, brought in for questioning, been found guilty in the court of public opinion.

And still, somehow, he had found a way out of what he had been born into. He had focused his energy on justice. He had pursued law enforcement the way other people might have pursued drugs or alcohol or crime.

She was fascinated by that, curious about the spirit that had driven him, the people who had stood behind him, the strength of character that had sustained him when his entire world had crumbled.

Maybe that was why she wanted to help him find the Emerys' killer. She wanted him to have closure so that he could move on without wondering if there were whispered accusations following him. Granted, all that was lodged in his gut. But she understood.

That wasn't why she had agreed to go to the beach with him and King, though. Yes, it would be an outing, not focused on work, where she would be safe in the presence of an armed detective.

The real reason: she liked Bradley.

She was interested in learning more about him.

Not for the cable show. For herself.

"There," she said, setting her laptop on the table and crossing the room. She pulled back the curtain that covered the window and stared into the dark night. "You admitted you like him. Was that so hard?"

Not as hard as having another broken heart would be.

Just take it one day at a time. See about the business of living today before you worry about what might come tomorrow.

That was what her father would say to her if he was around.

It was good advice, but harder to live than she wanted to admit. She liked to have a plan. She liked to know what was coming next. The unknown scared her.

And relationships?

They were filled with unknowns and dark corners and unexpected twists and turns.

Her cell phone rang, and she jumped, nearly tumbling in her haste to grab it from the charging port. "Hello," she said breathlessly.

"Sasha? It's Bradley. Is everything all right?"

"Fine," she managed to say, her foolish heart jumping with joy at the sound of his voice.

"You sure? You sound out of breath."

"The phone startled me."

"Still on edge after the incident at work?" he asked, his voice warm with concern.

"A little. Do you have news?"

"Not as much as we'd like. After the bomb squad disarmed the bomb, the evidence team was able to get a fingerprint off the adhesive that was used to stick it to the underside of my Jeep."

"Any matches in the data bank?"

"Unfortunately, no, but I put a call in to the DNA lab. I have a friend there who is expediting the test on the blood we found on the note."

"Do you really think it belongs to the perpetrator?" she asked. "He isn't stupid, and leaving DNA evidence is."

"He's smart enough to be cocky. Or thinks he is. Perps like that make plenty of mistakes, because they think they are too smart to get caught."

"I hope you're right. I hope it's his, and I hope there's a match in the system."

"Even if there isn't, we may be able to find him. Our tech guru is looking for family connections to Martin Roker. And there are ancestry registries online that give people an opportunity to connect with long-lost family members. One of our officers knows how to run DNA through the system to look for family matches. I also asked the local police station that handled your mother's case if there was anything left in connection."

"It's a closed file. Why would they keep evidence?"

"An officer-involved shooting is a big deal. Sometimes family shows up years later and claims undue force."

"It's been eighteen years."

"Right. I wasn't sure there would be anything," he said. She heard people talking in the background. Phones ringing.

"Are you still at the office?" she asked.

"Yes. The team is meeting in a few minutes. I wanted to call you before then."

"It's your day off."

"I'm not sure I know what that means," he said with a quiet chuckle. "Regarding the evidence in your mom's murder investigation, the handgun Roker used was in the box, along with his wallet and gloves he wore when he committed the crime. I had the evidence team swab for DNA, and I sent that and the gloves to the lab. Just in case the person who is after you is related."

"For someone who has a day off, you are certainly working hard."

"I want this guy behind bars. The sooner it happens, the happier I'll be. You're still in your room?"

"Locked in and not going anywhere."

"Good. I'd worry about you if I thought you were wandering around without protection. My meeting is about to start. Try to get some rest, Sasha. I'll check in before I leave tonight and call after my shift tomorrow to see if there's anything you want me to bring when I pick you up."

"Talk to you later," she said, not wanting the call to end.

But he disconnected, and she set the phone back in the port, her stomach doing a crazy little flip of excitement. Bradley wasn't trying to be charming. He didn't seem to want to impress or disarm her. He was doing his job the way he always did and taking the time to update her on the steps he was taking to find her stalker.

It was what she imagined he would do for the victim of any crime. She couldn't see him changing his routine to impress a woman or trying harder because he wanted to seem more driven or more interesting. From what she had seen, Bradley was exactly who he seemed—a focused police detective who gave everything he had to the job.

She found that very attractive and very intriguing.

That scared her, but not enough to make her back out of tomorrow's beach run.

She grabbed her computer and settled into the chair again.

Warm, fuzzy feelings were great, but until her stalker was behind bars and the Emery murders had been solved, there wouldn't be anything else. There couldn't be. They were both too focused and intent to veer from the course set in front of them.

Meetings were about as much fun as root canals.

And usually took three times longer.

The entire team had gathered, some of them with their dogs. Some alone. King was under Bradley's chair, huffing quietly every few minutes. Obviously miffed about the long day indoors.

Bradley shifted in his seat, the pad of paper in front

of him covered in notes about Sasha's case and about the Emery murders. Since the arrest of Randall Gage, the man who had murdered Bradley's parents, the Emery case had grown too cold for his liking. The newest information they had was from Gage, and it hadn't helped much. Detective Tyler Walker, Bradley's future brother-in-law, had gone to see Randall Gage in prison and had asked for help—his take on why the copycat killer had acted. Gage had said that they needed to look for someone the Emerys had wronged. Maybe a drug deal gone bad. Money owed. Something that made the need for revenge or repayment paramount. He had also claimed that if the killer had seen Lucy Emery being neglected the way he had seen Penelope McGregor being neglected, he had probably figured they deserved everything they got. Children deserved better than parents like that, and Randall Gage seemed to think he and the Emerys' murderer had done the world a favor. He also thought that if the police wanted to find the killer, they needed to find someone who knew the family well, someone who knew Lucy well.

"That brings us back to Andy," Bradley said.

Gavin looked up from notes he was reading through. "What does?"

"The information Tyler got from Randall Gage. If he's right, we need to find someone who was close enough to Lucy Emery to care that her parents were neglecting her. Someone who might have used that as a secondary reason to murder them."

"Right. If we find Andy, I think we may just find the perp," Tyler agreed from his place across the table.

Someone knocked on the door to the conference room. It swung open, and his sister walked in, a large box of carryout coffee in one hand and a stack of disposable cups in the other. Anyone looking at him and Penny would know they were siblings. They were both tall, and though Penny's hair was red and his was more auburn, they had the same dark brown eyes.

"Don't expect this every time," she announced with a grin as she set everything on the conference table. "I have more important things to do with my time than keep you all awake."

She glanced at Tyler, a soft smile on her face.

They made a good couple.

That didn't mean Bradley hadn't warned his future brother-in-law about the consequences of hurting his sister.

"Thanks, Penny," Bradley said, and she turned her smile in his direction.

"No problem. I'm heading home. I'll see you when you get there." She bustled out of the room. Quick. Efficient. Cheerful. The K-9 unit wouldn't function as effectively without her. Bradley hated the flashes of memory that would overtake him at the most random times. His sister being hunted by Randall Gage last month, determined to "get rid of the witness" he'd left behind twenty years ago. With Gage awaiting trial and sure to go down for a long time, Penny would be safe. Especially married to a detective Bradley knew well and trusted.

Bradley was proud of his sister, proud of what his Penny was accomplishing, the reputation she had built for herself in the short time she had been there. She'd survived so much and was stronger for it. He hoped Penny knew how much he admired her. He had a feeling she did.

For a few moments, the group chatted as coffee was poured and cups passed around. Bradley sipped his, ignoring King's impatient nudge.

"I think we should go back to the Emerys' neighbors," Henry said, drawing everyone's focus back to the case. "Ask around again. Someone has to know Andy. Someone who wasn't comfortable saying so before. Who knows—maybe this Andy guy got to the neighbors and threatened them when we first started coming around asking about him."

"We've been through that neighborhood dozens of times," Jackson Davison pointed out. "But if it'll help, I don't mind asking around again. Maybe a new face will bring new answers."

"We can only hope," Gavin responded with a tired sigh. "This case is dragging on, and the media is still having a heyday with it. Hopefully Ms. Eastman isn't going to do a show on it."

"Sasha Eastman?" Officer Vivienne Armstrong asked. "From that cable television show? Good news only, or something like that. What's she have to do with the Emery case?"

"She was here last week, hoping to get an interview with Penny and Bradley," Tyler said, an edge of disgust in his voice. "Now she's claiming that a stalker is after her."

"She's not claiming," Bradley cut in. "A stalker *is* after her. I saw the guy going after her today at her office building. He's the same person who planted explosives under my Jeep. And the one who shot at her the other day."

"Her mother was murdered eighteen years ago," Gavin said. "Whoever is after her seems to have a connection to that. Any news on the DNA evidence, Bradley? You said you asked to have it expedited?"

"Right. They can usually move it through quickly. My friend at the lab said they might have something for us by the early a.m. And Eden is checking deeper into Roker's past."

Tyler nodded, stifling a yawn before taking a quick sip of coffee. Everyone was running on fumes, but adrenaline and the call for justice kept them all going. "I may have needed this more than I thought."

"We've covered everything pressing," the sergeant said. "If you want to visit the Emerys' neighborhood, I'd appreciate it, Jackson. I'm ready to close this case."

"No problem. I'll head out there during my shift Sunday. See what I can dig up."

"Good. Let's set another meeting for a couple days from now. Hopefully by then we'll have more answers than questions." Gavin stood, the rest of the team following suit. The group filed out, officers, dogs, the quiet murmur of voices and rustle of K-9 fur a familiar and comforting melody.

Law enforcement had been Bradley's life for more than a decade. He enjoyed what he did. If pressed, he told people he felt called to it.

But there was more to life.

The members of the K-9 unit seemed to have been discovering that over the past few months. One by one, they had found love, and he had watched with shock and amusement as they had fallen hard and fast.

The romances had begun back in April, when his friend and colleague Detective Nate Slater answered a homicide call at the Emery house and met newly orphaned Lucy and her aunt Willow. The tragic case had brought them together, and now Lucy was safe and well cared for, Nate's K-9 partner, Murphy, a gentle yellow Lab, the little girl's extra protector.

Bradley glanced over at narcotics officer Raymond Morrow, who'd been reunited with an old flame when a dangerous drug dealer had come after Karenna Pressley. Ray sure was happier these days. As was Officer Belle Montera, her German shepherd partner, Justice, walking beside her to her desk. Belle had had the difficult task of convincing a known relative of Randall Gage to give up his family member for the sake of justice. Thanks to the efforts of both Belle and US marshal Emmett Gage, the killer of his and Penny's parents was behind bars and facing trial.

Detective Henry Roarke's K-9 partner, Cody, a cute beagle, let out a little bay. Everyone glanced over as Henry gave Cody his favorite new toy to play with beside his chair. Bradley had been worried for Henry for a while when he'd been under investigation by IA, but he and investigator Olivia Vance were now planning a wedding. Officer Vivienne Armstrong passed by Henry's chair with her own K-9 partner, Hank, a black-and-white border collie, grinning at Cody, who was enjoying his stuffed moose. Vivienne was now engaged to Caleb Black, the FBI agent who'd been on Randall Gage's trail. Then there was Officer Jackson Davison, who'd managed the impossible: convincing forensic scientist Darcy Fields to give up her rule against dating cops for him.

Of all the new couples among his friends and co-workers in the K-9 unit, the one that brought him some measure of peace, allowed him to get a little more sleep at night, was Penny and Tyler. With Randall Gage in prison, Penny was safe—and always would be with Tyler by her side.

Lots of happy couples. As for Bradley, he figured his path was already written in stone. When Penny had admitted her love for Tyler, he had been happy for her, but there had been a hint of something beneath the surface of that. Emptiness. Longing. The sickening feeling that life was passing, and he had devoted himself to something that would never devote itself to him.

Law enforcement was his calling, but one day he would retire. He and his K-9 partner would spend their days on the beach or exploring parks. Maybe he would have nieces and nephews. Obviously, he would have friends, but there was loneliness in the thought of growing old without someone to talk to late at night or wake up with in the morning.

Years ago, he had made the decision to devote himself to his sister, to make certain she had the happiest, most stable upbringing possible. Once she was grown, he had put the extra energy and time into his job, telling himself that romance and relationships were for men who weren't committed to justice the way he was.

That used to satisfy him.

Lately, though, those reasons didn't seem strong enough to make him spend the rest of his life alone.

"Come on, King," he said, suddenly exhausted and ready to put the day behind him. Hopefully by the time he arrived home, he'd be ready to take King for a run. Even at this time of the night, the Malinois needed to expend energy. First, though, he'd check in on Sasha, even though it was late. He'd been busy tonight, but she'd been front and center in his thoughts. He knew she was safe at the hotel, that she'd call him if she needed him. But he wanted to hear her voice.

That was unnerving.

He pressed in her number, relieved when she answered right away. She sounded tired.

"Everything okay?" he asked.

"Yup," she said. "Thanks for checking in. But I'm locked in, no trouble here all night." She let out a little yawn. "I'm ready to turn in. See you tomorrow, Bradley."

He was looking forward to just that a little too much. "See you tomorrow," he said, disconnecting and putting his phone in his pocket, Sasha's face, her voice, lingering in his mind.

The streets were nearly empty as he drove home. He didn't bother sitting down, just changed into running gear and headed out into the night. Chilly November air stung his cheeks as he and King did their normal three-mile loop. When they finished, he walked King to a small park and allowed him to sniff bushes and rocks before they returned home.

It was nearly two by the time they returned home. King was finally content, his tail wagging happily as he sprang onto Bradley's bed and settled down for the night.

Trying to be as quiet as possible so he didn't wake up Penny, who was asleep in the bedroom across the hall, Bradley showered quickly, anxious to get a few hours of sleep before the alarm went off and he had to get ready for work again.

He'd barely laid his head on the pillow when his phone rang, the shrill sound making King raise his head and huff softly.

Bradley grabbed the phone from the nightstand. "Hello?"

"Bradley? It's Mitch from the lab."

"You're working late," he said, suddenly wide-awake.

"We have a lot piled up, and I wanted to prioritize yours. We pulled DNA from the sample you sent. Male. European ancestry. No match in the criminal database that I can find."

"You already ran it? You've gone above and beyond, Mitch."

"Just doing my job and helping out a friend. I've sent you an email with information that you can use to find connections in public ancestry searches, but, to be honest, I got curious and ran it through a few myself."

"You're not calling because there wasn't a match," Bradley said, flipping on the light and grabbing a paper and pen from his desk drawer.

"You know me well," Mitch chuckled. "Okay. Here's what I've got. The DNA donor is related to Wanda Anderson."

"Not a name I'm familiar with."

"Would you be if I told you she'd once filed a restraining order against Martin Roker? I called Eden Chang and asked her to look into that connection, and guess what?"

His heart skipped a beat, and he scribbled the name, his mind racing with possibilities.

"The restraining order was a domestic violence situation," Mitch continued. "Wanda had been in a relationship with Martin. And since the donor is a close family relative of hers, Eden did some digging. Wanda had a child out of wedlock, a son named Landon Anderson.

He would have been in his early twenties when Martin Roker died."

"And in his early forties now," Bradley said, the puzzle pieces fitting together. Landon Anderson was no doubt Martin Roker's son.

"Roker has only one child on record with his estranged wife, a daughter, Ashley. The son with Wanda Anderson slipped through the cracks in the databases."

"I can't thank you enough for going the extra mile on this," Bradley said. "And thank Eden for me if you talk to her before I do."

"I will," Mitch said. "And no problem. Your dad and I went way back. He mentored me when I worked on the force years ago. He's the reason I went into this work. He was always looking ahead, thinking about the next thing on the horizon, as far as forensic evidence."

"He was a great guy and a fantastic police officer. I was very fortunate that he took me and my sister in."

"Funny you say that. He always used to tell me how blessed he was to have a son and a daughter he could be so proud of. Take care, Bradley. Call me anytime."

He disconnected, and Bradley dropped the phone on the desk, booting up his computer and logging in to the police database remotely. He input the names and birth dates, waiting as the system processed his request.

"Everything okay?" Penny called through the closed door.

"Yeah. Come on in," he responded as he scanned the information he'd pulled up.

She opened the door, yawning and stretching. "What are you doing?"

"I think I may know who's been stalking Sasha Eastman," he responded.

"Who?" she asked, walking across the room and leaning over his shoulder.

He tapped the photo on the screen. "Landon Anderson." He read the name on the man's driver's license. "Martin Roker's look-alike son."

"But why?" Penny asked, dropping onto the bed the way she had so many times in the past.

He would miss that when she was gone.

He would miss having late-night conversations with a sister who was more like a daughter to him.

"I don't know, but I plan to find out and stop him."

"Hopefully sooner rather than later. Being stalked by Gage was a horrible experience. I still have nightmares about it."

"Is that why you're awake?"

"I'm awake because I heard you come in, and I wanted to check in with you. Make sure things were going okay." There was something she wasn't saying. He could hear it in her voice.

"What's wrong, Penny?" he asked.

"Nothing."

"Something," he corrected, and she smiled.

"I just… Things are changing, you know? I'm going to get married and move away, and you're going to be here alone."

"King is offended by that statement," he joked, hoping to lighten her mood.

"King understands what I'm saying. He doesn't want you to be lonely, either."

"I'm not going to be lonely, and you don't need to worry about me."

"We've always been a team, Bradley."

"We still will be. You'll just have a slightly more important member added to your part of our little group."

"Slightly?" She laughed, standing up and swatting him on the shoulder. "How about differently important?"

"Fine. We'll call it that," he replied, looking into her face and seeing her as she was. An adult. Accomplished and hardworking. Smart. Loyal. She was nothing like their biological parents and everything that he had ever hoped for her.

"Why are you looking at me like that?" she said, grabbing his hand and pulling him to his feet.

"Because I'm proud of you and happy for you, and I don't want you to waste another second worrying about what's going to happen to me when you're gone."

"That's like me telling you not to worry. Say it all you want, but I'm still going to be concerned. I love you, Bradley. You are the best big brother a girl could have."

"I love you, too. That won't ever change. Now go back to bed! You have to work in the morning."

She gave him a quick hug and walked out of the room, closing the door behind her. The little girl he would have done almost anything to protect now a grown woman in love, getting married, planning her future.

He prayed she would be happy. That her life would be all the things it hadn't been when their biological parents were raising them.

And he prayed that she would never know the truth: that the house was going to feel a whole lot emptier without her in it.

NINE

The phone rang at just after five in the morning.

Sasha was wide-awake, doing her best to focus on the script she was writing for Wednesday's show. She'd had a restless night, filled with nightmares. In all of them, Martin Roker was chasing her through the streets of Brooklyn, screaming that she was next.

She shuddered, pushing the thought from her mind as she grabbed the phone. "Hello?"

"It's Bradley. Sorry for calling so early, but we've had a break in the case, and I wanted to keep you updated."

"What kind of break?" She sat up straight, her pulse racing with a mixture of excitement and dread.

"We got a DNA hit from an ancestry database, and we traced the sample to Roker's forty-one-year-old son, Landon."

"He had a son?" she asked, shocked by the news. She'd thought he had only had a daughter with his estranged wife, the woman he'd left to pursue Sasha's mother.

"Landon Anderson. The result of an affair Martin had with a woman named Wanda Anderson. She'd filed a restraining order against him. According to records, Landon was a computer tech for a public school on Staten Island until recently."

"Like his father." That was how Martin and Sasha's mother had met—in the computer lab at the school where she taught.

"Right. From what I've been able to gather, he had a few other of his father's…characteristics."

"Like?"

"He became obsessed with a teacher at the school. She filed a protective order, and he lost his job. After that, he moved to Brooklyn."

"Why?"

"That's a good question. I'm hoping to ask him. We have a search warrant for his residence and are outside his apartment complex. I've got to go, but I wanted you to be in the loop."

"Be careful," she managed to say before he could end the call.

"I will be," he responded, his voice so soft and warm, she was smiling when she set the phone down.

She expected he would call back within the hour.

She'd worked the crime beat for enough years to know how quickly the police moved in on suspects. She'd interviewed witnesses and knew that a person could be in bed one minute and in a police car the next.

She tried to concentrate on the script.

When that didn't work, she turned on the television, flipping through news channels, hoping to find a story about Landon Anderson being led from his apartment in handcuffs.

Nothing there.

She tried the internet, googling the name.

Tried the police beat.

If they'd found him, they weren't making it public.

She glanced at her watch, talked herself out of calling Bradley. He'd said he would contact her with updates. She didn't want to interrupt whatever he was doing. Especially if what he was doing was dangerous.

But she was on edge and filled with nervous energy.

If she hadn't promised that she would stay in the room, she would have jogged up and down the hotel stairs a few times, just to get rid of some of her restlessness.

She made the bed, opened the curtains and tried her best not to think about what Bradley and his team were doing. She wanted Landon Anderson caught. She didn't want anyone hurt in the process. Knowing that a police officer or his K-9 partner had been injured or killed pursuing the son of the man who had killed her mother would only compound the heartbreak.

She shut down her computer, too preoccupied to try to work.

When her phone rang, she answered quickly, not even looking at the caller ID.

"Bradley?"

"No, sorry. It's Prudence."

"What's up?" she asked, crossing the room impatiently and staring out the window. There was nothing to see. She was twenty stories up, overlooking the busy street.

"How are you feeling? You went through quite a scare yesterday."

"I'm good. A little sore, but nothing that a few aspirin won't cure."

"Camera ready for Monday? If not, we can run next weekend's programming early."

"A couple bruises. They should be easy to hide with makeup." She glanced at the mirror, hoping that was the case. She hadn't paid much attention when she'd taken her shower. She hadn't bothered drying her hair, not planning to go to the office until Bradley could bring her there.

She had learned her lesson the previous day about leaving the safety of a locked room. She planned to stay where she was until Bradley told her Landon had been arrested.

"I'm glad to hear it, Sasha. You know how much I care about you, and I hate to put pressure on you, but I've told some higher-ups that we're going to run your story next week, and they're planning to do a preview Monday. I won't be in the office from noon today until early Monday morning. They're planning on stopping by at nine. I really need you to come through for me on this."

"You know I will, Prudence," she promised, her stomach churning with anxiety.

She enjoyed her job.

She didn't want to lose it because Martin Roker's son had decided to stalk her.

"Then you'll be here by eleven? That'll give us plenty of time to review the tape and discuss the changes I'd like you to make. I hate to ask you to work tomorrow—"

"I'll get everything done. You have my promise," Sasha assured her, glancing at her watch and frowning. It was closing in on nine. With traffic, it would take at least thirty minutes to get to the office. She could leave as late as ten and still make it in time, but she didn't dare leave later than that.

She brushed her hair, pulled it into a loose bun, swept on a coat of mascara and slid into slacks and a turtleneck. She layered with a bright yellow cardigan and slid her feet into ankle boots. No heels. Just a dab of concealer over the bruises on her cheek. A coat of clear gloss, and she was ready to go.

She paced the hotel room until ten, glancing at her watch so often she grew impatient with herself. Either things hadn't gone as Bradley had hoped, or he was busy at the station, questioning Landon or booking him into the detention center.

Either way, she was between a rock and a hard place.

If she left the hotel room, she'd be breaking her promise to him. If she didn't, she be breaking the one she had made to Prudence. She had no desire to do either, but she knew Bradley and the K-9 team were searching for Landon. For all she knew, he'd left the city and was deep in hiding. He'd be a fool to keep coming after her now the police knew who he was, and she had no doubt he was aware of what they'd discovered. By this time, they'd been to his apartment, searched it, had probably put out an APB on him and any vehicle that might be registered in his name.

His minutes of freedom were numbered.

And if she wasn't careful, her days with a job would be, too. Prudence had always been fair and reasonable, but people who didn't do their jobs, and do them well, didn't last long. She had no problem praising news anchors who did good work, and she had no problem firing ones who did not.

For the past three years, Sasha had stayed in the for-

mer category. She couldn't afford to slip into the latter
one. Her father hadn't had life insurance. His life savings had been eaten up by medical expenses. By the
time he'd passed away, he'd been broke, and she had
been paying co-pays and deductibles for his treatment.
Her finances had been stretched thin, her savings ac-
counts emptied.

Two years later, and she was finally out of the hole,
building a nest egg and standing on secure financial
footing. Losing her job would ruin that, and it was a
chance she didn't dare take.

She checked her watch one last time, searching her
phone screen as if a call might have come through unnoticed.

She knew it hadn't, and she left the room with her
purse hiked over her shoulder, a wool peacoat thrown
across her arm. If she needed to stay at the hotel for another few days, she'd have to return home to grab more
clothes. She'd worry about that after her meeting with
Prudence was over.

She waited in the hotel lobby while a concierge called
a taxi service for her, then sat in the back, fidgeting
with her phone as they made their way to the office.
She didn't want to interrupt Bradley's day, but she didn't
want to go to the office without letting him know she'd
be there. If he went to the hotel, and she wasn't there,
he'd be worried.

On the other hand, he might be in a dangerous situation.

A phone call might distract him.

If he was meeting with his sergeant, he might not
appreciate his phone ringing.

She listed pros and cons, worrying over the decision

like a teenage girl trying to decide if she should contact her first crush. That thought, more than any other, helped her decide. She was a grown woman. She needed to act like one. She needed to contact Bradley. He had given her his number. There was absolutely no logical reason not to give him a call.

She dialed his number quickly as the taxi approached her building. The phone rang once and then went to voice mail. She left a brief message, letting him know what had happened and that she would be at the office for the rest of the day.

She dropped the phone into her bag as she exited the taxi and hurried into the building. There were several people chatting in the lobby, their dark suits and polished shoes making her think they were part of the financial adviser group that owned an office suite down the hall from the studio.

She was glad that she wasn't alone, that the building had people moving around and conducting business. She didn't think Landon would dare come to the office building again, but from what Bradley had said, he wasn't in his right mind. It was difficult to predict what he would do.

She took the stairs two at a time, hurrying down the hall and through the cable network's doors. As it was most days, the receptionist desk was empty, the computer screen dark. The light next to the door behind it glowed green, indicating that there was no one in the broadcasting studio.

That wasn't a surprise. On the weekend, most programming was recorded, and the station ran on a bare-bones crew. She hung her coat on the hook and headed to her office. She'd arrived in time to review the work she had done the previous day. She had been too emotional to judge her work then. Today, she should be able to see it through clearer eyes.

She had locked her office door when she'd left for the day, and she pulled out her key. But the door was open. She stepped back, her heart slamming against her ribs as she peered through the doorway.

Everything looked the way she'd left it. Laptop closed, chair pushed in. Phone on the corner of the desk. Coffee pot washed and sitting upside down on a pile of paper towel.

"Maybe you didn't lock it after all," she murmured as she stepped into the office and closed the door.

"Of course you did," a man said as the cold butt of a gun jabbed into her side.

She froze in terror, every thought flying from her head as she met the cold dead eyes of Martin Roker's son.

"Don't scream," he said. "Don't try to run. I can kill you where you're standing and sleep like a baby tonight."

"What do you want, Landon?" she asked, hoping that using his name would throw him off-balance and make him lower his guard.

"Justice for my father," he responded, his eyes a clear gray-blue that was as cold and hard as a frozen lake.

"What do you mean?"

"Don't pretend you don't know. That will just make me angry." He shoved the gun deeper into her side.

"I'm not pretending. I really don't know. I was only fourteen when my mother was killed."

"Your mother," he nearly spit, "was an adulterer. My

father was going to marry my mother until he met your mother. Her sin cost my father his life."

"Your father had a wife and daughter," she pointed out. "He cheated on his wife with your mother."

Rage flashed in Landon's eyes. "No. My dad would have married my mom. He was leaving his wife to be with my mother, Wanda Anderson. That's why I hold no grudge against his wife or daughter, my half sister. But then he met your mother."

Sasha had no idea of the timeline of all this—whom Martin had met first. Bradley had said Landon's mother had filed a restraining order against Martin, so clearly she wasn't trying to get back together with the man. Likely, she wanted to keep herself and her son away from Martin Roker.

Sasha was filled with regret over her mother's choice to get involved with Martin and would never understand it. But that wasn't the point here. Landon Anderson was clearly delusional and had shifted the blame for what happened or didn't happen in his own family to Sasha's mother. And now to Sasha herself.

"My parents would have been happily married if it weren't for your mother!" he growled at her.

"You're delusional," she said, the words slipping out before she could stop them.

"Grief will do that to a person."

"I've been grieving my mother for eighteen years. It hasn't driven me mad yet."

"Because you're as coldhearted as your mother. You don't care about anyone but yourself." He jabbed her again, pushing her to the door. "We're going to walk out of here, take the elevator down to the lobby and go out the rear entrance of the building. My car is just outside the door. If you scream, if you call for help, if you do anything to try to escape, I will shoot you and anyone who happens to be nearby."

"I'll cooperate," she said, unwilling to risk other people's lives for the sake of her own. Maybe when they stepped outside, she could fight for her freedom. For now, she had no choice but to walk out of the room and lead the way to the elevators. She hoped that Prudence would appear, or that a security guard would notice how tense and scared she looked and ask if everything was okay, but they made it out of the office and into the elevator without drawing the attention of anyone.

She was relieved.

She was also terrified.

Once they left the building and she got into Landon's car, there was every chance she'd disappear. Never to be seen again. There. Gone. Vanished without a trace. There would be news stories about her, speculation about where she had gone and whom she had been with. Anniversary vigils where people prayed for her safe return.

If Landon had his way, she never would.

She understood that.

She just wasn't sure how to stop him without hurting anyone else.

"Move," he demanded as the elevator doors slid open.

She did as he said, stumbling off the elevator, her body nearly numb with fear. The group of people who had been in the lobby were gone, and her boots echoed hollow against the tile floor as she walked toward the back entrance.

When her phone rang, she let out a quiet shriek.

"Shut up or I'll make you sorry you didn't," Landon hissed.

"I need to answer my phone," she responded, her voice shaking with fear.

"No."

"It's the police detective who helped me yesterday. We were supposed to meet here at eleven," she lied, knowing that the time would worry him. "He's probably calling to confirm."

"Answer it. Tell him you can't meet."

"He'll ask why, and then—"

"I said answer it," he growled.

She pretended to do so reluctantly, her head down to hide the relief in her eyes. "Hello?"

"Sasha? Bradley. Sorry it took me so long to get back to you. We were tied up at Landon's apartment."

"No problem, Detective McGregor," she responded, pressing the phone tightly to her ear and hoping Landon couldn't hear Bradley's end of the conversation.

"Everything okay?" Bradley asked, obviously noticing her use of his title and last name.

"No," she replied. "Not at all. Work is hectic. I won't be able to meet you at my office."

Please let him realize I'm in trouble. Please, God.

"Work?" he repeated.

"The project? It's more complicated than I thought, and I'm going to need more time to prep for it. If you don't mind, I'd rather meet with you tomorrow."

"That's fine," he said, a sharp edge to his voice.

He'd caught on. She could hear the concern mixed with cold determination.

"You're at the office now?" he asked.

"Stepping out for an early lunch."

"I see. Any idea where you're going?"

"Finish the conversation and hang up!" Landon whispered, pushing the gun into her ribs with so much force she knew she'd have a bruise.

If help didn't come quickly, that would be the least of her worries.

"Listen, I've got to go. How about you call me later?" she said.

"Is he there?" Bradley asked.

"Yes. I'll do that. Thank you," she responded, pretending to end the call and dropping the phone back into her purse.

"Leave it here," Landon demanded.

"But—"

"Drop it. On the floor. Now." His face was red with rage, his eyes blazing.

She pulled it out of her bag and dropped it, hoping the line had stayed open. "Where are we going?" she asked.

"One of my father's favorite spots," he responded.

"Your father was a computer guy. A computer store? A technology museum?" She didn't move as he had told her to, just stood near the phone, hoping the conversation was getting through to Bradley.

"That's how much you know. He loved the ocean. He used to spend his days off at Manhattan Beach Park. He always thought it was odd that there was a neighborhood in Brooklyn named after a different borough."

"Manhattan Beach Park?" she repeated loudly. "There are a lot of people there this time of day."

"Not this time of year, and not when the sun goes down. I'm willing to wait for that," he responded, shoving her forward. "Now move!"

She had no choice but to obey, so she took one slow step after another toward the exit, praying all the while that Bradley had heard every word she'd said.

Bradley and King waited on the east side of a rocky outcropping that jutted out into the ocean. Cold air seeped through Bradley's jacket, salty spray coating his hair and skin. He'd been in place for fifteen minutes, his body tense as he waited for the call he was hoping to hear: Roker's son had arrived, and he had Sasha with him.

If he had heard right, if Landon was telling the truth, this was where they'd headed after they'd left Sasha's office. Landon's apartment complex was just a few blocks away. No water view, but a nice enough property for someone who didn't seem to have a way of supporting himself. They'd just finished collecting evidence when Bradley had called Sasha. He had planned to give her an update and let her know he was on his way to the hotel. Instead, he had interrupted her kidnapping.

His blood ran cold at the thought, and he prayed that he wasn't mistaken, and that Sasha and Landon were on the way to Manhattan Beach Park. His sergeant and Henry were waiting with their K-9s near the entrance of the park, hidden from view. They'd radio and trail Landon when he arrived.

Bradley was on the beach, ready to release King as soon as the perp was in sight. They'd cleared the area, stationing plainclothes police officers at entrances to the beach and to various areas of the park, but Bradley thought Landon would come here. The sound of waves would mute a gunshot, and a body could easily be tossed into the ocean and carried out with the tide.

If that was the plan, it wasn't flawless. As a matter of fact, it seemed more an act of desperation than a planned effort. Either way, the results would be the same, if the team didn't stop him.

He shivered. And not from the cold wind carrying off the Atlantic.

His radio crackled, and the sergeant's voice carried over the sound of crashing waves. "We've spotted them leaving a black Honda Accord. Heading toward the beach. I'm following."

"Copy," Bradley said, staying where he was, stomach to the ground, gaze focused through a crack between boulders. He needed to bide his time and wait things out. If he showed his hand too soon, Sasha could be injured.

As he watched, two figures appeared, walking from the area of the beach closest to the parking lot. A tall, stooped man, his arm around a slim woman.

"I've got them," he murmured into the radio, never taking his eyes off the approaching figures.

"Copy," the sergeant replied. "We're a hundred yards behind. There's a clear path, if you want to release King."

"They're too far away. If I let him go now, Landon might have a chance to shoot him or Sasha."

"Copy. We're hanging back. Don't wait too long, McGregor. This guy has already proved he's a loose cannon."

He was right.

There was no question about that, but Bradley resisted the urge to give in to fear. Sasha and Landon were in full view of several beachfront restaurants. There were patrons inside, looking out the windows and taking in the views. Men like Landon Anderson worked under the cover of darkness or in the shadowy corners of the world where most people never went. If he'd had to guess, Bradley would say the perp planned to cross the small sandy beach and lead Sasha into a less-visible area of the park.

They weren't going to get that far.

He waited, counting the seconds as the figures drew closer. He could see Sasha's pale face, her wind-whipped cheeks and sand-speckled slacks. He could also see the gun pressed to her side. One wrong move and a shot would be fired straight into her abdomen.

He tensed, and King shifted restlessly. The Malinois could sense his anxiety and was reacting to it.

"Wait," he murmured, knowing the dog wouldn't move until given the command.

Sasha stumbled, and she fell to her hands and knees, her hair falling out of the loose bun and hanging around her face.

"Get up!" Landon bellowed, the words carried clearly on the ocean breeze. "Now!"

She pushed to her feet, her hands fisted, the wind blowing her hair toward Landon. She lifted her hands, opening both so that sand flew straight into his face. He fell back, clawing at his eyes. She sprinted toward the outcrop, probably hoping to use it as a shield.

"NYPD! Down on the ground or I'll release my dog," Bradley shouted, hoping Sasha heard and praying she would obey.

She dropped to the ground.

Landon took off, racing back the way he'd come, perhaps thinking, mistakenly, that he could outrun a dog.

"I said, down on the ground!" Bradley repeated.

Landon kept going, obviously knowing that if he fired his weapon, he'd be shot before he could take his next breath.

"Get him!" Bradley urged.

King sprang over the walls, bounding across the sand in a blur of tan fur and unbridled energy.

TEN

It happened fast

One minute, Landon was running back toward the parking lot.

The next he was on the ground, the wrist of his gun hand between King's razor-sharp teeth.

"Call him off!" Landon screamed. "Call him off."

"In a minute," Bradley said as he walked past Sasha, knelt next to Landon and lifted the gun he had dropped, emptying the cartridge.

"Release," he commanded, and King backed away, still growling ferociously and showing his teeth.

If Sasha had been Landon, she wouldn't have dared move.

Landon didn't seem to have the same compunctions. He started to push to his knees, and King lunged for him again.

"I wouldn't do that if I were you," Bradley said dispassionately. "My dog doesn't like it."

"You've got no right to do this. I've done nothing wrong," Landon bellowed.

"Nothing? How about kidnapping and attempted murder?"

"Prove I wasn't just out here having a lover's spat with my girlfriend."

Sasha snorted, the dampness of the sand seeping through her slacks, the salty water making the cut on her chin sting. She didn't dare move, though. Not with King standing guard a few feet away.

She waited while Bradley frisked and cuffed Landon. When he finished, he turned in her direction. "Are you okay?" he asked, offering a hand and pulling her to her feet.

"Fine. Just glad you and King showed up when you did. I don't think Landon was planning to let me walk off this beach alive."

"You're as mouthy and obnoxious as your mother was. You know that?" Landon said, his cold blue eyes staring into hers.

"You didn't know her," Bradley said. "You were living on Staten Island with your mom until you moved a year ago."

"You've been doing your research, haven't you, Detective?"

"It's my job. And called your mother, too. She filled me in on some details."

Landon scowled. "She needs to keep her mouth shut."

"Not when she's being questioned by the police, and not when she could go to jail if she refuses to cooperate," Bradley responded, calling information into his radio and then reading Landon his Miranda rights.

Minutes later, two familiar K-9 officers appeared, striding across the beach and hauling Landon to his feet. She'd seen both of them outside her office when Bradley had called in the bomb threat and again at the K-9 unit the previous day. The taller man was Detective Henry

Roarke, who had a beagle named Cody. The other was Bradley's boss, Sergeant Gavin Sutherland, whose K-9 partner was a springer spaniel named Tommy. He'd assured her that they were doing everything that they could to find the person who had attacked her.

Now it was over, Landon Anderson in handcuffs and defeated, his eyes flashing with impotent rage.

"Are you all right, Ms. Eastman?" Sergeant Sutherland asked.

"Fine."

"You're sure? We can call you an ambulance, if you need one."

"I'm sure."

"You're going to pay for this one day," Landon cut in, shooting venom in her direction.

"I haven't done anything," she responded.

"Your mother killed my father."

"The police killed your father," Bradley corrected.

"No, his love and passion for a woman who used him and threw him away were what put him in the crosshairs of the police," Landon snapped. "If not for her mother, he would still be alive."

"And you think killing her daughter will bring your father back to life?" Detective Roarke asked.

"No, but it will make me feel like justice has finally prevailed."

Sasha knew Landon had everything twisted in his mind. The anniversary of her mother's murder was also the anniversary of his father's death, which had clearly triggered his rage, his need for revenge. There would not have been a marriage or getting back together or a family unit for the three of them. His mother had moved to Staten Island to get away from Martin Roker.

Now his look-alike son couldn't hurt Sasha anymore. It was over.

"You can explain all that to your lawyer, Anderson," Sergeant Sutherland said with a tired sigh. "Come on. Let's get you booked. We'll see you back at the station, Bradley."

He and Detective Roarke led Landon away.

Sasha watched them go, her legs weak in the aftermath of what had happened.

She'd been kidnapped again.

Nearly killed again.

"How about you sit for a minute?" Bradley suggested, his arm suddenly around her waist, his fingers curved around her bottom ribs.

She wanted to tell him she was fine, but that wasn't true.

She was far from it.

She dropped onto one of the nearby boulders, her hands shaking as she pulled her hair back into a bun.

"That was a clever trick," Bradley said as he took a seat beside her.

"What?"

"Sand in the eyes."

"I wasn't sure what else to do. I didn't know you and other members of the K-9 team were around, and I knew he planned to kill me if he got me far enough from prying eyes." She shuddered, and he dropped an arm around her shoulders, pulling her close to his side. He was solid, muscular and warm, and it felt right to lean her head against his shoulder.

"You were supposed to stay in the hotel room," he reminded her gently.

"Prudence insisted I come to the office. I left you

a message, so you'd know where I was. I figured you guys were handling Landon, and I'd be safe. It was a stupid assumption."

"Not stupid, but it could have cost you your life."

"I know. I'm sorry."

"No need to apologize. You're safe. The perp is going to be put away."

"All's well that ends well?"

"Exactly. And this has ended particularly well for King. We're in one of his favorite places. Mind if I let him chase a few gulls before I bring you back to the hotel?"

"That was the plan for the afternoon," she reminded him.

He smiled, brushing a strand of hair from her cheek, his finger warm against her cold skin. "You're right. It was. Not quite the way I imagined everything going down, but King won't care."

At the mention of his name, the dog's ears perked up, and his tongue lolled out.

"All right, buddy. Go do your thing," Bradley said, waving his hand toward birds that were swooping low over the water.

King leaped forward, springing across the sand with unbridled enthusiasm. Sasha stayed where she was, Bradley's arm still around her shoulders. He was a comforting solid presence, and she knew if she allowed herself, she could get used to having him around.

When Bradley's phone rang, she almost told him to ignore it.

She wanted to stay where she was, basking in the warmth of the sun and cool dampness of the ocean breeze as she watched King chase seagulls along the shore.

He pulled it from his pocket and frowned as he glanced at the number.

"Is everything okay?" she asked, all the peacefulness of the day slipping away.

"It looks like someone from your work is calling," he said as he answered. "Hello? Yes, it is. She's with me. She ran into some trouble, but she's fine now. All right. Sure. I'll give her your message."

"Was it Prudence?" she asked, jumping up and brushing sand from her pants. "I forgot. I'm supposed to be meeting with her." She patted her pockets, trying to find her cell phone.

"If you're looking for your cell phone, the security guard found it and brought it to your office. When Prudence realized you'd been there and were missing, she got worried and decided to call me. She asked me to tell you that she has to leave for her appointment, but she trusts you to have a great presentation for Monday. She'll see you then."

"That's not what she was saying an hour ago," she muttered.

"But it's what she's saying now, so how about I take you back to the hotel, you get your things and I bring you home? I'm sure you're ready to get back to your normal routine."

"I'm ready, but I'd rather get my things, go to the K-9 unit to make my statement and then go home. I can take a taxi if that's going to be any trouble for you."

"We're past the point of you worrying about that."

"What?"

"You being any trouble to me."

"How do you figure that?" she asked, laughing as King rushed over and shook water from his sleek coat.

"When you go through near-death experiences together, you become friends. Friends are never a bother to one another."

She laughed again. "Near death? I don't think it was that desperate of a situation."

"Landon would have shot both of us, if he'd had the opportunity," he said.

"Probably," she agreed.

"That's about as near death as I want to be today. Of course, if you'd rather back out of the friendship thing, I'll understand." He smiled, and her heart did a funny little flip.

"Back out? Just when I realized what one of the perks is?" she said, her gaze tracking King as he bounded back to the shoreline. "I don't think so."

"Perks?"

"Afternoons at the beach with a really handsome dog and a really nice guy."

His smile broadened. "In that case, how about we get out of here? Once we finish at the K-9 unit, I'll treat you to dinner."

"Another perk?"

"Something like that." He offered his hand, and she took it, her fingers threading through his as he called for King to heel and started walking back to the parking lot.

And it felt so right to be walking hand in hand with him, to have King loping along beside them. It didn't feel strained or scary or uncertain. It felt comfortable and sweet. It felt like belonging.

She wasn't sure how she felt about that.

But she knew when this was over, when her statement had been given and she said goodbye to Bradley and King knowing that the danger was over and they could all go back to the lives they had lived before Landon appeared, her life would feel just a little emptier than it had before.

Getting Sasha's statement and writing up his report had taken longer than Bradley anticipated. Not because the tasks were more arduous than usual. Because the team had been eager to hear the details of Landon's apprehension. Sasha had waited with good humor and patience while Bradley, Gavin and Henry filled everyone in.

Then she waited longer while he typed up his report.

She petted King and played with Cody, the adorable beagle, then poured two cups of coffee from the carafe and handed one to him. If she were bothered by the long wait, she wasn't letting on. If anything, she seemed to be enjoying her time with the dogs.

And, he had to admit, he enjoyed his time with her.

Even at the precinct, having her around made him feel more content than he had in a long time. He didn't want to read too much into that. He certainly didn't want to create something out of nothing.

But what he was beginning to feel for Sasha wasn't nothing. It was new, interesting, intriguing. Unexpected.

And now that Landon had been apprehended, she was safe. Free to go back to her life while he went back to his. He shouldn't feel disappointed about that, but he did.

"Thanks," he said, taking a quick sip before setting the mug down. He didn't meet her eyes. He didn't want her to see the softness in his gaze, the warmth he felt toward her. He didn't want to make her uncomfortable or make himself seem to be overstepping boundaries. "I'm almost finished here."

"There's no rush," she replied with a smile. "I'm sure if I get bored sitting here, I can find more dogs to play with."

"Easily. Everyone on the K-9 team has a partner. And we also have a mama dog named Brooke and her puppies. She was a stray."

"The one with five puppies? I read a story about that in the news. You guys spent a couple weeks trying to locate her puppies, right?"

"Right, and once we found them, someone came forward and claimed them as his."

"Then why do you still have them?"

"When one of our officers went to deliver her to the owner, he found a backyard breeder and a lot of sick German shepherd dogs. We closed it down and arrested the guy."

"And the dogs?"

"They got the vet care they needed, and they went to good homes. Brooke and her puppies are staying with the K-9 unit. Brooke is currently training to be in the program."

"Really?" she asked, glancing around as if she expected to see them romping through the precinct. "Are they here today? I'd love to meet them."

"I can introduce you one day," he said, watching her as she reached down to pet King again. "You know, it's funny."

"What?"

"When we met, you didn't seem much of a dog person."

"When we met, I'd never been around a dog like King," she replied.

"He is quite the dog," Bradley agreed as he finally typed the last sentence of the report and saved the document. "You ready to go back to your apartment? Maybe you need some rest after what you've been through. I can take you to dinner after that."

She smiled. "I'm not tired. As a matter of fact, I've been thinking a story about your K-9 unit might be in the future. Unless you think that's not a good idea?"

"It'll be a better idea after we solve the Emery murders," he said as he powered down his computer and stood.

"Why do you say that?" she asked.

"The public isn't pleased with how long it's taking."

"Maybe because they don't understand everything else your team does," she suggested. "A clear look at how the team operates, how the dogs are trained and all the time and energy that the K-9 unit expends making certain the city is safe might open people's eyes."

"You might have a point, but we're swamped right now and pretty focused on our goals." He didn't want to discourage her. He thought the story sounded like a good idea, but now really wasn't the time. Until they found the person who had murdered the Emerys, every spare minute the unit had was being poured into solving the case.

"Is that a kind way of saying you don't want me to do it, Bradley?" she asked as they walked outside.

"Not at all. I'm just saying now might not be the best time."

"Because of the Emery case."

"Right." He fished keys out of his pocket and walked

to his Jeep, opening the passenger door so Sasha could slide in. He opened the hatch so King could hop in his crate, then slid in behind the wheel.

"Can I ask you something?" Sasha said.

"Sure."

"Is the Emery case more important because of its similarities to your parents'?"

He wanted to tell her it wasn't.

That was the correct answer.

It was the one an objective law enforcement officer would be able to give.

He wasn't objective. Not when it came to this.

"Off the record," she added. "Of course."

"Why do you ask?"

"Answering a question with a question is a great way of shifting the focus of a conversation."

"Maybe it is, and maybe that's what I'm trying to do," he admitted. "I can tell you honestly that the team hasn't put any more time into the Emery case than we would any other investigation."

"But?"

"I'd be lying if I said the investigation hasn't hit close to home on two levels. First, one of our own fell in love with Lucy Emery's aunt, remember? Detective Nate Slater was the first responder to the Emery house, and he and Willow are now raising Lucy. Finding the killer is personal for the Brooklyn K-9 Unit on that end. And for me, yeah, the case has stirred up old memories. The killer chose the twentieth anniversary of my parents' murders to strike. Wore a similar clown mask with blue hair, gave Lucy a stuffed monkey." He shook his head and ran a hand through his hair. "How can the killer still be on the loose?"

"You'll get him," she said, having no doubt he and his dedicated, hardworking colleagues would do just that. "Just like you got your parents' murderer."

He nodded. "That was an unexpected bonus. After twenty years, I'd almost given up hope that would happen. The copycat case led to the retesting of old evidence from my parents' crime scene—a watchband. We'd been hoping to find a DNA connection between the two cases and didn't, but at least retesting resulted in a match from a genealogy site and right to Randall Gage."

"I can't imagine having to wait that long for justice."

"Then you'll understand why this particular case is so important to me. I don't want Lucy Emery to have to wait. Not like Penelope and I did. I want her to have her answers, so she can move forward with her life and not be chained to the past by a bunch of unknowns."

"I do understand that," she said. "Maybe I shouldn't have asked such a personal question."

"I don't mind. If I hadn't wanted to answer, I wouldn't have," he replied, surprising himself with the comment. Even more surprised that he meant it. He didn't like sharing pieces of himself. In the past, people's questions had felt intrusive and accusatory, unwelcome and unnecessary. But Sasha was different. She had a sincerity about her, a genuine curiosity and desire to understand that he both respected and admired. It was her warmth, though, that made him willing to open up to her, the fact that she had lived through her own heartache and that she so carefully approached the pain and heartache of others. There seemed to be no voyeurism, no desire to do anything other than understand. And there was a small part of him that wanted her to know the way he thought, the things that had shaped him, the way the past had made him the man he was.

"I'm glad you did share," she responded.

"Since I did, maybe you will."

"Will what?"

"Share."

"You won't know unless you ask a question," she said.

"All right, how about this," he began.

"Ask a reasonable one," she added hurriedly, the humor in her eyes making him smile.

"Are you hungry?"

Her eyes widened in surprise, and she laughed. "I'm always hungry."

"Want to sit down or bring something home?" he asked, wanting to reach forward and brush a stray strand of hair from her cheek, feel the softness of her skin. She was a beautiful woman. He had noticed that the first day they'd met, but her spirit—the essence of who she was—made her nearly irresistible.

"What will King do if we eat in?" she asked, her concern for the Malinois only making her more attractive.

"Behave while he waits. Get rewarded when we return."

"I'd rather he not have to wait."

"Then we'll grab something and bring it home. Your place or mine?"

"Mine. Then you won't have to leave home to drop me off after we eat."

"I don't mind."

"I do," she replied.

"Okay. Here's another question for you—burgers, Chinese or Italian?"

"I think King prefers burgers."

"And you?" he pressed, amused and still very touched by her concern for his K-9 partner. This was what he would want if he wanted a relationship—a woman who understood his commitment to the job and his relationship to King, who thought about those things when she planned meals or outings. Someone who was laid-back and accepting, but strong, too. Sasha was all those things.

"Tonight, I prefer burgers, too."

"Burgers it is," he said, pulling out of the parking lot and onto the busy street. The Emery case was still weighing on him, the desire to solve it and provide the closure Lucy would one day need something he woke with every morning and went to bed with every night.

But as he drove to a burger place to order their meals, Bradley felt lighter than he had in years, his focus on more than work, dog training and Penny.

Maybe his future didn't just have to include those things.

Maybe there was room for more.

A life outside his job. Relationships that weren't built in the confines of the headquarters building.

Maybe he could have what his adoptive parents had—the warmth of a family and of home.

It was something he hadn't dared to consider before, but every time he looked into Sasha's eyes, he felt like he was glimpsing a future he had never dared believe he could have.

He glanced her way, realized she'd been watching him, a soft smile playing at the corner of her lips.

"What?" he asked, wondering what she was thinking.

"I like you, Detective," she responded.

"That's it?"

"Does there have to be more?"

"No," he replied, surprised by the simplicity of it, by the easy way they had fallen into each other's lives. His life had never been easy. He had devoted his teenage years and his adulthood to making certain Penny was okay and to proving himself as a police officer. He had gone after justice the way other people chased after dreams. He had never considered himself to be a family man. He certainly hadn't thought of himself as husband material. Relationships were for people who had more time and energy to devote to them. For people who were hardwired for love and who were open to it.

He had spent too many years observing his parents' relationship, too many decades seeing the heartbreaking truth of what could happen in romantic relationships. He had ridden in ambulances and listened to beaten women sob because the person who had hurt them was the person they loved the most.

And he had told himself that he was better off without romance and love, better off keeping his thoughts and energy focused on his job.

He wasn't capable of physically hurting a woman, but he didn't want to be responsible for neglecting the feelings of someone who cared about him. He didn't want to have children waiting at home for him to return after a long weekend spent working homicide cases. He didn't want to hurt anyone with his absorption with his job and with justice.

But he couldn't deny the truth of how he felt about Sasha.

He reached for her hand, squeezing it gently as

he pulled up in front of the burger place. "You know what?" he asked.

"What?"

"I like you, too."

She laughed, and he leaned across the console, kissing her gently as King shifted impatiently in his crate and sighed. Maybe the dog knew better than Bradley did just how deeply he would feel the kiss, and how desperately he would long for more. Not just physical touch, but conversation, communication, laughter. All the things he had told himself he didn't need and shouldn't want.

All the things he suddenly wondered if he could have.

Without hurting anyone.

Without sacrificing his commitment to the job.

If he was willing. If she was.

ELEVEN

Life had a way of going on.

Sasha had learned that after her mother's death.

Then relearned it after her divorce.

Both times, she had thought her heart was broken beyond repair. She had wondered how the world could remain unchanged when her entire life had fallen apart. Somehow, the sky was just as blue, the bird songs just as cheerful. Summer grass remained soft green. Winter snow still tasted like childhood dreams. One day chased after another. Weeks passed just like they always did.

When her father died, she had already learned the lesson well. She'd grieved, but she had accepted that eventually some of the pain would fade, the heartache wouldn't hurt so much, and she would wake up one morning without the sick feeling of sorrow in the pit of her stomach.

At thirty-two, she was old enough to understand that there were life-changing events.

But Bradley's kiss? That one sweet, gentle touch of his lips?

It hadn't just been life-changing. It had thrown the

world out of orbit, left her dizzy and unsure of her footing.

She wasn't supposed to fall in love again.

Because she wasn't willing to have her heart broken again.

That was why she hadn't dated since the divorce.

It was why she had turned down invitations to dinner and lunch, refused blind dates, told her coworkers and friends that she was not interested in entering the dating pool again.

She had meant it.

She *had*.

But somehow that slipped her mind every time Bradley called or texted.

In the week since Landon Anderson's arrest, she had done her best to put some distance between them. She had refused an invitation to lunch, using work as an excuse. When he'd invited her to the dog park one evening, she'd said she was still trying to get a recording edited for the weekend's broadcast.

She had been, but there was more to it than that.

She was afraid of crossing a line with him. One she would never be able to step back over again. He had called them friends, but she knew they were moving toward more than that. Every night, he called her after work, and they chatted for an hour, catching each other up on the details of the day.

Every morning, she told herself that she wouldn't answer the phone the next time, that she'd pretend to be asleep, that she would claim fatigue every night until he stopped calling.

She sighed, pulling her hair up into a high ponytail. She'd pulled on yoga pants and a long-sleeved T-shirt.

Most Saturdays she worked in the office for a few hours, but she wasn't in the mood. She had spent too many hours bent over a computer screen, splicing together pieces of the show she had recorded.

She had told her story with as much candor as she could, using old family photos to give viewers a glimpse of the kind of home she had grown up in and the kind of people her parents were. Prudence had previewed the finished product Thursday, and she had raved about the sweet authenticity of it.

Hopefully viewers would be just as touched.

Sasha didn't intend to tune in to the show, but she hadn't been able to sleep in. She was too wound up, too nervous. She hadn't ever told her story before. Not the way she had for the show.

She grabbed a down vest from her closet and slid into it. She'd go for a run. That would get her mind off the show and off Bradley.

She left the apartment, jogging along the still-sleepy sidewalk. The sun had barely risen, and Saturday traffic was light, most people enjoying a little extra sleep.

Her phone rang as she rounded the corner of her block.

She answered it, knowing without looking that Bradley was calling.

"Good morning," she said, her heart doing a strange little flip as she pictured him holding the phone to his ear and sipping coffee.

"Good morning. Sounds like you're outside."

"I decided to go for a run."

"You should have told me. I'd have joined you."

"You have the day off?"

"No. I'm working the afternoon shift. Want to join King and me at the dog park in an hour?" he asked.

She hesitated.

He noticed.

Of course.

"I'm getting the impression that you're not comfortable going out with me."

"I'm comfortable. Too comfortable. That's the problem," she admitted.

"Why is too much comfort a problem?"

"You know I was married before?" She had mentioned it during one of their long conversations.

"Yes."

"And that he left me for someone else?"

"Yes again."

"So maybe you can understand why I'm...nervous about getting into another relationship."

"Nervous? Or unwilling?"

"Just...nervous."

For a moment, he was silent. When he spoke, she could hear disappointment mixed with understanding in his voice. "All right."

"All right?"

"I'm not going to push you, Sasha. When you're ready, I'll be here."

"Bradley, it isn't that I don't want to be friends—" she began, wanting to stop the conversation before it went too far.

"*I* don't want to be friends," he said firmly. "Not *just* friends, anyway. I want more than that. It would be unfair for both of us to keep moving forward like we are—one of us wanting one thing, the other one something else."

"It's not—"

"Hold on," he said. She could hear a muffled conversation, and then he was back. "Sorry about that. I got called in to work for a meeting. We are about to begin. We plan to discuss our next steps in the Emery case."

"You still haven't located Andy?"

"No, and since that's the only lead we haven't been able to follow up on, we need to. I'm going to have to go. We can discuss things later."

"Bradley," she began, wanting to apologize and tell him that she knew she was being foolish, that in the deepest part of her heart, she wanted exactly what he did.

"I'll call you tonight," he said, and then he was gone.

She dropped the phone into the inside pocket of her vest, then zipped it. The morning was crisp with the first hints of winter, dead leaves skittering across the sidewalk as she continued jogging.

Sheepshead Bay was waking, people rushing along the sidewalk on their way to work or to breakfast. Like Sasha, some people were jogging, dodging through the burgeoning crowd like Alpine skiers dodging slalom poles.

She turned off Ocean Avenue, taking a quieter route on a less-traveled street. She didn't realize where she was heading until she saw the limestone facade of the K-9 unit headquarters.

"Oh no you don't," she muttered, turning off on a side street before she reached it. The last thing she wanted was for one of Bradley's coworkers to see her wandering around outside the building.

She'd talk to him later.

Just like he'd suggested.

When she did, she would try to explain things a little more clearly. Hopefully he would understand.

She turned another corner, jogging into an area of Bay Ridge that wasn't nearly as well kept. Houses were close together, the yards cluttered and overgrown. Several properties were boarded up. There was a day care just ahead. A few blocks down and to the left was the house where Lucy Emery had lived with her parents.

Sasha had spent time in this area when she worked the crime beat, talking to men and women who lived in the area. She slowed down as she passed the day care, smiling at a few parents who were dropping their children off early. Several smiled back, but she didn't want to interrupt their morning routine. Trying to get information from someone heading into work seldom produced results.

She continued down the street, waving at a few older men who sat on rickety porch furniture, smoking cigarettes. "Good morning!" she called.

"You're that lady doing the good-news stories, right?" one of the men said, offering a nearly toothless grin.

"That's right."

"You gonna do a story about this neighborhood?"

"That's why I'm here," she said. "To find out what stories there are to tell."

"Good. Good," the man said, leaving his buddies and crossing his overgrown front yard. An old wrought iron fence surrounded the patch of dead grass. He leaned against the gate and nodded sagely. "Too much bad news coming out of this place lately. Time to change that."

"Bad news? You mean like the murder that happened a few months ago?" she asked.

"I sure do. We might have crackheads standing on some of our street corners at night, but we ain't a place where little girls should see their parents killed."

"No place should be," she agreed.

"I don't understand why the cops ain't found the guy responsible. They got that fancy new dog unit and all those fancy trained dogs, and little Lucy is still waiting for justice."

"You know Lucy?"

"Of course I do. Everyone on this street knows her. Cute kid. A shame her parents were losers." He took a cigarette from a pack in his shirt pocket and tapped it against his palm.

"I've heard they may have been killed because they weren't good to her," she said, throwing out one of the reasons she'd heard speculated about on the news.

"Yeah. Well, that's what the talking heads on TV say. You want to know what Buddy Morris says? That's me, by the way." He patted his chest.

"Sure."

"I say they owed someone money."

"Why do you think that?"

His eyes narrowed. "You working with the cops?"

"No. I work for a local cable station."

"But the cops aren't paying you to pick my brains?"

"If they were, would you care? You did say you wanted them to solve the case."

"You've got a point, kid. I do want it solved, and I don't care how the police make that happen. They want to send spies into the neighborhood, that's fine with me."

"I'm not spying. I'm just curious."

"The Emerys were crooks. They made deals and didn't follow through on them. That can get a person killed," Buddy said quietly.

"So, you don't think their murders have anything to do with the way they treated Lucy?"

He shrugged. "Maybe. Maybe not. You want to know more, you should ask CJ. He lives in the house behind theirs."

"CJ? What's his address?"

The man laughed. "Lady, you don't need an address. The Emery place still has yellow bits of tape stuck to the front door. Find it. Walk into the backyard. Go to the chain-link fence and scream his name a couple times. Maybe he'll answer."

"You're not sending her out to CJ's, are you?" one of the other men asked.

"She wants to know what was going on at the Emery place," he responded, the cigarette dangling from his fingers.

"CJ isn't going to talk to her. He doesn't talk to any-one," the man argued, his focus on Sasha. "I'm telling you right now, don't bother. He's not going to talk to you."

"He'll talk to her if she says I sent her." Buddy flicked ashes onto the ground, tossed the cigarette and ground it out with his foot. "You tell him I sent you. He'll talk to you."

"You two are good friends?" Sasha asked, trying to get a feel for how the interpersonal connections worked.

"Wouldn't say we're good friends. I wouldn't even say we're friends. Went to high school together. He doesn't get out, so I bring him groceries once a week. Grab his mail for him. Stuff like that."

"I don't suppose you'd be willing to introduce us?"

He studied her for a moment, his dark rheumy eyes taking in her running clothes, her scuffed shoes and her empty hands.

"If you'd like some cash for your trouble," she began, knowing she had two twenties tucked into her phone case.

"I don't want your money, lady. I just want you to find that good-news story in our neighborhood and air it."

"I can't promise anything, but I can tell you I will do my best."

"We have a deal," he exclaimed gleefully. "Come on. I got things to do, and I don't want to lollygag around. Of course, I'm sure I'm not as busy as a famous news personality like yourself, Ms. Eastman." He stepped through the gate, walking quickly along the crumbling sidewalk.

"You can call me Sasha. And we both know that I'm far from famous," she said, hoping that maybe this lead would pan out.

She knew how important it was to Bradley that he solve the Emery case. Whatever happened between the two of them, Sasha wanted him to accomplish his goal.

"More famous than me. There it is," Buddy said, pointing toward a dingy house with bits of crime scene tape still dangling from the doorjamb. "The Emery place."

"Did they have a lot of friends?" she asked as they approached the property.

"Probably the same as most people. I used to see them out smoking in their backyard when I dropped stuff off for CJ. Even if they weren't out there, it seemed the kid always was. Rain. Shine. Heat. Cold. Poor kid."

"Did anyone ever live here with them? Like, maybe someone named Andy?" She knew the police had been asking, but she felt compelled to do the same.

"Nah. No Andys. Police keep asking that."

"How about in the neighborhood?"

Buddy rubbed his nearly bald head. "Nope. I know everyone who lives in a five-mile radius, and not one of them is an Andy."

A few houses up the street, a door opened and a man walked out, a silky-haired brown dachshund in his arms. "Hey, Buddy, what are you doing over there?"

"What's it to you, Vernon?" Buddy replied.

"It's private property. You can't just go traipsing across the yard every time you want to take a shortcut to CJ's house." Vernon hurried across the street, the dog still in his arms.

"That's a funny warning coming from you. Every time I'm here, Brandy's in the yard."

"Brandy?" Sasha asked.

"That thing." He pointed at the dog.

"She isn't a thing," Vernon huffed. "She's a dog, and she's only over here because she's searching for Lucy."

"Guess I can't say anything about that. The kid loved that dog, and the dog loved the kid. It was mutual admiration society. Lucy always said Brandy was her bestest friend." Buddy laughed.

"Her friend?" Sasha repeated, the last square of the Rubik's Cube suddenly sliding into place.

"Animals can be our friends," Vernon said, a hint of defensiveness in his voice. "And if any human needed a friend, Lucy did. Always wandering around the yard alone. Half the time she was dirty and wearing clothes that weren't appropriate for the weather. Brandy knew she needed someone. I couldn't keep her inside if Lucy was out, and as soon as I opened the door, she'd fly across the street to visit." Vernon patted Brandy's silky head. "She misses her friend."

"Kid use to dress her in doll clothes," Buddy said, smiling at the memory. "Old Vernon here would half-near have a heart attack every time."

"Dogs don't need clothes. Especially not my dog."

"If you thought that, maybe you should have kept the critter in your yard," Buddy replied.

"Maybe you should keep your mouth shut," Vernon responded.

Sasha studied the dog while the two men argued, her mind racing.

She'd listened to the news conferences. She knew the police had been looking for someone named Andy. Andy with brown hair. Who the three-year-old missed.

A three-year-old who might mistake the name Brandy for Andy. Who might not ever mention that the "Andy" was a dog.

"You okay?" Vernon asked, his eyes narrowed.

"Yes. Fine. Just thinking about all the great human-interest stories I might find in this neighborhood."

"That's why you're here?" Vernon asked suspiciously.

"Why else?"

"Nosiness? There's been too many people wandering around asking questions lately. And the police come through every other day, asking the same questions over and over again."

"They want to find the Emerys' murderer," she pointed out, trying to drag her gaze away from the dog.

"Seems to me, those people got what they deserved." Vernon nearly spit the words, his tone filled with venom.

Surprised, Sasha met his mud-brown eyes. "Why do you say that?"

"They didn't take care of their kid. They didn't take care of their property. They didn't take care of their neighbors. Eventually someone decided to take care of them." He let out a snort of laughter. "I got to get back inside. Brandy is waiting on her breakfast."

He hurried away.

Buddy shook his head. "That guy is downright weird."

"Is there a reason you say that?"

"Just a vibe I get. Plus, he doesn't seem to like anyone. As far as I know, he doesn't get along with his neighbors, and he doesn't have any friends. Except his dog. I'm heading around. You'd better stay here. CJ will be more likely to meet with you if you don't go into his yard without permission." He walked through the yard, disappearing around the house.

Sasha stayed put, her heart beating frantically.

She had to be mistaken.

There was no way Andy was a dog named Brandy. Was there?

She took her phone from her pocket, dialing Bradley's number before she could second-guess herself. He had said he would be in a meeting. Hopefully he would check his voice mail as soon as it was over.

She left a detailed message, explaining what she had discovered and telling him where she was. No apologies. No excuses. If the information was helpful, great. If it wasn't, no harm done.

She shoved the phone in her pocket and tried to see around the side of the house.

She didn't want to get on CJ's bad side. Better to stay out of sight until she was summoned or told to go home.

"No success with CJ yet?"

She jumped, whirling to face Vernon. He was just steps away. A coat now pulled over his stained T-shirt.

"You scared the life out of me!" she exclaimed.

"Actually, it doesn't seem that I have," he responded. "You're still very much alive and breathing."

She didn't laugh.

She didn't get the impression he wanted her to think it was funny.

"Where's Brandy?"

"In the house eating."

"Shouldn't you be with her?"

"I usually am, but I looked outside and realized that you were still standing here. I thought I'd come back out and find out why."

"I'm thinking of doing a story on the neighborhood," she said. "I work for a local cable show. WBKN. I do feel-good stories about people and places in Brooklyn."

"Nothing feel-good about this neighborhood," he said with a narrow-eyed glare that made her take another step away.

"Look, Vernon, I'm not here to cause any trouble."

He laughed, something evil and ugly just beneath the sound. "Of course you aren't."

"Why would I be?"

"Because you think you're better than we are, walking around in your fancy coat and expensive shoes, acting like you have a right to ask your questions."

"Freedom of speech is a constitutional right, Vernon.

I'm not doing any harm by engaging in that right," she replied, suddenly nervous and a little scared. Anxious to get away from Vernon.

"Freedom of speech has gotten people killed, you know that?" he responded.

"I have an appointment soon," she said, glancing at her watch, ready to make her escape.

"Right. A meeting. Like I said, you're too important for this part of town."

"Goodbye, Vernon." She turned away, realizing her mistake a moment too late.

She heard the rustle of fabric and a quick swish of air behind her.

She swung toward the sound, caught a glimpse of something arching through the air.

A heavy baton?

A baseball bat?

She put up her arm and tried to dodge.

The object crashed into her forearm, glancing off her temple with enough force to send her flying backward. She fell, the world spinning. Darkness edging in.

Flying.

Floating.

Realizing she was being carried somewhere.

She managed to open her eyes just enough to see a bright orange car. Vernon opened the trunk, dropping her unceremoniously inside.

"You really should have minded your own business," he grumbled as he shut the trunk.

She lay where she was, allowing her eyes to adjust as the car engine rumbled to life. He was taking her somewhere. She was terrified of what would happen when they reached their destination.

You have your cell phone. Use it! her mind shrieked.

She reached into her vest pocket.

The phone was still there, her fingers clumsy as she pulled it out. Her head was pounding, her arm throbbing, her stomach churning. It hurt to keep her eyes open, but it would hurt more to die before she had a chance to see Bradley again.

She had fallen hard for him.

She didn't know how.

She just knew it had happened.

Everything good she had thought she'd seen in Michael actually existed in Bradley. Kind, generous, gruff and tough, he had a deep love of God, family and justice that shaped everything he did and said. She hadn't been able to resist that.

She didn't want to resist him.

If she got out of this situation alive, she would tell him how she felt. She wouldn't hold back, wouldn't let her fear keep her from pursuing something wonderful.

If she did?

When she did.

The car stopped. Not idling. Stopped cold. She tensed, certain Vernon would open the trunk and finish what he'd started. A minute passed. Two. She thought she heard him walking around the vehicle, his heavy footsteps crunching on gravel or crumbled asphalt.

Where were they?

A park?

She tried to hear past the fear roaring through her head.

Were those waves crashing?

She didn't dare call Bradley again, afraid Vernon

was lurking outside and would hear her. Instead, she turned off the sound and texted, grateful she'd left him the detailed voice mail earlier.

Andy/Brandy's owner kidnapped me.

I'm in trunk of orange car.

Maybe near the bay or ocean.

Track cell phone.

Hurry.

She wanted to say more. She wanted to tell him she had fallen in love with him. She wanted to explain how sorry she was that she had let her fear hurt him.

She should have said everything she'd meant, everything she had felt, when she had had the chance. Should have told him just how happy she felt when she was with him and just how eager she was to explore the depth and breadth of their friendship.

She had missed her opportunity.

She could only pray she would have another one.

A quiet click warned her the trunk was about to open.

She hit Send, shoved the phone back into her pocket and closed her eyes, praying desperately that God would show her a way out of the mess she was in.

Sunlight speared her eyes, and Vernon dragged her out by the arm. Her head hit the edge of the trunk, and she stumbled as her feet landed on pavement. She blinked, trying to get her eyes used to the bright light. She hadn't been in the trunk long. They hadn't gone far.

"Where are we?" she asked, her voice shaking. She couldn't stand that. Couldn't stand that this hate-filled man had her so terrified.

"Figure it out yourself," he grumbled.

She glanced around and realized they were at a beach. That was good. A beach meant people. People meant safety. She hoped.

"Vernon, I'm not sure what you think I've done, but if you just leave me here, we can pretend none of this ever happened."

"Shut up! I'm trying to think. This is not where I wanted to be. The docks would have been better. Easier to drown you without someone seeing, but I need gas to get there and money is tight. This'll work. I'll make it work."

"I think—"

"Shut up, I said!" he yelled, flashing the gun that he had hidden beneath his coat. "Or I'll kill you right here, and I won't care who sees."

It had been ten minutes and fifteen seconds since Bradley had received Sasha's voice mail and text. He had tried to call her three times since then. She hadn't answered.

Every available K-9 team was being gathered; a BOLO had been issued for a bright orange car; her cell phone was being actively traced.

Everything that could possibly be done to find her was being done.

It didn't feel like enough.

"Staring at that phone isn't going to make her respond," Henry said, barely looking up from a map he was studying. Vivienne was beside him, placing marks where Sasha's cell phone had pinged.

Near the K-9 unit.

Why hadn't he answered his phone when she'd called earlier? He'd been about to head into a meeting with his team, trying to figure out how they could finally track down "Andy," while she'd had the information he and the K-9 unit needed. He shook his head, furious at himself. He should have answered.

But he'd figured she'd been calling because she was worried about the way their conversation had ended, and he hadn't been ready to talk about it.

He should have made it clear that he wasn't upset, that he would give her all the time she needed, that he absolutely understood how desperate she was to not be hurt again.

He'd been too anxious for the meeting, hoping for new leads, and to get out on the street and start asking about Andy again.

He thought about the message she'd left. And looked at the text she'd sent.

Andy is a dog named Brandy...

Andy/Brandy's owner kidnapped me.

"Where's Nate?" he asked. Nate was engaged to Lucy's aunt Willow. If anyone could get in touch with her quickly, it was him. He believed Sasha but he wanted the information confirmed.

"Right here," Nate responded, striding across the room with his K-9, Murphy, beside him.

"Can you call Willow? Have her ask Lucy if Andy is a person or a dog?"

Nate's eyes widened, but he didn't ask questions. He knew Sasha had been kidnapped, and he knew time was of the essence.

He pulled out his phone, made the call, his voice terse, his expression grim, and he asked for the information he needed.

When the conversation ended, he met Bradley's eyes.

"Andy is a dog with brown hair. Apparently, Lucy's very best friend."

"A dog?" Henry repeated, looking up from the map. "The guy we've been searching for has fur and can't testify in a court of law?"

"But his owner can," Bradley responded, pushing Play so that the voice mail Sasha had left played again. She was breathless. Apparently unharmed. Giving quick, clear details. The Emerys' house. A neighbor across the street named Vernon with a little brown-haired dog named Brandy.

Suspicious.

Trouble.

May need help.

The words skipped and tumbled through his head, adrenaline pumping through him.

"We need to find her. Now," he muttered.

King whined, sensing his tension and fear.

"We will," Vivienne assured him. "This map is leading us straight to her." She pointed to the marks she'd made. "Cell phone tower pings all the way to Manhattan Beach. She's been there for a little over twenty minutes."

Bradley's stomach churned. Manhattan Beach again.

Bad guys liked the place. Desolate spots and an ocean to dump their victims. "Let's pray she stays there for another twenty more," Bradley said, grabbing his coat and heading for the door.

The sergeant grabbed his arm, pulling him to a stop.

"I understand why you want to rush, but I want to remind you that a sloppy plan leads to a sloppy outcome."

"Sloppy plan?" Nate said. "We don't have any plan at all."

"Exactly," Gavin agreed. "We can take five minutes to hash it through, come up with the best message of approach and then move in. The last thing we want is for Sasha to be injured."

"The last thing we want," Penny said loudly from her desk, "is for Sasha to die."

"So, let's be clear-thinking. If they're on the beach, what approach is going to keep us out of sight?"

"There are plenty of people who walk the beach this time of year. I'll just go out there and pretend to be enjoying the view," Penny offered. "Once I'm close enough—"

"No," Bradley said harshly. "You aren't trained, and we don't need more civilians involved."

Her eyes flashed and her lips tightened, but she must have realized now wasn't the time to argue. "I suppose you have a better plan?"

"Every K-9 officer dresses as a civilian. We go in plain clothes, surround the orange car and take this guy down. Until we actually see where the vehicle is and understand the situation better, that's about as good as it's going to get."

Gavin frowned. "I hate to agree, but if this guy murdered the Emerys—"

"He did," Bradley cut in.

"If he did, he's already killed once. There's nothing keeping him from killing again. Everyone understand what we're doing?"

The team gave agreement as a group.

"Good. Go to your lockers. Change. Do whatever you need to do to not look like a K-9 police officer. We'll meet back here in ten. Head out immediately."

The group took off, everyone moving quickly.

Bradley should have been relieved.

All he felt was terror.

A murderer had Sasha.

Every minute that ticked away was another opportunity for him to hurt her.

It took him five minutes to change out of his suit into casual clothes he kept in his locker. Less to get King out of his work vest. He kept the same lead and collar. Just as he would if he were working undercover. King understood what that meant. He knew he was still on the job, and he pranced excitedly as he waited, whining under his breath every few minutes.

"I know, boy. I want to leave, too," Bradley said, his voice husky with concern and fear.

"It's going to be okay, Bradley," Penelope said, wrapping her arm around his waist and offering a quick, firm hug. He had been her protector, her mentor, her supporter for as long as he could remember, offering advice, lending an ear, giving her a shoulder to cry on when she needed it.

Now she was an adult. A strong, accomplished woman who knew her mind and her heart, and who was now offering him the things that he had spent so many years giving her.

"I hope so," he said.

"You should know so," Henry said as he stepped into the room. "Our entire team is working on this. Our track record for success is excellent."

"It is," Gavin agreed as he joined them.

Within minutes the remainder of the team had returned, dogs out of vests, uniforms off, guns hidden beneath their coats. Ready to do what they did best. To work as a team, to protect the innocent and to bring justice to the guilty.

Gavin gave one last brief, reiterating the need to be careful, cautious and aware. They had pinned down the location of the orange car. A patrol officer had confirmed that it was in the parking lot near Manhattan Beach Park.

Now all they had to do was get there, and then use the dogs to track down Sasha and the man who had kidnapped her.

"Ready?" Gavin asked. "Let's head out."

Bradley didn't wait for a second invitation.

He was in his Jeep and heading for the beach before most of the team had left the building.

Sasha was in danger.

He was going to do whatever was necessary to save her.

TWELVE

Sasha was digging her own grave.

She knew it but could do nothing about it.

Vernon was standing a few inches away, watching as she scooped another shovelful of sand and tossed it toward the lush tree that shaded the area.

In late spring or early summer, the park would have been too crowded for this. Every bit of sand taken up by humanity. There would have been families and laughter, games of beach volleyball and rows of sunbathers. As far as beaches went, this stretch of sand was small, the area more for the community of Manhattan Beach than for tourists who flocked to the other beaches during the hottest summer months.

In the fall, it was empty except for a few die-hard beachcombers, runners and dog walkers.

"How about you spend a little more time digging and a little less time daydreaming?" Vernon snapped, the gun still tucked under his coat. She could see the barrel poking toward her beneath the fabric. If he shot her now, someone would see him. He certainly couldn't push her into the pit she was digging and bury her without garnering attention.

"I'm trying, but I'm sick from that knock on my head, and I think my arm is broken." She lifted her left arm. The area below her wrist was black-and-blue, the skin tight from swelling.

"And?" he asked dispassionately.

"It's difficult to dig quickly when you're only using one hand."

"Then use two and deal with the pain. Either that or don't. We'll just go back to the car, and I'll bring you to a place where no one is going to notice if and when I shoot you. Any alley will be fine. I can toss you in a dumpster, and it may take days for anyone to find you." He scowled. "That should have been my first plan. I'd be done with you by now."

"You're asking me to dig my own grave, Vernon," she said, hoping there might be some compassion in him, a bit of humanity that would make him rethink his choices.

He laughed. "Do you think I'm that stupid? There aren't many people around, but there are enough. Right now, all you're doing is digging sand for a nice big sand sculpture. If anyone remembers me here, that's what I'm going to tell them."

"And? Then what?" she asked, tossing another shovelful of sand to the side.

"I haven't decided yet. Tragic accident when the sand caves in on you? Tragic drowning when you accidentally fall off the pier? I think deaths should be appropriate to the person. Don't you?"

"Sure," she agreed, eyeing the surrounding area. If she ran, would he shoot and hope that he wasn't seen? "But I have never done anything to hurt you. And there is no need for either of those things to happen."

"That's my decision. Not yours. And I don't like nosy people. Ridding the world of one is a favor to the cosmos."

"I'm a journalist. It's my job to be nosy," she argued. Good thing she *was* because she'd set her phone to record while she was still in the trunk. If she could get Vernon to confess to killing the Emerys before he killed her, at least the K-9 unit would have that. The thought made her shiver and she purposely tripped over the pile of dirt she'd removed, causing a good amount of it to fall back in the hole.

It would be very easy to stage an accident like the ones Vernon had described. People drowned every year. People died when sand pits caved in. Beaches were lovely, but they could be dangerous. She shuddered.

She wasn't afraid to die.

She had just been hoping to do it a little later in life.

"Be careful!" Vernon bellowed. "We don't have time to redo this."

"We? I'm the one doing all the work." She purposely goaded him, hoping to distract him and make him focus on something other than the timeline he had in his head.

She had to believe that Bradley had gotten her messages and her texts. She had to believe that he and his team were on the way to help.

She just had to slow down the process of being murdered.

She needed to stay alive long enough to be saved. She knew that not getting caught was everything to Vernon. He could have easily dragged her into his house, killed her there and then stuffed her in a suitcase to get rid of her body later. He clearly wanted no evidence in his own home that she'd been there. Perhaps he was even hoping to make her death look accidental. Anything to throw the police off his trail.

She could use his fear of being caught to her advantage, manipulate his fears. Somehow.

"Please, God," she prayed out loud, hoping Vernon might feel a twinge of guilt. "Help me."

"No one is going to help you, lady. So shut up and keep working."

"You don't have to kill me."

"Sure I do."

"Why?"

"You know my secret."

"All I know is that you have a dog named Brandy."

"You know Lucy called her Andy. You know that my dog is the man the cops have been looking for." He cackled gleefully. "It's been a riot watching them canvass the neighborhood looking for some guy with brown hair named Andy. You know they even brought Lucy out one day?"

"No," she said, swallowing down bile as she scooped up more dirt.

"They did. Drove her up and down the streets hoping she would spot her special friend. I heard about it before they reached my street. Brandy and I stayed inside that day."

"You have to know that they'll find you eventually. Buddy and Gunner both know you're the last person to see me alive."

He scowled. "Those guys won't talk to the cops. Why would they? They don't really know you, so they won't care about you one way or the other. But they did know the Emerys. And those two were low-level criminals. They cheated everyone they dealt with. They neglected their kid. They let a nice house go to ruin. Got away with it for years, too. They'd still be getting away with it if I hadn't stopped them. The way I see it, the community owes me a favor for killing the Emerys."

There it was. The confession. And it was all caught on her phone, recording in her pocket.

"Then go home and ask them to throw you a party. Leave me alone. I won't say anything to anyone about this."

"Of course you will. You're a reporter. You can't help yourself. Dig faster. There are some people on the beach over there. I wouldn't want to have to kill them, too."

Terrified, she glanced in the direction he was looking.

A woman was walking her dog near the water's edge. Closer to the parking lot, someone else was throwing a ball for his...

Malinois?

Her heart skipped a beat, her gaze dropping quickly.

They were there, and she knew if she looked around she would see more team members, slowly moving closer, trying to get an opportunity to take Vernon down before he could fire the gun.

"Dig faster," he growled, and she scooped another shovelful. A dog suddenly appeared. A beagle. Brown, white and black with a sweet face and a wagging tail, heading right for her.

Cody!

If he was there, Henry was, too.

"Get away!" Vernon snapped, stamping a foot in Cody's direction. Undaunted, the beagle kept coming, his tail wagging wildly as he watched the shovel.

He thought Sasha was playing a game, and he was excited to play, too.

"No. Stay." She tried to stop him, but he just kept coming, his lean body moving like he had all the time in the world.

"I said, get away," Vernon shouted, raising the gun, pointing it.

She couldn't let it happen.

She swung the shovel at his head, too weak from her injuries to get much force behind it.

He grabbed the handle, twisting it from her hand and tossing it away.

"Die!" he said quietly. Coldly. Then he lifted the gun and pointed it straight at her heart.

She braced for what she knew was coming, praying that God would make it painless, that He would watch over the people she was leaving behind. Coworkers. Friends. The K-9 unit that had worked so diligently to keep her safe.

Bradley.

Because she wanted him to always be happy, to always have joy in his life.

Instead of a gunshot, she heard a vicious snarl and saw a flurry of tan and black launching through the air.

The gun went off as King latched on to Vernon's gun arm and dragged him to the ground, shaking him until the gun fell from his grip.

Vernon howled, his cries ringing through the air and mixing with the wild screams of the gulls.

In seconds, it was over.

Vernon cuffed and lying facedown on the ground.

King still snarling as Bradley called him back.

Sasha stumbled a few steps away, collapsing onto the

warm, soft sand, her head pounding, her arm throbbing, her heart soaring with gratefulness.

"Are you okay?" Bradley asked, crouching beside her, his dark eyes filled with concern.

"I am now," she responded, wrapping her hand around his and looking into his eyes. "I'm sorry," she said.

"Sorry? You deserve an award for finally giving us the information we needed to bring this guy down."

"Not for that," she murmured, watching as the sergeant pulled a wallet from Vernon's pocket, opened it up and read his ID.

"Vernon Parker, huh?"

"What's it to you?" Vernon spit.

"Not much. Just wanted to know whose name we're writing on the paperwork. Vernon Parker, you're under arrest for attempted murder." He read Vernon his Miranda rights before dragging him to his feet. "And in case you think that will be the only charge, we'll be filing murder charges, too. We have no doubt that your DNA will match evidence our forensic scientist has been painstakingly working to retrieve from evidence found at the Emery crime scene back in April."

"You're crazy. I would never hurt anyone," Vernon protested.

"You're saying that while you stand three feet from the grave you were making me dig for myself," Sasha pointed out. "Oh, and guess what? The phone in my pocket recorded your confession to killing the Emerys and why."

He lunged toward her, nearly breaking free of Gavin's hold.

"Let's go," Gavin said, dragging him away. "Good job, Ms. Eastman," he called over his shoulder.

"Very good job," Bradley said, holding her gaze. "That was some excellent detective work on your part. We were working on finding Andy for months and you're the one who uncovered that Andy was really Brandy—and a dog. I didn't realize how closely related our skills are."

She smiled, appreciating his praise, but she was still too shaken to think beyond being safe.

"We should get out of here, too." Bradley helped her to her feet, slid his arm around her waist. "Are you sure you're okay?"

"I will be," she replied.

"Looks like you might need an X-ray." He touched her arm.

"I don't think it's broken. Some ice and some ibuprofen, and I'll be fine."

"You might be, but I'll spend the next few days worrying that something is broken or bleeding internally."

"You have too much on your plate to worry about me."

"Like?"

"Your job. All the people in Brooklyn who count on you and the K-9 unit."

"My job is important to me. I'll admit it takes up a lot of my thoughts, but you are always on my mind, too. And now that we've made progress on the Emery case, I'll have more than enough time to focus on worrying about your health and well-being."

She looked into his eyes, saw the humor and relief there.

"You know what?"

"What?"

"I really do like you, Detective McGregor."

He laughed. "Good. So, how about we get you checked out while my colleagues take Vernon in for questioning?"

"This is your case. You need to be there."

"I'll be there when they book him for murder and when he is convicted and tossed into prison, where he belongs."

"If it happens." She frowned. She knew how the criminal justice system worked. Even airtight cases could be lost.

"I have no doubt it will. Between the confession you have on your phone and the DNA evidence our forensic scientist will likely be able to match, we'll be able to close it fast and, hopefully, get him to plead guilty."

"Since when are you the optimist in this relationship?" she joked, then realized how it sounded. "What I mean is—"

"I hope what you mean is what you said. I like the idea of a relationship with you. Now. How about that X-ray?"

"Only if you drive me to the hospital. I'm not keen on another ambulance ride this month."

"It's a deal," he said, calling to King as he helped her across the beach, the bright sunshine dancing on the waves, gulls calling wildly, King chasing waves and birds. K-9 officers huddled in groups, discussing the successful rescue, the capture of a murderer they'd been hunting for seven months. She could see their smiles, feel their joy, and all of it was so breathtakingly perfect, tears filled her eyes.

"You're crying," Bradley said quietly, stopping to study her face, his palms cupping her cold cheeks, his touch as gentle as his gaze. "Are you in more pain than you told me?"

"No."

"Then why the tears?" he asked, brushing one from her cheek.

"Relief, I guess," she said, glancing at the beach and the men, women and dogs she had come to admire, respect and care about. "And joy."

"Because you're alive?" he asked, a tender smile curving his lips.

"Because I'm surrounded by the family I never thought I'd have, looking into the eyes of the only man I've ever truly loved, and it feels like I have finally found a place where I belong."

"We are your people, huh?"

"You are my person," she corrected.

He leaned down so that they were eye to eye, his forehead resting against hers, his palms still warm against her cheeks. "And you're mine. I love you, Sasha. More than I ever imagined I could love anyone."

He kissed her then, his lips warm, his hands gentle, and she knew that if she lived a hundred more years, she would remember the way it felt to feel so cherished, valued and loved.

"You're an extraordinary woman, Sasha," he whispered against her lips. "And I'm going to spend the rest of my life thanking God for bringing you into my life."

He stepped back, allowing his hands to drop away. "But first, I'm bringing you to the hospital."

Sasha laughed, taking his hand as they walked to his Jeep, all the heartache and pain of the past forgotten, and she stepped toward the future God had planned for her.

EPILOGUE

Sasha had never been part of a large Thanksgiving celebration. Even as a child, before her mother's murder, Thanksgiving Day had consisted of their small family gathering around the kitchen table, thanking God for their blessings before they ate the meal her parents had prepared. As an adult, she had avoided attending Thanksgiving meals with coworkers or friends. Not because she didn't see the value in doing so, but because the people she knew had families and relatives who would fill their homes and make the day complete.

She hadn't wanted to be an add-on or an extra.

She had wanted to belong.

And now she did.

Her heart swelled at the thought as she stepped into the large meeting room that the K-9 unit was using for their Thanksgiving meal. Not just any Thanksgiving meal. This was a celebration of the closing of the Emery murder investigation, and the entire unit would be there. Bradley had invited Sasha, and she hadn't even considered saying no. After years of sidestepping invitations and making excuses, she was finally going to be part of a wonderful time of thanksgiving and praise.

"Sasha! You made it!" Bradley said, moving through a small crowd of people and dogs that were congregated in the middle of the room.

"It looks like I'm a little late," she murmured, allowing him to take the covered dish she had brought from her apartment. Her mother's dressing. She had found the recipe in an old cookbook stored in the back of her closet.

"There are plenty of people still on the way, and you are right on time," he responded, kissing her sweetly, gently. Right there in front of the members of the K-9 unit and all their loved ones. "And I am very glad to see you."

"You saw me three hours ago when you stopped by to tell me that Darcy Fields finally extracted DNA evidence from the doorknob at the Emerys' crime scene and that it matched Vernon's," she reminded him, smiling into his eyes, her heart filled to overflowing with gratefulness. She hadn't expected to fall in love again. She hadn't wanted to. But she didn't regret it. She didn't doubt it.

She knew that Bradley was the man she was meant to love. He was her friend, her partner in beach exploration and late-night conversations. His loyalty, his passion for truth and justice, his love for his sister, his friends, for King and for Sasha, were undeniable, and she couldn't have liked or admired him more if she had tried.

Love was the frosting on the cake of happiness they had found with one another. She couldn't deny it any more than she could deny the sunrise in the morning or the dusky blue of the sky when the sun set at night.

"Three hours is a long time to be away from someone you love," he said as he took her hand and led her to a buffet table laden with covered dishes.

"It smells great in here," she murmured, her stomach growling loudly.

"Hungry?" he asked with a smile.

"Always," she replied, laughing as King nosed the edge of the table, sniffing loudly as he tried to determine what was there. "I think King is, too."

"Looks like the last few people are here," he said, pointing to the door.

Penny and her fiancé, Tyler, walked in.

"Hello, brother!" Penny called, rushing over to hug Bradley.

"And Sasha," she added, offering Sasha a hug, as well.

"Looks like we're all here," Sergeant Gavin Sutherland said, his springer spaniel Tommy prancing near his feet as he approached the front of the room. "Before I offer the blessing on this Thanksgiving feast, I want to thank each and every one of you for the hard work you do for the team. You are vital assets to the K-9 unit and to the New York City Police Department. Thanks to your efforts, we have finally solved the Emery murder investigation."

He glanced to his right, and Sasha realized Willow Emery, little Lucy Emery's aunt, was there, Detective Nate Slater's arm wrapped around her waist, his dog Murphy near her feet. Lucy was a few feet away, sitting at a child-sized table coloring in a coloring book.

"I know that Willow is grateful for your effort in making that happen. And I want to share some news I received early this morning. The perpetrator of that crime, Vernon Parker, was told about the DNA evidence we found at the scene. Faced with that and the taped confession obtained by Sasha, he agreed through his lawyer to plead guilty."

"Thank You, Lord," Willow said quietly, leaning her head against Nate's shoulder. "We'll be saved from a long trial."

A murmur of agreement filled the room, couples talking quietly about the case and about the newest development.

"It's over," Sasha said quietly, her arm slipping around Bradley's waist.

"As close as it can be before he is sentenced and locked away," Bradley agreed. "It's been a long seven months. I think everyone on the unit will sleep well tonight."

"A long seven months that accomplished a lot of things for a lot of people," she replied, scanning the faces of people she had come to know and love. Not just people. Couples who had come together because of the work the K-9 unit had done. Henry Roarke and Olivia Vance. Raymond Morrow and Karenna Pressley. Vivienne Armstrong and Caleb Black. Belle Montera and Emmett Gage. Jackson Davison and Darcy Fields. Penny and Nate.

"I hope they all have their happily-ever-afters," she said.

"They will," Bradley assured her, not asking what she meant. He knew. They had talked about the people in the unit many times, and they had both been awed by the way God had brought love into so many of their lives.

"You say that with authority, Detective McGregor. So I'll assume you're right," she responded.

He laughed quietly, his dark eyes soft and filled with love. "I'm glad you think so," he said, taking both her hands and looking straight into her eyes. "Because there is something else I plan to be right about."

"What's that?" she asked, the room suddenly quiet, all the attention focused on them. No one spoke. Even the dogs had gone quiet, the soft swish of their tails against the floor the only sound.

"We'll have our happily-ever-after, too," Bradley said, all the amusement gone from his eyes and face. "If you want one."

"I can't think of anything I want more," she admitted, all the fear she'd once had, all the certainty that she would spend the rest of her life alone, gone. Love was not a scary thing. Not when it was made of friendship and kindness and respect and faith, all of it bound with hope.

"I hope you know how much I love you, Sasha. Not just for today, but forever, I want to stand beside you. Through the good and bad. The hard and the easy. Every day. For as long as I have breath in my lungs and life in my chest. Will you marry me?"

He reached into his pocket and pulled out a small box, opening it to reveal a simple rose-cut solitaire, the band a braided ribbon of gold.

"Yes," she said, her throat clogged with tears, her voice raspy with love and hope and joy.

The room exploded in cheers and barks and howls of joy, everyone moving closer as Bradley slipped the ring on her finger.

She knew people were talking, issuing congratulations, but all she could see was Bradley, all she could hear were his words as his lips brushed hers.

"You are my forever. My happily-ever-after. The place I will always call home. Today and every day, I thank God that He brought you into my life."

Then he was kissing her with passion and with promise. And, for today and for always, she was grateful.

* * * * *

Had he really just offered employment to the woman
who'd broken his heart? There was no way he wanted to
be stuck working with her day in and day out, a constant
reminder of how she'd chosen the big city over him—
over them. Then again, she could accuse him of doing
the same thing to her.

But that was different. This was his home.

And hers, too, whether she wanted to admit it or not.

"Seriously," he found himself saying, "it would be
full-time with benefits and everything."

"As what, Creed?"

"A deputy. And leader of the K-9 unit."

"You don't have a K-9 unit."

"We would if you started one."

She gaped at him. "I need to talk to you about Fawn, but first I have something I need to take care of."

"What?"

"Scarlett was real antsy around that fallen tree trunk," she said. "I want to go take a look at what she was reacting so strongly to."

Creed nodded. "I'll go out there with you, and we can talk on the way."

Lacey studied him for a moment, then gave a short dip of her head. "Can you keep Regina and the others here until we finish checking out that tree trunk?" she asked.

He narrowed his eyes. "Why? Don't tell me Scarlett is trained in cadaver search, as well."

Lacey shook her head. "She started out that way but hated it and was terrible at it. She apparently just really did not like the smell and would be very skittish when she got close to a dead body."

"Can't say I blame her," he muttered.

"And she would sneeze. She was acting that way out by the tree."

Creed froze. "I see. And you think there's a dead body out there?"

"I don't think so, I'm…afraid so."

Don't miss
Following the Trail *by Lynette Eason,*
available February 2022 wherever
Love Inspired Suspense books and ebooks are sold.

LoveInspired.com

IF YOU ENJOYED THIS BOOK, DON'T MISS NEW EXTENDED-LENGTH NOVELS FROM LOVE INSPIRED!

In addition to the Love Inspired books you know and love, we're excited to introduce even more uplifting stories in a longer format, with more inspiring fresh starts and page-turning thrills!

LOVE INSPIRED

Stories to uplift and inspire.

Fall in love with Love Inspired—inspirational and uplifting stories of faith and hope. Find strength and comfort in the bonds of friendship and community. Revel in the warmth of possibility, and the promise of new beginnings.

LOOK FOR THESE LOVE INSPIRED TITLES ONLINE AND IN THE BOOK DEPARTMENT OF YOUR FAVORITE RETAILER!

LOVE INSPIRED

Stories to uplift and inspire

Fall in love with Love Inspired—
inspirational and uplifting stories of faith
and hope. Find strength and comfort in
the bonds of friendship and community.
Revel in the warmth of possibility and the
promise of new beginnings.

Sign up for the Love Inspired newsletter
at **LoveInspired.com** to be the first
to find out about upcoming titles,
special promotions and exclusive content.

CONNECT WITH US AT:

f Facebook.com/LoveInspiredBooks

🐦 Twitter.com/LoveInspiredBks